THE ~~EDGE OF SHADOW~~

BOOK 5, THE FINAL OF THE KIN OF KINGS SERIES

THE KIN OF KINGS SERIES

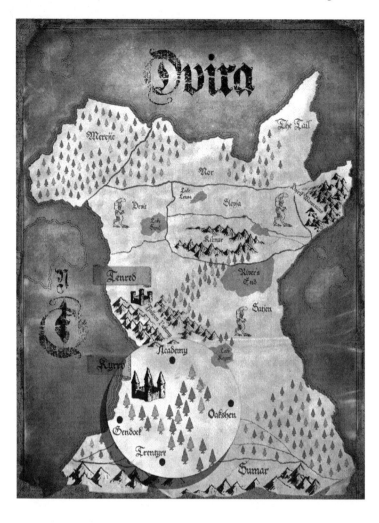

CHAPTER ONE

Basen felt as though everything was finally right, and then he saw Sanya and realized how wrong he must be. A swarm of guards surrounded her as she hobbled past Basen with a bloody bandage around her leg. At least a day old, it didn't look to be helping much anymore. Taking Sanya's cloudy eyes into consideration, it was clear she'd walked through the night to make it to the Academy by morning. Whatever brought her here was dire.

She didn't notice Basen until he was right in front of her. "What is this?" he asked.

"The war isn't over," she told him.

"So who leads the army now?"

"Ulric."

But he died...it must've been a trick.

"The announcement of his death was for what purpose then?"

"I'll tell you at the stadium, with everyone else."

"You can't go there! Mages bring their wands with them everywhere. You'll be burned alive before you can get two words out."

"No, they'll have to listen." She set her gaze ahead of her and walked with purpose. "After I'm done, I will accept whatever fate they decide for me."

"Sanya, stop. Sanya!"

"I will not."

Basen looked down past his bare chest at the towel around his waist and muttered a curse. This had been the only opportunity to bathe and change out of his soiled clothing since returning to the Academy. With Alabell looking after Neeko, Basen's assistance was no longer needed in the medical building. He'd hoped to clean himself swiftly and hurry to Redfield to catch the end of Terren's announcement. Surely, the headmaster would be proclaiming Tauwin's death and the end of the war at any moment now.

The bathing house was close to Basen's student home, so he hurried back, dressed as quickly as he could, and started for the door, only to stop short. He went back for his wand, hoping he wouldn't need to use it.

He sprinted to catch up to Sanya, thankful she was slow. When he rejoined them, he spoke to the guards first. "You can't let her enter the stadium. They'll kill her."

"If she wants to go there, we'll take her there," answered one of them.

Basen scoffed as he came around to Sanya's side.

"Stay back," one of the guards warned him. "She's dangerous."

But Sanya's hands were tied behind her back, her lips dry and cracked, her eyelids heavy. Basen counted an even ten guards around them.

"She's not going to do anything to us," Basen said. "Are there more of you watching the land from the walls? This might be a trap."

Most seemed offended by his question. "Of course," a couple muttered.

Good, then he could focus on the dilemma at hand. "Sanya, why must you go to the stadium at this moment? Effie is there, along with many others who want you dead."

"Terren can't wait a moment longer to find out the war isn't over."

"Just tell me what he needs to hear, and I can interrupt his announcement. Was it Ulric himself who wanted everyone to think he was dead, or was it someone else who planned it?"

"Keep me alive long enough to say everything I need to and you'll find out."

"I can't do that alone. And look at yourself, Sanya. You can't even run if you need to." He gave her a tiny push. She stumbled and then let out something between a hiss and a growl.

"You idiot! I'm trying to help you."

"*I'm* trying to help *you,* as you can't seem to realize you're walking toward your death."

"I've already faced death and ran. I'm tired of running. Just make sure I'm protected until I'm done speaking. It's for the Academy's benefit."

They weren't far from the red walls of the stadium. It was here that all the names of the students who'd fallen in war were written. Would Sanya's name go on the wall after she was killed? Basen doubted it.

He groaned in frustration. "I have little control over sartious energy, which might be the only thing that can stop the onslaught of fireballs that will rain down upon you as the fury of hundreds of mages—"

"Then get someone else!" she snapped.

He put himself in front of her. "Give me time to figure out what to do."

She lifted her hand and hit him with a spell of pain.

The surprise of it alone was enough to take him to his knees as she limped around him. She released him, but not without a warning. "Do not get in my way again. It took me too long to get here, and the Academy doesn't have much time."

He shelved his anger for the moment. "Before what?"

"An attack. Hurry to get someone to protect me if *you* cannot." She showed no sign of stopping as she approached the open gate of Redfield.

"You won't need anyone to protect you if you listen to me." Basen hurried out in front of Sanya to stop her, then held up his hands as he walked backward. "Don't move. I'll get Terren, and you can tell him what you need to say."

"He won't believe me. I need a stadium full of psychics as I speak. Only then will it be impossible for me to lie."

"Do you *want* to die?"

The question was rhetorical, but her cold look made him wonder if it was actually a possibility.

She thought for a little while, then said, "I will accept whatever the Academy decides to do with me."

Basen cursed and ran into the stadium. Sanya yelled after him, "I'm following you in a few moments! I must face Terren inside."

Sanya had always been stubborn in her refusal to listen to logic, but this was bordering on madness. Expecting to find Terren in the center and everyone else in the audience, Basen was shocked to see the sandy arena crowded with the entire army of the Academy. Lines had been formed, separated by factions.

Nearest to the only exit were the original troops of

the Academy, all students and instructors in somewhat organized lines with a psychic facing them at the front to question one person at a time. In the center of the arena stood the men of Basen's father. All in uniform, and holding perfect lines, they made the students and instructors of the Academy look messy. But the least organized were on the far side, Abith's men. Or were they allegiant only to Crea?

Basen had spent enough time training with Abith by now to wonder if he really had any power over those who'd come here from Tenred. Up until the recent battle, Abith had spent nearly every hour of each day helping Basen learn how to manipulate energy to increase his speed and strength as he fought with sword. It didn't seem possible that he had any time to plan something with Crea. Though she was Basen's cousin, there was no love lost between them.

Basen looked for Crea briefly among the thousands of them and soon figured she was still missing. She'd left before Basen's mother had returned, certainly frightened of Henry's wrath for putting Juliana in prison. But Crea was much more of a threat out of sight than she would be here at the Academy where people could keep watch over her.

Basen sprinted over to Terren and asked, "What's going on?"

"Everyone's loyalty needs to be questioned before I announce Tauwin's death. If Abith has a takeover planned with his men, we're going to find out now."

"Sanya is moments away from entering the arena," Basen said in a hushed voice.

"Captured?"

He was amazed at Terren's lack of surprise. "No, she came willingly. Ten guards surround her, but none seem interested in keeping her from entering where mages like Effie will certainly burn her with fire."

Terren pointed at Reela, who was just about to question Abith. "Hold your questioning!"

She spun. "What's wrong?"

Basen muttered to Terren, "We need Abith. He's the only one who can shield Sanya well enough from fireballs to keep her alive."

Terren gave Basen a look as if he'd claimed they all had to bow before Sanya. "That's absurd. I won't have Abith involved in this. I'll speak with her while I take her to prison, and then I'll return."

Basen didn't question how the headmaster expected to get her to prison because it didn't matter. "Sanya won't allow that. She'll come in any moment now."

"Why?"

"She says there's no time and you won't believe her unless she's questioned in a stadium full of psychics. She might be right about at least one thing she told me—we have no time. We need Abith now." Basen looked over his shoulder at the entrance and saw Sanya emerging. Fortunately, no one else in the stadium was looking yet.

Unfortunately, Terren wasn't either. He was too focused on his potential rival. "If Abith is planning a betrayal, he will do anything to get out of this questioning. We can't let him move."

Sanya stopped and looked around nervously. Movement among Henry's troops turned Basen away from her. Henry seemed to be covertly organizing his men to surround Abith's line as if to prevent escape. He and Terren were sharing looks of understanding as Terren pushed Basen toward the exit.

"Go," Terren demanded. "I don't care what she says. You will keep her from entering and disrupting this questioning."

With no time to spare, Basen sprinted back to the entrance. All eyes were on the commotion around Abith. Questioning on every line had stopped, the air laden with hostility.

"Not yet," Basen whispered to Sanya with a hand on her back. "Just wait a moment."

She refused to move. "No."

"Yes!" he hissed and scooped her up.

"Put me down!" She elbowed him in the side but he gritted his teeth through the pain and rushed her out. He set her on her feet, but she fell to the ground as if she hadn't the strength to keep herself up any longer.

"I despise you, Basen," she whimpered. It sounded as if she was holding in tears. "Can't you see that I want to face them all!"

She pushed herself up and trudged toward the stadium's entrance again, looking as if she would ravage Basen with tooth and nail if he didn't get out of her way.

He did not budge. "Just *one* moment, Sanya."

"I will hurt you."

There was a surprising lack of reaction from all the guards, even as Basen looked at them incredulously. "Won't you detain her? It's Terren's orders!"

Many shook their heads. "She can get herself killed if

she wants," one muttered.

They'd tried to control her earlier, Basen realized as he looked closer at their faces of anger. *She'd pained them all.*

"Hurt me if you must," Basen told Sanya. "I'm not going to let you enter."

She took in a breath as if she might attack but then let it out as sadness twisted her face.

"Why go through so much trouble to protect me?"

"I'm not just keeping you from killing yourself," he explained. "I'm keeping you from sparking a battle. The politics within the Academy are shaky, ready to fall apart, and your sudden appearance would be like a boulder from a catapult striking the Academy. You're so caught up in making this into something about yourself that you don't see how you'll affect everyone else in that stadium. Just wait here, and you'll have your time in front of them soon enough." Anger had finally slipped out through his tone. "God's mercy, Sanya, I don't understand why you always have to be this difficult."

But then he noticed something about her that had been evident this whole time. Her ragged breathing, her sweating, the clinch of her face—she wasn't just exhausted; she was terrified.

"I can't be brave enough to face them all for much longer. I have to go now, or I might never."

Finally Basen was beginning to understand. He thought of a few choice words.

"You are brave enough. You've come this far."

CHAPTER TWO

Cleve had been watching Abith closely before Basen ran into the stadium and spoke with Terren. When Basen started back the way he'd come, Cleve watched Abith even closer. Something was wrong—everyone in the stadium could sense it as all focus switched to Abith and the line of men behind him.

"Resume questioning!" Terren announced, mostly for Reela's benefit as he looked straight at her.

Terren had allowed Cleve to go without examination, a privilege shared only by the Krepps. But it wasn't as if Cleve's uncle trusted the savage creatures as much as he did Cleve. They just didn't have the capacity for something as complex as an organized betrayal. But with Abith—everyone knew he wanted to be headmaster. If something was planned to further that goal, it would happen now, when the war was all but over.

The leader of the Krepps leaned down close to Cleve's ear and asked in Kreppen, "How we know when to *attack*?" The breath of the massive creature was as hot as a blast from an oven. The word he favored most, *kirjek*, was spoken with a languid role of his tongue, as if it gave him great pleasure to utter. Rickik and his Krepps were the only ones excited to be in this cramped arena, with battle ready to ignite at any moment.

"Don't attack," Cleve answered in Kreppen. He had learned much of the language, but he could convey only simple ideas when speaking. "Attack only if I attack."

"You give me orders?" Rickik asked, already perturbed. "You are not leader of Krepps."

Cleve held back a grumble as he tried to think of the right words. He'd been practicing Kreppen every day, though he could barely stand the company of any of Rickik's Krepps except for his son, Nebre. There were no two Krepps more different than the two of them. Nebre had been accepted by the Krepps into their group, but that didn't mean they gave him the same honor as they did each other. All Krepps, male and female, were better with sword than Nebre and therefore more respected. But among the humans, Nebre was the most revered of the savage creatures.

"I request you call son to you," Cleve said. "We need his help."

As Rickik called out to Nebre, Reela leaned close to Abith and squinted. Cleve had come to recognize this expression as her putting her full concentration into reading energy—detecting for lies. Everyone fell silent to listen to her first question.

"What do you plan to do with Terren after the war is won?"

Nebre joined Cleve and Rickik and asked in common tongue, "What's wrong?"

"Wait," Cleve said as he strained to listen to Abith's reply.

"That depends on what Terren plans to do with me." A hint of sarcasm came through, perhaps showing that Abith was unafraid in this tense situation. *Or it might be to hide his fear.*

Reela squinted as she tilted her head from one side to

another, staring into Abith's eyes. She glanced over at Terren. "Would you like me to push on this question?"

He rolled his hand through the air "We can return to it if need be. Go to the next."

Reela's Elven half-brother, Vithos, had been positioned beside her, questioning more of these troops from Tenred. But now he came over to join her. Cleve hoped this didn't mean the Elf had sensed aggression.

"You've proven through Basen that you have the capacity to train a new class, but do you have the loyalty?" Reela asked.

Terren had clearly prepared these questions specifically for Abith, presumably with the help of the headmaster's loyal staff, but Abith training a new class came as a shock to Cleve. Whispers fluttered around the audience as he wondered why neither his uncle nor Basen had told him what Abith had been doing. Why keep it a secret unless there was something to hide?

Abith continued to smirk, even as he answered. "It's not a question of loyalty, like you suggest." He glanced at Terren before returning his gaze to Reela. "It's a question of whether I'll be satisfied with taking a lower position than I deserve."

Reela frowned. "But there's no one better to instruct battle mages. There's great honor in that."

"Honor?" Rickik whispered to Cleve. "They say what?"

Cleve didn't have the ability to describe the complexity of the situation in Kreppen, but he tried his best. "Terren asks Abith to train men with sword and wand. Much honor. But Abith wants to be leader of the Academy."

Nebre elaborated for his father as Cleve waited for Abith to speak. Abith was not a large man, but his skill with sword and manipulating energy made him imposing. The line of men behind him was in disarray as many had come forward to listen.

"More honor as leader," Rickik told Cleve in common tongue. "Do Abith and Terren fight for leader?"

They might. "No, because a human leader needs to be good at more than winning a duel."

Abith was taking his time to reply as he glanced back at his men. How allegiant were any of them to him? It was Crea who'd paid them to join this war, and it was she, not Abith, who would continue to pay them for their loyalty when it was over.

"You." Terren pointed at an older man behind Abith. "Come forward and answer questions about Abith if he refuses to answer them himself."

The man glanced at Abith before moving, as if asking permission. Abith shook his head and pushed out his palm. He shot an annoyed look at Terren.

"You would've stood no chance of killing Tauwin if it wasn't for me," Abith said. "And hundreds more would've died during the battle if these men weren't supporting your troops. I heard about the chaos under your leadership, and not just from my men."

Abith's implication almost made Cleve reach for his weapon. He stepped forward and fired back in his uncle's defense. "No one in Ovira knows the speed and power of horses. Terren did everything right, as he always does."

"No, Cleve," Terren surprised him by announcing. "I am to blame, and I do hold myself responsible for their ambush succeeding." Cleve eased back into the group of Krepps as shame colored his cheeks. But Terren wasn't done. "I live with the deaths of our soldiers and officers on my conscience, and I would gladly pass the burden of leadership to anyone more suitable for the task. But Abith, you are not the man to lead the Academy. You would do no better than I have. You said yourself that it's out of boredom that you've taken such drastic measures to be standing before me now in hopes of stealing my position. You can't honestly believe everyone here at the Academy would be better off with you leading them. Do you? Let's hear the truth."

Jackrie stepped close to Terren and whispered something in his ear.

"It's all right," he muttered to her.

She shook her head and stepped back.

Abith had his arms folded. "The truth, Terren, is better left unspoken."

This was it, then. Battle. Cleve gripped the handle of his bastial steel sword. The brawl would be messy, as only a few people had brought swords, but most were on the Academy's side. It should be an easy victory.

Terren looked into Abith's eyes...and made no demand for him to answer. Cleve didn't understand. *Force him to speak the truth. We all know he means to kill you.*

But Terren found some sort of understanding in Abith's eyes, nodding to the smaller man.

Rickik whispered, "I'm confused."

"So am I," Cleve admitted.

"We attack?"

"No." This was one of the many problems with Krepps. Confusion led to fighting more often than not. There were many Kreppen words for settling problems with combat, while no such words existed in common tongue.

Rickik spoke a few of them in his language to Cleve, one to settle dishonor with fighting, another to prove strength with fighting, and the last to end a hostile situation with a duel. Cleve told the Krepp "no" more forcefully each time until Rickik was seething.

"We're done with him for now," Terren told Reela.

Everyone voiced shock and disagreement, though Reela was the loudest. "He's worried, headmaster! Are you sure there are no other questions you'd like to ask him?"

"I have no more questions for Abith."

"Terren," Cleve tried to plead, but his voice was lost among hundreds of others.

Terren raised his arms. "There is one thing I need to know, actually."

Everyone quickly settled, the silence swelling with tension.

"Where is Crea?" Terren asked.

"I don't know." Abith sounded glad for that fact.

"Then what do you know about her?"

"All that I know is she didn't go back to Tenred."

Terren waited for more information.

Abith shrugged. "That's it. I have no idea what she's doing."

Terren pointed at the older man behind Abith again. Cleve didn't know anything about this particular swordsman. He just seemed to be next in line. "And you.

What do you know about Crea?"

"She continues to pay us to serve her."

"What does she expect you to do?"

"Fight." He shrugged and said the word as if it were a simple thing, like he'd been told to clean a room.

"Has she given you any instruction to go against me or anyone at the Academy?" Terren asked.

"No."

"Have you seen her since she left?"

Why had Terren let Abith off so easily to focus on Crea instead? There was something the headmaster wasn't telling them. Normally, Cleve wouldn't worry, but he'd seen a different side of Terren on the way to battle. The news of Jackrie's terminal illness had changed his view on life. It had weakened him.

"I haven't seen her," the man answered.

Terren didn't seem to believe him as he glanced at Reela, but Reela nodded at the headmaster and said, "True."

"You must know of someone who's seen her," Terren accused the man.

"I do."

Terren sighed in clear frustration. "Who?"

He pointed at another man, who came forward. Terren muttered something to himself as he shook his head. He finally seemed to notice everyone had stopped what they were doing to watch. He lifted his arms. "Finish answering your own loyalty questions. We could be here a while."

As psychics begrudgingly resumed questioning their classmates—an unfortunate necessity with the history of betrayal at the Academy—Cleve moved closer to his uncle to escape the growing din of voices. Rickik stayed with him, his Krepps not far behind.

"When did you last see Crea?" Terren asked the man. He was younger than the last, with a sinister face that made it seem as if he would rip a coin out of a child's hand just to watch him cry. Cleve had seen him on Warrior's Field, training men of Tenred. Clearly, he had trained long before these days. He could have very well fought against Cleve in the war between Kyrro and Tenred. *He could have even killed some of my allies.*

"I saw her two days ago," he answered.

Terren swept the hair off his forehead, gave a quick glance toward the exit, then showed a look of annoyance at the man Cleve was beginning to assume was their enemy.

"Where?" Terren demanded. "It would be appreciated if you elaborated in your answers."

"Near the mountains."

Terren looked as if he wanted to grab him by the neck. "Which mountains?"

"West of the Fjallejon Pathway."

"How did you know to meet her there?"

The man's mouth twisted as if he tasted something sour. He glanced at Reela, then back at Terren.

"Don't embarrass yourself by trying to lie," Terren warned. "You're going to tell me everything you know about Crea, so stop stalling."

The man looked as if he wanted to make the headmaster regret his words. "I knew where to meet her...because...she..." Each word was spoken slowly, as if

Terren was too stupid to follow otherwise. "Told...me...where...to...meet...her...last time we spoke."

His disrespect for Terren was so palpable that even Rickik seemed to know what was going on, taking an aggressive step toward the man. Cleve quickly followed, unsure if he had the will to stop Rickik. The man noticed the enormous creature but showed no fear.

"Did you discuss anything that would lead to the injury or death of anyone here at the Academy, including myself?" Terren asked.

"No."

Crea probably knew this man could be questioned by psychics.

"What did you discuss?"

"Nothing."

Terren looked confused, glancing over at Reela. She turned to him and said, "It's the truth, as strange as it seems."

With a triumphant smile, the man took his spot back in line. Terren opened his mouth as if he might object but said nothing. His attention returned to Abith.

"Give them all the normal questions so we can be done with this," the headmaster told Reela. Then he stepped back and crossed his arms as he watched.

Reela proceeded to ask Abith, and then everyone else from Tenred, the same questions posed to every student and instructor. Where are you from? What is your name? Why did you come to the Academy? Do you harbor any grudges toward Kyrro or anyone at the Academy? And finally, do you have any intention of betraying or doing harm to anyone at the Academy?

Abith was intentionally vague during some questions, answering that he came to the Academy because it was in his best interest at the time, and that he had the best interest of the Academy at heart.

"But do you have the intention of betraying or doing harm—?" Reela began, only to be interrupted by Terren.

"Move on to the next person."

Abith nodded as if thanking Terren, then stepped out of line. Disappointed, Reela asked the same questions to every man after that. They each answered clearly and without hesitation, but many seemed nervous or upset by the process. The third man to be questioned, the one who'd met with Crea, held an expression as if he were above all of this.

When all were finished, Cleve joined Vithos and Reela as she spoke with Terren.

"None were lying," Reela said, "but many were worried and did seem to be keeping something secret."

Vithos nodded. "Many secrets, especially with one." Cleve didn't need to look to know the Elf was pointing at the one who'd spoken with Crea.

"Thank you, Reela and Vithos, but that's all I need for now."

"I think they're dangerous, headmaster," Reela said as Terren turned away.

"I know they are."

"And Abith is definitely hiding something," she added.

"I know what it is. I'll explain later." Terren raised his arms and yelled, "Return to the benches."

Cleve didn't move, noticing Reela and Vithos standing there as well against Terren's order. The two of them looked at Terren the same way Cleve did. They needed to say something, but what?

"Trust me," Terren told the three of them.

He gestured for them to leave.

Rickik came to join Cleve as they walked toward the benches. "No battle?"

"No, but there might be one later."

"Good."

After a long while, everyone was seated in the now quiet stadium. Effie had come earlier with nearly her entire torso bandaged. Reela sat next to her, with Cleve on Reela's other side. They spent a few moments trying to convince Effie to go back to the medical building now that the questioning was over, but she refused to miss this announcement.

Terren let out a long breath, then smiled in what appeared to be relief. "I'm glad that's done. Now I can finally tell you the good news."

He held the silence of the audience for what felt to be an eternity. Everyone knew the battle had only been to distract Tauwin so the trio of Basen, Abith, and Neeko could surprise and slay the young pretender to the throne. Now they were just waiting to hear the results.

At first Cleve thought Basen and Abith had gone with Neeko to get him to the capital. As two men who could fight with sword and fire, one able to make portals, it seemed they were a good choice. But after hearing how Basen had been training with Abith, Cleve was beginning to see there was a lot more to Terren's choice than Cleve had first realized. Terren had never kept secrets from Cleve before, and he didn't see why it had to start now.

People began to murmur excitedly as Terren's smile grew to split his face. "I can see many of you already know what I'm about to say."

Tauwin's name drifted around Cleve. He pushed away his worry about Abith to let himself enjoy this moment.

"Tauwin is dead!" Terren shouted with a shake of both fists.

Applause erupted, scaring the Krepps behind Cleve until Nebre calmed them with a quick reminder of what clapping meant.

But everyone stopped suddenly as screams were heard at the entrance of the stadium. Not a single person was sitting when Sanya limped in.

Basen ran in after her. "She used psyche, Terren! I couldn't stop her."

The headmaster was already sprinting toward Sanya. "Abith! Abith, get here now!"

Sanya lifted her arms as if mimicking the gesture Terren made before each of his speeches. "The war is not over." Her voice did not carry well, partially muffled by everyone's sounds of shock. "Ulric is still alive and *planned* for Tauwin to be killed. It's what he wanted! All of this is exactly what he wanted. Ulric now leads the entire army against you, and they could be here as soon as today. I came here to tell you everything I know and to face my punishment for my crimes!"

Effie took out her wand and made a face of concentration.

"Don't," Cleve said at the same time as Reela.

It was too late. She was the first to cast, her fireball zipping over the heads of her classmates close enough to singe their hairs. Some shrieked as they ducked, while others spun around and cursed at her. The fireball landed short of Sanya, sending out a wave of sand as she covered her face with her arm.

Abith was there by the time Effie cast her second fireball. He made a sartious shell around himself and Sanya, a thin shield of green energy that protected them from every angle. Effie wasn't the only mage casting by then, as ten fireballs rained down on Sanya and Abith for every breath Cleve took. Abith's protection only incited more mages to stand and cast, which caused the troops of Tenred to stand and draw arms.

"Everyone stop this instant or you will start a battle!" Terren yelled, his deep voice thunderous as it reverberated around the stadium.

All mages stopped. Dying flames sizzled across Abith's energy shield.

Effie didn't lower her wand.

"He can't keep that up for long."

Cleve glanced around the stadium to see a number of mages—Alex's friends—with the same smug look on their faces as Effie.

CHAPTER THREE

Cleve and Reela moved closer to Effie's sides, neither daring to reach for her wand yet.

"Eff, you've just gotten out of the medical building," Reela reasoned. "You shouldn't even be standing, so you certainly should not be casting. You must still have caregelow working through you and altering your mind. Don't do anything you might regret."

Effie gritted her teeth and lifted her shoulder as Reela's hands came closer. "Don't use psyche on me. *You* don't get to protect her, Reela! You didn't lose someone precious to you."

If this had been the first conversation Cleve heard between the two young women, he would've guessed by Effie's spiteful tone that they were enemies.

"But I did," Cleve interjected. "I spent every day training with Alex. His death opened an old wound so deep, it was as if my parents had been killed all over again."

Effie ground her teeth, looking like a dog about to bite. "So you should be charging down there and throwing Abith out of the way so we can kill her!"

Reela put her hand on Effie's shoulder. "Please—"

"Don't touch me!" In her hurry to get away from Reela, Effie fell into Cleve. He had just enough time to steady her before she pushed him off. "You don't touch me either!"

"All right," Reela said. "We won't."

"We won't force you to do anything," Cleve added.

"This has to be your decision, something you can live with."

"You said you wanted her dead," Effie growled. "Why not anymore?"

"I still do, Effie. But not by mages' fireballs in the middle of Redfield. Not before she tells us whatever she came here to say."

Several mages continued to cast, ignoring Terren's shouting. Their fireballs splashed against Abith's green energy with flickers of light. Cleve caught glimpses of Sanya's horrified expression in the short gaps between the spells.

"She came here by her own volition," he argued. "It would be different if we'd caught her trying to run, but she's here to face her punishment. There will be a trial, Effie. She'll get what she deserves, and you won't have the guilt of murdering her before she's done everything she can to help us."

Effie did not lower her wand, but at least she wasn't casting.

Terren eased toward Abith, his voice rising to a level Cleve had never heard before. "Put your weapons away, now!"

The fireballs stopped, but Effie and many other mages still refused to lower their weapons. It wasn't until Terren promised, "She *won't* escape," that Effie finally holstered her wand.

Unfortunately, there were mages even more stubborn who did not budge. Brawls broke out as other students tried to force them to put their weapons away. A few shouted in vain about Sanya killing Alex or Nick, but it wasn't long before they were overwhelmed by the people around them and were forced to give in.

Abith let his sartious shield come to rest, the energy sprinkling down and coloring the sand with a green ring. Basen stood stunned at the entrance to the arena with ten wall guards behind him. From the other side of Sanya, Terren called, "Has she been checked for weapons?"

"Yes," Basen replied.

"The war is not over!" Sanya repeated. "Ulric wants you to believe that it is." She fell silent suddenly, spinning to look in every direction as if expecting more fireballs.

"Psychics!" Terren called. "Come down here— everyone who questioned people earlier."

Vithos and Reela joined the psychics powerful enough to detect lies as they came down to surround Sanya. There were only about twenty of them, plenty for interrogating just one person. But with fifty psychics entering the school per year, and six instructors, Cleve would've liked to have seen more. Like chemists, many of them were nearly useless during battle, and it seemed as if yesterday was not the last time they would fight.

"I have nothing to gain by lying," Sanya said. "I came here because you need my help now more than ever." Softly, she added, "And I can't run from my guilt anymore."

"Get out everything you know," Terren said.

Sanya seemed nervous as she tried to speak, her words catching. "Troo-many of the troops who came here with Ulric from Greenedge have fought before. They're...are skilled and more dangerous than Tauwin's men...and none of them left Kyrro like Ulric made you believe." She seemed to be finding her voice. "That's why there were so many on the battlefield yesterday. But even they did not know Ulric was still alive. Now they do, and they are eager to finish this war. I have no idea when Ulric will order them to attack, but it could be as soon as today."

"If all of this is true," Terren said, "then why didn't you come here to tell us after the battle yesterday?"

"I tried, but my injuries kept me from covering the necessary distance. Injuries that I got fighting your enemies, alongside Abith Max." She took in a deep breath and addressed the audience with a slight turn as she spoke. "I know I've done some terrible things, but—"

"This isn't your trial, Sanya," Terren interrupted.

She froze with her mouth still open. The fresh fear on her face reminded Cleve of how she'd looked when she'd faced Peter during evaluation week. It was right after she'd found out that he wanted to punish her for trying to join the warriors.

"Tell us what else you know," Terren urged.

"And then what?" she asked him so faintly that Cleve could barely hear.

Terren answered loudly, "And then you'll be put in a cell until your trial."

"But I'll be killed if you send me back to the capital— so will anyone who escorts me there."

"There is a cell for you here at the Academy," Terren said.

The audience sounded confused as questions arose all around about where a prison could be on campus. But Cleve knew exactly what Terren was referring to. In the storage house, there was a cage of metal bars in the far corner of the weapons section.

It wasn't exactly private, as dozens of people would be in and out throughout the day for weapons and armor, but it would do. How they would execute Sanya when she was found to be guilty, however, Cleve had no idea. He supposed someone would take off her head. He felt a chill as he wondered whether Terren might give the choice to him. He had been Alex's close friend and had a bastial steel sword, so it seemed appropriate.

"Speak," Terren demanded. "Or was that already everything you have to offer us?"

Sanya scowled in sudden anger. "I came here to fight against Ulric's army with you." She spoke as if they would all be fools for not taking her in. It brought out a roar of snide laughter from many in the audience, Effie included.

"Terren would never," Effie whispered, as if to reassure herself.

But while she was whispering, Cleve caught Basen speaking to Sanya. "Tell them what you told me."

Sanya stared at Basen, hesitating. He stepped back and pointed at the audience. "Tell them," he said loudly enough this time for everyone to hear. "Tell them what you said while we were waiting. Go on."

She shook her head and looked at Terren, still waiting for the answer as to whether she could fight with them.

"Nothing will be decided right now," Terren said. "You will now be taken to prison."

Sanya visibly tensed as if preparing to fight. It caused Cleve and many others to stand.

"Stop," Terren commanded. "Sanya will be taken

there peacefully, and she will cooperate. She must know that doing so is her only chance of survival."

"She cannot survive, Terren!" Effie yelled.

"And even with her cooperation," Terren announced, "of course she might still be executed for her crimes."

"Might?" Effie replied with many others.

"I'm prepared to face whatever is decided," Sanya yelled.

Terren gestured for the guards to approach, then gave them instructions too quiet for Cleve to hear.

As people began to complain, Terren shouted, "Return to battle training!" He turned and said something to Abith, who nodded.

"She's a fool to come here," Effie muttered to herself, then scoffed. "She thinks we'd let her live just because she feels guilty and wants to help?"

Cleve hurried down the stairs and jumped into the arena, then made his way through the dispersing crowd to get to Terren. His uncle was already out of the stadium, escorting Sanya with the help of others. Abith strolled casually at his side. *Damn*, Cleve needed to speak to Terren without Abith there. He had to know why his uncle hadn't forced his rival to answer harder questions, especially after Abith had shown he was hiding something. Cleve came upon them as they were in the middle of a conversation.

"You know she's not the one you have to worry about," Abith said, then looked over his shoulder and spotted Cleve. Abith said nothing as he turned back, while Terren hadn't yet noticed his nephew.

"I know," Terren said in an even tone. "What's his

name?"

"Cassius Lane," Abith answered.

Probably the man who'd met with Crea. Where have I heard that name before?

"Are you sure that's him?" Terren asked.

"So you've heard of him."

Then Cleve remembered. Cassius was an officer in the last war. His name had been spoken in conversation between Alex's older brother and other officers of the king's army. Terren seemed to care little about Sanya in front of him as he glanced around to check for eavesdroppers, finally catching sight of Cleve.

"What is it?"

"I was going to tell you the same advice as Abith," Cleve lied. "Cassius should not be let out of sight."

"What else?"

"Nothing."

Abith smirked. "You're not a good liar, Cleve." He put up his hands. "Don't worry, I have to go anyway. I won't hear all the flattering things you have to say about me." He casually walked away from the group, toward a few of his men who had noticed him beside Terren and didn't seem to approve.

"You don't need to worry about Abith," Terren said, not quietly enough to keep it from the ears of the guards around them. They did well to hide that they were listening, as did Sanya, all looking straight ahead.

"You should be more worried about Abith," Cleve told his uncle.

But Terren shook his head. "You have to trust me, Cleve. I know what I'm doing. That's all I can tell you for now." He made a quick sweep of his hand to gesture at Sanya and the others around them.

At least there was some reason why Terren wouldn't push Abith to answer direct questions about his loyalty in front of psychics. Perhaps he was still the old Terren, always a step ahead of his enemies, and Jackrie's illness wasn't affecting him as much as Cleve first thought.

Jackrie. Cleve looked around until he found her walking the opposite way, toward the mage classrooms with many of her students. Were he and Terren the only ones who knew the truth about her? Cleve thought of who he should tell but couldn't come up with any names.

Sanya limped ever slower. This was not how Cleve imagined her capture. There was supposed to be a chase, an epic struggle, and then a celebration. There was still time for the celebration part, however.

After her execution, there had better be the satisfaction he greatly anticipated. Only then would the hole in his heart finally close.

CHAPTER FOUR

Basen spied on Abith after everyone left the stadium. He saw Abith speaking with Terren, then briefly with Cleve before sauntering over to his loyal troops and probably offering up some explanation as to why he was with the headmaster. Basen wondered if anyone besides himself would find out the surprising truth about Abith and Terren: They'd become friends during all their sparring, probably even trusted each other. Abith was wise not to answer some of those questions, and Terren was wiser not to force him. It wasn't that the Academy would revolt at hearing the truth. Quite the opposite, actually. They would welcome Abith. But his men—they would do more than just revolt.

Abith seemed particularly busy organizing his troops. Perfect. It gave Basen time to return to the medical building and inform Alabell, Neeko, and Shara what had just happened. But not before first fetching the food Basen had promised to get them from the dining hall.

When he finally made it to the medical building, Neeko was asleep and looking much better than when Basen and Abith had brought him in that morning.

"The food is here," Shara said, waking Neeko with a gentle stroke of his hair. Basen was thankful Neeko had short hair when he'd crashed down onto the burning grass, or his scalp might've burned with much of the rest of him.

He weakly sat up and formed a pained smile.

By the time Basen was done telling them what had happened with Sanya, everyone had eaten and Neeko was back asleep. They moved away from him to resume their conversation.

Shara pursed her lips petulantly. "Her name is too similar to mine. San-ya. Shar-uh."

"You probably won't have to worry about that for long," Basen said.

"She'll be killed?" Shara asked without a hint of joy at the idea.

"I thought that would be good news for you."

"I don't want anyone to die if it can be helped."

If Basen was being honest with himself, he didn't much care what Shara or Neeko thought about Sanya, but Alabell...he gave her a questioning look.

"Will she be killed in front of everyone?" Alabell asked.

"I believe so."

Alabell's mouth twisted as she huffed out a breath. "She must not believe she's going to be executed. Otherwise she never would've come here."

"I think you're right," Basen said. "But that doesn't stop her from being terrified she might be wrong. I spoke with her a while before she forced her way into the stadium to face everyone. She told me something that, for reasons I can't understand, she refused to mention in her short speech to the Academy. She said she'll fight for us no matter what we decide. It's up to us whether we include her in our army or exile her. But no matter what, she'll find a way back to fight with us."

"Not if she's in prison," Alabell pointed out. "Or dead."

"I told her the same thing. She said both would be a mistake because we would be losing a powerful ally."

"Maybe she didn't mention all that in the stadium because she couldn't lie while surrounded by so many psychics."

"I'm hoping it's not that, but you might be right."

Looking at Alabell, Basen still found it hard to believe she felt the same about him as he did about her. If she was out of his reach, it was as if an ocean separated them. When they were close enough to touch, he felt sparks in his chest. It didn't matter what they spoke about. Nothing could diminish the dizzying effect she had on him. He'd wonder at times like this whether she experienced the same desperate longing to be closer. Then he'd look into her eyes and the question would be answered. She didn't just admire Basen for avenging the grief that Tauwin had caused her. This was much deeper.

Every time Basen saw that look, he felt as if he'd been given the world.

"You need to rest," he told her as he suddenly noticed that, while she seemed happy, she was also completely drained. She'd been caring for the injured for an entire day with hardly a chance to sit. "I don't know how you're still on your feet."

"I don't either," she agreed with a wan smile. She noticed something over Basen's shoulder.

He turned to find Effie and Reela coming in, Reela's hand on the small mage's upper back. Half her torso was wrapped in cloth with a red stain just under Reela's hand.

"My wound reopened," Effie said.

"Your sister and I both told you it would," Alabell

chided. "But you refused to stay here."

"I'm glad I went."

Gabby hurried over to them. "I told you—"

"We already covered that," Effie interrupted.

"You need to stay in bed!"

The two sisters walked off while arguing with each other, Reela close behind.

Alabell glanced around the medical building, looking to be judging whether she could leave without anyone dying.

"There are plenty of healers here," Basen assured.

She nodded. "Shara, Neeko should be sleeping for a while, and I need—"

"Yes, go. Please, thank you. Go."

"I'll walk you," Basen said.

As they left the medical building, he offered his arm, but Alabell took his hand instead. They smiled at each other, making Basen wonder if he could possibly be happier. The news of Ulric had faded to the back of his mind the moment he'd seen Alabell again.

"Tell me what I should be feeling about Sanya coming here," Alabell said with a tired smile. "I'm too exhausted to decide."

"Confusion. Some satisfaction. Perhaps a small amount of worry for her and for us."

"Why for us?"

Basen hesitated. Alabell didn't need to worry about anything other than helping the injured.

She stopped and turned to face Basen. Letting go of his hand, Alabell said, "Promise me you will stop trying to protect me."

"I can't."

"I mean by not sharing your thoughts. You must agree to tell me everything, even if it might cause alarm."

"Oh. All right, I promise."

She nodded, smiled, and they resumed walking.

"So you have no problems with me protecting you otherwise?"

"No, I encourage it." She chuckled, and he laughed.

"Sanya's presence is a cause of concern to us because she might be a trap. She could distract us at just the wrong time."

"You really think it's possible she's here to betray us again?" Alabell sounded as if she couldn't fathom it.

"I don't. I'm just being cautious."

She yawned, then again, and then once more.

"Yawn attacks," she commented. "Unfortunately common when I need sleep."

"Before we get there, I have to ask something."

"I already know what the question is."

"Then what's the answer?"

"The answer is it's too late now."

They walked in silent reverie for a while, Basen unable to stop smiling. Alabell seemed to have the same affliction. She'd already opened her heart to him, and it was too late to change her mind, as she'd done in the past.

After another yawn attack, Alabell said, "The last time I saw you before today was when Annah screamed during the night and I ran into your room. You told me you were training with Abith Max and then *rudely* fell asleep before Annah and I could ask you anything."

He chuckled. "Sorry about that. I was sworn to

secrecy."

"So you're not anymore?"

"I'm not sure, but there will be no secrets between us now."

"I'm glad. What are you doing with Abith? I won't tell anyone."

"He's training me. You can say what you want about it because the Academy already knows."

"I'm the last?" she complained.

"Besides those in the medical building. Everyone found out today at Redfield, and I've noticed glares ever since. It didn't help that I came into the arena shortly after Sanya, as if I support her, and it's even worse that I encouraged her to share something that she only said to me. I think people are starting to worry I might be making allies with the wrong people. But it's not because I'm involved in anything complicated or devious. It's just that Terren wants Abith to be the first battle-mage instructor, and I'm his only student because he's too picky to take on anyone else."

"Why not spend half your time training with the warriors and the other half with mages? Then you don't have to put your trust in someone like Abith."

"Because we don't just alternate training sword and energy. It's a combination of both together. Being a battle mage is about using bastial energy in ways no other mage does—for long- *and* short-range combat."

"It's unfortunate that he's the only one who can help you with that."

"Actually, I trust him, and not just because he trains me. I have another secret for you—he and Terren have been sparring with each other for quite a while. I think they've become friends."

Her head whipped back. She stared for a moment. "You're not joking."

"You're the first to know, and I don't recommend telling anyone."

"My bastial stars." She clasped her hands in what looked to be excitement. "That's wonderful news!"

"Most people would be concerned for Terren. You must really trust his judgment."

"I've known Terren for more than three years now. Yes, I do." There was deep respect in her voice, as if Terren were her father.

Basen wasn't as trusting, fearing for Terren's safety. *I'll be lucky to know the headmaster as long as Alabell.* With all the mortal challenges Terren had faced so far, it didn't seem likely he would live another three years. The thought deeply saddened Basen.

He wanted to change the subject to liven his spirits, but Alabell was hit with yawn attacks all the way to their neighboring student homes.

"I would sleep in the medical building," she said, "if I was able to rest well there. But I can't get the same sleep anywhere else that I do in my own bed."

"I'm surprised you don't miss your bed in Kyrro's castle. Is it because you spent more time here?"

"The castle can never be 'home' to me again. But the Academy always will be."

"I feel the same about this place compared to Tenred castle."

She stopped at her door and took out her key, but

moved toward Basen instead. Without meaning to, he cupped the back of her head as they embraced, showing how precious she was to him.

"Rest well," he said.

"Thank you."

As soon as she closed her door, the dread of being late to Abith's class returned with such force that it sent him sprinting. Abith had told Basen their training location would change to Warrior's Field after it became known they were working together. It was closer than over the north wall but less private. Basen had always hoped fire would be involved in their practice, but the grass of the field made that unlikely.

He rushed into his student home to grab his training sword. With his new skill to focus bastial energy into his legs, he enjoyed a good run even more than in the past. He made it to the enormous field in little time and frantically searched for Abith.

The smell of grass reminded Basen of hard work, probably because he used to train with his sword on a field like this one, only a tenth the size. Eventually he spotted Abith on the northern end of the field. He stood impatiently with folded arms, so Basen ran straight through the various training groups in his way to get there quicker. Warrior instructors yelled out mistakes in their students' forms, while grunts of effort and cracks of wooden swords rang out around Basen.

He decided to give a wide berth to the Group One warriors, most of them enormous Krepps. He wasn't sure how Warrior Sneary had managed to keep order among these creatures when they'd first arrived, but now the routine of training appeared to keep them focused.

"You'd better have a good excuse," Abith said when Basen arrived. "And don't tell me you were so foolish as to go back to our old spot. I told you we would be meeting here as soon as everyone found out."

"Yes, I remember. But I had to get food to the healers in the medical building."

"You alone were tasked with bringing food to *all* the healers?" Abith asked incredulously.

Basen quickly realized his mistake. Abith never let him get away with bending the truth even a little. "I'm sorry. I don't have a good excuse."

"That's better. Always admit to your mistakes with me and never lie, no matter how small it may seem to you. What we're doing now is bigger than the two of us. We need complete trust."

He didn't give Basen a moment to think about his words as he drew his wooden sword. Basen got his own ready, then quickly wiped the sweat from his brow. But in just that brief time, Abith had disarmed him with a powerful swat to his weapon.

Abith gave Basen a disapproving look as he went to retrieve his training sword. His instructor had made the same demands as when they used to train with manipulating energy back in Tenred. Basen was to arrive on time, mentally and physically ready to improve. He was certainly not supposed to be tired from running and busy wiping sweat off his face when Abith engaged him.

As punishment, Abith came at Basen without mercy. He quickly got through Basen's fatigued defenses and tripped him with a perfectly aimed sweep of his foot.

Basen popped up as quickly as he could. He would not apologize twice. He'd learned years ago that it only brought on more punishment.

"Will anyone else be joining us now that secrecy is no longer needed?" Basen asked to stall Abith.

"Not today. Terren first needs to find out when we're expecting battle. That will determine whether it's worth starting someone new knowing it might take weeks before their time could be put to use."

"What about your men?" Basen asked. "What do they think of our training?"

Abith ignored the question. "Today we'll focus on the one thing you can do better than me. You're not taking full advantage of your ability to control the immense amounts of energy that you're capable of. Attack me, and I will show you something."

Basen sighed. He would be in for some pain as soon as he attacked, but the worst part was not knowing how or when it would happen.

He charged. Abith made no motion of aggression, waiting for Basen's first attack. The older swordsman was so quick that Basen had little hope of reaching flesh, even if Abith never attacked. In fact, it was only when Abith attacked that Basen found the opportunities he needed. So it wasn't easy to motivate himself to put his full strength into his overhead swing, and Abith easily sidestepped it.

He swatted Basen in the thigh, pulling out a hiss.

"That's for not trying harder. Come on, I'm trying to teach you."

Basen charged again, only he stopped short this time

in hopes of tricking Abith into revealing his plan. It worked. Basen felt his instructor gathering energy. Abith tried to let it disperse as he realized what Basen was doing, but it was too late.

"You're going to send hot energy into my eyes when you block my attack," Basen said dryly. "You could've just told me."

"You're too smart for your own good sometimes. First, you should know that anyone attacking with sword is extremely unlikely to feel their enemy gathering energy like you can. Second, you can gather and use bastial energy quicker than anyone, so it will be less obvious when you perfect this skill. Third, now you'll never know what it feels like to be surprised by this defensive trick."

"I can live with that. So how do I go about training this? I've never been able to gather energy while fighting."

"You might never be able to on a whim in the heat of combat, but you can train yourself to gather energy during one specific moment. You do it enough times, and you no longer have to think about it. I know these troops of the Takarys—your enemies. Many of them will poke, but more of them will slash with their first attack. They will go for your torso. Block and gather energy, then unleash it into their faces and stab them in the chest. For the next hour, I will attack you with the same slash over and over. For now, just focus on blocking and gathering energy at the same time. Before lunch hours start, I expect it to be easy. And before the day is done, I expect a blinding retaliation every time I attack."

"So that explains the blindfold you're hiding in your

back pocket."

Abith didn't seem impressed that Basen had noticed.

They trained for hours. Basen made quick progress, training his mind to gather energy while his body put his arms and feet in the right position to protect himself from Abith's sword. But soon he started losing focus as he began to wonder about Sanya. He wanted to know when her trial would be. Would it take place in secret or in front of the entire Academy?

His feelings about her would be easier to figure out if she had never saved his life by stopping the leader of the Elves from killing him. Then there would only be anger. But as it was now, Basen wanted her to live even after what she had done. No doubt she had been trying to change, but what place did a murderer have at the Academy?

In battle, we are all murderers. But there is a difference there, even if I can't find the words to describe what it is.

Abith, clearly frustrated, put his full strength into his next swing. It knocked Basen's sword out of his hand.

"Why are you so distracted!" Abith complained. "I'm teaching you how to stay alive, and you act as if you're doing me a favor by being here."

"Sorry," Basen said, forgetting that Abith never let a moment of training go by wasted. It would be admirable how focused the man could be if it wasn't so frightening at times. "It's Sanya," Basen admitted. "Did Terren tell you when her trial will be?"

"If I answer, will it satisfy your curiosity or make it worse?"

"Satisfy," Basen lied, knowing it meant he could not ask another question as much as he would want to.

"It's tomorrow. Now focus."

CHAPTER FIVE

Sanya's prison cell was just large enough for her to pace back and forth, which she began doing as soon as she entered. She figured she would continue until they came to bring her to her trial. She'd prepared parts of a speech, but she still had to decide how they would fit together.

This had to be the only prison cell on campus. The fact that it was empty until she'd been locked inside meant she was the only criminal here. But she knew for a fact that she wasn't the only one who'd killed someone. The reason she was the only one pacing around in here was purely because of who she'd killed and when.

She had to stop herself from feeling indignant. It would get her nowhere. She needed to focus on what she would say tomorrow.

As she whispered her speech in practice, searching for the right words, one question kept coming back and distracting her. What did she *hope* would happen, compared to what did she *expect* to happen?

Just before leaving her, Terren had asked her to consider both possibilities. He would want an answer during her trial.

She knew what she wanted: to fight. She hoped they would let her join them, but that wasn't what she expected. How could they trust her to fight with them? And even if they did find some way to trust her, what were they supposed to do with her after the war was over?

She needed not only to prepare a speech outlining why they shouldn't execute her for her crimes but also a plan for how she could be useful to them into the future.

No one was on her side in this.

The storage house was as large as the dining hall, but it was separated into three sections: one for everything required to prepare food and raise animals; one for maintaining the enormous Academy garden; and the last for weapons and armor. She was in the warrior's section, and it wouldn't be long before people began to come in and out to get gear.

She was just beginning to feel hunger pangs piercing through her anxiety when a boy entered and fearlessly walked straight toward her cell.

"Hello, I'm Micklin," he said. "Your name is Sanya Grayhart, right?"

"Yes."

"People are talking about you a lot today. Did you really kill two of Kyrro's Allies?"

He spoke quickly enough that it seemed easier to answer him than to tell him to leave her alone. "Yes, but they weren't part of *Kyrro's Allies* at the time. That name came later."

"Oh, but did you do it because you thought one of them was making portals when it was really Basen?"

"Ye—"

"And the other was defending Basen?"

"Yes."

"But..." Confusion stopped him for a breath. "But you let Basen live later."

"You'd rather I'd I killed Basen?"

The boy scoffed. "Of course not! I'm trying to understand why you'd kill Nick and Alex if you were going to let Basen live?"

"Because I'm a fool."

"You don't look like a fool...or a murderer."

She could feel from his energy that he wasn't believing her answers. She really should send him away, but now she was too curious to find out what people of the Academy like him thought of her.

"You don't look like a murderer either, and yet there's a good chance you'll have to kill someone if you stay at the Academy."

"I would never."

"Not one of your allies, you dolt, an enemy. This is the second war in two years. With a life-long contract, you'd face almost certain odds of a third war breaking out in your lifetime."

"That doesn't make me a murderer. I'll never be one."

"I thought the same thing when I was your age," Sanya said.

He swallowed. "When did you...realize you could...do it?"

"At fourteen, when I decided I was going to kill my father."

The boy gasped. "And you did?"

Sanya had never told anyone. The only person who knew was also the only person to have seen, Bliss. But Sanya had killed her, too. *That makes four.* She would only be on trial for two. She really was a fool, especially for saying anything to this blabber.

She sensed someone else in the room and held silent

as he or she approached.

"Micklin," Reela scolded. "I'm sure you were told by whoever sent you here not to speak with her."

"Why?" he questioned rather than denying it. "Warrior Sneary wouldn't tell me."

The boy wasn't short, but Reela was still taller than he was, making him look even more like a child as she put her hand on his back and turned him away from Sanya.

"I can tell from using psyche that you know not to ask me if Sneary wouldn't tell you. Whatever questions you have, ask them of yourself as you leave. I'm sure you'll find the answer if you think hard enough."

He looked back at Sanya over his shoulder as he walked away, disappearing behind the turn.

Reela returned and opened her mouth, only to close it again. She and Sanya exchanged an annoyed look as they both felt the boy hiding to listen.

"We know you're still there," Reela announced.

Micklin muttered something as he finally left.

"Terren sent me," Reela said. "I'm not going to try to hide how much I want to stay away from you, so if you need to ask me anything about my emotions before we get started, then do so now."

"Get started with what?"

"Does that mean you have no questions about what you're sensing?"

"Fine, give me a moment to search you."

Sanya accepted Reela's invitation and delved into the man's emotions as if diving into a lake from a peak.

Sanya found shocked her. Reela's feelings reminded f the speech she was working on. Complicated, layered, and full of contradictions. Reela was angry, yet she wanted to feel peace. She was sad for Alex but even sadder for someone else unfamiliar to Sanya. She forgave Sanya, yet she wanted Sanya to be punished. This made the least amount of sense given what Sanya had felt in others. Every time she'd detected forgiveness in the past, there had been no need for vengeance among the person's emotions.

"How can you forgive me yet still want me to be punished?"

"You killed two innocent people. Classmates. Friends. I don't want you to be punished, but you need to be. Otherwise, what kind of message would that send?"

Sanya wouldn't have argued even if she thought Reela was wrong.

"What's the reason you're here?"

"You'll find out as soon as Vithos joins us, which will be at any moment. Is there anything else you want to ask or say to me?"

"No." Why was Reela hinting that there was?

Sanya felt sudden anger from Reela's energy. "Really, nothing?"

"What is it?"

"You should apologize!"

Completely baffled, Sanya turned up her palms and shrugged. "Why? An apology will do nothing."

That only seemed to anger Reela more.

"It will accomplish *everything* that you're trying to do by coming here! How can you not get that?"

Sanya had to think for a moment. Her lack of sleep was making this social situation even more difficult than it would be normally. Fortunately, Reela helped her with the answer.

"You're trying to show guilt and a desire to change. That must start with an apology."

Sanya somehow knew Reela was right. All of Sanya's ability to interact properly with others had been destroyed by her father's experiments over the years. Only after his false death and their separation did she have the capacity to train herself to act "normal." She desperately needed help with her speech. This was becoming frighteningly clear.

"I'm sorry, Reela. I'm sorry for…what I did. It's difficult for me to even label my actions as what they are, murders. I think back to that time, and it seems like I was a different person."

"That's good. Say that to Vithos when he comes in, and everyone you see who knew Alex or Nick."

Perhaps Sanya did have at least one person on her side: Reela. Sanya wiped her wet eyes.

"Why are you so happy all of a sudden?" Reela asked with a tilt of her head.

Sanya swallowed past the lump in her throat. "It feels good to have someone care about me, not that I understand why you do."

Reela tossed her hand. "Because I can't help but care about everyone."

That sapped Sanya's happiness quicker than a punch. Still, she appreciated Reela's support. If it amounted to nothing else, at least Sanya knew to start her speech with an apology. It would set the foundation for everything else she had to say.

Someone else joined them in their section. Sanya wasn't familiar enough with Vithos' energy to confirm it was him until the Elf came around the standing shelves filled with boiled leather tunics and smiled at Reela.

"Ready?" Vithos asked his half-sister.

Reela nodded and turned to Sanya. "Terren sent us here to accomplish three things: learn how to use psyche to cover up lies, learn how to figure out when you're lying, and learn how to break the bastial energy in the air."

"I hope you're expected to be here for weeks."

"One day," Vithos said in his Kreppen accent.

"That's impossible."

But Reela shook her head. "It has to be in one day."

"I don't care what it has to be, it's impossible."

"We will be here all night if we need to," Reela said.

"I still have to finish preparing my speech, and I didn't sleep at all last night."

"Neither your speech nor sleep will matter if we can't tell when you're lying." Reela moved close to the bars. "Your trial is tomorrow, but only if you teach us before then. Otherwise there won't be one."

Sanya sighed as she sat on her straw bed. The overwhelming news had exhausted her more than the trek here. Her head throbbed and her leg stung. The rest of her body fared no better, feeling tenderized like a piece of meat.

"Teaching you how to lie and how to detect when I lie is the same lesson." She shook her head. "But there's no way you'll learn how to do either before tomorrow, and there's definitely no way you'll learn how to break bastial energy in one day. You might never be able to even if I spent years trying to teach you."

"Then explain how we can catch you lying," Reela said. "And you'd better be able to prove it works on you. I'm not going to tell Terren we know when you're lying unless we are absolutely certain. I can't be responsible for a betrayal."

"There won't be another betrayal. At least not from me. Don't you see how tired I am of all of this? Everything I've done has failed. Even when I appeared to succeed, like bringing my mother back from the dead, it still failed!" Sanya lay down and closed her eyes.

A mistake—she'd almost fallen asleep, and now getting up was like struggling beneath the weight of someone sitting on top of her.

"I need something to eat," Sanya said as she forced herself up. "And my injuries should be treated to help me focus."

"Someone will come with food and potions soon. We should start the lesson."

"Don't worry, Sanya," Vithos added. "Reela and me learn fast."

"Fine, but pay close attention. We don't have time for me to repeat anything." Sanya came to the bars to stand close, shaking the grogginess from her head. "You have to read and manipulate energy differently than you're used to. All psychics pick people's personal energy patterns out of the BE in the air. This was the first step you were taught: familiarizing yourself with how particular energy patterns appear—reading the energy. It's the same way we learn to look for specific colors while glancing around, and similar to colors, there are thousands of variations but far less groups. Emotions can be bundled in groups, like frustration and desperation. There are many different types of greens and reds, just like there are different types of feelings of frustration and desperation. But there are other emotions that take more practice to identify, specific feelings like stress from not being given sufficient time." As Sanya was feeling now.

"We already—"

"I know you know this," Sanya cut Reela off. "But what you know is wrong. Let me explain without interruption. Detecting lies is about picking up specific emotions, then making a judgment about what they mean. Some people, when they lie, are obvious because they feel a surge of worry or anxiety. But there are others who are better at lying, and it takes more than an amateur psychic to tell. Can the two of you tell if this is a lie? I regret killing Alex and Nick."

"It's not a lie," Reela said.

Vithos agreed.

"How do you know?" Sanya asked.

"Because I feel your sincerity," Reela said.

Sanya pointed at her. "That's the problem I'm trying to get at."

Reela and Vithos shared a look before he spoke for them. "We don't understand."

"Detecting lies has become easy for you because you only try to read a person's sincerity or a lack of it. It's this training that allows any good psychic to detect lies, but it's also because of this that I'm able to fool every good psychic. All it took was finding a way to manipulate my own energy into the form of sincerity without actually being sincere."

Reela put out her hands. "I hope you know not to be lying about any of this. If we can't confirm when you're telling the truth, you'll be killed before the end of tomorrow."

"I know. You can stop hinting at that," Sanya spat. "I already have enough pressure on me. I'm not lying now, nor will I again. You'll have your chance at the end of the lesson to confirm that for yourself."

"All right, go on."

"The key is to focus on the feeling of sincerity more than you ever have before. Describe how you detect it so I know where to start."

"It's dull and calm, like ocean waves."

Sanya waited, but Reela seemed to be done. At seeing Sanya's disappointment, Reela furrowed her brow.

"It's like asking me to describe what it feels like to breathe," Reela protested. "Sincerity is normal—as everything should be. I know sincerity because there are no irregularities to detect."

"Let me help you." Sanya cleared her dry throat. "Sincerity is almost like desperation but without the same *need*. If desperation were bright red, sincerity would be a darker red, less sharp. Dull and calm like you say, but also unique. It's not normal. Sleep is normal to me. When you first learned to detect sincerity, did you associate it with calm ocean waves?"

"I don't remember," Reela said, then looked at Vithos.

"I don't, too."

"That's what happens to all good psychics. It's how you can manipulate energy quickly and efficiently.

Unfortunately, it's also why I can lie to all of you without you knowing."

"You still haven't explained that."

"Psychics spend their time training to read and manipulate bastial energy, but you don't spend much time *perfecting* the manipulation of energy. You never strive to bend energy to mimic exactly what people would feel naturally. And why not? It doesn't matter in any circumstance. If you wanted to use psyche to make Vithos want to smile, you'd just have to move his energy so it resembles the form it naturally takes when he smiles. But any good psychic can tell the difference between his energy when he's smiling naturally compared to when it's manipulated. But can you tell me the differences? Describe them."

"I can't," Reela admitted after a moment of thought. "I can only feel that they are not the same. The differences are obvious yet impossible to describe."

"I will help you. Think of two paintings that are almost identical. At first, you can only see they are different. Once you look closely, you can you spot the differences. But think about someone who has spent years painting the same image over and over again. In the end, she can paint two that are so close to being identical that only she can see the differences while everyone else thinks they look exactly the same."

Reela hummed and nodded. "I see what you're saying. You've trained yourself for years to mimic sincerity almost completely."

"Exactly. I have painted the same scene over and over again, and that scene is sincerity. Other psychics don't bother to learn it in such detail because they focus on a broader training regimen. They put no effort into being able to hide their manipulation. Like I said earlier, in order to catch me, psychics have to change the way they use psyche. You have to retrain yourself to manipulate energy into the shape of sincerity. It's the only way to tell I'm lying."

"And it will also teach us to lie without detection," Reela added. "I see how they are connected."

"Fortunately for both of us, I don't believe perfect mimicry is possible every time I lie, but I'm good enough that no psychics, no matter how many are around me, can catch me unless I make a mistake or they are trained to be as good as I am. Now do you see this is not something that can be done in a day?"

"We will do it," Vithos said with surprising confidence.

"We will," Reela agreed.

"Did you miss the part about it taking me years to get to this level of detail?"

"You were learning psyche while teaching yourself this sneaky skill," Reela said. "We already know psyche, and you already know how to teach it."

"And we learn fast," Vithos repeated.

Reela added, "I always thought you used a trick of some kind. I didn't realize it was possible to mimic emotions completely."

"Not completely," Sanya reminded her. "No two things are the exact same, no matter how hard we try to make them be."

CHAPTER SIX

Basen made great progress training with Abith that day. After lunch, he'd been able to push away the distractions caused by Sanya and his desires to see Alabell. Abith's demands for improvement required his full attention.

Forcing his body and mind to work in harmony reminded Basen of the brief dancing lessons his mother had made him take. Getting his feet to match the steps of his instructor required first ignoring how they wanted to move. Only then could he train himself to move in a new way. Gathering energy while blocking an attack was just like a dance step. He was required to hold up his weapon, brace for the impact with one foot back, and pull bastial energy into a cluster between him and his attacker. He had to momentarily ignore his impulse to counterattack because when he mastered this ability, it would be a better version of counterattacking.

No one could cast continuously while engaged in fierce melee combat, but Basen could teach himself to pick the right moment to gather BE once he progressed. Sending hot bastial energy into his opponent's eyes would be predictable to anyone who'd fought him more than once, but that was highly unlikely to happen.

Without meaning to, his defense slowly changed from intercepting Abith's sword with solid wood to swiping his sword in front of him to deflect Abith's attack. It was more effective and reliable, and it didn't slow Basen's ability to gather energy after enough practice. He could see from Abith's smug grin that he would take all the credit for Basen's new ability and quick improvement. In the end, that didn't matter.

With enough training and tricks like this, Basen hoped to reach the same lethal level as Cleve. Basen's cluster of bastial energy wasn't hot enough to singe skin or cause any permanent damage, but no man should be able to keep his eyes open through the brief spell. Abith put on the blindfold eventually, his eyelids not allowing sufficient protection.

When it was time for dinner, Abith took off the blindfold and rubbed his red eyes. "That's it for today," he said.

They headed to the dining hall, where they would sit apart even though everyone knew by now that Abith was his instructor. The implication of sitting at a Tenred table was still too much of a stain for Basen's reputation to stay clean.

"You still haven't mastered the skill," Abith said as they waited in line for their food. "I expect you to return to the field after you eat. I want you so comfortable gathering energy during combat that you can open a portal while defending yourself, if you so desire."

It was what Basen wanted to do anyway, not that he thought it was possible. That wouldn't stop him from trying, though. He noticed Abith glancing at the group of tables composed of all the Tenred troops as he spoke his next words. "There are other matters I need to take care of after I eat." His tone told Basen he would rather go back to Warrior's Field.

Basen looked around the dining hall for someone to

eat with. Even though his time was short, he longed for the company of a particular beautiful woman, but Alabell wasn't there. He did spot his father, though, sitting with Terren and a few instructors. Basen didn't have the clout to join them, but the pride of seeing his father there made him smile.

Cleve no longer sat with the Krepps, but with Steffen and Effie. Even though Reela and Vithos seemed to be elsewhere, Basen hoped Cleve's change of seating meant he and Reela had overcome their differences.

Unfortunately for Basen, their table was full. He hadn't seen Annah anywhere, though there was a good chance he couldn't see her from where he stood in line because the dining hall was so large and she was not. There was one other person he wanted to speak to. But he didn't have the spare time to visit Sanya. It would be dark in a couple hours, and Basen wanted to improve even beyond what Abith required of him. Besides, what could he and Sanya discuss that wouldn't anger or sadden him?

As Basen got his food, he found out from the server that his mother was still helping the kitchen staff. Although he couldn't find time during the day to see her, it was good to know she was keeping herself busy.

With his dinner in hand, he started toward Cleve's table figuring they could make room for him. Then Basen realized there was something he needed to discuss with the Krepps. He stopped and stared in their direction, intimidated by the lack of humans around them. Only a few Krepps sat and ate quietly, while most seemed to be fighting to be the center of attention.

Finding courage, he walked over as confidently as he could to where they had taken over four tables. He sat down in front of Nebre.

"We need to talk."

"What is it?"

Basen noticed yellow eyes shifting toward him as well as the boisterous conversation quieting a bit. A few of them spoke his name, though only to each other. Rickik came toward him, so he stood.

The Krepp grabbed Basen by the collar of his shirt and looked him up and down.

Basen could feel Rickik's strength as he tugged on the shirt. The creature was probably powerful enough to lift Basen with one hand if he wanted.

"*You* are the human to kill Tauwin?" It seemed hard for Rickik to believe.

"I am."

"Bastial steel," Rickik said slowly, as if he could taste the words and had never sampled anything sweeter. "Where is his sword?"

"It was the only thing that saved my life."

Confused, Rickik glared at his son. Nebre stood and translated into Kreppen.

"You use my sword?" Rickik asked.

"No. When it fell out of Tauwin's dead hands, his army fought over it. That was the only reason I escaped. They had just won the battle, so there were thousands of them and only me."

Rickik stared at Basen as Nebre translated, never letting go of Basen's collar. It was impossible to tell if Rickik was angry, as he always wore the same scowl.

When Nebre was done, Rickik laughed and let Basen go. "You must run fast for human."

"I am the fastest."

Many of the Krepps laughed with Rickik.

When their deep clucking came to an end, Rickik asked, "Where is bastial steel sword now, human?"

"In the hands of one of our enemies. I don't know who."

Rickik's scowl returned.

"But there is another man who has a bastial steel sword," Basen said, "and an axe, both larger than Tauwin's sword. This man is still alive, and he's the greatest fighter I've ever faced. He cannot be hurt by psyche or fire. He bravely fought against one hundred of his enemies—and won."

"One hundred?" the Krepps started to mutter.

It was an exaggeration, for Abith and Sanya had fought on the giant's side outside Tauwin's castle. But these Krepps needed all the inspiration they could to forget about Tauwin's sword, which would probably never be identified among the few other bastial steel weapons of their enemies.

"Yes, one hundred," Basen confirmed. "The size of his weapons are more suitable to you. It is him you must kill. But..." Basen let his voice trail off for dramatic effect, getting the attention of all the Krepps watching. "He is larger than you are, Rickik, and stronger."

"No human is!"

"He is," Basen confirmed. "And like many Krepps, he was born only to fight. I met him briefly in battle, but it was long enough to see that he was a man like no other."

Rickik thumped his chest. "I will kill him!"

The Krepps began to chant in their language, attracting uncomfortable looks from everyone around them. It brought Cleve over from his table.

"I'm glad you're here," Basen said before Cleve could ask about the uproar. "You need to help me explain something important."

"What?"

But Basen noticed Krepps snatching his food. He was hungry and refused to wait in line again. He grabbed his tray to protect it.

"It's about the Krepps who died in Tenred castle," Basen said.

That got Rickik's attention again. "I honor Cleve for killing Javy Rayvender, the coward leader of the dishonor ambush!"

"There might be someone else who was involved, though," Basen told Rickik, giving Cleve a knowing look. "It's time," Basen told him.

Cleve thought for a moment, then nodded. "He's right, Rickik. I think someone else was involved in that betrayal besides Javy."

Rickik bumped his chest against Cleve's, sending Cleve back a step. "You lie, human?"

Cleve bent back his shoulders as aggression took hold of his face.

"No," Basen answered for him. "Javy was responsible, and Cleve did the right thing by punishing him for his crime."

"Then what you speak?" Rickik asked.

"We later figured out that someone might have told

Javy what to do," Basen lied. They had known from the start, but telling Rickik this earlier would've helped no one.

"Who betray with Javy?" Rickik asked, his Krepps gathering around to listen.

"My cousin, Crea Hiller."

"Who? Your what?"

The Krepps all began to chatter until Nebre translated for Basen. Then they roared.

"Crea," Rickik said, looking at his Krepps as if he wanted them to chant the name. "Crea!"

Basen raised his palms before they caught the attention of the troops at the Tenred tables. "Stop, secrecy is important here."

Nebre's tense Kreppen translation stopped the creatures.

"Secrecy no honor," Rickik complained.

"There will be time for honor," Basen said. "But your enemies have no honor. If they hear you plan to kill Crea, they will stab you in the back. She's always wanted control over Tenred and Kyrro. From what I saw at Redfield stadium, it looks like she's still plotting to take both territories. Tenred already belongs to her and her sister. For Kyrro, she's going to start with the Academy and then eventually try for all the cities." Basen didn't know any of this. Most likely, his cousin would settle for the Academy and Tenred, as she couldn't stand up to Ulric's army, but that didn't help Basen's cause.

After Nebre finished translating, the Krepps no longer looked confused. By then, they'd drawn the glances of every human around them. It was a good thing there were dozens of tables between them and Crea's troops, but word of this conversation still might reach them. Everything would have to move quickly to stay one step ahead of their enemies.

Rickik made it worse as he pointed toward Abith. "What about him and them?"

Basen risked pulling the Krepp's arm down and was relieved when Rickik didn't resist.

"Abith doesn't want to fight against us," Basen said, fearful he might be igniting a brawl between the Krepps and his trusted instructor. "He certainly had nothing to do with the cowardly ambush in Tenred castle, but some of the men over there were involved in the plot to kill your Krepps, and Crea definitely was involved. You must give Cleve and me more time to figure out what they are planning here at the Academy before we decide how to handle them. I think Crea is plotting another cowardly ambush here, yet she needs the help of those men to do it. We all must be prepared for an attack as we try to figure out who's guilty so we can prevent it."

Nebre struggled with this translation for a while, but eventually the Krepps seemed to understand. Rickik bent his back to put his glaring eyes in front of Basen's. "How you figure this out? No lie!"

It was a surprisingly insightful question from the simplistic creature. Almost all of this had been based on feeling alone. As Basen thought of a way to explain it, Cleve answered for him.

"At least one of them has to be communicating with Crea. The incident at Redfield confirmed this. While we figure out who is communicating with her, as well as how, where, and what they're saying, we need more eyes watching for people leaving the wall during the night. Kreppen eyes are best in the dark."

This was exactly what Basen was getting at. He nodded in agreement. "We need your help."

"We watch," Rickik said. "But no kill without…see betrayal or see ambush."

Basen was thankful Rickik already knew this without Basen having to remind the savage beast.

"Yes, and it's important not to let our enemies know what you know. If asked, your Krepps are watching for Ulric's troops because battle is coming."

"Are you able to recognize my Uncle Terren?" Cleve asked. "And Jack Rose?"

"Yes, many Krepps recognize Terren," Rickik answered. He transitioned to Kreppen to ask his Krepps about Jack.

They moved their hands through the air as they seemed to be describing him.

"Yes for Jack," Rickik told Basen and Cleve. "Dark skin. Easy face."

Basen figured he meant "friendly" by that. There was one important question left. "Do you know what Crea Hiller looks like?"

Rickik asked his Krepps. Many of them used their hands to draw the shape of her head and hair in the air.

"Yes," Rickik answered. "Light skin. Dark and short hair. Hard face."

It seemed accurate enough.

Cleve took Basen aside. "Next time, warn me before you incite these creatures into doing something." He waited for Basen to nod before continuing. "The psychics questioned everyone except Abith. It's him we need to worry about speaking with Crea. I still don't know why my uncle—"

"Terren trusts him, which is why he didn't force him to answer. If Abith revealed that he has no intention of leading these Tenred men against Terren in the future, they'll turn against him and choose someone else to lead them."

Cleve cast his eyes down at Basen in disappointment. "His training with you has bought your trust."

"He hasn't just been training with *me*, Cleve."

"Who else?"

He would have to break his promise to Terren. Too much had been set in motion to stop now.

"Your uncle. They spar together." Abith wasn't training with Terren any longer, as Abith's time was better spent with Basen so the both of them could improve their battle casting, but Cleve didn't need to know this detail.

"Abith told you this? He lies."

"No, I stumbled upon it by accident a while ago, before I started training with Abith. I've seen them go at it for hours. They look like friends."

Cleve glared incredulously toward Terren's table. "I think he's losing what makes him a great headmaster," Cleve whispered, adding in an even softer voice, "It's Jackrie."

Even if Basen hadn't heard the rumors about Terren and Jackrie, their relationship would've been obvious from the times he'd seen them sitting close in the dining hall. He didn't hide his disappointment at Cleve's statement.

"A relationship won't weaken a leader."

Cleve shook his head. "Never mind. I misspoke."

Krepps pounding on the table while laughing distracted them for a breath. He and Cleve moved farther away.

"You're taking a risk turning the Krepps against Crea without proof," Cleve complained. "They are not subtle creatures, yet you ask them for subtlety. This could all go wrong too easily."

It wasn't exactly a question, but Cleve seemed to be waiting for Basen to defend his actions.

"Crea has to be planning something against the Academy. Why else would she meet with an officer from my late uncle's army?"

Cleve let out a breath of distress. "I was hoping you had more to go on than Cassius Lane's vague answers in the stadium."

"I don't, but it's enough to be sure."

CHAPTER SEVEN

The next day, Basen noticed many Krepps on the wall. He hoped they had been there throughout the night because it was during the darkness that a betrayal was most likely. The human guards around them seemed to be spending as much time watching the creatures as they did looking out for signs of an attack.

Basen knew a worry would distract him for days to come. His allies could not set up scouts anywhere along the Fjallejon Pathway because Ulric had control of the mountain, so if an attack came from the north—from Tenred—they wouldn't know until their enemies were already upon them. He hoped Terren had a plan for such an event, but it wasn't his place to ask. Perhaps most of Tenred's army was already here within the walls. Basen wished he knew how many they had in total.

During his training with Abith, Basen got a surprise visit from someone he never expected to seek him out. Reela called his name from the wall.

"Attack?" Basen feared as he and Abith rushed over to the rope so they could climb up.

"Not that," Reela said. "No need to rush up here."

Basen didn't know the psychic too well, but he was familiar enough with her to notice her heavy eyes. She looked as if she hadn't slept a wink last night.

"Sanya chose you to speak on her behalf," Reela said.

"What?"

Reela repeated herself, but it only made Basen more

confused.

"Do you accept?" Reela asked.

"Would this be during her trial?" Basen assumed.

"I didn't say that?"

"No."

Reela placed her hand on her forehead. "Forgive me, I'm exhausted. Yes, her trial. Do you accept?"

"Why does she need me?"

"She doesn't need you. She'll be speaking for herself, but Terren has allowed her to choose someone to speak for her as well. She wants that person to be you."

Basen had feared something like this would happen. Sanya had no one else. What would Effie think of him if he supported Sanya? What would Cleve?

"When's the trial?"

"As soon as I can find someone to speak on her behalf or if I come to the conclusion there's no one."

"Have you asked any others before me?"

"No. Yours was the first and only she's given so far. She said you're the closest thing to a friend."

A sound of disappointment slipped out of Basen's mouth. It was too sad a notion for him to be Sanya's closest friend when even he wanted her to pay for her crimes. Reela should know this.

"But I want her to be punished," he said. "Severely."

The psychic shrugged. "Do you accept or not?"

Basen scratched his head. "Should I?"

"I don't know, Basen. It's up to you."

He looked down as he thought. "Does she expect me to say only good things? Because I would run out of words quickly."

"I believe she's just expecting you to help her tell the truth."

"Which is what?"

"She repents. She wants to fight." Reela paused for a long while but didn't seem to be done, gazing up at the clouds as if in thought. "She believes she can contribute to this world—and specifically to our cause."

He supposed there was a lot of truth to that. They could use her, but then what?

"I'm tired," Reela said with a sigh. "If you aren't going to accept, I need to find someone else."

"I accept." He'd known he would as soon as she'd asked. He'd just wanted more information.

Abith interrupted, "Basen, you have a lot of work to do to reach your potential. Do you *owe* this woman something?" The question was asked rhetorically.

"Yes. I might not be alive if it wasn't for her."

"Yet she might be dead if it wasn't for me," Abith countered. "Seems fair to go back to your training."

"What's fair would be if she does a favor for you later, not for me to ignore her."

"Then go." Abith frowned. "Just be quick about it." He started up the rope first.

"Where is the trial?" Basen asked Reela as he climbed the rope after.

"Redfield," Abith answered to Basen's surprise. "We'll be walking there together because I'm part of the jury."

*****

Nick and Alex's relatives couldn't be at the trial, as there was no way for word to reach them safely, nor was there a way for them to get to the Academy. Only Ulric's men could travel between the cities without risk of death or capture. So it was Nick and Alex's friends, Basen soon learned, who would have to argue what kind of justice they wanted on the victims' behalf.

"This is a matter of justice, not forgiveness," Terren explained soon after Basen and Abith arrived. "This trial will not be about whether there is sufficient evidence to execute Sanya, as she has already admitted to her crimes and has come here to face her punishment. It's about deciding whether executing Sanya is the right choice for the Academy and everyone outside these walls. Normally a matter like this is decided by the king or his representatives of justice, but because of circumstances we are all aware of, we're forced to settle this matter differently."

There weren't many people present in the vast stadium. Terren's trusted instructors made up the jury: Jack, Trela, Sneary, Abith—who probably came as a surprise to the others—and Wilfre, which surprised Basen.

Effie stood facing the jury, surely to argue for Sanya's execution. Sanya was a good distance from everyone, sitting on her own side of the audience section. She looked even more tired than Reela as her head wavered. She had chains around her hands and presumably her feet. Reela and Vithos had taken their own solitary spot in the arena. They were probably here for psyche, but Basen didn't see the point if Sanya could lie without detection.

Vithos looked no better than Reela—and that's when Basen realized it: *They've spent all night with Sanya learning to detect her lies.*

There were no seats in the arena, no tables, no podiums, no stage. Steffen scribbled away like a madman while seated in the first row of the audience, probably writing down every word to keep a record of the event. The whole thing felt too informal. It seemed wrong for this group of individuals standing in partially organized clusters to decide a woman's fate.

Basen had been told to take any seat in the audience benches, so he sat next to Cleve. Terren had probably invited his nephew to watch and possibly speak if he wanted to. But Basen didn't know whether the warrior would speak for Sanya or in support of Effie.

"We will start with Effie," Terren said. "I want to remind you again, Effie, officially, so that our scribe can write it down this time, that it is not your responsibility to convince us of anything. Even if you choose to say nothing, we still understand the importance of upholding our laws and are able to come to a fair decision in this matter. The reason we give you the chance to speak is in case there's anything you might want to add, having been so close to one of the victims, that someone in our position might fail to consider. You may begin, Effie."

"I don't have much to say, headmaster. I trust that you and everyone on the jury already know that we can't have a woman walking around free who has murdered people in their sleep." There was fury in Effie's tone as she spoke each word with force. "I miss Nick, and I didn't even know him that well. So Alex..." Her voice broke as emotion overwhelmed her. "The pain that I feel..." Effie started to cry. "It seems like it will never end, made worse by his murderer living and breathing...while he is not. Sanya might have helped us, and she might continue to help us, but that does not mean she should go free. There's only one thing she can do that will make me feel better about losing Alex, and that's dying."

Damn, Basen whispered to himself. Effie's sharp tone had made the hostile air even more volatile. A tense moment of silence passed as Effie visibly forced herself to stop crying.

"I don't like the person I've become," she said and almost began crying again. "Sometimes I hear myself talking about killing Sanya, and it doesn't feel like me. But I wouldn't have to be like this if I knew she would finally receive the punishment she deserves. I'm somewhat relaxed for the first time since Alex's death, now that she's here, and that you, headmaster, and the rest of you on the jury will decide her fate. Thank you."

"Thank you, Effie," Terren said. "Would you like to call Cleve down here to speak?"

That immediately made Basen uncomfortable for sitting so close to Cleve. He should've taken a spot farther around the bend of the curved stadium. They glanced at each other, then looked away. Each of them shifted.

"I don't know," Effie told Terren, then glared up at Cleve behind her. "That depends on what he's going to say." Beneath her words was a warning. He had better not go against her or he would forever regret it.

A cold sweat came over Basen as Effie shifted her gaze to him. He showed her a look of apology. She turned away.

Cleve stood with purpose and swung his long legs over the wall. He dropped down into the arena and walked over to Effie.

"Terren said this wasn't about forgiveness but justice," he began. "In that case, it's simple." But he stopped. The pause went on long enough for everyone to tell he was having second thoughts. Sanya's chains clinked as she shifted on the other side of the stadium.

"May I speak?" Sanya asked as she stood.

"Only once Cleve is done," Terren replied.

Cleve took his time, glancing first at Reela, then at Effie. The small mage to his side gestured for him to go on.

"I'd like to hear what Sanya says first," Cleve told the jury.

Terren and the rest of them looked at each other. Wilfre shook his head at Cleve. "That's not the procedure we agreed upon."

Cleve waited for his uncle to confirm his request. That seemed to offend Wilfre, as he crossed his arms and glared at the headmaster.

"Say what you need to say now, Cleve," Terren told him. "We don't have time for this to draw on."

"I suppose I just want to say that I agree with Effie. Now that Sanya's here and her fate will be decided by people I trust, I feel better." He grumbled in what sounded to be frustration. "I'm not sure what I'm supposed to be talking about."

Terren put up his hands. "That was fine, Cleve. Thank you for your input."

Cleve shrugged and muttered something as he

returned to his seat. For reasons unknown to Basen, the big warrior seemed embarrassed.

"Now, Sanya, you may come down here to speak," Terren said. "But stay close to Reela and Vithos, and don't make any sudden movements."

Sanya tried to get down into the arena by slowly scooting her rear toward the edge. The chains at her wrists and ankles made the short drop dangerous, yet no one came over to offer assistance even as she looked around for help. Murmuring to herself, she edged closer to the drop then looked up once more. Everyone else held still. She slid off the edge and landed hard on her side. She murmured more as she pushed herself up and then slowly made her way over to Reela.

The long walk was painful to watch. Basen was thankful when Abith walked over to her, lifted her up over his shoulder, and carried her the rest of the way. It earned him disapproving looks from everyone on the jury but Terren.

Sanya seemed in discomfort as all focus returned to her. She looked as if she was too tired to care about anything but sleep, her shoulders slack, her head atilt. But then she licked her lips and took in a breath, and her visible fatigue disappeared.

"If I were an enemy, then the decision would be simple." She paused. "If my being alive continued to threaten your system of justice, then the decision would be simple. If I might take more lives of your allies, of your friends, or of your family, then the decision would be simple. But I am no longer an enemy and never will be again. By being alive, I will only help bring others to justice—others who do threaten the Academy. I will take no more lives of your allies, of your friends, or of your family. I will only take the lives of your enemies…who I hope to be our mutual enemies soon. This is not a simple matter. We can claim it is simple by saying that all murderers deserve to die no matter the circumstance, but we know that's not true. Most of the people in this stadium have killed others. The only reason I'm on trial is because I killed the wrong people at the wrong time."

Sanya looked at Reela and stopped for a few breaths. "I'm sorry," she told the jury, then turned to Effie. "I'm sorry." She looked back at Cleve and Basen. "I'm sorry." Finally, she glanced back at Reela. "I'm sorry. I wish I could tell everyone how sorry I was, and if you let me live, then eventually I will. There *is* a difference between the people I've killed and the people the rest of you have killed. I agree that it should be the reason I'm here on trial. I only bring it to light to further explain that there is nothing simple about this. All murderers are not executed. Please don't let that idea cause you to make a decision that will hurt the Academy.

"I came here to help the Academy and to face my punishment. I was with Ulric before this. I had won his trust." Her voice rose. "He wanted me to counsel him. I would've had a life in the castle. It was the very life I had planned for myself from the beginning: I was going to bring my mother back, marry Tauwin, and eventually take control of the castle from him, killing him if necessary. He was one man who, I knew from the start, didn't deserve to live. He's done nothing but hurt Kyrro, and I wanted to be the one to take him from this world. Ulric and I had a plan, but it was disrupted by a man whose name I learned to be Neeko. When he couldn't kill Tauwin, he tried to kill me instead. Because I figured out he was allied with the Academy, I risked my own life to help save him as a psychic disabled him. Ask him, and you will see that he might be dead if it were not for me."

She pointed at Basen. "He might also be dead if it weren't for me." Emotion put a strain in her voice, as it sounded like the planned part of her speech was over. "Ask him. Ask the both of them! And I plan to save many more lives by fighting against Ulric. My power should not be ignored! I can help. I want to help. I need to."

Her chains complained as she shuffled about. "I'm not asking you to forget about my terrible crimes. I agree with everyone here that I deserve punishment, but let that punishment be a life of reparation. I promise to spend the rest of my time in this world helping those who deserve it, the allies of the Academy and of my victims. It's these people who deserve to win this war, your people. Let me help them. By killing me, more of yours will die. Don't let my horrible mistakes cost any more lives."

Basen's pulse increased at the end of her speech. Soon it would be his turn to speak, giving him the unfortunate responsibility of concluding the trial. He wished he could hear from Cleve and Effie again, especially Effie. He needed her anger to remind him of his own, as Sanya had done too good a job of convincing him that it would be a waste to execute her.

"Basen," Terren called. "Sanya requested one person to be here to support her, and you will be the last to speak today. Come down here and stand next to Reela.

Sanya, go back to where you were."

Abith came out of the disorganized line that was the jury to carry Sanya back into the audience section. He dumped her on top of the arena wall and let her get herself onto the bench. Basen still hadn't figured out what he was feeling. It was even worse that psychics would be right next to him.

"Go on," Terren encouraged. "Or is there nothing you want to add?"

Basen caught Sanya gesturing for him to speak. He felt sick.

"I think both Effie and Sanya have a point," Basen said. "We can't let a murderer go free, yet Sanya could be of great benefit to us." He asked Reela and Vithos, "Were the two of you able to confirm she meant everything she said? She wants to fight with us?"

"Yes," Reela answered as Vithos nodded. "She can no longer lie to us without us knowing."

He thought for a few breaths. "Sanya, I wish you'd never put us in this situation. You could've stayed with the Group One warriors and fought beside us all along, yet now you're forcing people to make an impossible decision. Like Effie, I'm still angry. But it's not like I can ignore what you've done to help me."

He turned to the jury. "And we especially cannot ignore how much she can help all of us. In the end, what matters most is whether she's changed, whether we can trust her, and whether the others who aren't in this stadium right now can live with the results. I think it's that final question that's the most difficult to answer. Personally, I can live with my anger. But Effie and others might never be able to. Sanya's presence here might cause more problems, even if she does nothing directly to harm us. You as the jury have no correct answer in this. I don't envy you. But I do trust that whatever you decide will be the best for all of us."

"Thank you, Basen," Terren said. "The jury will speak now. In the meantime, Reela and Vithos will escort Sanya back to her cell."

They won't decide and tell us now? The lack of a culmination was unsettling.

Sanya fell down off the wall. "I'd like to say something else!" she tried.

"It's over," Terren said with finality.

Reela and Vithos came for her. She didn't resist, but she didn't keep quiet either. "No matter what you decide, I'm going to fight for you. I'll find a way." The psychics escorted her out of the stadium as she yelled back at the jury. "It would be wise to work with me instead of against me as I'll do everything I can to help. I will make up for my mistakes!"

Basen glanced at Effie and Cleve but found nothing neighborly about the way they looked back at him. He gave a questioning look to Abith, who fluttered his hand for Basen to leave, then pointed north to imply he should be training.

It was strange to go back to his normal routine as if nothing had happened, but he didn't see another choice.

*****

"How long will they take to decide?" Sanya asked her escorts. She could probably fight her way free, but there was no chance she would make it up and over the wall without anyone stopping her.

"I'm not sure," Reela answered. "Terren didn't tell us."

"Sleep," Vithos advised.

None of them had taken more than a short break from their training in the last day, but Sanya had been up since the day before last. She was beginning to feel dizzy, her body in constant pain.

Reela and Vithos locked her back in her cell and left. She had a bad feeling about all of this.

Forcing herself to stay awake, she began to gather energy around the base of two bars. But after just a few minutes of effort, the prison cell began to spin around her. She fell to the cold, hard ground and then crawled her way up onto the bristly bed of straw.

She would just sleep an hour.

CHAPTER EIGHT

Basen returned to Warrior's Field to practice. He trusted himself not to catch the grass on fire as he tried to familiarize himself with dodging while gathering energy. Thoughts of Sanya distracted him, but soon he was pushing himself too hard to worry about her.

After several hours, he needed a break, and thoughts of her returned with such force that the grunts and clangs of the warriors and Krepps around him fell to near silence in his mind. Guilt roiled in his stomach before he realized why it was there: He would partly be relieved if she died so this confusion and anger could be over.

But she could've killed him when she had him roped and gagged, yet she didn't. And she had saved him when Fatholl had him pinned.

Did he really just tell himself he wanted her dead so he wouldn't have to deal with any more confusion or anger? What a terrible thought. Her execution wouldn't even put an end to it all. Only if he forgot or forgave her would the anger stop, and he would never forget.

He acutely missed Alabell the same way a patient might crave medicine, feeling that her presence could heal his misery.

Abith did not come back before lunch hours. Basen looked for him and the rest of the jury in the dining hall but eventually came to the conclusion they weren't there. Unfortunately, neither was Alabell. Cleve and Effie sat together at a table full of students. There was a spot for

Basen if he wanted it, but he would be more comfortable with the Krepps at this point.

When he noticed Micklin, he sat with the boy. At seeing Micklin's eyes go wide, Basen was glad he could at least make this dining experience special for one person. Micklin chatted away about his growing ability with pyforial energy and how he missed Neeko's instruction. Basen was glad he had almost finished his food by the time the boy asked him about Sanya.

"I don't know what will happen," he told Micklin. "Unfortunately, I have to get back to training."

The boy nodded. "I do, too," he said proudly.

Basen didn't see Abith in their spot past the north wall, so he went back to Warrior's Field to feel less alone. Abith should see him here when he came looking.

But he didn't that day. By the time dinner hours began, Basen had made great progress gathering energy while performing several defensive maneuvers. He didn't see anyone from the jury in the dining hall, where he ate quickly and then made his way south. On his way to his student house, he stopped at the medical building.

Neeko was looking much better as he sat in his bed and made two towels hover in front of him. He was so concentrated on circling them around each other that he didn't notice Basen come up.

"You seem well."

The towels dropped. "Alabell says it'll only be a couple more days before I'm fully healed. I told her I'm ready to go back to teaching tomorrow, but she advised against it."

"I'm glad you're listening to her. She's wise."

Neeko looked down bashfully. "I wouldn't have, but

Shara demanded it."

Basen chuckled. "Is Alabell here?"

"She went home to rest."

"I see." Disappointed, Basen said good night to Neeko and headed out of the medical building. But just as he turned into the hall, he nearly bumped into Alabell.

"You're here!" he blurted.

"It's still early."

"Oh, he must've meant Shara," Basen said to himself. Neeko was still healing with the assistance of potions. His mind probably wasn't all there.

"What?"

"Never mind." As Basen drank in the beautiful sight of her, he forgot all his worries.

"It looks like I have a few moments," Alabell said, her smile warming his heart, and other parts of him. "Tell me about your training."

"It's boring to talk about."

"Boring is what I want right now. And hearing about your improvements makes me feel more secure. It's how I know you'll protect yourself."

So he told her about his training, and she grinned as if he'd given her hope.

"I'm glad for Abith," she said. "I'm looking forward to hearing what else you can accomplish with him."

"Yes, Abith is great." Basen hurried to get to the reason he'd come. "So are you headed back to your student house soon?"

"You would like to walk with me?"

"Yes."

"I need to check on a few people first, and then I'll be

leaving."

"Good. I need to tell you something."

"Now I'm eager to find out." She scowled. "I hope you're not saying that to get me to hurry."

"No, I don't like to play those kinds of games. There really is something."

"All right. You should keep Neeko company while you wait."

So Basen returned to Neeko's bed and watched him as he juggled towels with sleepy eyes. When Neeko noticed him, the towels dropped again.

"You're back."

"Thought you could use some company as I wait for Alabell."

"Thank you."

"I spoke to Micklin. Is he improving as much as he would like to think he is?"

"He is," Neeko confirmed.

"So when can we expect him to fly?"

Neeko chuckled. "Not for a very long time."

"What about controlling swords in the air like you do?"

"The same." There was no chuckle like before. "I should've come to the Academy as soon as Shara and I arrived in Kyrro."

"I'm glad you're here now. Has anyone told the two of you what happened during the Redfield announcement?"

"Effie did."

"I've seen her in the dining hall, still wearing bandages." *Though the bandages were off during Sanya's trial. She probably didn't want to look weak.*

"She comes and goes for treatment, like many people here. I'll be one of them soon enough."

"Shara must be happy the scars of your burns are nearly gone."

Neeko scoffed. "*I'm* the happy one. But it could be a long time before my eyebrows grow back. I made the mistake of looking into a mirror recently."

"It's not that bad."

"Right," Neeko said sarcastically. "My eyes look so small and naked. It's even worse when I smile. I look like a crazed Krepp."

"I'm sure you're exaggerating."

But then Neeko smiled wide and Basen couldn't stifle his laugh quickly enough. As Neeko's face stretched, he looked bordering on mad, as if he would be delighted to taste Basen's flesh.

"I told you," Neeko said as the two laughed together.

✳✳✳✳✳

It was night by the time Basen and Alabell finally walked toward their student homes. "Don't keep me in suspense any longer," she said as soon as they left the medical building.

"Sanya's trial was today."

"Was there an announcement?"

"No. It doesn't seem like most people even know it happened."

"How do you?"

"Sanya wanted me there to speak on her behalf."

Alabell looked surprised. "What did you say?"

"Before I tell you—and I will tell you everything that happened—I'm curious what would happen to Sanya if it were up to you."

Alabell blew out a long breath. Basen expected her, as a healer, to want to preserve life in all circumstances. So he was shocked when she gave her answer. "As callous as this might sound, I think all murderers should be punished in the same way. Even if Sanya wants to help us or she repents for her crimes, it shouldn't matter."

Alabell had danced around saying Sanya should die. Basen doubted she would've advocated execution if she had to be the one to take Sanya's life, but he wouldn't challenge her on that.

"What do you think?" Alabell asked.

"I think it's easy to talk about what Sanya deserves, but it's difficult to answer what's best for us. Her power cannot be ignored."

"I think about that, but then I imagine that she killed someone I loved, and none of it matters anymore." Alabell showed him a sad smile. "I'm feeling guilty now."

Basen took her hand. "The same thing happened to me."

"Why do we feel this way?"

"I think it's important for you to ask yourself that instead of hearing my answer."

She nodded. They walked in silence for a while.

"Are you ready for more pleasant thoughts?" he asked.

"Sarcastic pleasant or actually pleasant?"

"Actually pleasant."

"Yes, please."

"What will you do when the war is over?"

She forced out a light laugh. "I haven't thought about that for even a moment. When the war is over—bastial stars, it doesn't even matter what I'll do. I'll be happy." She hugged him.

He could hold back no longer, cupping her face in his big hands and pressing his lips to hers.

When their kiss came to an end, he said, "You should stay at the Academy afterward. I'm sure there will be a position for a woman of your talent."

Her eyebrows lifted. "Would you say the same if you were sent elsewhere after the war?"

"Of course not. I would be talking about how your talents could be put to great use wherever I go."

She smirked.

When they arrived at their neighboring houses, Basen had grown more curious about something she'd said. Even though their conversation had taken many turns since then, he had to revisit one part or he might never get to sleep.

"Why would I be sent somewhere when the war was over?"

"You have abilities. Depending on the war's outcome, those abilities might be needed."

He couldn't tell if she was scared or worried about this, though it was one of the two.

"You'll be needed as well," he said, confused. "So will Cleve and Effie and Steffen and Reela and Annah...I could keep going."

"But not in the same way as you, Basen." Alabell

produced her key and shoved it in the door lock.

"You could join me in my house," he offered. "So we could finish our conversation."

She gave him a knowing look. "Is that all we would do?" As his cheeks reddened and he tried to think of something to say, she continued. "We can *finish our conversation* in the future. When we're ready."

*****

Abith still didn't show up the next morning. Basen checked both training spots, asking some of the students on Warrior's Field and the guards on the wall if they'd seen him. None had.

Basen decided to take advantage of this time and visit Sanya. She was already calling to him before he rounded the corner and saw her in her cell.

"Basen! Have you heard the results of the trial?"

"I haven't," he said.

She clung to the bars as if she might fall if she let go. After a moment of staring at him, she muttered a curse and spun away.

"They're going to kill me," she said to the floor. "It's the only reason they haven't told me anything yet." She glared at him over her shoulder. "You could've argued more for my cause."

"I wasn't going to lie, Sanya."

She straightened her neck to stare at the wall. "Why are you here?"

"To talk about portals. You must know something about them. You were going to kill me for making them, after all."

"And you've come to get all the information out of me while you still can, because even you think they are going to kill me."

"I don't know that."

"But it is the reason you're coming now." She spun and came at him. He tried to get far enough away from her, but it was too late as she reached out and grabbed his shirt. "It's fine. It's good! Allow me to help as much as I can, but then you must leave."

She sounded insane.

"Why must I leave?"

"I cannot tell you," she said. "Ask what you need to ask. What about portals?"

"Let go of my shirt first."

She released her grasp.

"You must've opened a portal to the world of the dead in order to retrieve Alex, and then again for your mother. Do you have the same limitations as I do?"

"Which are?"

"I can only open a portal where energy has been gathered many times, and I can only go somewhere I've been before."

Sanya shook her head. "I don't have the same limitations, and neither do you."

"I do. Have you slept at all?"

She swatted her hand at him through the bars. "Don't waste our time with your worries. You *do not* have those limitations. You made a portal to the eastern edge of

Ovira. Had you been there before?"

"That was different. I had tried to make a portal to the Academy from the Fjallejon Mountains, but we ended up in the Dajrik Mountains because..." He stopped to think.

"Because what?"

"I figured it was because the energy between the two sections of akorell metal was linked somehow. I don't fully understand it, I'm realizing now."

"Energy is alike everywhere, and you can't see how it all fits together. These limitations might prevent you from creating a portal to a specific place, but they aren't rules. You've obviously made a portal to a place you've never been before, as have I when I went to the spiritual world. The first time was in Raywhite Forest and the second was in the Takary mansion. I doubt energy had been gathered over time in either of those specific spots."

"You can make a portal to anywhere?"

"Only to the spiritual world. But I can make a portal there from anywhere." She made a claw, drawing in all the bastial energy around them. Then she groaned as she spread her hands apart. A small sphere of red—an opening—appeared between them. She dropped her arm, and it collapsed into nothing. She sat on her bed.

Basen was beginning to believe these rules could be broken.

"What kind of damage do these portals do to our world?" he asked.

"I don't know, but like I told you earlier, they are changing the shape of the spiritual world."

"So I suppose you don't know how these portals might affect us?"

"A strain like that probably isn't good, but I don't know more."

He noticed her looking down at the bars in front of his feet. He bent down and put his hand on one of them. The air felt different here, denser yet familiar.

"Have you been gathering energy here?"

"Tell no one."

He rose and scratched his head.

"If that's all, there's something I need to tell you," Sanya said.

Then he realized what she was doing. "I thought you said you didn't need an area where energy has been gathered before in order to make a portal."

"To the spiritual world, yes. But the portals to the spiritual world aren't as powerful as yours."

"But you've never made one like I have, yet you expect to now?"

"Just because I haven't doesn't mean I'm incapable." She grabbed the bars. "You're wasting your time with this. I need to tell you about Rockbreak so you can leave and let me get back to it."

He thought for a while until he decided that he would allow her to drop the subject. He could always tell someone about her plan to escape later if he changed his mind.

"All right, who's Rockbreak?"

"The dajrik of a man you faced on the mountain and saw again outside the castle before you chased after Tauwin. The one who cannot be affected by psyche."

Basen hadn't quite forgotten Rockbreak. He'd just been happily unencumbered by worries of the giant until now. "Is there a secret to defeating him?"

"Not that I know of. I've been considering how he's resisting psyche. He must put himself in a mental state that ignores the shape of his energy. I don't think he does it on purpose, but it might be something others can learn. Psyche is not the ultimate weapon people perceive it to be. Broken bastial energy, like what I can do, or a solid mental state, like what Rockbreak can do, are perfect examples of complete counters to psychics. I was hoping to research ways people like us can resist the manipulation and teach it to you and your allies, but I might not have the chance. I forgot to mention this during my trial. I want you to tell Terren."

"All right."

She bit her lip, looking as if there was more she wanted to say.

"There's a Slugari colony in Raywhite Forest," she whispered. "It's been abandoned."

"I know where it is."

"If something happens, I want you to meet me there."

"I can't do that, Sanya. In fact, I probably should leave and tell someone you're gathering energy."

"Basen, *please!*" She fell to her knees as she grabbed his hand. "You can't tell anyone. Don't you trust me? I'm trying to help your side."

"I do, which is why I won't say anything. But you must promise you won't hurt anyone."

"I promise. No matter what happens to me, I'm not hurting any more allies. Now promise me you will meet me in the Slugari colony."

"I'm not sure I can do that. Ulric has people watching

the Academy, and I can't exactly tell Abith I'm leaving for the day."

"Promise you'll try," she pleaded, pulling him down to the floor with her.

"I'll try."

"You're lying! You must mean it."

"Let go."

"Not until you mean it!"

Someone was shouting Basen's name outside the storage house. He tried to stand, but Sanya continued to tug on his shirt.

"Promise you'll meet me!" she growled.

"I promise! Now let go."

She finally did. He put his ear to the nearest wall.

It sounded like a Krepp's voice. "Basen...Basen...where are you?"

"I have to go," he told Sanya as he ran out.

"Keep your promise! You must!"

He was gone before she could pain him.

"I'm here!" he yelled.

Nebre ran around the side of the building. Relief washed over his face. "Krepps saw someone leaving over the wall. We've been looking for you for a while. He has already come back."

"Did he have long hair tied behind his head and a mean face?"

"No, not Cassius. It was Abith."

Abith? "That must be a mistake."

"Don't you know? He's the one who wants to betray Terren. It does make sense!"

"No, you don't know everything about him. He

wouldn't do that."

"It was him! Many Krepps confirmed."

"Where is he now?"

"But you don't believe he is a traitor! You will destroy the surprise if you tell him anything. He doesn't know we saw."

"I'm sure he knows. Leaving at this time—human guards probably saw him as well. He needs to explain himself."

"No, do not tell him!"

"Nebre, you need to trust me. He wouldn't betray us. Where did he go?"

The Krepp took his time before eventually pointing south. "Toward the stadium."

Why would Abith go that way? "Don't lie to me. Where did he really go?"

Nebre heaved a sigh. He pointed west. "Toward the faculty housing."

Basen ran as quickly as he could. The distance he had to cover was about a mile, and he was seeing spots by the time he got there. Abith was just coming out of his home with his bastial steel sword, a weapon Basen hadn't seen for quite some time. Abith looked determined as he started toward Basen, then shocked when he noticed his student.

"What are you doing here?" Abith asked.

"Never mind me. What were you doing past the wall, and what are you doing now?"

"Investigating. I need to speak with someone."

But the way his instructor spoke told Basen it wouldn't be a conversation but a fight. Basen stayed at his side as Abith walked quickly.

"I've been training alone," Basen pointed out. "It can't possibly take more than a day to come up with a verdict for Sanya."

"Of course not. We found her guilty as soon as she left. She will be executed tomorrow. There are other matters that are more important now."

The news was like a punch to the stomach, stopping Basen completely. He wanted to keep up with Abith; he needed to. But he couldn't move.

Sanya would escape her cell. They didn't keep her chained in there. More might die trying to stop her, even though she'd promised not to hurt anyone else at the Academy. Basen was now obligated to say something, but as soon as he told, Sanya would be killed.

Sick with the terrible choice, he ran to catch up with Abith. "What did you find past the wall?"

Abith stopped and spun with a furious look in his eyes. "Who told you I left?"

"The Krepps. They think you're a traitor."

He cursed. "I don't have time to deal with them right now." Then he broke into a jog.

"What's happening?"

But the loud and clear call of a clarion came from the south. *Battle—an army approaches!*

Abith cursed again and grabbed Basen by his shoulders. "Go," he said. "Join them in the fight, but first tell Terren that I think there's going to be an ambush from the north." Abith pushed him. "Go!"

Abith sprinted northeast and was too far away before Basen could think of a single question.

A needle slid down Basen's spine. His skin hardened as it fell, his bones becoming rocks, his heart bursting with energy. Fire burned in his legs. He would not let the Academy crumble.

He made it to the medical building in no time and yelled his way through. "Ambush from the north! Everyone move to the south wall!" He stormed into the main room, where Alabell had already begun organizing the injured to leave.

"Bring nothing!" she yelled. "If you can run, help those who can't." She shot a look over her shoulder at Basen. "Can you carry someone?"

"I have to warn Terren."

"Then go."

He darted past the people already evacuating and was first out of the building. He raced all the way to the wall. With Basen coming from the far north, Terren had already organized much of the army here.

"It's their full force!" Terren yelled. "Show me your bravery. Mages and archers on the wall!"

"Terren!" Basen screamed, but he was stuck behind hundreds of his allies as most people were still making their way to their spots. Basen pushed his way through, but by the time he got to the base of the nearest ramp, the battle had begun.

"Fire!" Terren called.

Mages shot their fireballs, archers loosed their arrows, and Basen screamed for Terren's attention. The wall was too packed for him to force his way up.

"Terren! There will be an ambush from behind!"

Many troops heard and stared at him with dread, but

no officer was among them.

Basen strained his neck for a glimpse through the gate and witnessed the horrifying sight of thousands charging the wall. There were so damn many, did an ambush really matter at this point? Could anyone be spared?

But then Basen got his answer when an explosion of stone shook the earth beneath his feet. He fell, though he was glad to be on the ground as debris flew overhead.

When the rumbling came to an end, he rose up and was sickened to see that it wasn't just chunks of stone that had moved through the air above him but the bodies of his comrades.

The gaping hole in the Academy's wall looked like a dog with its teeth missing, a dog Basen had always relied on to protect him.

"Where's the catapult?" Terren yelled. "There are none in front of us."

"It's our own!" Basen answered as he realized the unfortunate truth. "It's an ambush from behind us."

"We can't hold them much longer," Sneary announced. "They're coming directly to the hole in the wall."

CHAPTER NINE

The armored horsemen were the first through, the strength of the beasts too much for even the Krepps in the front line. Basen took a risky shot with his allies so close to his target but managed to strike the lead cavalier with a fireball, sending the enemy soaring off his horse.

It was too little too late, as a horde of other invaders followed the horsemen into the Academy.

Another explosion rocked the wall farther down as a boulder broke through the stone and toppled many archers and mages shooting from atop.

Then came the horde from behind that Basen had anticipated with terror. This was all too perfectly synchronized—this had to have been planned in advance. He noticed the Redfield clock above the charging army of betrayers. It was only a few minutes past the hour. They had planned to strike right at ten. Thousands of them from Tenred, thousands! Every single selfish man who'd come here with Crea now charged to finish off the last of Kyrro's Allies. How had this happened after psychics questioned every one of them?

Anger struck Basen like a lightning bolt. Was this Abith's doing all along? No. It had to be someone else. Cassius. Basen saw him at the head of the charge, a sinister grin on his face. Basen was one of the only mages firing upon them, the rest of them panicking with the archers on the broken wall. He struck down dozens, his fireballs large enough to kill two, sometimes three at a time.

But it was not enough. The fight against these betrayers from Tenred would take every ally Basen had, but there was an army of an even greater number pouring through the wall.

"To the east!" Terren yelled. "We cannot be between them. Everyone get to the east."

The fight raged, swords piercing flesh, many of Basen's comrades running, others standing to face their enemies against the headmaster's order.

"If you stay here you will die!" Terren screamed. "You must move now."

Everyone who disobeyed him was quickly cut down, overwhelmed by enemies. That didn't stop Basen from disobeying as well, but not by staying put. He had to get to the medical building.

His nerves steeled as courage dissolved all fear. He ran straight for the betrayers, Cassius still at the head, still with his wicked grin.

"Basen, what are you doing?" Cleve yelled somewhere behind him.

"Alabell and Effie were in the medical building!"

If Cleve replied, Basen didn't hear it. He was too busy focusing bastial energy into his legs. Just before colliding with Cassius, he leapt up and jumped off Cassius' shoulder. It gave Basen the boost he needed to land on top of the wall of the Group One mage training area. He scampered across as knives sailed by him and quickly scaled the flat roof of the connected classroom.

He halted as he saw it would be quite a leap to the next roof. He took off his training sword and cloak to discard as much weight as he could, then dug deep to push himself to the utmost speed he could reach. He jumped.

Basen braced himself for impact when he realized he couldn't reach the roof with his feet. He grabbed hold of the edge with his forearms, his chest and knees slamming into the wood. He pulled himself up as more knives barely missed him. Going around the side of the building, many betrayers circled in hopes of him coming down in front of them.

Basen didn't have it in him to make another jump like the last, and his enemies seemed to know this as they taunted him to try. He dashed across the roof at a speed he was certain none of the men below him could reach. Their taunting came to an end as they struggled to keep up. But Basen didn't jump for the roof as he'd led them to believe. He leapt off at an angle and came down straight upon the last line of the betrayers. None of these men seemed to have a clue why the rest of their comrades had been shouting about jumping, but a few looked up to find Basen just as he landed on top of them.

He felt their bones break beneath him. Rolling, he avoided enemy swords that accidentally impaled the flesh of the enemies behind him.

"Grab him!" some yelled. But the others ignored the suggestion, swiping wildly at Basen, who zipped around them like a feral cat avoiding capture. They cut more among them as Basen barreled into the few he couldn't avoid. Hands grabbed at him, but none could keep hold.

He broke free. Some gave chase only to give up after a breath when they saw how much faster he was. Soon he came to the clearing between the classrooms and the stadium. There were many enemies still in front of him. He didn't know what to make of these men trailing behind their comrades—perhaps they were cowards—but there was no way to trick them into thinking he was one of them. They all wore black uniforms, and Basen recognized some of them from his time in Tenred. Most were too confused to go after him as he ran around them, but others chased him.

They were slow. Basen wished he'd had time to grab a real sword so he could at least kill a few of these men. They deserved worse than death. The entrance to the medical building was blocked by enemies going inside, so he had to go around and hope for an open window. If Alabell was even there.

Basen yelled her name as he circled with many enemies still trailing him. Soon he made it to the first window outside the largest room of the building, where Alabell spent most of her time. A healer in a white coat was crawling out, her face bloody from a head wound. Someone grabbed her from the other side and pulled her back in. Basen jumped in and kicked her attacker off her.

Screams rang out around him as the horrible scene burned in his memory. There were equal numbers of enemies and allies, but hardly any of his allies here were trained to fight. And just like him, they had no blade to defend themselves. None of his allies were being taken prisoner. This was a massacre in the making!

He took out his wand and shot two men cornering a group of injured who were trying to get to Basen's window. It freed them to escape.

Basen noticed movement from his side. He ducked as he stepped back, his enemy's blade slamming into the wall. Basen pushed the man's arm against the wall to keep his weapon pinned. He blocked a punch from the man's free hand, then delivered his own punch to the man's wrist.

The sword dropped out of the man's hand as he squealed. He and Basen fell to the ground in hopes of retrieving it, grabbing each other's limbs as best they could while trying to pull the other away. Basen got his hand around in front of the man's face and gathered energy there. It burned his palm, but it did far worse to the man's eyes. He screamed and turned away as he covered his face.

Basen got the sword and started to stand, but there was another flash of movement so he fell down onto his stomach to avoid the blade. Another enemy got his foot on Basen's new sword.

Basen let go and rolled away before the inevitable boot could stomp on his arm. He backed away from the two enemies and glanced around the enormous room. Alabell wasn't here, and neither were Neeko or Effie. Basen rushed the back of a man focused on two injured women hobbling away from him, leaping as he got close and kicking his enemy in the spine. The man lost his sword as he fell forward. Basen grabbed it and spun to face his two attackers.

They advanced without hesitation. Basen blocked the first blow and blew bastial energy into the face of the next attacker, causing him to scream out and recoil. Basen deflected the first man's following swipe and ran his sword through his chest. The other had recovered, but he wasn't quick enough to stop Basen's onslaught of pokes and slashes. One got through to his leg.

Basen turned and swung his blade as he felt someone coming up on him. His blade sunk into the man's arm, the force of it buckling one of his knees and sending him down on his side.

The other enemies seemed to notice Basen then, calling to each other for support as they all started to circle him. The injured quickly made their way out the window and doorway, now completely ignored.

There were at least twenty men, all waiting for someone to attack Basen first. This was a grave error. He aimed his wand and fired, then again. His first took out two of them at once and the second took out one more. Some charged while others cowered. Basen gathered more energy and blasted the first man in the face, then danced around the two others swinging wildly at him.

Their feet got tangled, causing both to trip. Basen stabbed one man on his way down, and then the other who'd already hit the floor. The Tenred bastard he'd just burned tried to rush him with his arm up to protect his eyes, so Basen went one way and then the other to get around and stab him in the leg.

All others seemed more hesitant to approach by then. They looked behind them as if waiting for something. Then Basen noticed two men fetching bows from the ground.

It was his turn to run. He bolted for the window. Someone got in his way. Basen batted the enemy's sword out of his hand and rammed his shoulder against him to send him flying. With the window clear, Basen jumped through, but his own stolen sword had fallen and become lost without him realizing until it was too late.

He ran as they came through one by one to chase him. Alabell and the others must've escaped already, but which way did they go? Basen had no way of knowing. His best choice was to turn back to rejoin the rest of the Academy's army.

Terren had ordered everyone to retreat to get all their enemies on one side. They were probably in the southeastern corner of the campus by now. Basen veered in that direction.

He ran for quite a while without anyone blocking his path, eventually thinking he would make it. But the closer he got to the battle, the more enemies started popping up in front of him. He changed course to avoid them all, but soon there was no route to take him straight there. Eventually they caught sight of him coming from behind.

He'd created a wide gap between the enemies behind him by then, but he'd also exhausted himself as he'd covered probably a couple of miles since this had begun. He held up his wand and tried to look less fatigued.

Most of these men looked far less confident than Cassius, reluctant to approach and wearing expressions of worry. Basen recognized one of them, a stonemason from the castle. He didn't know the man's name, but they'd spoken on a few occasions over the years.

"Why do this?" Basen asked to buy himself time.

Their approach slowed. The stonemason stopped and shuffled to get himself behind his comrades, presumably ashamed by his betrayal.

"Crea made a deal with Ulric," answered the lead man.

"When?" Basen asked. He already knew the answer. It had to have been a while ago. She knew her loyalists would be questioned with psyche, so she'd told them nothing until it was time to strike. Today. But he needed more time to figure out how to get through to his army.

There were about a dozen easing toward Basen, trying to avoid getting out in front so they wouldn't become his first target. That didn't include all the enemies approaching from behind.

The clamor of battle sounded so far away. Terren's voice was almost completely lost against the roar of other shouts. From what Basen could make out, the headmaster seemed to be ordering them to shift once more.

No one answered Basen's question. Enemies were beginning to catch up from behind. He would have to run again soon, but he still needed to catch his breath and figure out how to get around these men.

"Take me to Crea," Basen demanded.

Two of the men snickered. One told him, "Put down your weapon and we will."

He shot at the snickering men first, putting a permanent end to their laughter. The rest charged, but they underestimated how quickly he could gather energy for another fireball. He shot another group of two, but there were still many more.

He would have to wrench the sword out of the first enemy's hands quickly enough to defend himself from all the others. He shot one more time, taking down the first and second fastest of these men, noticing the stonemason still staying behind.

The next assailant came in contact as Basen was backing away. Basen stepped in just as the man raised his sword, turned his back as he grabbed the man by his arm, and flipped him over his hip. The sword came loose. Basen spun around to ready himself for the next...four of them. *God's mercy.* And the sword he'd taken was iron and rusted.

An arrow embedded itself in the neck of one man. Another arrow pierced an arm and sprawled the enemy as he lost his sword, which slid to a stop at Basen's feet. He started to pick it up but had to stop and roll backward to avoid more attackers.

As he created some distance to buy time to plan his defense, two more arrows found homes in the bodies of his enemies. Basen finally had a moment to glance in the direction they'd come from. Cleve and Peter stood atop neighboring buildings, both men firing with speed.

It was good to see that Peter had chosen the right side in this separation between Tenred and the Academy. The betrayers must've excluded him from the battle plan knowing he would've warned the Academy leadership.

The enemies began to take notice and started using the many classrooms around them for cover. They yelled to each other to shoot the Academy archers, but it seemed that Tenred betrayers with bows were rare. Cleve and Peter continued to shoot down any black uniforms, giving Basen the opportunity to get over to the mage classroom Cleve stood upon and climbed up.

Basen joined in the shooting, using his wand to hurl fireballs down onto the corners of buildings where enemies scurried for protection. The splash of fire caused these unseen men to scream. It would've given Basen great satisfaction if he wasn't in such a hurry to get back to the rest of the Academy's army.

Cleve rained arrows down onto the backs of betrayers closing in around the allies until he had no arrows left.

"I'm out!" he told Peter.

"Same."

But Basen continued to shoot balls of flaming destruction, killing all that he could.

An arrow flew by between him and Cleve, making Basen realize how dangerous this was now. He and Cleve lay flat.

Cleve yelled, "Peter, get—!"

But Peter screamed before Cleve could finish. Basen rose up to see Peter with an arrow in his stomach, collapsing to his knees.

More arrows flew overhead as Basen and Cleve crawled to the edge of the roof and jumped down. Basen followed Cleve as he leapt up to grab the lower awning of Peter's building, got himself onto it, then climbed up to the roof.

Peter lay on his side as he groaned. "What are you doing here?" he complained. "Get somewhere safe. I'm done."

"We have to get to everyone else," Basen agreed.

Arrows soared over them, too high to hit them so long as they stayed down, but Basen had to risk a look to see where his enemies were. The battle had shifted past the southern wall, many of Basen's allies climbing up and then jumping off with enemies following.

"It looks like Terren is having everyone retreat to the south," he said. "Ulric's troops have come around to join Crea's."

"You mean Abith's," Cleve corrected. He sat up for his own glimpse.

"Watch out!" Basen called as he noticed a couple enemy archers climbing up onto a classroom not too far from theirs.

"We have to get down onto the other side." Cleve grabbed Peter by the arm and dragged him.

Peter helped with his feet as he screamed in agony. Basen covered them by shooting a fireball at the archers, causing them to duck and drop the arrows they'd nocked. He helped Cleve get Peter down to the awning, and then to the ground. Peter fell with a grunt.

"We have to go," Cleve urged, trying to pull Peter up again.

"Leave me," he groaned. "Find some way to live so you can kill them all later. This battle is lost."

"Cleve." Basen pointed at a horde of Ulric's soldiers in blue who'd spotted them and were approaching quickly.

Cleve cursed. Peter forced himself up. With surprising strength, he ripped Basen's sword out of his hand and then stuck the hilt of his own into Basen's palm.

"Use mine," Peter gritted out. "Ten times better than that shoddy blade." He took a fighter's stance, his face showing great pain. "I'm fighting until my last breath. Go!"

"Peter—" Cleve began.

"Go!" Peter yelled. "Don't let my death be meaningless. Get to Terren. Win this war."

"Thank you," Basen said and started to turn. But Cleve, the brave fool, took a spot beside Peter.

"I'm dead anyway, Cleve!" Peter spat out, his face red. "Don't be an idiot. Go!"

Basen pulled Cleve away. They ran around a building, then another, heading south away from the horde. The wall was close by then. The battle had shifted to the east, sounds of it growing from outside the wall.

Basen and Cleve ran through the broken gate and found themselves parallel with the rest of their allies backing away from enemies pouring over the wall like ants.

"Terren's retreating into the forest," Basen realized.

Cleve turned to Basen with a dire look. "It was by accident that Peter and I found you. We climbed up to the building to shoot, and before we saw you, we noticed Effie and Steffen with others going north. They were being chased. I'm not sure what became of them, but someone needs to go in case they need help."

"Where north?"

"Veering west toward the third-year student homes. Alabell and Neeko were with them. I'll stay with my uncle."

"I hope we see each other again," Basen said as he turned and sprinted.

"Be safe!" Cleve called after him.

CHAPTER TEN

Sanya began to gather energy again at a furious rate as soon as Basen was called away by some Krepp. They would execute her—it was the only reason they hadn't come to tell her the decision of the jury yet. She had to escape, and she wasn't sure if Basen would do anything to help.

It was difficult to tell the time with only a sprinkle of daylight gliding in through a far window. But it didn't seem as if more than an hour had gone by before she heard screams. Some seemed to be people calling to each other, while others yelped out of fear. None were close, but the increasing number of screams made up for that as they came from nearly every direction.

Eventually it sounded as if an entire army was running around the storage building. The walls were too thick for Sanya to pick up anything with psyche except that there were hundreds if not thousands of them. Whatever was happening, it might be her best chance to escape.

She had almost gathered enough energy to make a portal; she could feel it. But the air at the base of the two bars had felt like this for the last few hours, unchanged. As she had never made a portal to anywhere but the spiritual world, she had no idea how much more energy it would take.

She'd already tried to break the bars with a portal to the spiritual world, and as she'd told Basen, the portal wasn't strong enough. She'd tried to make one that would envelop part of the bar, but it would not hold steady as the metal started to pass through it. Perhaps with an akorell stone, she could make one her size and force part of her prison inside, but right now she had nothing but the clothes on her body.

The army marched past her, and the screams seemed to move ahead of them. Sweat down her temples made her hair stick to her face, her breathing ragged. She leaned forward and grabbed hold of the bars as she looked down and made energy beneath her.

She tried and tried, then tried some more, but all she accomplished was burning her shins. She fell forward when she lacked the strength to keep herself up, her shoulders ramming into the bars. She cursed and sank backward to sit on the cold ground.

She lay there until she'd regained her breath, then rose up again. This time the feeling was different. The door was there, waiting for her to open it. She forced energy together once again and finally felt the beginning of a portal. It was like falling into a familiar dream, as she lost sense of where she was to focus on where she was going.

She found herself encased by stone walls, the dim glow of the ceiling above. Back in the Fjallejon Mountains, she'd spent much time here preparing herself to make a portal to the spiritual world after she'd finally found the spot. She'd needed the boost of energy from the akorell metal, which she used to open a portal to the red steppes of the spiritual world and toss in the weapon of death. Now she was back—no, she was still imprisoned. *Focus!*

Her mind was split between her location and her

destination, reality and memory. She regained sight of the cage and the dark sphere hovering between the base of two bars. The mental strain felt like trying to keep three enraged rams from colliding into each other. There was no way to fully control this beast, its edges bending inward in hopes of collapsing on itself as she pushed with all her strength to keep it whole. The bar rattled as she forced the portal wider, one edge brushing against solid metal.

But just like with the small entrances to the spiritual world she'd made here, the metal was too sturdy to be broken. Sanya sucked in a deep breath and pushed with all of her strength to double the size of the portal. It went from half to the full size of her fist, finally growing to reach past the bar. It bit off a chunk of the base.

The rest of the bar crashed down on top of the portal, breaking the portal apart. Sanya gasped as she fell to her knees. She neither heard nor sensed anyone nearby. She begged for her stamina to return as she crawled toward the opening in her cell. It would be a tight fit, but she would get through even if she lost a damn nipple in the process.

*****

After a short time and a bruised chest, Sanya made it out of the storage building. No one was around her. She could easily run to the north wall, make her way over...but then what? The only route available would be through the

Fjallejon Pathway and into Tenred unless she risked going around the Academy once she was past the wall.

Where were all the wall guards? Where was anyone?

She could risk going east. If she made it to Lake Kayvol, she should be able to hide in the copse of trees on the eastern side and drink from the lake until she decided what to do.

No, she'd promised to do everything she could to make up for her mistakes. Something was happening to the Academy, and she might be needed.

She had to get somewhere high before she could figure out anything. She did make the short trip to the north wall after all but only for a glimpse of the rest of the campus.

A large army of Tenred troops marched south. Something flying through the air caught her attention—a boulder! It looked to have been flung from within the Academy. It smashed down somewhere on the southern wall, shattering part of it to pieces. She faintly heard screams of horror as she scanned for the catapult.

There, in the wide path between the housing for staff and the psychic classrooms. It was the Academy's own war weapon being used against them.

A betrayal. Tenred! The very troops who came here to help fight against the Takarys have now joined Ulric against the Academy.

It was time for her to fight.

The wounds she'd come here with had healed, but she was weakened from exhaustion and the stress of her whole ordeal. She needed a weapon. She would go back to the storage building—a scream stopped her from descending the ramp of the wall. She shielded her eyes from the morning sun to make out the Tenred army separating to chase after students trying to get away.

Sanya's mind would be her weapon. She rushed down the ramp and toward the army. A voice nagged her to run the opposite way, to escape and forget about those who would've executed her. She ignored it as she made her way down the wide southern path, traveling between the dining hall and the storage building, and then between Warrior's Field and the farms. A group of Krepps encircled a single man toward the center of the enormous field of grass. Sanya stopped for a moment, unsure what to do, before deciding to listen to her curiosity and turn toward them.

Three of them attacked the man, who turned out to be Abith. "I'm not responsible for this!" he yelled. "You're attacking the wrong man, and you're keeping me from helping everyone else!"

"You lie!" one Krepp responded, then spat in Abith's face.

Another Krepp dived on top of Abith, but he rolled backward and flung the creature off. He deflected and dodged blades, refusing to attack back as he continued to yell at them.

"It's Cassius Lane who you must kill! Stop!"

Sanya came up behind the Krepps. "He's telling the truth," she said. "I can tell with psyche."

The Krepps stopped fighting. "Who are you?"

But another Krepp answered in their own language, probably recognizing her from the stadium.

They had a brief conversation among themselves,

then darted off while glaring back at Abith and Sanya.

"Who let you out?" Abith asked. "Never mind." He ran in the same direction as the Krepps, calling to them, "I'm joining you against the traitors."

Her nagging voice grew louder. Abith's tone had confirmed what she'd assumed: She was to be a prisoner until executed.

She didn't move as she reconsidered her options. North to Tenred or east to Lake Kayvol. Abith and the Krepps headed west until they left the field and disappeared around student homes. Again, Sanya had to remind herself of her promise. She would help them no matter what. But it was to the south where she seemed to be needed more than the west, where most of the Tenred troops had gone. Abith and the Krepps had probably headed off to meet up with more of the lizard creatures.

By the time she'd caught up to Tenred's army, the last of them were making their way past Redfield at the center of the school. They'd separated into many smaller groups by then. Some veered west, others north, but the rest continued south. Soon she heard the sounds of the raging battle, and she gritted her teeth in determination.

The troops running in her direction glared at her and asked something among themselves. She had no weapon, no armor, but she was still confident she could take on the six of them if needed.

"Who are you?" one asked her.

"Come closer and find out."

Insulted, the man started toward her. But another put his arm out to stop him and told Sanya, "If you are staff of the Academy there is no need for you to die. You will continue to work here but for Crea and the rest of us."

"I'm not."

He shook his head at her answer, as if disappointed by her stupidity when she could've lied. The first man she'd insulted charged while the others stayed back to watch.

She took him down easily with psyche. As he lay coiled on the ground, she snatched the sword from his weakened grip and plunged the tip into his neck.

The others began to curse as they all ran in different directions. She pained them all and walked after them as they tried to crawl away. One by one, she killed them and took the best sword among them.

An arrow caused her to flinch as it missed to the side. She ran around the nearest wall of the round stadium for cover. Locating the archer to the south, she saw him put his bow back on his shoulder and join the rest of his moving army.

She took a different route than the wide road to the south, going around the mage and psychic classrooms to keep herself safe from other archers. As she neared the southern wall, she heard the battle shifting. Terren was in retreat.

She climbed up the nearest building to find out exactly why he would run from a few thousand Tenred troops, most of them hardly skilled in comparison to the Academy's warriors.

The wall was broken in several parts, the gate collapsed. Ulric's troops had broken through and come around to join Tenred's, forcing Terren's army out of the Academy.

An arrow flew over her shoulder.

She'd been found. Archers shot at her as she jumped down for cover. The sound of rushing boots forced her to flee. There were too many to face alone. She needed to get around these men to join the rest of the Academy.

She ran west until she no longer heard the patter of boots chasing her. She went south again to put herself in line with the last of the southern classrooms and risked a look. Only enemies were left within the school, now chasing the last of Kyrro's Allies over the wall.

Sanya ran through the gaping hole where the gate used to bar entrance. Terren seemed to be taking his army into the forest, outnumbered an estimated five to one. But at least there were no more enemies behind him and his troops.

Unfortunately, Sanya was stuck between her enemies and allies, and she refused to let herself think of the Academy's troops in any other way. It would be too easy to give up on them and leave to make a life for herself somewhere else.

She had to find some way to get around.

CHAPTER ELEVEN

Cleve fought like a jungle cat trying to evade capture as men came at him from every angle. He'd left his longbow, the gift from his father, at the Academy. He promised himself he would return for it somehow, even though it appeared this battle would be lost, as Peter had said.

He'd cut and lunged his way through his enemies to make it to Terren's side. There was no doubt about it; his uncle had been the target from the start. But Cleve wasn't the only one protecting Terren, as everyone left standing would fight until they could no longer lift a weapon.

"We have to separate," Terren told Sneary as they got behind the cover of the first trees of Raywhite Forest. "They're coming around for me. We don't have the numbers to keep them from flanking. Just leave me Groups Seven and Eight."

"Got it," Sneary said with surprising speed, too easily giving up on Terren. "All Groups but Seven and Eight, follow!" he ordered.

Almost the entire army moved southwest with Sneary, half the enemies following and still outnumbering them. Many family members of the Academy had been recruited to the school weeks ago. Half had left when the Takary army threatened them with the destruction of their homes. The rest who stayed now fled with their kin.

There were no more than thirty mages and warriors left from Group Seven and Eight, none with family beside them. *One thousand against thirty*, Cleve estimated.

"Go with them!" Terren ordered Cleve.

"I will not leave you no matter what you say!" Cleve screamed as he blocked an attack and cut two men with one swing.

"They focus all their efforts on me. We have to use it against them."

"Cleve." It was Reela's voice. "We must go with the rest. It's the only way they'll have a chance."

"You go," he screamed back. "I'm staying. Keep them alive and we'll meet again soon." Reela had her mother to worry about. Airy would follow Reela wherever she went, though she was smart enough to stay at the back of the battle.

"Cleve!" Reela implored.

He chanced a look over to see Vithos dragging her away with the rest. Soon she stopped resisting and disappeared behind the dense trees.

"Basen, where are you?" Terren yelled.

"I sent him north to help Effie and others escaping from the medical building," Cleve said, dread tightening his chest. So his uncle had hoped to use a portal. Cleve didn't see how that was possible in the forest. Perhaps in all this chaos Terren hadn't remembered the limitations.

"That's fine, Cleve. We'll find a way out of this."

One enemy stood out above the rest. Cleve had no name for the giant in full steel armor, not until his comrades yelled to him. "Rockbreak! The headmaster went this way."

Rockbreak had proved to be an unstoppable force with no weak spot on his body, a boulder. The only thing keeping him from demolishing Kyrro's Allies was his slow speed. He yelled in frustration as Terren continued to retreat.

From behind the enemy army, Rockbreak's deep voice sent a chill down Cleve's spine. "Terren's head is mine!"

Enemies ran to come around on Cleve's side. If he wasn't already busy fighting two or three at once no matter how many he killed, he could've done something about it. But all he could do now was shout a warning. "Flanking us!"

Suddenly the skilled swordsmen working their way through Cleve's defenses dropped and screamed. Annah stepped toward them and yelled to Cleve, "Block those going around!" She bent toward her enemies with her knife drawn. She was supposed to have left with the others, but Cleve was glad she was here.

Their screams became gargled with blood as Annah killed them while Cleve put himself in front of the flanking dozen of swordsmen. None of them had armor like Rockbreak, but they had twice the skill that those from Tenred possessed.

Cleve attacked like a swarm of bees, his bastial steel sword too quick for them to stop. He'd cut down half of them when he heard screaming from behind.

"Flanking other side!"

Cleve moved backward as he fought to keep in line with the small group of his army remaining around his uncle. Their enemies began to charge.

We have to give the rest of our allies more time.

Terren must've been thinking the same thing as he screamed for them to run.

They rushed through the trees while chased by as

many men as could fit in all forest lanes. There was no chance to hide, nowhere to take cover. They could keep running to stall these enemies from meeting back with the rest and overwhelming their Academy allies, but was there any way for Terren to get out of this alive?

I love you, Reela.

It felt as if Cleve's heart had shattered to pieces when another group of enemies appeared in front of them. Terren cursed and came to a stop. He dropped his sword and put up his hands.

"Nothing we can do now," Terren told them. His teeth bit down on his lip in obvious anger, while his eyes squinted with a sad look. He glanced at Cleve coming over to join him, then at Jackrie on his other side. "Let them take you prisoner," he whispered.

Everyone dropped their weapons as the circle of enemies closed in on them. Everyone but Cleve. He valued his bastial steel sword almost as much as his life. To be captured was the same as losing it, nearly the same as death.

"Put it down, Cleve," Terren demanded.

Cleve compromised and put it in its sheath instead.

The enemies made a path for Rockbreak. The giant came through huffing, removing his helmet and wiping the sweat from his forehead. He did not have the face of a man but of some gargantuan creature, with a bulbous forehead and a square chin.

"You will suffer for making me run!" Rockbreak boomed.

Cassius pushed through to stand beside the giant and frowned at the sight of Terren giving up.

"I expected more out of you," Cassius complained. "I admired you when we were enemies in the last war. You were hailed as the best swordsman in Ovira, the leader of the courageous Academy army, outsmarting the best of your enemies. This should've ended with a duel between you and Abith, but you've become soft and made him so as well somehow."

"I'll cooperate with whatever you want so long as you take the rest here prisoner," Terren demanded.

"Soft, like I said."

Furious, Cleve almost drew his blade and charged Cassius right then. But as Cleve took a step, Terren put a hand on his arm to stop him.

"It's over," Terren said.

"Almost," Cassius corrected. "I'm sure Rockbreak will agree with me that we want to see the old Terren one last time before you die."

"Agree," Rockbreak said.

"Spread out," Cassius ordered. "Form a circle."

Rockbreak moved into its center. He jabbed his bastial steel sword into the ground to remove his armor, the weapon nearly the same height as an average man. With his mammoth arms, he had the advantage of reach over Terren, an advantage Terren was used to having over his own opponents. Cleve feared the worst was inevitable. Even if his uncle won, the archers would shoot him down.

Enemies shoved Cleve and his allies into place to make up the center ring of the wide circle. Then they were pushed down to their knees. The men behind Cleve grabbed his bastial steel sword out of his sheath and let out a sound of surprise. "Where did you get this?"

Cleve didn't answer. It took all his will to remain still as he desperately wanted to fight the person who had laid hands on his sword.

"There will be time for questions later," Rockbreak grumbled as he continued to take off his steel armor.

Cleve was beside Jackrie and Annah, the three of them glancing around for a way to escape, fight back, anything to avoid what was about to happen.

Something blunt struck Cleve in the back of the head and blurred his vision. "Keep your eyes on the duel," said the man behind him.

Rockbreak finished removing his armor. Basen was right—the man was larger and stronger than any Krepp. It was as if he had legs for arms. No doubt his shirt had been made specially for him, though it still stretched to contain his chest as if all the fabric from the tailor had been used and it still wasn't enough.

"If you want a fair fight," Cleve said, "you will let Terren use my bastial steel sword."

The man behind Cleve grumbled a curse at him.

"Give Terren the sword," Rockbreak demanded. "He will lose anyway."

Terren approached and let out his hand. The man gave the weapon to Terren blade first, letting go of the handle before Terren had a safe grip. But Terren pinched his fingers and twisted his wrist, spinning the light weapon so the handle flung toward him. He grabbed it out of the air with familiarity as if he'd used the sword for years.

He looked down to send Cleve a message with his eyes. What he was trying to say, though, Cleve had little idea. In his uncle's eyes was sadness but also love. Terren stared for a bit, then looked to Jackrie. He turned his head slightly, lifting his eyebrows. She jumped up and hugged him before anyone could get their hands on her.

Cleve heard her whisper, "Cleve, come here."

"Enough of that," Rockbreak complained. "No time. More people to kill!"

Enemy soldiers closed in but not before Cleve jumped up and squeezed through to join the embrace. Jackrie whispered, "I will distract them so you and Annah can escape."

"Not until the end of the duel," Terren said. "Let them fight each other over your sword, Cleve, and then run."

Tears stung Cleve's eyes as enemies pulled him and Jackrie away from his uncle. Terren and Jackrie had just accepted their fate. Both of them would soon be dead.

Terren had cared for Cleve like a father. He was the last of Cleve's family...there was so much Cleve needed to tell Terren. There was no one left in this world who Cleve loved in the same way that he did Terren. There was no other man like Terren. But Cleve could say none of this, as the duel had already begun.

Terren tried to circle around Rockbreak to get a better feel for his opponent, but the giant charged him. Faced with an overhead attack too powerful to block, Terren's only choice was to get out of the way. Rockbreak seemed to know he would, swiping at Terren in the same moment he dodged. Had Terren simply stood still, he would've had a clear opening to stab his weapon in Rockbreak's chest. The giant was a smarter fighter than he appeared.

It took a master like Terren to get his weapon up in

time to save himself. He seemed surprised by his own agility, but it was really the light weight of the bastial steel, Cleve knew, that caused his shock.

I should've given him the weapon to train with long before this.

Terren attacked as if he had a heavier sword, putting more than enough power into each swing to slice his blade through bone. Speed was what he needed, not additional power. It took no more than a moment for Cleve to see that Rockbreak was indeed a master like Terren.

The giant fought fluidly, better than he'd spoken. His movements looked instinctive as he moved his weapon as if it were an extension of his body.

Terren soon had to look out for more weapons than just Rockbreak's sword. The giant swung his elbows with enough force to crack Terren's skull if they connected. Later he tried to smash his head into Terren's as he came in close.

Cleve had trained his whole life to fight like Rockbreak, with his entire body, and much of his time had been spent with his uncle. Terren should know what to do—he had to create opportunities to attack by taking risks, putting himself closer than he clearly wanted to be. But there seemed to be no weaknesses in Rockbreak's defense, just as there were none in his offense. He was stronger than any human should be, yet he matched Terren's speed. His sword covered every part of his body and attacked from every angle.

Unfortunately, Rockbreak soon caught onto Terren's strategy of attacking and then retreating. He charged

Terren again, just like in the beginning, only this time he smothered Terren with attacks and continued to press.

Terren retreated to the edge of the circle, where he was just about to trip over his own troops until they told him he was coming to the edge. He planted his feet and defended all of Rockbreak's blows, but they never seemed to end. Trapped against the edge of the circle, Terren almost looked to be defending his own people from an inhuman creature. Terren's size over the kneeling students made him appear fatherly, the determination on his face showing everyone that he would protect them until his last breath.

Rockbreak chipped away at Terren's strength as he slashed down and swept his weapon across over and over, forcing Terren to block every attack. Terren amazed Cleve at how precise his defense had become since the last time they'd sparred. There was no doubt that his lessons with Abith were the only reason he still hadn't been cut. But time was not on his side.

He finally found an opening and darted around Rockbreak. Frustrated, Rockbreak charged for the third time. Terren ran at him, to Cleve's surprise. At the last moment, both men dodged to opposite sides and slashed hard. Their weapons clashed with a deafening ring. But Rockbreak's strength was too much for Terren, knocking Cleve's weapon out of Terren's hands.

Without giving Terren a moment to turn for the sword, Rockbreak spun to keep up with his momentum and cut Terren deeply across his chest. Terren fell backward, toward the fallen sword. He grabbed it before Rockbreak could stomp over to him, but his grievous injury made his movements slow as he put it up to defend himself. Rockbreak slashed the weapon out of his hand again, then turned his grip to bring his sword straight down into Terren's heart.

Cleve screamed in rage.

"Don't," Jackrie wailed, her cheeks wet with tears. He didn't realize until then that he was struggling against his captors to get to his now dead uncle.

"Cleve!" Jackrie yelled again.

Suddenly he remembered their plan. Annah was weeping beside him. He turned and grabbed her for a hug only so he could whisper in her ear. "Jackrie will distract them. We run."

Slowly, their enemies began to move toward the bastial steel sword. Rockbreak left to put on his armor once again, not seeming to notice one of them picking up Cleve's weapon. A few dozen glared as they closed in on the man.

"Such a disappointment," Cassius commented, nudging Terren's body with the side of his boot. He didn't seem to care that half of the men vying for the bastial steel were his own.

Cleve almost gave his life for the chance to kill the traitor, his whole body burning with the urge to leap on top of Cassius and strangle him. Fortunately, Jackrie was the first one there.

She'd gathered a ball of bastial energy the size of her fist, rushing Cassius with it floating out in front of her. He screamed as the heat of it reached him, instinctively falling away from her before it touched his flesh.

She screamed as well, her mage robe blackening

around her stomach. She pressed toward Cassius as he scampered backward.

"Shoot her!" Cassius yelled.

But Jackrie spun toward where the archers hurried to load their weapons and set her bastial ball aflame as she unleashed it. The fireball hit one archer directly, sending two others spiraling away like chunks of the Academy's wall.

The swordsmen who weren't busy brawling over the bastial steel sword swarmed her. She formed another ball of energy that burned so bright Cleve could barely look. It stopped all her assailants, the heat sending them back. She screamed as her flesh singed, but she wouldn't stop.

Cleve grabbed Annah and started to run. Their comrades jumped up and joined them, some even managing to snatch away enemy swords first.

"They're trying to escape!" shouted the one who'd first grabbed Cleve's weapon.

Annah threw out her hands and every enemy around them collapsed. Her spell only lasted a breath, but it was enough for the two of them to get ahead.

"Again!" Cleve told her, looking back at his comrades. "The others need help escaping."

As Annah took down more of them, Cleve grabbed the arm of someone trying to cut him and bent until the sword dropped. Cleve took it and stabbed into the stomach of the next man to reach them. He kicked someone coming from behind to give himself time to pull his new weapon out of the body, then plunged it into someone else's chest.

All men had given up on Jackrie to chase the fleeing

Academy troops, and she took this opportunity to shoot fireballs at her enemies. Many more of Cassius' troops had joined the brawl over the bastial steel sword, while others started to turn back for Jackrie. Cleve finally saw her fall beside where Terren lay as she was stabbed from behind.

She had done a marvelous job to give them the opportunity they needed.

Cleve ran with at least fifteen of his allies, many now holding the swords of their enemies. Annah continued to hurt anyone who came close, and soon there was a large gap between them and their enemies. Eventually Ulric's and Cassius' troops gave up the chase.

Cleve found himself leading everyone as they looked to him to choose a route. For now, he headed toward the river where they could cover their tracks.

He had no idea what they should do after that.

CHAPTER TWELVE

Basen stayed on the western wall during his search for Alabell and the others except when he crossed by his student home. He stopped inside to take his akorell stone, thinking for a moment whether he should trade Peter's sword for his own but then deciding to keep Peter's. Not only was it of better quality steel, but it meant more to Basen.

He ran the rest of the way along the wall while surveying the campus to his right. It would've appeared deserted if it weren't for the betrayers looting bodies. Some looked up and seemed frightened by the sight of Basen and his glowing stone, making him remember many of them were not soldiers but men Crea had convinced to come to the Academy and fight for coin. He would exact his revenge against all of them somehow, but not today.

He ran all the way to the north wall and still saw no signs of Alabell. The Academy was really deserted up here. He needed to get back to the fight, which continually moved closer and closer to Raywhite Forest.

Please be safe, Mother. He didn't have time check the dining hall for her. She had probably run somewhere else by now and wouldn't be harmed so long as she didn't resist.

Basen gave a silent prayer for Alabell and set a quick pace back to the battle. He watched the fighting the whole time he ran, dread slowly creeping over him as the last of Terren's troops and the troops of Basen's father disappeared into the trees with thousands upon thousands following, hardly a gap between.

By the time Basen made it to the forest, everyone was long gone. He didn't follow the same path directly, as there were too many enemies. Bodies were everywhere, most of them his allies. Each time he recognized another student or instructor, he felt more weight on his back to make this right.

He pressed on, slowing to regain some stamina before the inevitable encounter. He just had to stay near enough to the trail of dead to come upon his enemies.

Eventually it stopped. Dirt and grass had been thrown into shrubs and against trees. It seemed as if combat at range between archers and mages had dictated whatever happened here, tracks showing separation of two large groups. He followed the trail of footprints of what seemed to be the bigger group and was thankful to jog for quite some time and only see the bodies of men in black or blue uniforms, his enemies. His father's troops always wore their ugly gray uniforms, most blanched and dirty, but students of the Academy had on their normal training clothing. Their bodies created the most depressing sight. They were the youngest, the least prepared for such a savage betrayal. He dearly hoped Alabell was not just another body somewhere.

Distracted by the sharp sting of thirst, he began to search the bodies along his way until he found one with a water skin. He drank it down, listened for anything he could hear, and then followed the trail again.

He didn't know what Terren hoped to accomplish by continuing to run. Perhaps escape had been the only option for survival. Bodies became fewer, with more distance between each one. There were equal numbers of ally and enemy bodies, so clearly the plan was working, whatever it was.

Finally, Basen heard voices. He put himself behind a tree and looked out. Enemy troops of both uniforms looked to be taking a reprieve by the main river of Raywhite Forest. They were removing their armor and drinking the water, all visibly fatigued. There were more of them than Basen could see, at least a thousand here. A few got fires started as if they might be making camp.

He gleaned that his enemies had given up on his allies for the time being. But these men didn't seem too concerned about letting the Academy escape.

No reason to be, Basen realized with dismay. *Walls have been built around every city, and they probably have guards watching for us.*

He wished he had some idea where Terren and his father were now.

"That's enough rest!" someone announced. "We need to keep them from coming back around north. Get your gear on. We're moving."

They started to come Basen's way. Careful not to make a sound, he used tree roots and rocks whenever he could as he hurried northwest in hopes of getting around them to look for his allies.

His heart trilled when he glanced left and saw an enemy soldier relieving himself on a tree. Basen froze. He hadn't been seen yet. Painfully aware that movement was more likely to attract his enemy's eye, he shifted slowly.

The bastard looked over and screamed.

"K R!"

The enemies along the river started into a frenzy as if they were bees detecting a threat. He focused energy into his legs and sprinted in the only direction he could go, north toward the Academy.

A man's voice rose up above all the others. "Fast little rebel! But there's nowhere for him to run."

This wasn't true. It couldn't be true. There had to be somewhere in the forest where he would be safe.

He ran until he was winded, nearing the edge of the forest. He made a sharp turn to the west and pushed himself to keep up his speed. Finally, he felt as if he'd covered enough distance to make another turn and start back deeper into the forest.

He had to find his allies.

*****

For the entirety of that night and the next day, Basen scavenged for food and water as he went deeper into the forest. He'd snuck in a few hours of sleep when he felt safe enough to rest, but he couldn't let himself relax until he found the others. Unfortunately, the only people he did come across were more enemies.

He was thankful for his speed, as he was able to evade capture each time. But all it would take was one mistake for his enemies to surround him. He had to be careful, but he didn't know how to reduce his risk of running into them unless he cowered in a hidden nook until he died of thirst. He removed the energy from his akorell stone every time it started to glow. Spotting enemies before they saw him was paramount.

K R...he wondered what it meant. Other enemies had yelled the same upon seeing him.

As more encounters resulted in some shouting "rebel," he realized his enemies were probably thinking of him and his allies as Kyrro's Rebels. It was true, he supposed. They were the "rebels" of this situation now. How many of them were still alive? Did anyone in the cities support them?

The weight of this tragedy had grown to feel as if a small beast clung to him at all times. A fog of fatigue filled his head.

It was during the morning that he heard the first drum. It awoke him from a fitful slumber. The interminable beating was nowhere near Basen, but that didn't stop it from instilling him with fear. He had a feeling he didn't want to know what it meant.

The drumming continued throughout the day, but the low booms that frightened the birds were sparse and too sporadic to be measuring minutes or hours. It had to be for something else.

As Basen found nothing but living enemies and bodies of his allies, he started to realize he would die like so many others if he didn't come up with a better plan than searching randomly. His allies had to still be in the forest, as a plethora of enemies were constantly searching for them. If Henry had retaken Trentyre, for example, all enemies would be surrounding the city in preparation of stealing it back.

There could be others like Basen, searching for each other. *Others who can't match my speed or stamina.* It was a dreadful thought, his allies being hunted down like animals. Completely alone. He needed to help them, but how?

There were a few thoughts that waded around in the back of his mind. He feared for the safety of his family, of Alabell, and his friends, but he also wondered about Sanya. If she had escaped, she might be waiting for him in the abandoned Slugari colony.

It was time to admit that his chances of surviving and finding his allies were much greater with her.

The abandoned Slugari colony was no secret, so he was just as likely to find enemies searching for his allies there as he was to find Sanya. But he had to take the risk.

When he arrived, he saw the rocks barring the entrance had already been moved. He didn't hesitate to enter.

It was a long descent down the dark tunnel. He didn't risk making light as he traversed into complete darkness. He stepped slowly and carefully, as there were dents in the ground deep enough to trip over. Dajrik footprints, he soon realized, remembering the story of Sanya and Reela controlling the creature that had found his way down here.

There must be akorell metal. It was the only way a dajrik had gone from the Dajrik Mountains to here, the world's energy balancing itself out with a temporary portal after one of Basen's.

Sanya wasn't at the end of the long tunnel, but she might be waiting near the akorell metal. Basen just had to find it. *Easy*, he joked silently. The Slugari were known for building mazes to keep out predators, and even though they'd purposely collapsed parts of the colony to keep anyone from following them to their new location, there was still much of the old colony left.

Now hopeless without light, Basen created a dim glow through his wand. The forest had been filled with the sounds of trees and branches swaying in the wind, of birds chirping and bugs buzzing. But here the air was dense and eerily quiet. Darkness lurked around the edge of Basen's light, swelling behind him no matter which way he turned.

A creeping fear began to overwhelm him that he wasn't alone down here.

He carefully made his way through the vast caverns. There were only a few different routes, but there were many alcoves to explore.

He felt as if he'd been abandoned by everyone he'd ever known.

This must be how Sanya feels all the time.

His imagination began to play tricks on him as he sensed movement. He would flash his light in the direction he thought he saw something, only to find nothing but more dirt walls. That only heightened his fear.

Eventually he was absolutely certain something had moved. He couldn't describe how he was sure, as he'd seen nothing, but something had come out of one of the alcoves ahead of him to investigate Basen's light, then darted back in before Basen shifted his wand. It wasn't a sound but more of a disruption of air that raised the hairs on his neck.

"Hello?" he called. "Sanya?"

There was no reply.

He swallowed the dread creeping into his throat as he made his way close to the alcove. Alarm bells chimed in his head that something alive was near. He drew Peter's sword and steadied his shaking hand.

"Hello?" Basen tried again as he entered the alcove.

He came around the turn. The alcove opened into a small square, as if Slugari had used this little area to sleep. He guided his light from wall to wall.

There was nothing here. Or perhaps there was, and he couldn't see it.

Chills ran down his back. He took a few shaky breaths, then continued his search.

The great cavern turned, eventually bringing him back to where he'd entered. There was one more cavern to go through, but he wasn't sure he wanted to search every alcove like the last one, as his heart was ready to jump out of his chest.

He picked up his pace and covered a good distance before the cavern split into two smaller ones. Basen figured none of the alcoves he'd passed would lead anywhere, akin to the last cavern, but both of these routes in front of him could go on for miles.

There has to be akorell metal here, he told himself for the hundredth time. Even though it would put him in total darkness, he let his light die out for a quick reprieve.

Excitement bubbled up as he noticed the faintest glow coming from the cavern on the left. He made light once more and rushed toward one of the alcoves. He could feel the energy warming his spirit as he neared.

He glanced around the corner. No one was there, but at least there was akorell metal above. The ceiling was quite low, about an arm taller than his highest reach. With the rest of the cavern being enormous, it was clear the Slugari had wanted to dig out a greater ceiling here to match the rest but couldn't get around this wide block of metal.

They must have no use for it. How deep does it go into the dirt?

It didn't take long for his akorell stone to start glowing again, absorbing some of the energy from above. Basen couldn't tell if a mage had been here recently to draw the energy out of the akorell metal, but it didn't seem to be glowing as bright as when he'd crossed beneath it in the mountains. That might've meant Sanya had come and taken out the energy to let Basen know she'd been here, or it might've meant nothing.

Eventually he could think of nothing else to do but lay down and catch up on his sleep. He hoped to be awoken by Sanya.

CHAPTER THIRTEEN

Basen awoke to his sense of danger flaring. There were voices in the distance, too faint to make out the words. If they were enemies, they would come toward the light. He peered out into the cavern. Ahead was a long stretch of darkness, then a dim glow. They'd come with either lamps or wands.

He left his akorell stone as he rushed out of the glowing alcove and into the darkness. He headed toward them at the quietest yet fastest speed he could manage, a little slower than a jog.

Their light would disappear and then reappear, making it seem as if they were investigating the alcoves as Basen had. They were still well before the fork. He needed to protect the akorell metal. If seen, it might be reported and others could come to mine it. That would leave nowhere for him and Sanya to meet.

But he couldn't kill these men, either. Their absence would be investigated. He needed to find some way to get rid of them before they found the light of the akorell.

Basen darted into the first alcove of his cavern, before it reconnected into the larger one where the men were coming from. He stayed just inside the turn, going down to his knees and collecting a few hard clumps of dirt big enough for throwing.

He waited as they came closer.

"It doesn't seem like anyone's here," said one.

"We've barely searched at all," said another.

Their voices were full of fear.

They came closer still. Basen had to act now while he had the cover of darkness. He leaned out and tossed one of the clumps of dirt, then waited.

Nothing.

He tossed another, farther this time.

"Stop, did you hear that?"

"No. Don't be a coward."

"You weren't part of the army yet when we fought the Academy outside this tunnel. A dajrik came out! If there's still one in here, we're dead unless we leave now."

"I heard about that battle. You *are* a coward if you fled."

"I would rather be a coward than dead. At least admit that we can't search the entire cavern."

"We have no idea how big it is. It could be small. And we were told to search the entire thing."

Basen threw the rest of the dirt from his hand. He listened to it sprinkle on the ground.

"I know I heard that!"

"Quiet."

They'd soon be close enough to see Basen if he remained there, so he went farther into the alcove and searched the ground for something else he could throw. There was nothing but more dirt.

He gathered some saliva and silently spit. With the added moisture, he made a small ball of dirt. There was just enough light for him to make out the edges of his alcove. He threw hard, but up at the ceiling this time above where he thought them to be.

"I saw movement, there!" one yelled.

There was a faint crumbling sound as Basen's dirt ball must've hit the ceiling.

One of the men screamed, "Something's here!"

"Lower your voice."

"I'm leaving. You can stay and finish the investigation if you want." The echo of his voice was different as he must've turned and begun walking away.

The second man grumbled something.

After a moment, Basen distinctly heard two sets of footsteps receding. He returned to his alcove with the akorell metal and fell back asleep the moment he lay down.

He awoke several more times. With nothing to soften the hard ground, it was difficult to stay asleep.

He lost track of the hours. He slept and shifted and slept and shifted some more, but eventually he heard someone coming.

He or she walked faster than the last two men. Footsteps were already too close for Basen to chance a look without showing himself.

He started to draw his weapon as silently as he could, but the metal against his sheath was louder than grinding rocks.

Whoever it was stopped. Basen drew the rest of his blade and jumped out in hopes of catching the person off guard.

Sanya raised her hand as if to pain Basen but then froze. Both of them lowered their weapons.

"Did anyone hear or see you come in?" he asked.

"No. How long have you been here?"

"I think more than half a day yet less than a full day."

"I was here yesterday."

"You went straight here after the battle, then."

She nodded. Her face looked as dirty as his felt. Her hair was tied back, and she wore different clothing than he remembered. "And you've acquired a different outfit," he commented.

She nodded again, though this time there was a hint of shame. "My clothes were filthy."

"I took things from the dead as well," he said to help relieve her guilt, as well as his own. "Have you seen anyone else?"

"I've seen lots of people." She spoke as if locating others was a simple thing.

"Who? When?"

"Enemies. You care for the details?"

He let out his frustration with his next breath. "You made me think you came across allies."

She muttered something that he didn't pick up. Figuring it was something about how his allies weren't hers, he didn't prod.

"Have you heard the drums?" he asked.

"Yes, what are they for?"

"I don't know. Is there anything else you've seen or done that might help us figure it out?"

"I've seen and done little, so no." She crossed her arms. "If you'd come here yesterday, we wouldn't have wasted a day."

He ignored her statement. "I have a plan."

She didn't seem particularly interested in hearing it.

"Do you want to help?" he asked.

"Tell me what it is first."

"There have to be more of Kyrro's Allies like us who've been separated from each other. What we need most is to be able to gather somewhere safe, where we can coordinate. We'll need food and water, and it has to be somewhere we can rest."

"There's nowhere in the forest like that. Your enemies are searching everywhere for you."

He didn't like her choice of words but let it pass for now. "I know they are, which is why we need to get everyone somewhere safe as soon as possible. I must bring everyone to one of the cities."

"That's impossible. They are blocking all routes of escape out of the forest, and each city is surrounded by—"

"A wall, with guards watching at all times," he interrupted. "I know. But there's a safe way into the capital." He pointed toward the white light pouring out of the alcove.

Her chin lifted as she appeared to understand.

"We need to go there first to find the best place to bring our people. It needs to be somewhere they can eat and sleep without worry of being turned in to Ulric. Then I'll figure out the next steps to win this war."

"There is little chance of this working, and a high chance of capture."

"Not with you coming with me. Your psyche will help tremendously. We can accurately judge people's loyalty and tell if they're lying."

"Before I help with anything, I need to know something."

He knew what she was going to ask...and god's mercy,

he couldn't lie. "Don't, Sanya. Everything's changed now anyway. Don't let yourself think about it."

Her head fell, then began to shake as if in disbelief.

"You're thinking about it," Basen said.

"After everything I've done...it doesn't make sense." She whispered the words to the ground. "How could they?" She looked up with sudden anger. "When did you find out?"

"Right before the attack. Abith told me."

"You could've come back to help me get out!"

"There was no time." Her look of fury was starting to worry him. He stepped away from her. "I had to warn Terren about the ambush."

"And I see you failed!" She came at him. He put up his hands, but she pushed them out of her way to grab his tunic. "Was it a difficult decision?"

"The jury deciding your punishment or me going straight to Terren?"

"Both."

Basen would feel no better about delivering this news than if he had to tell someone a loved one had fallen. He would've rid the world of psyche if it meant he could lie for this one moment.

"Answer me," she demanded. "Was any of it difficult to decide?"

"No," he muttered.

She shoved him with what seemed to be all her strength, sending him down. She grabbed at her hair and pulled as she screamed, looking like a madwoman. She thrust her finger at him.

"And you *still* expect me to help you and the

Academy?"

He got himself up and watched her right hand carefully. If he could resist Fatholl, he should be able to resist her. *I hope.*

"They *had* to choose to execute you, Sanya. You murdered two people. They couldn't allow you to do that and live. And I had to get to—"

"So there's no point in helping if they'll kill me after this!" She walked away from Basen.

"Where are you going?"

"Leaving."

"Sanya, wait. I can't do this without your help."

"Why should I care? You didn't help me."

He put himself in front of her and took a slow breath in the hope she might mimic him and calm down.

"Our situations are different," he tried to explain. "At least they used to be. You came back to the Academy knowing you might be executed for your crimes. Now that the decision has been made, you're going to...what? Flee Kyrro?"

"It makes more sense than fighting for the Academy. Would you help someone who planned to kill you?" She started to go around him, so he stepped into her path. "I will go through you if I must!"

"I'm trying to tell you that everything's different now. Don't you see? They will decide to give you a lighter punishment after you've done all you can to help us."

"I've already done so much, and they still condemned me to death." She walked into him, their arms entangling as they each tried to gain control. "Get out of my way." She tried to throw him to the side, but he overpowered her and pushed her back.

"We have to talk through this. I know you'll agree with me if you just let go of the anger for a moment."

"They didn't even bother to tell me of their decision! When did they decide?"

"Soon after the trial, but that doesn't matter—"

"I would've only found out when it was time!"

"I'm sure they didn't want you to fight them, which is what you would've done if you'd known."

"I would've had another chance to change their minds, at least. Don't I deserve that? *You* have been redeemed for your betrayal of Kyrro last year when you supported your uncle. Why is it impossible for me to redeem myself?"

"You did a lot worse than I did by killing Nick and Alex."

"Shut up. Just shut up."

Basen didn't know what else to say, so he took her advice. She stood still for a while, anger never leaving her shadowed face as she glanced down in thought.

"Did you want them to execute me?" she asked almost shyly as she looked at Basen's feet.

"What?" He felt fear grabbing his throat. Sanya was as unstable as a rabid animal, her mood swinging from fury to depression in the span of a breath.

"Answer me." Her voice was quiet but powerful, like distant thunder. "I know you heard."

If anything would start a brawl between them, it was this. He stepped back before he answered.

"I can't say for certain."

"Then tell me what you believe, and we'll let psyche

decide. Did you want them to execute me?"

He sighed. "You wanted to kill me—you almost killed me—but you decided against it. That's akin to saving my life. Then you really did save me from Fatholl. Many people, myself included, might be dead if it wasn't for all that you've done for us. It makes my decision that much harder because I do believe murderers should be removed from society permanently. I was so glad I wasn't on the jury, and I'm thankful you chose me to speak on your behalf. But I'm angry, Sanya, like everyone else. And I'm sad. You took away two great people who did nothing to deserve it. No matter how many good deeds you do, I can't forget that."

She stared into his eyes and hadn't blinked until he was done. At the end of Basen's short speech, he realized something about himself that warmed his whole body.

"But I do forgive you."

She looked confused. "Say that again."

"I forgive you."

He heard her swallow air. She extended her hand to read his energy. "One more time."

He took her hand with both of his. "Sanya, I forgive you."

She fell down to her knees and put her free hand over her face to hide her tears. She said nothing for a while, only cried. Basen came down with her to embrace her.

She smiled as she cried, but soon her mouth shifted into a frown. Her weeping no longer contained any joy as she stood and forced herself to stop shedding tears.

"What's wrong?" Basen asked.

"Your forgiveness isn't enough for me to risk my life to

save the people who want me dead. I'm leaving."

Before he could even protest, she ran. There was no stopping her now.

"Is it night outside?" he yelled after her.

She didn't stop to answer.

"Sanya, is it night? I have to know!"

"Yes," she answered without slowing.

CHAPTER FOURTEEN

With Sanya gone, Basen had no one. Despair was a gaping hole beneath his feet, growing larger the more he thought about how alone he really was. If he went back into the forest to search and found no one, no doubt he would fall in the gaping hole and might never be able to climb back out.

Psychic or not, he could wait no longer. He kept a small pouch of coins with him at all times, and he'd collected more money from the bodies of his allies and enemies when searching for water, but it wasn't nearly enough for what he needed to accomplish.

He walked beneath the akorell metal, then prepared himself for the mental strain of a portal. He ripped the energy clean out of the metal and pushed it in on itself until the familiar feeling of a gateway came to mind. He pried one out of the energy but was too distracted to see it form. In his mind, he was already at the capital.

He suddenly saw the shimmering black gateway ahead of him and tried to push himself toward it. But he didn't move.

He felt mired in a dream, his legs disobeying his commands like they belonged to someone else. It was as if he was already in the capital looking at himself through a mirror, trying to pull the image of himself into reality.

This wasn't working. He shut his eyes and bent to touch the ground. The feel of the dirt brought him back to the abandoned colony so violently that it dizzied him. He almost lost control of the portal as he fell. With a groan, he pushed himself up from his hands and knees and marched into the gateway.

He tumbled out into the city's training center. It took a few moments for the metal fence to stop turning around him. The training center was empty, as he'd hoped it would be at night. He walked out and down the main road.

All shops were closed, no one on the street. It was strange to walk through town as probably the only rebel here. He needed a bath so he didn't look like he'd been living in the forest for the last day and a half. His stomach grumbled, reminding him that he also needed food.

He had to be careful, though. Without a psychic, there was no way to know who would report a suspiciously dirty and hungry young man who might've come from the Academy. He walked in the opposite direction of the castle, constantly looking back at the enormous structure as it loomed over him.

He didn't know the capital very well. In Oakshen, he could've returned to the district of his old workhouse where he and his father had spent the worst months of their lives. At least he knew the area enough to be confident that none of the owners of the shoddy taverns would think twice about a filthy man coming into their establishment.

He believed he'd heard something about the outskirts of the capital being poorer than the center, so he kept walking straight.

There was a faint hint of morning light behind him, telling him he'd been walking west. He came to the first homes of people who were clearly poor. Even from here, he could still see the top of the castle, but at least he felt less like someone was going to grab him and yell for guards.

Hunger was gnawing his stomach by the time he saw the first of what turned out to be many buildings burned by fire. Some had collapsed, while others were missing chunks of walls. It looked as if there had been little effort to put out the fire once it began, roaming freely all over the inside of every shop or home it had touched. Even the neighboring houses sometimes had signs of recently repaired damage, like an ill-painted wall. The fires were strange in that there had been so many, yet each appeared to be an isolated incident. Never were there more than three buildings showing signs of fire on any one street, and in every case it was a big fire, as if it had been started to cause great damage.

Not only were all of these structures long deserted, but there seemed to be little life left in this district. It was well into morning by the time Basen had a good look around the entire area, where hardly anyone walked the streets.

There were other strange things he noticed. Each time he walked past an open wooden window, he peered inside to see what he could glean. He often noticed chairs and tables sitting in buckets of some kind of liquid that seemed too dark and thick to be water. He crossed by an abandoned inn that had taken considerable damage from fire, and here too remnants of beds stood with their posts in buckets, now dry. Although Basen was concerned about what he saw, he could think of no better sanctuary for him and his kind than this district. He began looking for a suitable place to use as a headquarters.

He came across nothing better than the abandoned inn, as it was the largest of the uninhabited buildings, and eventually returned to it for a closer investigation. He made a mental list of everything he liked: It was the last building on the street before an intersection, or the first if Basen was coming from the west. This made neighbors less of an issue. It was still a good distance from the wall so he wouldn't have to worry about guards. There was an alley between it and the neighboring building, which seemed to be a large tavern from which the scent of food emanated. A cellar door with no lock sat along the side of Basen's new sanctuary—at least he hoped it would be. He still had to make sure the partially charred floor wouldn't collapse under his weight.

He made each step with precision, testing the creaky wood before putting all of his weight down. His first slow trip was through the dining area, past the kitchen, and into the first bedroom. There were few walls left separating it from the others on either side of him, but the ceiling didn't look as if it would fall down on top of him.

The insides of the discarded buckets were burned to the blackest of black. Whatever substance had been inside must've fed the flames. There was only one bed left that still had full buckets under each post. Basen squatted over one for a close look at the substance. He risked a small swipe of his little finger to feel and smell it. *Oil.* He didn't understand.

Very few items still looked supportive enough for his weight. One was a chair flipped over against the corner of this bedroom, which was the least damaged room of all. He continued to look around in hopes of finding a bed to sleep in when the time came, though he doubted he'd find one better.

Eventually, he came to the conclusion that the only sturdy bed was the one he'd already passed, with buckets of oil under each post. This one seemed special, some sort of carving along the head that the flames had mostly licked away. It was almost as if someone had protected this piece of furniture. There was a pile of rubble in a ring around it, possibly from some sort of barrier.

Basen sat slowly, though he wasn't too concerned it would collapse. He shifted to lay flat on his back.

There was a loud crack. Suddenly he was falling! But it was a much longer fall then just through a rotten bed frame.

The moment he realized the bed was falling through the floor and he'd better prepare for impact, he struck the ground. His back bounced off the mattress. He spun through the air and landed on his back again, this time with no mattress beneath him.

Pain traveled up and down his spine. He considered himself lucky not to be seriously hurt. Glancing over, he saw the bed frame had collapsed upon impact, but the mattress still held. He stood and looked around.

The basement had been burned separately from the first floor, purposely so. Heaps of rubble had been clumped together in the center of each room, not one piece of furniture in sight. All of the walls were intact, supporting the ceiling. Someone had sectioned off what seemed to be different storage areas, with the brass rings of barrels still evident among piles of ash.

"Is someone here?" a woman asked from somewhere above Basen. He set down his now glowing akorell bracelet and walked back to the main room to find her poking her head through the cellar doors. "Bastial hell, are you all right? I heard something come down."

"Fine, thank you." She looked strangely familiar. "It's too bad you weren't here earlier. I had quite a bounce off the mattress after it all came down, but there was no one to witness it."

She smiled and that's when he realized it was Jackrie who she resembled. This woman had the same mouth and understanding eyes. Her hair was brown like healthy wood—exactly what Basen needed to fix this place.

"What's your name?" she asked him.

"Ba…" He stopped himself. It was unlikely that any enemies knew him by name, but he still couldn't take that risk. "Bayris. And yourself?"

"Millry. What are you doing here? I understand you might not be able to answer honestly."

"If I don't have to answer honestly, then why ask?"

"I'm going to need to tell people something when they see me feeding you."

He couldn't help his smile. "That's very kind of you, and I would be happy to pay."

She gestured for him to come up the stairs. "That's not necessary." But she didn't say the words as if she meant them.

It took him a moment to realize that she didn't believe he had coin.

"I would like to pay." He carefully made his way up

each step.

She seemed concerned as he reached the top and stood in front of her. "Now you really have to tell me what you're doing here."

Second lesson: Don't make it obvious to others you have coin. You'll stand out more than if you'd sauntered through with a fancy cape. For the first time, he was thankful he had left his cloak on the roof of a mage classroom. The beginning lesson had been not to trust the floor. He hoped he wouldn't fail the third lesson, whatever it may be, like he did the last two.

"I'm looking for a place to sleep," he said with what he hoped was the right amount of shame for someone without a home looking for help. *God's mercy, that's really what I am.* "I don't have much money, but it should be enough for some food."

She put up her palm. "You don't have to say anything more. Come with me, but grab that sack of potatoes. Be careful with them; they're twice as expensive as they used to be before all this started."

He noticed as they walked that the sleeve of her right arm covered her entire hand as if she was trying to hide it. "Glad to help."

"Many people are glad to do a lot these days if it means eating." She spoke as if this was common knowledge.

He nodded. "It's been difficult for me as well."

He was pleased when she led him right into the tavern next door, and even more pleased when she told him she owned the place. "Yes, that is pride you hear and yes, I'm aware that it's empty. More will come soon, don't fret."

"I was hoping to speak to you more anyway, so I'm glad it's empty."

"What would you like to know?" She brought him into the kitchen, its cleanliness a welcome change from the abandoned inn. "Set the potatoes down there." She pointed at the counter.

"I haven't been to this area of the city before," he said. "Why are a number of buildings burned?"

"We have a terrible problem with febeetles. If you haven't been to this area of the city yet, you might not have heard of them." She reached for a knife, then stood in front of the sack of potatoes. "You're going to see something not pleasing to the eye," she warned, then pulled back her long sleeve to reveal a horribly burned hand.

Basen cringed before he could fix his face. "I'm sorry."

She used that hand to fetch the first potato from the sack, pressing it with her last three fingers against her palm. It didn't seem as if she could use her thumb or pointer, where most of the damage showed. The injury made her hand look as if someone had pulled back her skin, revealing red and white splotches.

"I'm sorry you have to look at it."

"It's not that bad," he said truthfully. "But it does look painful. What happened?"

She set down her knife to show him a smirk. "Did you not hear the part about the febeetles?"

He shrugged. "I'm hoping to learn about both, but your hand is in front of me and they aren't."

"I had a knack for fireballs before I was old enough to realize how dangerous they were."

That's what Basen had figured. Unfortunately, burning a hand was a common injury among younger mages. "You didn't start with training gloves?"

"I was foolish and overconfident, a dangerous combination."

He stayed out of her way when he realized she needed her concentration to prepare a big enough breakfast for at least six people. Eventually, when she had everything cooking, she wiped her hands and took a deep breath.

"Febeetles," she began, "are a lot more horrific than my hand. They must've come with Ulric, Yeso, and all the men and Elves with them. They look just like black beetles but bigger. They have a taste for meat and nothing else that we know of." She walked toward him with a menacing look, as if pretending to be one of these little monsters. "They wait until it's dark, then they climb up your body until they find your flesh. They bite hard, like they know they're about to be crushed or flung and want the biggest piece of you they can manage first." She pinched his arm with her good hand.

"Ow. Your description was good enough. I didn't need a sample." She grinned mischievously, making no doubt about her flirtation. He figured there wasn't any real interest, as he was four or five years younger, just that she was having a bit of fun.

"The owner of the building—with the floor you fell through—was frustrated with the infestation of febeetles. He tried to get rid of them, like so many people here have, but they multiply quickly. I told him not to go to the guards. All they do is burn down the building. He had to get a psychic, I kept telling him. It was worth the money for a good one who could get all the pests out of hiding where he could kill them." She busied herself with her cooking, but that didn't stop her from shaking her head in disappointment. "He didn't listen. He thought the guards would help, as they should, but they never do."

"Are the creatures still there?"

"I don't think so. The fire is usually as effective as it is destructive, but that doesn't stop me from worrying that some of them have made their way into the nooks of my place."

"Do you know where the inn's owner is now?" Basen asked.

She gave him an inquisitive glance. "I haven't seen him for days."

"What kind of man is he?"

"The kind who won't understand someone trying to use his property, even if he isn't using it himself." She showed him eyes of pity. "There's nowhere else for you to go?"

"I'm fine."

"Remember that you can come here for meals whenever you want so long as you don't mind the company of a few older folks who have everything to complain about."

"I hope you're not referring to yourself as one of these older folks. You don't look past twenty."

She flicked her wrist to point at him. "Smart to compliment your chef."

After he was full, he returned to the basement of what he deemed would be his new sanctuary and that of all his surviving allies eventually. He set himself to gathering energy in one spot over and over again. Millry invited him back for lunch and supper and politely said nothing of his dwelling in the abandoned basement, where he always returned to gather more energy.

He slept a few hours when night came, then got up and went straight back to gathering more energy. Soon came the familiar feeling. He wouldn't get much done in the forest at night, so he slept the rest of the hours of darkness away and joined Millry for breakfast. He indulged himself with a quick bath when he was done, and then it was time to go back to the forest.

He used the energy from his akorell stone to create a portal to the underground Slugari colony. With a revitalized spirit, he jogged through the colony to leave it. He faintly heard drumming that went on and on just like before. It even continued as he made his way up and out into the forest.

Smoke was in the air. There was a hill nearby, so he climbed up for a better vantage point. The drumming finally ceased.

A pillar of black, too thin to represent a forest fire, puffed up and spread out over the tops of trees. It was a good distance away, but there might be allies like Basen who would go to investigate. His sole purpose now would be finding as many as he could until he had enough for the next step of his plan. He had to risk a look, knowing all too well that it might only be enemies waiting for him.

Basen didn't have much practice walking silently through the woods, so using common sense was his only tool. He wouldn't step on leaves if he could avoid them, choosing rocks or roots instead. He knew he was leaving tracks whenever traversing through the soft dirt, but he covered all he could around the Slugari colony with gentle swipes of his feet.

His stomach turned when he edged close enough to see what was causing the fire.

CHAPTER FIFTEEN

The fire was still burning when he made it there. The stench was unlike anything he'd smelled before. It was both putrid and sweet, and so rich he could almost taste it. The sight crushed his spirit all over again. Hundreds of his allies lay dead and burning, melting away as if they'd never existed.

Ulric had wanted Basen to see this. Basen wished the Takary was somewhere in this forest, but he knew the forgery of a king sat comfortable on his throne as he waited for his men to hunt Basen down along with nearly everyone he knew. The only thing that could stop this was to kill Ulric and replace him with someone else. Basen could feel his plan changing while fighting back the claw of anger reaching up to grab his thoughts, trying to drag him down into an abyss in which all hope would be lost.

The terrible sight had put him in such a stupor that he didn't notice the sound of someone coming up behind him until a leaf cracked a few feet away. Instinct took over as he dove to the side. He heard a sword crash into the tree he'd been hiding behind.

"Rebel!" shouted a man in a blue uniform. "Here!"

Suddenly Basen found himself chased by an entire group of them. "Rebel, rebel!" they continued to yell, sparking more voices to sound out around Basen. "Which section?" one asked. "Which direction?" asked another.

"Running toward section twelve! Northern half!"

The bastards had organized! It terrified Basen as he

struggled to focus on the bastial energy in his legs.

Just when he was gaining some distance, he was spotted by another group. They obviously knew he'd been seen earlier, because they called to the others that he'd entered section twelve but the southern half of it.

There were even more of them than he first thought. He sprinted around the trees as fast as he could, veering toward the Slugari colony in hopes of losing them. But more kept coming, their shouts never too far behind and always revealing his location.

With a burst of speed, he made it to the colony and finally seemed to be out of sight. But he hesitated before going down through the tunnel. If he was wrong about losing them, and they came down to his sanctuary to fight him, there was no other exit to get back into the forest. He would be trapped, in the dark. He could teleport out, but if they confirmed he'd gone down here only to disappear, they might realize how he escaped and search the cities. Surely there had been talk of a portal mage given everything Basen had done. As soon as Ulric knew to look elsewhere, hope really would be lost for Basen's allies.

But his gut told him this was his only chance, and it had kept him alive thus far. He'd left the stones scattered around the entrance instead of blocking it, for he wanted no one to know he'd gone down at any point. Thankful for this now, he sped down the tunnel. His head start gave him an opportunity to make light for a while, but eventually he let it out and was forced to slow.

He kept one hand on the wall for guidance, looking back into the glow of day above. His heart shot into his throat when shadows passed into the light.

"Are you sure he went this way?"

"No, we'll go back and check the tracks as we wait for a mage."

They would be coming down for sure. But the abandoned colony was enormous. Even with a mage, it could take them hours to search all of it. Basen had to figure out something. Perhaps he could teleport back to the capital and recruit a small army to stand against them. It would make it seem as if Basen had been leading the enemy troops down here for a trap, hiding his ability to make portals.

No. No one would join him, and word of a rebel in the city would spread.

After a while of wading through the sea of darkness, he figured he was a safe enough distance and created a dim glow of energy. He made good time the rest of the way to the akorell metal, but he still had to figure out—

"Basen!"

He jumped and screamed. Then relief washed over him as Sanya made light to show her face. But the relief lasted only for a breath before panic set in again. "There's many behind me," he informed her.

"Then we fight."

"There could be fifty of them coming. They're just waiting for a mage."

"Doesn't matter. We fight." She grabbed his arm.

He could feel by her grip that she was as weak as she looked. "Have you eaten or slept at all?" he asked.

"Not much, but I'm still willing to trust our odds in battle. Please, Basen." Her tone was so desperate, it sounded as if she was about to get down on her knees and beg.

Suddenly he realized what this was all about. She'd given up. This was her glorious exit.

He wasn't about to let this be it for them.

"I have plans to win this war, Sanya. I can't die here."

She took in a breath, already looking stronger. "We won't."

"Promise me that you fight to live, not to end it all."

"I promise."

He wasn't sure he believed her, but fighting still seemed to be the best choice. He might be able to keep her alive even if she planned to die here.

"Come with me this way." He led her farther into the cavern, away from the light of the akorell metal. There were many alcoves on either side, but none went very deep into the walls. Eventually he found one that would provide enough cover from fire if a mage shot at them.

He crouched down and continued to make light, but he was disappointed at the sight of Sanya's tired and worried eyes.

"Here," he said as he gave her his water pouch. "And I have some food as well. It could be hours until they come, so eat."

*****

It took a while for Basen to realize how surprising it was for her to be here. "You said you wouldn't come back."

Sanya had eaten all the provisions Basen brought. She'd stared at her lap the entire time, and Basen hadn't disturbed her until now. She swallowed the last morsels and finally glanced over to where he stood resting his back against the wall.

"It isn't the first time I've changed my mind about you," she said, then stood and brushed crumbs from her pants.

"Why did you change it this time?"

"I had promised myself that, no matter what, I was going to help your side in this war. Anger made me lose sight of it, briefly."

"I'm glad you changed your mind, but you should've stayed with me. You look awful. What did you do after you left?"

"I hunted and killed. I scavenged."

It was unclear whether she hunted and killed animal or man. Basen supposed it was probably both. The same went for scavenging from the forest and from bodies.

"They guard most of the river," she said. "And they've set up camp in the north of the forest."

"What of our allies?"

"I haven't found any. I think they must be gathered somewhere, most likely to the south. I haven't looked there yet."

"Then we'll go there after—"

"Wait," she interrupted. "Listen."

They held their breath. The soft crunch of boots against the hard dirt came closer. Basen's akorell stone was not charged enough for any kind of energy boost, so he pulled out the small amount of BE within and let it disperse into the darkness. No light was on them yet, so he took a look.

There were so many! At least twenty. They headed straight for the akorell alcove and started to move around to cover all avenues of escape, but one man in their group waved his arms as if this was wrong. He pointed in Basen's direction.

Sanya pulled Basen back into the alcove. "They have a psychic," she whispered.

"I saw."

"They'll know we're in here."

"We have a plan for this. Stay in control."

The enemies slowly came toward them.

They stopped and began to whisper amongst each other. The light from a mage blasted into their alcove.

"We know you're in there," announced one man. "We have a psychic. There are two of you, and you are both afraid. But if you come out, we will let you live."

Sanya shook her head at Basen. He didn't know if this meant their enemy was lying or if she disagreed with letting them be captured. No matter, Basen was with her. He was sick of these men bullying him, and they had no idea of the power he and Sanya possessed. Every muscle in Basen's body tensed as he drew Peter's sword with his left hand, his wand with his right.

She handed him her dagger. "This will serve better."

He put his sword back in his sheath and took the dagger. "Ready?"

"Go."

Basen flew out like a bat. He startled the mage into letting out his light, leaving only the glow of the akorell metal behind the lot of them. Panicked archers hurried to get their arrows nocked, clearly expecting Basen and Sanya to give up.

Basen jumped on top of the first archer he came to and drove knife into neck. The others dropped from Sanya's spell, screaming out their agony.

Hearts and throats became his targets, whichever were more exposed. He was quick with the dagger, extinguishing all archers and the single mage in a frenzy of gore and shrieks.

Sanya began to scream, taken down by the psychic. Everyone she'd pained rose and turned on Basen.

"Don't break the energy!" he called out to Sanya.

Basen backed away to give himself distance to burn as many as he could. He got off three fireballs before they swarmed him. His training with Abith came back like instinct as he dodged and retaliated with hot energy into their faces.

But soon there were too many, forcing him to circle around in retreat to get back to Sanya.

"Take them down!" he yelled.

"I can no longer discern your energy," she groaned.

"Doesn't matter!"

It felt as if a pair of claws had dug into his torso and begun to rip him apart. Meanwhile, his legs cramped, his muscles refusing to obey. He fell with the rest of them, screaming as he remembered all too well this helpless feeling against Fatholl.

He thought of his family and of Alabell needing his help. These were the very men responsible for their separation, standing between him and his loved ones.

Determination more powerful than hunger drove him to his feet. He felt as if he were struggling against a hurricane as he trudged over to the enemy psychic and ended him.

Sanya's screams ceased. She came to join Basen, her hand extended toward the pile of squirming men. He passed her the dagger, which she skillfully flipped to shift her grip. With grunts of anger, she stuck each man in the neck.

She gained momentum as she killed, spitting out a sick sound of satisfaction that could only come from exacting revenge.

"Haa! Enn! mmMM!"

Basen searched deep within himself and brought out his darkest side, getting rid of all sense of mercy as he plunged his sword into their bodies.

"Leave him alive," Basen told Sanya as she came to the last one.

Sanya held her dagger up as if contemplating whether to disobey.

"He can answer our questions," Basen specified.

She plunged the knife into the man's stomach, then ripped it out. It was strange to see his screams of agony softening afterward, as Sanya released her spell over him. His hands covered his wound. He suddenly looked frightened as if realizing what was about to happen. He tried to get up and run, but Basen tripped him.

Basen grabbed the man and flipped him over, reminding himself that these were people who came to kill and take land just because they could. His blue uniform said he was one of Ulric's, a slight disappointment to Basen, but it didn't change anything.

"What do the rest of your men know about this colony?" Basen asked.

He said nothing, just gaped in obvious fear.

Sanya plunged two fingers into his wound. He screamed and grabbed her arm. She pulled out and let him be as he writhed in agony.

"Answer the question," Basen ordered.

Again, he said nothing. Sanya clawed her way back inside his wound as he tried to block her. His scream sounded inhuman.

When she finally released him, he seemed defeated and accepting of death as he looked up with vacant eyes.

"Tell us," Basen said.

"They don't know anything," he replied. "This colony is just another place to look for hiding rebels every so often."

"What about the glow?" Basen asked. "What do your people know about it?"

"Just that it's some kind of metal."

"Is it useful to Ulric?"

"Not that I know of."

Good, the akorell metal should be safe for now. "Tell us everything you know about the location of your comrades."

He heaved a ragged sigh. "We're all over the forest, but mostly in the north. We move." He seemed reluctant to say more.

"How many are in the Academy?"

"I don't know. Crea Hiller is in charge there."

Basen felt a spark of excitement. He could teleport in

during the night, find and kill Crea, and get his mother...no. There were other matters more pressing. Juliana would either be dead already or remain unharmed to be used as leverage against Basen and his father. He could leave her be for now.

"What about in the cities?" Basen asked.

"I don't know. I only know the forest. There are three to five thousand of us here at any one time. There are many different officers. Most stay in our northern camp. The cities have all been taken and their walls are being watched, so there is nowhere to run. Your only chance of survival is to bring me back to the others and let yourself be captured. I will make sure they don't harm you."

Basen glanced over at Sanya. She nodded. "It's what he thinks the truth is." Her arm was covered in blood. At first Basen thought it belonged to others, and some of it might have, but as he looked closer he noticed a gash.

"Your arm," he said.

"I feel it," she replied without moving her eyes from their enemy. "Finish your questions for him."

He put her out of his mind for the moment. "After your investigation of this colony, where and when do you give your report?"

"My officer will expect me back in less than a few hours. In section ten." He smiled like he thought he was smart to tell the truth without actually saying much. Basen didn't care, as there was only one thing left that was important.

"When none of these men report back, how long until more come to investigate?"

This, he did not want to answer. Sanya motioned as if

she was going to jab her finger into his wound again.

"Very soon!"

"Liar!" Sanya threw his hand out of the way.

"Not until tomorrow!" he yelled. He seemed disappointed as he sighed. "Or never."

"How can that be?" Basen asked.

"All who knew about you coming down here followed you. We don't keep track of each other as well as we do you rebels."

Keep track of us? "The drums," Basen realized. "You're tallying kills."

He nodded.

But there had been so many...

"The drum must beat more than once for every kill," Basen said. "In hopes of scaring us."

The smug look returned as the man shook his head. "No, and I'm glad psyche can confirm this. Every time you've heard the drum, one of your own has died."

Basen's pity for this man was gone. "I have nothing left to ask."

"And I don't have anything either," Sanya added.

"If you're smart, you'll realize you cannot win this war!" the man yelled through his teeth as he continued to grimace. "We've killed over half your army. Now we outnumber you ten to one. Your only chance of survival is to let yourself be captured. Take me back to my men and they will put you in chains, but you will live."

"That's very generous," Basen said. "But I'd prefer to kill you."

Weakened by his injury, the man could only crawl away as he let out a small yelp. Basen opened his hand for

Sanya to give him the knife. She didn't appear to want to.

"You're hurt," he said.

"Doesn't matter. You can take care of the others."

Others? As she walked over and slit the man's throat, Basen painfully became aware that this man wasn't actually the last one alive. Some of the ones Basen had burned still squirmed. He felt sick to his stomach as he realized what he had to do. Sanya gave him her dagger.

After he was done, he ran over to one wall and vomited. Then he buried it, as well as his dark side.

"Let's go to the Academy and kill Crea," Sanya suggested.

"You're letting your emotions decide your actions. That will be the death of us."

"No, I'm going to die from bleeding or infection. Might as well kill Crea before then."

Basen cut off the cleanest sleeve of an enemy uniform he could find. "I told you that you need to stop thinking you're going to die. I need you alive." He wrapped her arm. "But you're right about infection. I have to get you back to the capital to have your wound properly treated."

"Back? When did you go?"

"After you left me here. I've been busy figuring out how to continue fighting. You must realize by now that we can't win going against them in the forest."

"I know we can't, and that's why I was prepared to die."

"Have hope, Sanya. I'm going to get us through this."

"If only you believed that."

Damn psychics. "I half believe it. At least give me a little hope to match mine."

"All right. But I can't blend in with the citizenry dirty and bleeding."

"You won't have to be seen. My portal will take us to the outskirts of the capital, and I'll get what I need to treat you. Go beneath the akorell metal and rest. In a moment, I'll come help you."

"While you loot the bodies and keep everything for yourself?" she asked snidely.

He gave her an incredulous look. "Do you honestly believe that?"

"Sorry," she said. "The old Sanya comes out when I'm tired or angry, and especially when I'm both."

"I'll be collecting the few uniforms that aren't stained with blood. I have a feeling they'll come in handy."

She didn't move, staring at him.

"And I'll show you everything I find," he said, insulted he even had to mention it.

She extended her hand not to shake, but to receive something. He realized then he still had her dagger, the Takary sigil of wings engraved on its handle.

"You're going to have to learn to trust me," he said.

"I'll try."

CHAPTER SIXTEEN

Once they were in the capital, Basen saw how deep Sanya's wound really was. The rough cloth of the uniforms made horrible bandages, so they'd brought the undershirts of their enemies to use instead. Ideally, Basen would wash and dry them first, but Sanya was bleeding too much to take the time. It was a disappointment that so many of the uniforms were marred by blood or rips. A few of Ulric's men had fancy blue hats, but the only one that fit Basen's big head had a tear down the side. He hid them in the small space beneath the burned wardrobe in one of the back rooms on the first floor.

When he went to see Millry, he was surprised to find her in the empty tavern gathering energy as if practicing. She didn't seem to notice him as she stopped suddenly, her head hanging as if a sad thought had struck her.

He made sure his footsteps could be heard as he entered. She looked over and put on a smile. "Bayris, how are you?"

"Not good, unfortunately. A friend of mine was cut down her arm. I'm looking to buy clean bandages and potions to help her heal. Do you know where I can get some?"

She put her hand over her chin. "I have bandages and allamale." She stuck her wand in her pocket and checked the cleanliness of her hands. "I can treat her. Is she at the neighboring building?"

"Um, it's all right. I would rather you sell me what I

need."

"Your hands don't look as clean as mine. Is that blood on your sleeves?"

"The allamale should work well enough against infection that I'm not worried."

She gave a sly smirk. "You should be. Clearly, you know little about healing." She put up her hands before he could object. "Just let me get the supplies and I'll meet you there. It'll give you enough time to convince your friend she can trust me."

Basen worried until he remembered that Sanya could sniff out the woman's loyalty after a short conversation. He silently prayed that Millry was everything she seemed to be, otherwise he would have to…he couldn't even finish the thought as his stomach turned.

He returned to Sanya. "A woman named Millry will be coming to treat you. I believe she can be trusted, but you will be the judge of that with psyche."

Sanya looked slightly more relieved than worried. "What does she know?"

"Almost nothing. She thinks my name is Bayris. You will be…what?"

"She doesn't need to know my name."

"She might ask, and it's suspicious to refuse to give one. She might be coming any moment, so—" He stopped himself as Millry came to the top of the stairs and started down into the basement.

"Let's have a look at your wound."

Sanya unwrapped the shirt-bandage. Millry didn't hide her alarm. "Bastial hell, you must've just gotten this or you'd have bled out already."

It only then occurred to Basen that no one had reached Sanya during the battle. She must've accidentally done this to herself in her fury for revenge once they were all incapacitated. *She has a lot of anger.* That might become an issue.

Millry asked no questions as she treated Sanya first with water, then by spreading on the thick potion, and finally by tightly wrapping a bandage around her arm. Though she did look at the two of them with more skepticism with each glance she took.

"You're going to need something more than allamale and bandages," Millry informed them.

"Do you have any caregelow?" Sanya asked.

Millry laughed. Then her face fell. "Oh, you weren't joking." She folded her arms. "All right, I must ask. What are you two really doing here?"

Sanya stood with a face full of aggression but immediately lost her balance. Basen caught her before she fell.

"It's best if you don't know," Basen said.

"It's not as if psychics are coming around here to question people!"

Millry tightened the fold of her arms when Basen didn't reply.

Sanya growled, "Are you allegiant to Ulric or Tenred in any way?"

"That's a dangerous question. How do I know you won't report my answer? They could take my head before sunset."

Silence followed. It appeared they'd come to an impasse, no one willing to speak.

"This is absurd," Millry complained. "Are you going to give me a false name like he did if I ask?"

Basen sighed as he saw no point in hiding it any longer. "We're from the Academy."

"And what else?" Millry spat back. "Will they come looking for you here? Will they accuse me of aiding you?"

"Not unless they're told," Sanya threatened.

Basen hurried to soften the conversation. "They have no idea we're here and won't find out."

"Then your secret is safe." Millry rubbed her chin in thought as she stared at Basen. "If you're from the Academy, then I believe I know who you really are. Basen Hiller, right?"

"How in god's world did you figure that out?"

"Jackrie spoke of you, the exiled nephew of Tegry who showed up in her training center and shocked everyone with his skill and courage."

No doubt she'd described Basen accurately enough for Millry to recognize him. *These two women must be close.*

Suddenly it occurred to him: "You're her sister, aren't you?"

Millry nodded. "I've barely slept since hearing the news of the attack. Where is she?"

Where would Jackrie be now? "I can only hope she's with the others. We haven't been able to find them yet."

Millry seemed shocked. "I find it hard to believe you had an easier time getting into the capital than finding others. Are there that few of you left? Ulric's loyalists spread that rumor around, and I fear people are beginning to believe it."

"Lower your voice," Sanya snapped. "This is talk that can get us all killed."

"She's right," Basen said. "We have to stop, but first I need to know one last thing. As the sister of an instructor, will the guards come for you?"

"They haven't done anything to the families of rebels yet, and if the rumors are true, they have no need to do anything more than continue hunting down the rebels in the forest to win this war."

"Sadly, that's true," Basen confirmed.

"I have to get back," Millry said. "If I'm away from the tavern for too long, people might look around. We have to be more careful about arousing suspicion. It's best if your friend..." Millry paused.

"Sanya," she said.

"If Sanya stays out of sight until she can hide her wound better. I'll see if I can find anything to help her heal faster, but I will need some coin."

Basen gave her a little bit more than he expected medicine to cost. "If you would kindly return what you don't use, I'll have more to pay you for food."

She nodded and hurried off.

Basen looked down at Sanya sitting on a chunk of charred wood. "How loyal is she?"

"Completely."

"Good." He sat on the floor in front of her and grabbed his knees. "There will be even more difficult times ahead of us. We could use all the help we can get."

"What do you have planned for us now that we're here?"

Unless it was his imagination, she seemed relieved to

take direction.

"You'll be charging my akorell stone as your injury heals. At night, we can make use of your power. In the meantime, I'm going to find out more about our enemies by taking a long look around the city."

"What will I be using my power for at night?"

"This is only one of many buildings that have been burned in this area. They have a problem with febeetles, which hide somewhere in the house and come out at night to gnaw on flesh. Guards have been burning the shops and homes instead of finding a better solution." He pointed at her. "You are that solution."

"What will I do with these beetles?"

"I'll make a portal back to the colony, and you will bring them there. They will get rid of the bodies we left there, and we will enclose them somewhere in the colony to be used later. That's why we need the akorell stone charged, but make sure you do it in one of the back rooms, in case someone opens the cellar doors."

"I might be able to make the portal," she said. "I made a small one to break the bar of my prison cell."

"But if you fail, we'll have to wait another day for it to charge again." There was a pause as they each pondered. "But I do need you to learn...if you are capable," Basen continued. "We will have to make many portals back and forth."

"We need another akorell stone for me."

Basen shrugged. "We do know where akorell metal is. A lot of akorell metal..."

He could see by the twinkle in Sanya's eyes that she had the same thought. Why don't they make ten?

*****

People noticed Basen everywhere he went in this poor district of the city, their gazes lingering long enough to make him certain that most everyone knew each other and could spot a stranger a street a way. Fortunately, there was nothing about him suspicious enough to be reported. He smiled at everyone who met his gaze, as a friendly face was more likely to get away with something than a mean one. He kept his bloodstained arms pressed against his sides until he found a shop and purchased a new outfit.

There was only one guard patrolling the streets, and the people of the district looked at him in the exact opposite way they looked at Basen. All had mastered a way of seeing without looking, of watching without moving anything but their eyes. Basen wasn't the danger here; the guards were.

As Basen left the district and came closer to the center of the city, people were less cautious around guards. Instead, their irritation was as plain as if they'd smelled something foul.

There weren't enough guards to stop an uprising unless everyone from the forest came to stand up to the citizenry, but Basen had no way of gaining the people's support. At least not that he knew of.

He roamed for hours, revisiting streets twice, sometimes three times to ensure he remembered key locations. Eventually, he witnessed two men fighting outside a bar. Two onlookers seemed to know the men but did nothing to stop the fight until a guard started down the same street. Then they grabbed their friends, threw them down, and jumped on top of them as if trying to put out a fire on their backs.

The belligerent men fought in hopes of freeing themselves until they became aware what their friends were telling them about the approaching guard. The two pairs jumped up and went in separate directions.

Basen circled around the castle, getting closer and closer the way a boy might test the feeling of fire against his hand. The only people who smiled at the guards were other guards as they walked past each other or stopped for a chat. Unlike in his new home district, no one seemed to think Basen was an outsider here, and eventually he found little reason not to venture to the castle.

There were a few guards outside the closed doors while others patrolled the main road. Most of them looked either content or resigned to boredom, while some glanced around almost mischievously as if searching for something to do. None were vigilant like the men on the eastern wall watching the forest.

Basen made his way over to the nearby training center. It was empty, so he walked inside to fortify the memory. He would probably have to make another portal here eventually if he were to win this war.

The road around the training center was almost as wide and well-paved as the road to the castle, but unlike that one, this road was empty. Weapon shops and teachers of magic for hire still seemed to be in business, but there were no patrons to serve.

Almost everyone who can fight is already doing so?

Basen wondered again about his mother, and now about the other family of students who'd come to the Academy. Hopefully they were safe with Juliana or they'd escaped with the Academy's troops. What about the others who'd come there previously because they'd been bribed with the promise of food—like Effie's and Steffen's parents? *If the war starts to turn in our favor, Ulric could use the safety of our families against us as leverage.*

The thought brought on the same discouragement as remembering how outnumbered they were. Basen had to find some sort of advantage in this war, and soon, something more than making portals. He could feel a plan for victory was there waiting for discovery, so close yet just out of reach.

Basen strolled by the castle again on his way back, this time going around back for a look at the stables. He knew little about horses and didn't see how they would be of much use in this war, but he was hoping everything would change soon enough. He'd better be prepared by learning all he could.

Either there weren't very many horses or most of the animals were kept somewhere more secure. A few guards stood outside the entrance while workers tended to the animals within.

Basen witnessed a man approach the guards and ask to join Ulric's army.

"It's too late," one soldier said. "You should've joined earlier."

"We're not recruiting," the other added in

punctuation.

The man wanting to join was twice Basen's age, but he looked in no way feeble. *They really must be confident to refuse any others to pad their ranks.*

Basen couldn't let himself succumb to the hopelessness that kept trying to drag him down. He refocused his thoughts on learning the city, finding out which locations had more enemies, and which had less.

He made his trip home using only moonlight. The longer he could keep his ability with bastial energy a secret, the better.

He opened the cellar doors. "It's Basen," he announced.

Sanya walked into view from around a wall. "What did you see?"

"First, what is that I hear?" It sounded like the walls were whispering.

"The febeetles."

He descended the stairs and cautiously peered around her. It looked as if hulking shadows had collected on the floor and along the base of the walls. He made light and could hold his ground no further as he backed away in a hurry. There were thousands of the black beetles squirming around, most as long and as wide as two fingers put together.

"It was night," Sanya said, "so I went to fetch them. I couldn't handle the boredom of staying here any longer."

"Did anyone see you?"

"A few people." She crossed her arms. "You couldn't have prevented that if you were with me. You would've just made it more likely for us to be seen."

He held back his annoyance at her leaving without his permission only because she was right. "Did they see you come back here?"

"No."

"What about guards?"

"There were none."

"And the febeetles—you have them under control?"

"Yes, relax."

He wasn't sure he could while standing in the same room as thousands of flesh-eating creatures, but he did need to at least get off his aching feet. He moved to the other side of their sanctuary, as far as possible from the febeetles, then took off his boots and lay down.

He told Sanya of the one image he couldn't get out of his mind. "I saw a man trying to join Ulric's army, yet they refused him because they don't need any more."

Her biting tone surprised him. "With so many more than us, what's the point to kill Ulric! Someone will just take his place."

"Don't lose hope, Sanya." Basen closed his eyes. "I'm trying to take your advice to relax."

"And while you're doing that, your allies are dying."

She sounded exactly like the old Sanya, always starting trouble whether it was on purpose or not.

He let out a frustrated breath as he sat up. "They are your allies as well now."

"No, they want me dead."

"We've already discussed this! Why are you reasonable at times and at other times you're denser than a brick?"

"I'm not. You're the one refusing to see the reality of

our position."

"What are you saying? You're not going to help anymore?"

"I'm saying there's no point. Ulric doesn't even recruit anymore!"

I should've never told her that. "What do you propose then?" he asked sarcastically. "That we die?"

"You can do what you want on your journey toward death. I'd rather leave and avoid the journey altogether. I'm going to steal some money and take a boat to Greenedge, when I'm able."

He felt as if he'd just stepped outside into a thunderstorm with no coat. But there was no going back to the beginning of this conversation. The door was closed behind him, Sanya's rage at a dangerous level.

He needed to stop inciting her. "I need your help."

"Would *you* help people who plan to kill you after you save them all?"

"When they see your dedication—"

"They will do nothing but use me and then kill me!" A river of febeetles poured into the room.

"Sanya!"

She spun and aimed her hand. The febeetles retreated out of sight.

"You're making me lose my focus!" she growled. "I've been dedicated to your allies by going to the Academy to turn myself in and by helping them in this war. But today I realized that nothing I do will take back what I've already done. It doesn't matter how horrible I feel for my mistakes or how much I want to help. No one cares."

"I care. I'm sure others will as well when they give

themselves a chance to accept your help."

She ignored him. "I'm not even asking them to take my guilt away by forgiving me. I'm asking for a chance to use my life for something good in this world. It's the only way to balance out the bad."

If Basen wasn't going to be heard, he saw no reason to speak. So they said nothing as they listened to the febeetles squeaking and scurrying about.

After a long while, Sanya shook her head. "There's nothing more we can do here, Basen. Ulric is too smart and too powerful. The Academy is lost. All cities are lost. Everyone loyal to the school will die if they don't give up or run, like that one soldier told us. He knew the truth. You need to decide what you're going to do now because I've made my decision."

She showed him a questioning look. Was she asking if he wanted to come with her?

He couldn't even look her in the eye, his disappointment too overwhelming.

"I refuse to give up. I refuse to leave. And I refuse to die."

"Then death will be chosen for you!" Fury colored her words, but his level of anger probably beat hers. She had made a choice not to listen to him even before he started speaking. He grabbed his boots, then stormed off to get as far from her and the febeetles as he could.

With her injury and the febeetles to manage, she wouldn't be leaving just yet. He needed her, as much as it pained him to realize. He would have to come up with a plan soon, something so solid that she could not fail to see their chance for success.

CHAPTER SEVENTEEN

Basen didn't see or speak to Sanya the rest of the night. He went to see Millry on business, apologizing for waking her while explaining why it was an urgent matter. Fortunately, she was happy to help and told him to wake her whenever he needed.

Late into the morning, he had figured out what to do and it was finally time to tell Sanya. He walked over to the other side of the burned basement to find her slumped against the wall, awake.

"I'm glad you're still here," he said.

"I won't be when I can travel."

"I think you're going to change your mind when you hear what I have to tell you."

She lifted an eyebrow, barely glancing at him. "You actually believe that." She spoke with surprise.

"I do."

Sanya shut her eyes and took a breath. "I don't want to start this again, Basen. Your time is better spent finding the people you care about the most and getting them out of this territory with a portal."

"No, we can win this."

She laughed bitterly. "I'm amused to hear how you expect to manage that, and it's not like I have anywhere to go while I heal. Tell me how you plan to win when we are severely outnumbered and in no position of advantage."

"We are outnumbered, but you're wrong about

having no advantage. Our numbers are the advantage."

The slight amusement was gone from her expression. "I changed my mind. I'm not in the mood to deal with stupidity."

He held back a sigh. "If you don't keep your mind open to new ideas, you won't believe my plan no matter how brilliant it is."

She let out one derisive laugh. "Brilliant, you say."

"You won't know until you listen to it."

"Fine. Go ahead."

"If there was to be a battle between all our forces and theirs, then you would be right. As badly outnumbered as we are, we would certainly lose. But there will be no battle like that if I can help it. Ulric has no objectives left to be taken. What was once ours, the Academy and Trentyre, are now his. There are no leaders or officers in fixed locations that he can kill to ensure a swift victory. He has to eliminate all of us, which means he has to find us first."

He paused to let the meaning of his words sink in. Sanya seemed slightly bored, offering no feedback.

"Don't you see it now?" Basen continued. "Terren told us to retreat for a good reason. If we'd stayed to fight, we would've been destroyed. Now we have an advantage."

"Not an advantage. Terren only delayed the inevitable."

"It *is* an advantage! You have to change the way you're thinking to see it."

She took in a long breath, then let it out in a sharp exhale. Her eyes drifted around as she clearly refused to believe him.

Basen knelt right in front of her. "Sanya, if we go back to the forest to gather our allies, we're doing exactly what Ulric wants and expects us to do. Their numbers will eventually lead to victory as they hunt us down. So we're going to fight in another way."

"How do you expect to do anything without gathering your allies in the forest?"

"We will *find* our allies," Basen specified. "But we will never *gather* because that's how we're going to lose. In fact, it's the only way we're going to lose. We will communicate with each other to maneuver around our enemies and engage them in combat only when we have the advantage."

There was no way Sanya could argue against this.

She rolled her eyes. "Those are just words." She sat up straight and spoke with mock heroism. "I will heal ten times stronger and kill anyone who dares stand in my way!" She slouched again. "See, it doesn't matter how good it sounds if it isn't true."

He paced away from her so he wouldn't scream, taking a few moments to breathe out his anger and gather himself. Then he returned.

"You're right," he said with controlled frustration. "Right now, everything I say is *just words*. But every good plan starts as *just words*. Before you run off to who-knows-where, give me more time to figure out all the steps needed to put this plan to action. I need your help with the beginning and probably the end. That's all I ask!"

"You *want* my help," she corrected. "You don't need it."

"No, I need it. You'll see why soon enough. Heal as

quickly as you can." He went back to his side of the basement. There was no time to waste. Although he couldn't hear the drumming from here, he knew more of his allies had to be dying each day.

"What are you doing now?" she called after him.

"Prepare to be surprised," he hollered back.

"You don't prepare for a surprise," she replied with irritation.

"It's a nice way of saying be quiet as you wait!"

He dressed himself in the full enemy uniform, the blue coat with bronze buttons and the regal pants to match. He even donned the cap covering all of his black hair that had gotten too long for his taste over the weeks. He didn't have a mirror, so Sanya's reaction was all he could use to judge his appearance.

He sauntered back to her and puffed out his chest. Her eyes widened but she said nothing.

"I look that good?" Basen teased.

"Yes," she answered, then in a flat tone, "I hate how good you look in that."

She didn't seem to be trying for humor, but he couldn't hold in his laughter.

"What about the tear in the hat?" Sanya asked.

"Millry. It turns out she's very talented at many things."

"What are you going to do dressed like that?"

"Begin my plan."

"With what exactly?"

"Prepare..." He stopped himself. "You *will be* surprised."

He started up the stairs.

"Basen, what? Basen! Come back here!"

He would let her curiosity run wild. "I might be a day," he called back. "I'll have Millry check on you."

*****

The real reason Basen couldn't tell Sanya what he was doing had nothing to do with surprising her. He needed to avoid the inevitable conversation about the impossibility of winning this war. If she knew how dangerous what he was about to do really was, she would've filled his mind with futility, which might very well be the death of him.

At least a hundred enemies had seen his face when he'd killed Tauwin. The uniform and hat should mask him well enough, but a skilled enemy psychic could discern if he was an imposter. His mission was his only focus. He couldn't let his thoughts veer off toward doubt or panic, as there was no way to know who might be reading his energy.

He had great plans for the enemy uniforms, but today his task was simple. As he walked toward the center of the capital, his uniform commanded respect in the most uncomfortable way. It made people fear him.

He almost gave in to his instincts to ease their fear with a smile or a greeting, but doing so would go against what he was hoping to accomplish.

"What are you staring at!" he growled at a little girl gawking at him.

Her mother swept her up. "I'm sorry, sir."

The girl cried as the mother ran off with her.

Guilt ate away at him. He needed more practice to get rid of this feeling before he came into contact with his enemies.

Basen told an old man to get his ugly face out of his way while purposely walking toward him. After that, he waited for a woman near his age to walk by and then turned back and tilted his head for a good long look at her rump, ensuring others saw him do so. A few streets later, he started to pass by a beggar, only to stop. Seeing the man's fear, Basen turned and stared right at him. Basen said nothing, but it was enough to get the man to take his bowl with his measly coins and hurry off.

These acts of disrespect left such a bitter taste in his mouth, he made sure to disturb these poor people only when there were many others looking on.

By the time he made it to the training center near the castle, he'd lost himself in the role so much that not even a psychic could tell he was an imposter. The training center was empty again. He walked down the road and into the first armory on the way. There were two men cooking up lunch. Basen was hungry, so he would be taking some of their food. One of the men was old enough to be the other's father, though both were considerably older than Basen.

The sneer he wore told these men he was there to make trouble, both of them grimacing before they could hide their annoyance behind false smiles.

"Do you need something, sir?" the younger one asked.

Basen sniffed the air the way a noble might sniff a glass of wine before drinking. "That smells good," he said in his roughest voice and watched their worry worsen.

They glanced at each other from the sides of their eyes.

"If both of you are busy eating," Basen continued in a sarcastic tone, "who will attend to all your business?" He gestured at the empty shop of weapons and armor.

They offered no reply yet somehow managed to look hungrier, as if barely resisting the urge to devour all the contents in their bowls before Basen could walk over and take them.

"I think you'll agree that you should leave the eating to me," Basen said. He'd been holding the figurative dagger at their throats and had finally run it across.

He came toward them, fully prepared for a brawl if they were stupid enough to take him on. The eldest stepped in front of his meager bowl of what turned out to be beans.

"Can I offer you a weapon instead?" he pleaded.

Pity almost broke Basen, but he kept the weak feeling at bay. "Get out of my way."

The old man shuffled aside with a whimper as if about to object. The younger stared until Basen glanced over at him, then he took a long look at the floor.

Basen took the bowl and had himself a hefty bite. He made a sound of disgust, then licked his teeth clean as he set the bowl down.

"I hope you have a better lunch for me next time." He walked out the door.

He proceeded to visit every shop on the street and outrage every last one of them. It didn't take much to sour their day when the mere sight of him caused such fear. It turned out that noon was the best time to go, as many of them had food for him to steal.

By the time he was finished, he was full to the point of nausea. Now that he was done, the sour taste from earlier came back with such force that it filled his mouth and traveled all the way down his throat into his stomach. He couldn't hold it in.

Basen stumbled into a nearby tavern and emptied his stomach across the entrance with a loud retch. Playing the drunken fool, he pointed at everyone reacting quite appropriately to his disgusting act and yelled at them.

"Shut up or I'll arrest you!" He spun on his heels, pretended to lose his balance, then walked off with a drunken swagger.

He made his way to the castle. It was just enough distance from the scene of his disaster for him to feel safe from recognition by the people he'd wronged. He exchanged a few nods with the guards as he made his way around to the back of the castle. The stone structure that protected the man he most needed to kill was, unfortunately and obviously, designed as a fortress. The back wall stretched out longer than most streets. There was no way to know how thick it was.

Even if he was able to make a portal into part of it, could the portal create enough damage to get through? The castle was built on a grassy hill, but Basen found one spot along the back wall where the top of a buried rock poked through the grass. It was the best marker he could find, so it was here he began to gather energy.

To make himself less conspicuous, he leaned against the wall while he worked, keeping his arms crossed as if taking a break. It didn't take long to draw the attention of the troops walking along the road at the bottom of the hill. They looked at him with curiosity but did nothing.

It wasn't until an hour had passed that two soldiers yelled up to ask him what he was doing.

"Looking for shade," he said in his drunken voice.

They glanced at each other, said something, then started up the hill toward him. A moment later, they were taking him away from the castle "for your own good, before an officer sees you."

"What happened to your hat?" one of them asked.

"Have you ever tried to put it on with a sword?" he replied.

"No."

"Don't."

They chuckled.

"Aren't you a little young?" the other man asked.

"I have to get back," Basen said, pretending he hadn't heard the question.

Fortunately, they let him go without voicing suspicion.

He would have to come back to the castle at night to gather energy without being bothered.

Basen ventured down the rest of the streets around the castle, memorizing the exact location of every place where he planned to return when it was time. The key locations were where people were most likely to be harassed by guards: brothels, armories, taverns, tailors, bakeries, and anywhere that employed women whose looks might garner attention.

It was evening by the time he arrived back in his district. He still wasn't used to the glances by then. He waited until his street was empty before walking down to his sanctuary, then made sure he hadn't been seen before opening the cellar doors and going down to meet Sanya.

"I thought you'd died!" she complained. "At least tell me where you're going when you leave like that!"

He stood silently in front of her, confused. She cocked her head to the side.

"What don't you understand?" she asked.

"You want to leave and never return, yet you can't seem to handle my disappearance for a day."

"I can handle it fine. It's the way you left without saying anything that bothers me. Where in god's world did you go?"

"I walked around the streets near the castle. Most of Ulric's troops are there, so it's where our spies will gather the most information."

She gestured at the empty basement. "What spies?"

"Our *future* spies."

"You could've told me what you were doing."

"I'm not sure how many psychics there are under Ulric's command. A conversation with you was bound to make me doubt the safety of my task."

She pointed toward the moving shadows. "I'm tired of controlling them."

"Is the akorell stone charged yet?"

"Yes."

"Then it's time to go back to the colony with our new pets."

"I've been practicing making portals," she said. "Let me make it."

"If you fail, we'll have to wait for the akorell stone to

charge again. The longer we leave our enemies' bodies in our colony, the higher the chances someone will find them. We'll figure out a way to make more akorell stones soon enough."

She glanced down at the stone for a while, then eventually handed it over. "First change out of that uniform. It's making me angry."

"What isn't?"

She grumbled as he went to his side of the basement to change.

CHAPTER EIGHTEEN

The sound of the febeetles munching on the carcasses was similar to crumbling paper. Once they were done, they would need to be put in a pen so Basen and Sanya could leave them here and locate their allies in the forest. But there were very few loose rocks to make an enclosure, so Basen decided to dig holes instead.

Sanya's arm was still healing, though Basen figured she could help him dig if she wanted to. But instead, she used her injury as an excuse and lay surprisingly close to the febeetles to shut her eyes and relax.

It wasn't easy to dig a hole in this hard dirt, but he managed to get many done in the next hour. Stretching out his sore back, he told Sanya, "Send them into the holes so we can see if they'll all fit."

She got up and pointed her hand. Basen hurried out of the way as the insect army flooded over the ground in front of him. Slowly, the sea of black began to disappear around the holes until they were all squirming around inside.

"They hate it in there," Sanya said. "They want to return."

"Release your control to see if they can."

"I can't release my control. Psyche doesn't work like that. Their feeble minds are different than that of humans. Everything I force them to feel alters them in permanent ways. They want to escape the holes, but I'm telling them that the holes are good. All I can do is stop telling them the holes are good."

"Then do that."

She bent a few of her fingers, and the creatures poured out of the holes in no time. Basen ran to escape as many came for him, possibly smelling his flesh.

"Sanya!"

"I'm trying. There are so many." The lack of urgency in her voice made Basen run even faster.

"They're under control!" Sanya shouted to him eventually.

He turned to see them receding like a wave sliding back from the beach to the ocean.

"The holes are no good," Sanya said.

"I hadn't noticed."

The last thing he wanted now was to spend another hour exhausting himself to create some other form of containment, only for it to fail.

The two of them thought for a while, the beetles returning to their feast of corpses.

Basen came to only one solution.

"You're going to have to stay here with them," he told Sanya.

"I'm not going to do that. I've spent nearly the last two days with them, hardly able to sleep."

"You just told me your arm is still too injured to dig," he chided. "How do you expect to run through the forest without reopening your wound?"

She heaved out her breath. "I'm sure I'll find a way."

"No, we can't risk the febeetles leaving the colony. We're going to need them."

"For what?"

"To kill Ulric."

She lifted her finger and opened her mouth as if to object but then stopped. "How?"

"They will help us get to him when it's time to attack."

She took a long look at the febeetles. "Fine, but you'd better come back soon and have thought of some way to contain them without me spending the rest of the war here. I'm too useful to waste away here."

"I can't deny that. But before I go, I need you to promise me something. Whoever I find and bring back, you will give them your best effort to be nice. I don't care if you have to act. Be like the Sanya who first came to the Academy, no matter how they treat you."

"Even if they treat me like Peter did?"

"Peter's dead." Basen cradled the handle of his sword.

"So what?"

"God's mercy, Sanya! This is exactly why I have to tell you to behave. You've regressed into your old self, a woman without empathy or knowledge of social conduct. I'm tired of it. At least try."

She rubbed her forehead as if scratching an itch with her fingertips. Then she threw down her hand and said, "Fine."

He'd been doing so much walking recently, his feet ached as he made his way out of the colony.

There was still some light left in the day, but it would be night soon. Determined to find someone before then, he hurried to cover his tracks near the colony entrance, then ventured out. Once he'd gone farther, he rushed around until he found a trail of footprints.

He was no tracker, so he couldn't follow them as

quickly as he wanted. Night fell upon him with no signs of whether his quarry was ally or enemy.

Eventually he started hearing sounds behind him that he first thought to be an animal. He stopped to listen but heard nothing else. He had to consider the possibility that someone was following him, or perhaps was following the same trail that he was.

He used rocks and roots to veer off the forest path and hide himself in a copse of bushes. He waited and listened. Moonlight illuminated the forest with a touch of silver as pillars of the faint light came down between the gaps of treetops. Basen had made sure to put himself in the darkest spot nearby, but that didn't make him any less afraid as he witnessed an army of blue uniforms seeping in through the trees. A giant led them, the same giant Basen had faced atop the Fjallejon Mountains, as there could be no other man of the same size.

Basen eased toward the back side of the shrubbery so he might be able to slip away if they came too close, but the sound of leaves was deafening as he tried to move. All he could do was shrink lower and hope he wasn't seen.

No doubt the hunt for his allies was still happening. At least it meant there were survivors for him to locate. He just had to find them before his enemies did.

First, he needed to get out of here alive.

The army stopped. He could catch only glimpses of them, but there seemed to be someone pointing in his direction. Then they began to circle.

A psychic! Basen had been sensed.

He stood and shot a fireball at the men coming around to block his escape, sending the one he struck rolling backward and the others jumping behind a tree for cover. Basen ran in the only direction he could without going straight toward them, the same direction as the footprints he'd been following.

These enemies did not yell out Basen's location like the others had. They gave chase for only a moment and then let him go. Perhaps they had witnessed his superior speed and didn't want to separate from each other in a pointless effort, or they had some trap planned.

He slowed to a jog and watched the ground for rope or string or net. He felt something coming down from above!

Basen dove as something crashed down where he had just been standing. He aimed his wand and pulled his sword as he spun back to face his enemy.

"Basen?"

"Neeko, thank god!" Basen put away his sword to give the other man a fierce hug. "I'm so glad to see you."

"And I you! Come, I'll take you to the others."

"Alabell?" Basen asked.

"And more."

Before Neeko could take a step, Basen grabbed him from the side and hoisted him off the ground with an excited bear hug.

"Basen, Basen! It's not safe here."

He let Neeko down. "I'm not sorry."

Neeko laughed. "This way."

"Did you hear the fireball?" Basen asked.

"Yes, was that you?"

"It was. What happened to you during the battle at the Academy? I came to the medical building to help but you and the others had already left. Cleve saw you going north and sent me after you, but I never found you."

"We tried to evacuate everyone, but there were many injured who were too slow even with our help. Cassius led the Tenred troops through the medical building, many of them stopping to slaughter everyone within their reach. We fought briefly, then ran. It was the only way to survive." There was heavy guilt in Neeko's voice.

"You did the right thing. We will get revenge."

"I almost did, but I failed."

"What do you mean?"

But Neeko put up his hand. They stopped to listen. Something skulked around behind them. Basen made light in its direction.

The small animal darted into the bushes and disappeared before Basen could recognize it.

"We shouldn't speak here," Neeko said.

Basen nodded.

They walked for a while before Neeko called out, "Here?"

It seemed to be some sort of signal, so Basen didn't ask.

"No," a voice responded from the darkness between the trees ahead. "And you?"

"Deadly," Neeko replied.

Sudden light made Basen shield his eyes.

"Who is that with you?" It was definitely Effie's voice.

"Prepare to be surprised," Basen teased.

"Oh my stars." The silhouette of Alabell hurtled toward him. He opened his arms and caught her. The feeling of relief was like a tidal wave, abolishing all his other fears and worries. He didn't care how many planned to kill them. So long as he was with Alabell, he would keep both of them safe.

Basen was about to show her with his lips how glad he was to see her again when someone demanded, "Do I get a turn?" He turned to see Effie with hands on hips. "Or are these hugs reserved for partners?"

"I hugged Neeko earlier," Basen said, reluctantly releasing Alabell. "Twice. So I'd like to think not."

Alabell sniffled as if holding in tears. "We figured there was a good chance you were dead," she told Basen as he and Effie embraced.

"There were a few close moments, but I'm unhurt."

They brought him to the rest of their group—Shara, Steffen, and Effie's sister, Gabby—and Basen hugged every one of them.

"Good. Chemists," he remarked. "And mages: bastial, sartious, and pyforial. I need all of you. I have a safe location. I will show you if you come with me."

Steffen made a sound of surprise. "We haven't been able to find anywhere to make camp safely. Where is it?"

"The abandoned Slugari colony." Basen walked toward it, but they did not follow. "Come on."

"Basen," Alabell said, "there's no way out if they find us in there. We would not be able to run."

"There is. Trust me."

Alabell didn't hesitate as she grabbed a bag she must've taken while fleeing the Academy and stood at his side. The others, however, looked at each other as if someone should object.

"How about you explain first?" Effie suggested.

"I know as well as the rest of you that we could be seen or heard at any point, so I'll explain everything once we are safe."

"If it means sleeping without fear of death, I'll go anywhere," Shara said.

"It does."

They gathered their bags and followed Basen. He got lost briefly on the way there but still made decent time. He hoped Alabell was comfortable holding his hand the entire time, as he never wanted to let her go again.

No one said a word until they'd reached the bottom of the tunnel and entered the colony.

"Now what?" Effie asked.

"It's still a walk from here, but at least I can talk now." His light brushed over something white scattered around on the dirt. As soon as he realized they were human bones, so did the others in his party. All of them spoke at once.

"What's down here?"

"We have to leave now!"

"The bastial hell is this?"

Sanya must've put these here. It was the only thing he could hope for that wouldn't mean she was dead and that his sanctuary was taken over by the febeetles.

"It's fine," Basen said. He led them forward, Alabell letting go of his hand for the first time. Around the bones were scraps of clothing. He lifted one of them in front of his wand. "These were our enemies. They tried to follow us down here, and we killed them all."

"Months ago?" Effie asked sarcastically, alarm in her tone. "There should be more than bones, Basen!"

"Are you sure there's nothing down here?" Alabell asked, taking hold of his arm and gently pulling him away from the bones.

He chuckled. "She must've done this on purpose to scare anyone who might come down here looking for us. I can see now that it works."

"Who?" Effie asked.

Before Basen could figure out how best to introduce Sanya, he heard her voice from the darkness behind him.

"Me." Sanya made light and didn't move. The many febeetles lurked in the darkness behind her.

"Effie," Basen warned, "there needs to be peace between all of us. Sanya has been invaluable to our effort in this war so far, as she will continue to be."

"They let her live?" Effie seethed.

"No," Sanya corrected. "They were going to execute me, but the battle interrupted their plans. I escaped and killed many of your enemies."

"Our enemies," Basen corrected.

Sanya refused to say it.

"What do you expect to happen to you when this is over?" Effie asked. If she was actually curious, Basen heard none of it from her furious tone.

"Obviously you have some idea," Sanya bit back. "Might as well tell me."

"Effie..." Basen warned again.

She put up her hands. "I will cooperate."

Basen knew this reprieve didn't mean it was over between them, but he gladly took the opportunity. He led the others toward Sanya and explained the febeetles as they carefully walked around them. Sanya waited until she was at the back to follow as Basen directed them toward the akorell metal too far ahead for any of its light to be seen.

"Sanya and I have established a sanctuary not only down here but in the capital. I can teleport to get us directly there. A woman named Millry has been helping us. She's Jackrie's sister, and Sanya's psyche confirms we can trust her."

He heard whispering behind him, something about Basen not knowing.

Alabell responded in a tone dripping with sadness, "Oh, that's right, he wouldn't."

"What is it?" Basen asked, devastation sliding its claws around his throat.

There was grief already in the air as they looked at each other. "I'll tell him," Effie said. The rest nodded.

CHAPTER NINETEEN

Effie took a long inhale, then approached. "Basen, this is going to be difficult to hear."

"Just tell me."

"Both Terren and Jackrie are dead."

Basen had expected something horrible about Jackrie, but Terren as well? "How sure are you?"

"Certain. Cleve saw it and told us."

Basen's stomach turned. He choked back vomit. They gave him some time as he turned away and tried to put the broken pieces of himself back together.

When his body allowed him to open his mouth without retching, he turned back to them and asked, "How did it happen?"

"Terren saw he was the target, so he made everyone else separate except for warriors and mages of Group Seven and Eight."

"I'm in one of those groups. Did he...expect me to be there?"

"There's nothing you could've done," Alabell said.

"What happened?"

They all stared at Effie. She lowered her head to look up through the tops of her dark eyes. "Ulric has a giant bigger than any Krepp."

"Rockbreak," Basen said.

"How did you know his name?"

"Sanya warned me about him a while ago. I had to run when I faced him on the Fjallejon Mountains. None of the

Elves, even Vithos, could do anything against him with psyche."

"He's barely human," Sanya added. "So it was him?" Even she sounded saddened by the news.

"Why do you care?" Effie asked sharply.

"Terren was a good warrior and an honorable man. I never would've gotten the chance to train at the Academy if it wasn't for him."

"You didn't seem to care about Terren when you sided with Tauwin, knowing what he had planned for the headmaster."

"I was foolish back then."

"Only back then?"

It felt as if Basen's bearings were coming apart as it took all of his focus just to remain standing. He didn't hear the rest of Effie and Sanya's bickering as the walls in his mind shifted toward each other while dark thoughts cascaded down the sides to bury him. Without Terren, was Sanya right after all? Did they really have any hope?

Basen couldn't let himself think like this. That's how wars were lost. Terren had been targeted. Ulric had wanted to create this very feeling of hopelessness. Basen refused to let it overwhelm him.

As he realized Effie and Sanya were still arguing, he touched Effie's shoulder. "This isn't helping."

She looked at him as if she might disagree, then let out her tension with a breath. "You're right." She made light and looked around the cavern. "Are you sure you can make a portal down here?"

"I'm sure. Follow me as you tell me more about Cleve. When did you last see him?"

She thought for a moment. "Bastial hell, it was only yesterday, but it felt like a week ago."

Alabell came up on Basen's other side. He took her hand and relished the feeling of comfort.

"We wanted him to join us," Alabell said, "but..." She looked behind Basen toward Effie.

"He's different," the mage said. "At least for now. Not only was his uncle taken from him but his sword as well. He strives for revenge."

"Don't we all?" Basen asked.

"Not like Cleve," Alabell said.

"He's going to get himself and Annah killed," Effie added.

"Who else is with him?"

"Five others who escaped, thanks to Jackrie sacrificing her life." Effie stopped. Basen could see the pain in her eyes as she forced out the next words. "Cleve and I argued about what to do. Now I'm not sure if we're going to see him again. Did you know they burn our bodies?" She made fists. "They just beat their damn drum and then burn us as if we never existed."

"The drumming has slowed," Steffen replied from behind them. "We can't lose hope."

"No, we can't," Basen agreed. "And there's no reason to yet. Sanya and I have already taken steps toward winning this war. You'll see soon enough." He wouldn't let out that his plan was impossible without finding more of their allies, but he trusted himself to get to them soon.

"Sanya was cut down her arm during the battle here," Basen continued. "Do any of you chemists have something to help her heal faster?"

"We've collected plants from the forest for many recipes," Alabell said. She smiled over her shoulder at Sanya. "One is the repair potion, and I know you can handle the pain just fine."

Sanya said nothing until Basen glared at her.

"Thank you," she told Alabell when she got the hint.

"Effie," Basen said, "I'm going to need you to make a sartious barrier to keep the febeetles from escaping until we need them. But we'll have to feed them, so it should be a structure in which we can create an opening when needed without compromising its walls."

"That's going to take at least a day. I'm no Jackrie."

"Sanya will keep them under control until you're done."

"You do realize," Sanya complained, "that I've barely slept for the last two days because of these beetles! Spending another whole day with them is no easy task."

"I'm sorry about that, but it can't be helped."

Sanya grumbled something unintelligible.

"Steffen, if anyone here knows about making akorell stones, it's you. We have the akorell metal, which is the gateway out of here that I mentioned previously. Sanya and I believe there's enough to make at least a few more akorell bracelets."

"Oh, I'll have to think."

"We need brass and a furnace," Gabby informed them.

"Yes," Steffen agreed, "and picks and chisels and a ladder, as well as other supplies I can't think of at the moment. Even then, my knowledge is based only on books. Without experience crafting the bracelets, I'm not sure how effective they'll be."

"We can figure it out," Gabby said, sounding excited about the idea.

"Good," Basen said. "I will get you whatever supplies you need."

When they arrived at the alcove with the akorell metal, Shara asked, "So is this where we'll be spending most of our time until this is over?" There was obvious dread in her voice.

"No, it's too dangerous here," Basen answered. "At any point, they could come down to investigate the dead and might not be scared off by the bones. I'll bring us to the capital when it's time."

Alabell asked, "And when is that?"

"Once we get in contact with enough of our allies."

It was silent for a breath. "Enough for what?" she asked.

All stared at Basen, clearly waiting for the plan. This was as good a time as any, so he went through all of it one step at a time. He paused after each part, expecting questions or objections, but no one said a word. Eventually he rolled on through to the end.

There was a noticeable change in the dense and damp air: a hopefulness. Even Sanya's scowl had softened. So it wasn't just Basen who believed this was possible. Knowing others believed in him bolstered his confidence in himself, dissolving the last bit of doubt Sanya had instilled in him.

Alabell asked, "How are we going to find our allies without running into our enemies?"

"With patience and psyche. Sanya's injury should heal in less than a day now with your help. As soon as the beetles are in their pen, she'll help us track down our allies and keep away from enemies. I assume Neeko has been doing most of that so far?"

"I have. Most people don't look up, but my rear could use a break from sitting in trees."

Steffen asked Basen, "Have you or Sanya seen any of the Krepps? I noticed them in the battle against Ulric's troops, but not after we got to the forest."

"They might not have fled with everyone else," Basen realized aloud. "If that's the case, there will be no Kreppen survivors."

"I don't understand something." Effie glared at Sanya. "Why wasn't psyche able to pick up Tenred's plan for betrayal? Did you do something?"

"I couldn't. I was outside the stadium, not that I would have, anyway. If you remember, I was there to turn myself in, and I had hopes of joining all of you."

Effie ignored her. "We won't know whether she's telling the truth until we find Reela."

"I am," Sanya argued.

"We can trust her," Basen said. "She saved my life more than once for no benefit to herself."

"She's probably just in love with you. She won't treat the rest of us the same."

Everyone fell silent. Effie suddenly seemed to realize what she had said, as her eyes widened and she raised both hands in a gesture of appeasement.

"It was a stupid thought that should've passed through my mind without being spoken aloud. I'm sorry."

Effie had made this awkward for everyone except Sanya, to Basen's surprise, as she stomped over to stand tall over Effie. "If you want complete honesty, here it is: I care about the lives of everyone here equally. Equally! And that includes my own! I'm done putting myself above others. The only person who I care less about than myself is you."

Shara cleared her throat loudly. "There is something that everyone knows but no one's saying. As an outsider, I think it's my responsibility."

"Shara, I don't think it's a good idea," Neeko said.

"I know we've had our disagreements about this, but it needs to be addressed. It's about Terren..."

"At least let me tell them," Neeko interrupted. "Please. I've thought a lot about it."

"All right."

Neeko looked as if he might be sick to his stomach. "Shara and I believe it's important to discuss the exact reason this happened, why we are all in this...unfavorable position. Terren didn't question Abith, even when Reela pointed out that he was hiding something. As we gather more allies, we will need to question them to make sure they are not spies or planning a betrayal so this doesn't happen again. It almost happened to Cleve." He appeared to be speaking only to Basen and Sanya now.

"What did?" Basen asked.

"Another betrayal. Someone in his group went to the enemy and reported his location, probably in the hopes of some reward. Many died because of it."

Shara spoke before Basen could think of anything to say. "We're sorry for bringing this up. We didn't get to know Terren as long as the rest of you, but we saw what kind of man he was. It fills us with sorrow to speak about him in any negative way."

"Terren did nothing wrong," Basen objected. "Neither did Abith."

"Basen, don't make this harder," Effie argued and turned to Neeko and Shara. "I know it was difficult for you to say that, but I believe the same thing. You shouldn't feel guilty for bringing it up."

"Yes, thank you," Gabby agreed. "I saw it, too. Terren refused to question him."

Everyone in their group began to agree, except for Alabell. "Basen knows something the rest of you don't."

That quieted them.

"I think it'll come as a relief that Terren is not at fault for this," Basen said. "I don't have proof, so you'll have to believe me."

Everyone edged closer to him, their eagerness palpable. They must've held anger for the headmaster if they believed this was all his fault. Basen knew what it was like to hate someone he loved—he'd thought his mother had betrayed his family—but he remembered the relief upon finding out the truth.

"Terren and Abith were friends. They trained together and eventually began to trust each other, but neither man could let anyone know this truth. The instructors and students would've questioned Terren's judgment for befriending a man who'd previously tried to kill him, and Abith's followers from Tenred might *actually* kill him and choose a new leader if they find out he'd changed his mind about taking over the school."

"Did Abith tell you all of this during your training?" Effie asked. "Because he might've lied."

"No, I saw it after I returned from killing Yeso. I was shocked at first, but then I started to realize how much they needed each other to stand up to Ulric and Tauwin, and it made sense. They learned to respect each other eventually—I could see it in the way they fought."

"But none of us saw Abith in the battle," Effie argued.

Sanya answered, "He was busy trying to defend himself from Krepps who accused him of being the traitor. I saw them fighting him while he tried to tell them it was Cassius Lane who they needed to kill. He was speaking the truth, which I told the Krepps. They stopped and ran toward the battle, but they were far behind. I don't know what happened to them."

Alabell pointed at Basen. "So it was Abith who told you about the ambush. I've been wondering how you knew!"

"Yes, Abith saw someone leaving over the wall and went to investigate. When he came back, he was headed somewhere as if about to kill someone. He probably found Crea and made her tell him the plan...she might even be dead already. He was on his way to kill Cassius as well, but he was too late. The battle had begun. A group of Krepps must've intercepted him. Meanwhile, many troops from Tenred tried to kill or capture me. When they were confident they had me, they revealed that Crea had spoken with Ulric to develop the plan. I don't believe any of them knew they would be attacking the Academy with Ulric until that day, when Crea relayed the message to Cassius."

"So they never actually lied," Effie said. "Now it makes sense why Terren and Abith wouldn't want the truth of

Abith's loyalty coming out at Redfield."

Neeko made a sound of pain, burying his face in his hands. Shara put her hand on his back. "It's not your fault. None of us knew the truth."

"What happened?" Basen asked, though he feared he already knew the answer.

"I saw Abith in the forest. I...he was alone." Neeko looked over at Effie. "We had assumed the ambush was his doing. I figured he was here hunting us like the rest of Ulric's troops."

"We did, too" Effie agreed. "Don't blame yourself."

"I figured it would be appropriate to send my sword through his back just as he organized an attack from behind us."

"Tell me you didn't kill him," Basen said.

"I tried, and two hells I'm glad I failed."

"Did you injure him?"

"No. I came down at his back, but he must've heard me as I sent my sword at him. He made a sartious barrier as he turned." Neeko shook his head. "He yelled out that we were on the same side, but I didn't believe him. I moved my second sword around his shield but he just extended the barrier. Then he drew his wand and shot a fireball at me. It landed in front of my feet, knocking me backward. He shot another, then another, forcing me to retreat. I thought he couldn't hit me while I was moving, but now I realize he missed on purpose. I returned to gather our group, but he was gone when we came back." Neeko grabbed the hilt of his swords. "But he left my weapons, which I thought was strange. It all makes sense now."

Basen tried to think of something encouraging to wash away the look of guilt on everyone's face, but this *was* bad. Now Abith had no reason to approach any allies. They all thought him to be the traitor.

"He's probably out of the forest by now," Sanya offered.

"Perhaps not," Basen countered. "Many would assume the same about you, yet you're still here."

"Why *are* you still here?" Effie asked. "You never explained that. I hope you don't expect to go free after this, no matter how much you help."

"Then why don't I leave right now?" Sanya snapped. "Is that what you want, Effie?"

Glancing at the swarming beetles behind Sanya, Effie gave no answer.

"Do you want my help or not?" Sanya prodded. "Tell me to leave, and I will right now. Or admit that you want my help and stop bothering me."

As uncomfortable as this was, Basen kept himself from interjecting. It was important for Effie to let herself accept Sanya's worth.

"I want your help," Effie grumbled to the ground.

"Then stop complaining and start making the damn sartious cage so I can be of better use."

"Fine." Effie walked over to the wall opposite the akorell alcove and started to gather clumps of sartious energy on the ground.

Basen smiled as he realized his allies were with him, finally. It was time for the next step.

He asked Neeko, "Have any of our enemies seen what you can do?"

"I don't believe so. Most don't look high enough to see me, and we killed every uniform we found."

Uniform. Basen liked that word for them.

"Good, we'll need to keep up that ferocity. After we get some rest, we'll go find the others. There has to be a large group of our allies hiding somewhere, which would explain why we have had so much trouble finding our friends. Unfortunately, the longer they stay gathered in the forest, the greater the chances of a battle they cannot win."

Basen didn't want to admit it—even to himself—but it was possible everyone else was already dead. Hope would dwindle quickly if they didn't find anyone tomorrow.

CHAPTER TWENTY

The news of Terren and Jackrie's deaths had sapped Basen's strength momentarily. Now that he had rested and was out in the forest looking for allies with Neeko, his fortitude had returned. A number of things were finally going right: Alabell was safer in the colony than she was in the forest; Effie worked to create a pen for the febeetles; and the three chemists would ensure Sanya healed quickly. Once Basen and Neeko had Sanya's help, it should be even easier to escape death whenever enemies found them.

The person Basen most wanted to locate, besides Abith, was Cleve. He feared what the young warrior's rage might cause him to do, as Basen knew how thoughts of betrayal had crippled him during his time in the workhouse. Basen wasn't angry with Crea. He could not be angry when he'd expected this deceit and selfishness from her. However, if he found out she'd done something to his innocent mother, he might put himself in danger with his quest for revenge in the same way Cleve was doing now.

"At least Annah is with Cleve," Basen told Neeko after they'd begun to share their worries. "She'll talk him down from doing anything too risky. But I want to find them as soon as possible."

"I'm not sure you'll convince him to do things differently than he wants. Effie pleaded to the point of tears, then seemed embarrassed and furious when he still left. She just kept muttering the same thing all day: Cleve's going to get himself killed."

"Where did he go?"

"He wants to kill Cassius and Rockbreak. He's looking for a way to attack them in their camp at night."

Basen stopped Neeko. "We know where their camp is for certain?"

"The northern edge of the forest. Why do you think we're going south?"

"What else should I know?"

"They guard the river as best they can, but it's too big for them to cover all of it at any given point, so they patrol."

So Sanya had been right.

"It seems like they patrol the entire forest," Basen added. "They've sectioned it off. Men are designated to certain spots."

"How do you know?"

"I heard them yelling numbers and directions while chasing me. There must be a system in place. If we can figure it out, we can use it against them. I assume they must be starting from the north and sweeping across the forest on their way south. It would explain why we see more of them in the north, and it would also make sense if their plan is to eradicate us completely. They don't want to miss anyone as they search the entire forest while guarding the walls of the cities."

"I hope you're right about everything. Food has been scarce for us, while I'm sure uniforms from the cities bring supplies to their comrades in the forest. Most of the food we've gotten was stolen from them."

"How many have you killed?"

"I'm not sure. A hundred?"

Basen stared with an open mouth.

"What?"

"I'm glad you're here."

"I fear the rest of our allies have had more trouble feeding themselves."

"We just have to find them," Basen reassured.

"Let's hope your theory is correct."

They walked straight south for a few hours. Basen soon became parched and hungry, but Neeko looked as if he wanted to keep walking so Basen did as well. Raywhite Forest was shaped like a Y turned slightly to the left. Its southeastern tail of trees ran down past Trentyre. Basen hoped his allies hadn't gone all the way there, as it would be difficult to get to them without their enemies taking notice.

The middle of the forest was almost as wide as it was long, but it narrowed the farther Basen and Neeko went south. This made it easier to search when they eventually came closer to the southern edge. They walked from east to west until they came to the western edge of the trees, then they made their way south again and went east until coming to the eastern edge.

For a few more hours, they repeated this. Basen began to worry when he noticed the sky darkening. He hadn't had a sip of water all day, and his throat tormented him for it. He could see the same pain in Neeko's grimace. If they didn't find allies soon, they would have to change their mission to get to the river instead.

"Don't move," someone said from above them. "Put up your hands."

No one looks up. Basen cursed inwardly. Neeko had said it less than a day ago, and both of them had now fallen prey to the same trap.

"State your loyalty," said the man. "Quickly."

If this archer or mage was a uniform, at least one of them was likely to die if they told the truth.

"Separate," Basen whispered.

"Now," Neeko agreed.

They darted in opposite directions. Basen spun around and drew his wand, but it wasn't needed. Neeko had already knocked the archer off the tree.

He did have a uniform on, but it was gray! "Ally!" Basen sprinted in a wild attempt to get beneath the screaming man before he hit the ground. He wasn't going to make it.

Something clear whisked in front of Basen and materialized into a blanket of dusty wind. The man fell into the pyforial energy, crushing it between his back and the forest floor. It slipped out and punched Basen in the stomach, but not before providing a cushion for the soldier of Basen's father.

He was getting up, albeit slowly, but it was a good sign.

"Are you all right?" Basen asked.

"You could've just said you're with Kyrro's Allies!"

"Sorry," Neeko said. "We didn't want to risk you being an enemy."

"Bastial hell, you nearly killed me!" Fortunately, the man didn't seem hurt, only angry.

Basen asked, "Couldn't you tell we weren't wearing

uniforms?"

"Yes, but Ulric and Abith have young men wandering the forest without uniform, pretending to be allies."

Basen frowned at the thought of that dirty tactic. Even worse was his allies thought Abith was guilty of it too, making it less likely they would trust him. By the time Basen convinced everyone Abith was an ally, he'd probably have found a way out of the forest, never to return.

The soldier collected his fallen bow. "So you're the pyforial mage I've heard about. Good, everyone will be happy I found you. What about you?" He pointed at Basen.

"I'm Basen Hiller."

The soldier chuckled. "I'm sensing a promotion in my near future. Come with me."

Basen couldn't wait a moment longer to ask. "Is my father all right?"

"He was injured during the battle, but he's recovered. He and Terren were targets, but Terren more so than Henry. Have you heard?"

"Yes."

There was a pang of sadness, but it was a cube of ice in Basen's warmth of glee. He was about to see his father, and possibly many more compatriots. "How many are with you?"

"Everyone still alive who we know of."

Basen shared a smile with Neeko. It had taken almost all day, but this was about as fortunate a turn of events as they could ask for.

"Do you have some water?" Neeko asked the man.

He gave over his water skin. "You two look as if you need all of it. Go ahead."

They traded gulps and emptied it in the span of a few breaths.

"I'm Teej," said the man. "You can speak with your father first, but do me a favor and tell him I found you wandering and recognized you. When I'm an officer, I'll repay the favor." Although his tone was light as if he might be joking, his stern eyes said otherwise. Except for his dark skin, he looked like most of the other soldiers allegiant to Basen's father, as if they'd been fighting in this war twice as long as the rest of Kyrro's Allies. It was something in their eyes. A hardness. A weariness.

But Teej's focus on a possible promotion made it clear he thought the war could be won. It was a refreshing change to meet an ally like him. Basen hoped there were many more.

Teej led them into a camp where Basen was blessed with the glorious sight of hundreds of allies and tents. They had fire, food, and water. His father was speaking with Warrior Sneary but stopped when he noticed Basen. Both of the high-ranking men came over.

Henry had never been an emotional man, so it came as a surprise when he threw his arms around Basen. "I thought you were dead!"

"I'm very much alive and have been getting much done. I have a plan for us."

Teej cleared his throat.

"Teej recognized us," Basen spat out quickly. "We can't stay here any longer. They could be coming any moment."

"Basen, relax," Henry replied. "You're safe here now."

"None of us are safe here."

"We have the perimeters covered," Sneary said. "Do you know of any others out there?"

"Yes, but we have to go to them."

Henry put his hand on Basen's shoulder. "I can send out a team to bring them back. You look exhausted; go see our healers. They're behind the first row of tents—"

"It's not safe here," Basen insisted. "They want us to gather just like this. They might even know you're here and are planning an attack."

His loud voice seemed to be gaining attention as the others nearby started drifting toward him. He recognized many faces that would've filled him with joy if he wasn't so worried he was about to be ignored. There was the master chemist, Jack, the master mage, Trela, and even Cleve and Annah and a few Krepps—including Nebre and Rickik. He didn't see his mother, however. She must've stayed at the Academy. Hopefully she was still alive.

"You're only guessing what they want us to do," Henry said.

"Yes, but logic is on my side. At least hear my plan."

A large audience was gathering, Cleve and Annah included. They looked surprised and happy to see Basen, but they knew not to greet him in this moment. Lives were at stake, and Basen's face must've revealed his worry.

"What's going on?" Cleve asked.

Wasn't the warrior supposed to be plotting out his revenge? Even Cleve must've been convinced that the best strategy was to gather here. This had to change right now.

"Nothing's going on," Sneary assured Cleve. "Basen just arrived, so he's unused to our method."

"It doesn't matter how well you've set up a perimeter," Basen argued. "They have ten times our numbers."

"Basen!" Henry chided. "Spreading misinformation will endanger the people you're trying to protect."

"It's been confirmed through interrogation. They've been keeping track of the dead with drums. They know exactly how many we have left, and they plan to kill us all. Once they realize we're here, they will surround us and engage."

"And we will win," Sneary said. "You don't know of our traps."

"It doesn't matter. There are too many…"

Basen stopped himself, realizing something. He *was* doing more harm than help if all he did was create panic.

"All I ask is that you listen to my plan," he said in a calm voice. "Everything is ready for us to begin."

"All right, Basen." Henry turned to address the crowd. "I know many of you are eager to greet my son, but let me speak to him first."

Everyone dispersed except for Henry and Sneary, but Neeko stayed at Basen's side. "I believe in Basen's plan."

"I hear you," Henry said with a single nod. "Now go get yourself some food."

Neeko walked off with a look back over his shoulder.

"You expect us to argue," Basen realized. During their time in the castle and the workhouse, Henry never wanted to argue or reprimand Basen in front of others.

He cared too much about the image of his family, but all he'd done now was send away many people who were sure to agree with Basen.

"We won't argue," Henry said. "I expect to convince you that we know what's best."

"Just keep an open mind as you listen."

"We will," Henry said for Sneary. Basen wasn't sure he believed his father, but he delved into his plan anyway. It could take weeks to set all of it up, and it would require trust, coordination, and devotion, but it was the only way to win. He could see Sneary and Henry's expressions becoming more doubtful as they realized what would be required of everyone. But they listened until the end without interruption.

"I know it would be difficult," Basen said. "But it will work."

"It might," Henry said, "but the chance of failure is too high."

"The chance of failure if we stay here is too high," Basen retorted. "How many do we have left, a thousand?"

"About," Henry said.

"They have ten thousand."

Sneary was a big man, leaning down to match his gaze with Basen's. "Many of them aren't trained like our troops."

"That doesn't matter when they have ten times as many as we do. We can't face them in open combat."

He could see by Sneary's surprise that the warrior wasn't used to people disagreeing with his decisions. Why were the warriors always the people to take command?

Terren had done an excellent job, but Sneary didn't have the experience to set up a proper defense. No one did. This war now required a different type of mindset, not a battle planner but someone who could outthink their enemies.

Basen had hoped there would be others like Teej who had faith they could win this war, but little did he realize that this trait would make people stubborn. It was because they thought they could win that they would go down in defeat.

"I can't allow us to separate," Sneary said, his voice sharp with irritation. "We won't be able to give our troops the guidance they need."

But separation was key to Basen's plan and essential to survive. *We'll die here,* he almost said before stopping himself.

Basen realized Sneary's problem was trust. He didn't have enough of it in his troops. Unfortunately, Henry seemed to agree as he remained silent with his arms folded.

"Get some food," Henry said as practically an order. "We'll talk about your plan later."

That meant never.

Dejected, Basen went to join Neeko for a tasteless yet satisfying bowl of soup. Basen couldn't tell exactly what was in it, and he wasn't sure he wanted to know as he didn't recognize any of the chewy textures.

"Any luck?" Neeko asked.

Before Basen could answer, his father surprised him by squatting down beside him. "There's something you need to understand," Henry murmured. "The people here are angry. They want to fight."

"Sneary included?"

"Yes. The need for revenge makes a man stubborn. There's a reason Ulric sent so many after Terren. He knew this would be the result."

"Are you actually agreeing with my plan?"

"No." The single word was like a stab to the back. "But only because there aren't enough people here ready to do what you need them to do for it to work."

"Sneary included," Basen repeated, finally feeling a glimmer of his father's trust.

"Yes. They follow him in the same way my men will follow me."

"Why didn't you say anything?"

"This has to be done delicately. We need *everyone* for your plan to work, especially Sneary. After you eat, greet your friends and put Sneary's worries to rest by smiling instead of wearing that stern expression you had while telling us your plan. Get your friends on our side, and have them speak to others. Eventually you should make your way over to Jack and Trela. They have the clout you don't to change Sneary's mind, but don't let Sneary know you're trying to undermine his strategy. Spend the night, and we will speak again in the morning."

"Thank you, Father."

He nodded and left.

Basen turned to Neeko. "It looks like we have a lot of work to do."

CHAPTER TWENTY-ONE

Basen saw many familiar faces, but there were even more people he didn't recognize who surprised him by coming up to tell him they were glad he was here. There was no chance to explain the plan to any of them without Sneary knowing, as an audience would be sure to gather. He waited until the commotion of his and Neeko's arrival died down, and that's when he approached Jack Rose.

"We're all glad to see you," Jack said as they shook hands.

"I'm glad everyone here is still alive and ready to fight, but if we stay here, we'll die."

"I realize that, but we don't yet have an alternative. I'm expecting you do?"

Basen let out a breath of relief. He could trust the chemist master. Without time to go over every detail of his plan, he could only summarize it. Fortunately, Jack was either able to fill in the missing parts himself or trusted Basen enough not to question any of it.

"And now you need me to tell others," Jack assumed.

"Yes. Once we have enough support, Sneary will be forced to join us. I'll need mages gathering energy within the camp in the meantime so I can make a portal here."

"I'll speak to Trela. She'll know who to choose."

They separated. Basen hadn't given himself the chance to look around the camp much until now. He glanced around as if taking in the scene while really looking for Sneary to make sure he wasn't watching.

Basen realized his earlier estimation of hundreds of tents was wrong. There weren't even one hundred, and those must've been stolen from their enemies. Wet clothes hung from low branches, strategically placed near the many fires. Most people sat or even lay on the dirt. To Basen, it looked like everyone was waiting for death.

Noticing Annah by herself, Basen took the opportunity to speak to her without Cleve. They'd already greeted each other, but that didn't stop her from smiling as Basen came up to her.

"Effie told me what happened," he said.

Annah bit her bottom lip. "We tried to find them again after we came in contact with this group, but we couldn't. We were going to look again tomorrow."

"Now you don't have to. Why did Cleve change his mind and join everyone here?"

"He didn't change his mind. Sneary convinced him they will get revenge soon."

"He means to attack them?"

She glanced around as if to check for eavesdroppers, then shook her head. "I felt with psyche that Sneary doesn't plan to leave anytime soon. He was concerned about Cleve, as I have been, so he lied. I wanted to join Effie and the others, but I couldn't abandon our group. I'm glad all of us will be together soon."

"That's what I need to speak to you about." Basen noticed Reela glancing over. She seemed to be speaking with an older woman who he didn't recognize but stopped when she noticed Basen. He beckoned for her.

Reela said something to the older woman, then came over to join them. "What is it?"

"I need both of your support," he told the two psychics. "There isn't much time."

Annah put up her hands. "If you mean to go against our leaders, I don't want to be part of it. I just told you how glad I am for all of us to be together. You shouldn't force us to separate again."

"I want the same thing as Sneary," Basen said. "To keep all of us alive and win this war."

"Don't you trust your father?" Annah accused.

"Yes, and he trusts me. But people who make a stand here will die."

"Henry *agreed* with your plan?" she asked with surprise.

"We haven't heard it yet, Annah," Reela said.

Basen touched her arm in gratitude. "Thank you, Reela."

*****

Most of Basen's conversations with others went similarly, with half the people having trouble understanding his wish to go against Sneary and the other half eager to hear Basen's ideas. He didn't like the thought of leaving Alabell and the others in the abandoned colony throughout the night, but he couldn't leave until a portal was established. Besides, he had much work still to do, and she was a lot safer there than these people were here.

He slept on the dirt, tossing throughout the night in a fruitless effort to get comfortable. When morning came, and there had been no attack, he got up eager to finish his rounds.

Breakfast was served to all, a mixture of oatmeal and rice. It was no wonder many people didn't want to leave. They'd been given order and protection here, as well as food and water. They couldn't imagine a sanctuary better than this because they didn't know one existed.

Fortunately, Basen was able to convince many people throughout the morning that leaving was the right decision. However, he was saving the most stubborn people for last. He had greeted Cleve last night but mentioned nothing of the plan yet, as Cleve would interpret leaving the forest as running instead of fighting.

Basen's former Group One instructor, Penny, never came over to greet him. Though the same could be said about Basen refusing to approach her. Now he caught her looking at him disapprovingly and began to worry she was a spy for Sneary. He walked over.

"Hello, Mage Penny."

"Hello, Basen Hiller." She didn't seem particularly pleased to see him.

"Do you wish to stay here and wait for battle or would you agree with me that it's not safe?"

"I do agree that it's not safe, but you haven't given me an alternative yet." She sounded offended.

"We've had our differences. I wasn't sure you would trust me."

"I can't be sure, either, until I hear what you hope to accomplish and how."

After reciting his plan countless times now, he was able to get through it at twice the speed. Most people would listen without question now, something about the confidence in his tone, perhaps.

Neeko came over as Basen reached the end. "Can we leave soon?"

"I'm not sure if we have enough to force the others into joining us. I need to speak with my father."

"I'll do that," Neeko offered. "Sneary's watching you, by the way. Don't look." He left Basen with Penny.

"What do you think?" Basen asked her.

"I think anyone who stays in this forest will die." She let out her breath. "I think even Sneary knows we have little chance of survival, but little is better than none."

"He's not listening to my plan."

"I'm sure he has listened, but his issue is accepting it. Try to imagine what it's like for an instructor to be forced to trust a student and to admit to being wrong. We were hired because we're supposed to know what's best for you. We've sworn in front of psychics that we'll do everything in our power to protect our students. It feels like we're betraying that oath if we give up responsibility to our students."

"So how do I convince him?"

"You can't, because you're his soldier. But perhaps I can. Don't say a word!" she whispered in haste.

A heavy hand took Basen by the shoulder and spun him around. "You openly defy me. If I'd known this was how you'd handle a disagreement with your leader, I would've sent you away before nightfall. Did you think I wouldn't notice, or do you just assume me to be slow?"

Basen gladly took Penny's advice and remained silent.

"Sneary, we already knew they outnumbered us,"

Penny said, "but not how badly until now. They must've only sent half their forces for the Academy, with the other half protecting the cities in case we escaped."

"That doesn't matter," Sneary said. "Our best chance is to stay together. We've trained harder and longer than any of them. We are the better fighters."

"They *expect* us to stay and fight them in the forest, where we are incapable of surprising them." Penny spoke with a hushed tone but it was in no way less severe than Basen had become used to as her pupil.

"We will surprise them when we take the river."

"But we can't hold it. There's nowhere to hide along the banks, and our enemies can use the trees to ambush us. They know we can't win here, so they are taking their time to search all of the forest on their way here. It won't be long before they come to the conclusion that we're this far south."

Basen remained silent, as much as it pained him not to add to Penny's argument. But then she surprised him by telling Sneary the exact line that Basen had been in torment trying to keep to himself.

"They aren't recruiting anyone anymore. They are *that* confident."

Basen had told this to everyone, including his father and Sneary. But Sneary only seemed to hear it when Penny said it.

"If they find out where we've gone," Sneary argued, "we'll have less of a chance than if we'd stayed together in the forest."

"It's a risk worth taking."

Henry and Teej ran toward them, Henry calling for

Sneary. A crowd of hundreds quickly formed around them as the two leaders faced each other.

"Tell him what you saw," Henry instructed Teej.

"Only scouts so far, but I fear there will be many more soon. There were two of them. They pointed in our direction, then walked away."

Basen shoved through. "We can't let them see us teleport out of here. It would ruin everything."

"Then we must go right now," Henry said.

"Run?" asked some of the people not privy to the plan.

"We're not running," Basen announced. "We're changing locations to surprise them when we're ready."

"Where are we going?" asked many.

"We're not going anywhere!" Sneary boomed.

God's mercy, keep your voice down. Basen gave a pleading look to his father. "There's no time."

Henry looked as if he was about to scream, though he kept his voice low. "My men are following me and my son, and I expect everyone from the Academy to come with us. You might disagree with the plan, but you have to see that you cannot fight here without us."

"Don't do this," Sneary said.

"I already gave the order." Henry gestured behind him at all his men gathering in support.

Basen's akorell stone was fully charged, but... "The portal! Trela, where are you?"

"Here," she called from amidst the crowd. "Only you can tell if it's ready yet."

"It has to be. Where are the mages?"

"Back farther into the camp. Follow me."

"Make room," Basen said as he pushed through the

crowd. He called back to his father, "Clear the camp and have everyone meet me back here."

But Sneary was already yelling, "Put on your armor and ready your weapons!"

Basen stopped. "No, collect your belongings and bring them with you!"

He could hear none of the following argument between Sneary and his father as he ran to catch up with Trela. There were about thirty mages in a line, but only one reached out toward a floating ball of white bastial energy. The mage let down her arm as the energy beamed into the dirt, and the next mage took over by gathering a new cluster.

"Every mage has been here gathering energy." Trela walked in front of the line to get their attention. "Everyone stop."

Basen put himself where the energy had been, closed his eyes, and opened his palms. He could feel the gateway partially there, like starting a familiar dream before fully falling asleep.

"It's almost ready, but we need more energy. I will take over while the rest of you get ready to leave."

They seemed confused as they looked to Trela.

"We aren't running," she assured them. "Plans have changed. Get everything you can carry and try to make it look like we were never here. Tell the others as well."

Basen squeezed all the energy he could into a single point, just like the beginning of a portal. It put the most weight on the world that he could manage and was the best method he knew of to create a doorway, but the energy packed so tightly was wild with power. He strained his mind and body to keep control as he packed more and more energy together.

It darkened as the heat lapped Basen's face. The cluster formed swirls of orange and red like Cleve's bastial steel sword. Eventually, Basen could hold it no longer. But there was too much power to let it go. He had to guide it into the ground as he released so that it wouldn't choose its own direction, a pillar of dirt shooting up as tall as some of the nearby saplings and then raining down in a loose line.

The door was becoming clear in his mind. He envisioned the burned basement in the capital and could feel a loose connection, as if grasping the door handle with his fingertips.

He gathered energy once again, mashing it together with his mind until he could hold it no longer. He released it into the dirt again and had to yell out a warning as the steaming clumps of soil scattered down upon people starting to line up behind him.

They moved away as he gathered his third ball of energy. He faintly became aware of hundreds moving into the space around him, all whispering as if worried their voices might startle him. Somewhere among them was Penny, probably internally having a fit. One slip, and Basen could kill more than a few of his friends.

An announcement almost broke his concentration. "Their army approaches from every side."

He shot the energy into the dirt. People leapt out of the way to avoid it. Panting, he looked around to see everyone ready.

"I can take over," Trela offered.

"No need," Basen said between breaths. "The gateway is ready. I just need a moment."

He could feel everyone's eyes on him as he struggled for breath.

"They will be here in minutes," Henry said. "And it might take that long just to get everyone through."

A familiar voice spoke out. "I believe you can do it, Basen."

He turned around to see Micklin. The boy looked older, tougher. His clothes and face were dirtier than everyone else near him, but he might be the most confident of them all as he looked at Basen with complete trust. Slowly, others' expressions began to change to mimic the boy's.

"You can do this," Cleve told Basen.

"We know you have the strength," Reela added.

Nebre, Rickik, and the dozen Krepps with them let out a quick chant of Kreppen as they stomped their bare feet and thumped their chests.

"Get us out of here," Neeko said.

"We must leave now," Henry urged.

"I can't keep the portal open long enough for everyone. I need a few more moments."

He heard a trumpet blaring in the distance, then a drum. The deep hoot of his enemies followed after each beat. They were close.

"You can do this, Basen," Annah encouraged.

Penny walked over to stand right in front of him. "Take us to safety, Basen. I know you can."

She stood back, and everyone else took her cue to make room. Encircled by all of his comrades who believed in him, he felt a sudden surge of strength. It was as if his body had a reserve of energy saved only for dire times like this.

"Form a line," he said. They began shifting around behind him as he focused.

He split his mind into this bright camp and the dark Slugari colony. Then he ripped the energy clean from his bracelet. This BE was a raging beast compared to the clusters he'd gathered just before, requiring all of his focus just to maintain his hold. But he had to do more than hold, screaming out his strain as he pushed the energy in on itself, then reaching through to take hold of the doorway and pry it open.

He tore the gateway out of the air, drawing out many gasps from the audience. It sucked up all the energy in the air, its edges rippling as it tried to overpower Basen in order to close.

"Go!" Basen told them. "Make room as soon as you enter, and help each other out of the way."

They poured in, most jumping and covering their faces. Almost everyone here had never entered a portal before, and their fear showed in their hesitance.

"Faster," Sneary urged them. "Find your courage right now!"

Everyone's pace quickened. The portal roared as wind whipped into it from around Basen's back.

A fire burned within his chest as he began to lose his strength. He clamped his teeth and clung to it with his mind.

"How many left?" Basen asked.

"Less than half," answered his father.

"You will keep it open for all of us!" Penny demanded. "I know you can."

Basen's body felt as if he'd been sprinting past his limit, his vision beginning to blur. Claws of fire ravaged his chest, but the worst pain came from within his head. It felt as if his skull was being split in half. The agony of it all took him to his knees, the portal shrinking. He screamed to put every last bit of his strength into keeping it from losing any more shape.

Somehow he held on longer and longer, every breath torture.

"Now, Basen!" Henry urged. "We're the last ones!"

But he lacked the strength to stand.

"Go," he said. "I'll hide."

"We aren't leaving you!" his father replied.

We?

Someone got his arms beneath Basen's legs and around his back and lifted him.

"I've got him," said Cleve.

Henry jumped into the portal, ducking to get his whole body inside.

"I hope we fit!" Cleve said with more worry than Basen had ever heard in his voice. He ran and half jumped, half fell in with Basen in his arms.

CHAPTER TWENTY-TWO

Basen came to and realized he'd been unconscious. A group of people stood around him, fanning him with their hands. His shirt had been removed. Why did he feel as if a fire had been lit inside of him? Alabell held a water skin to his lips. "Drink."

He gulped down the water. Remembering what had just happened, he sat up and shouted.

"Don't kill Sanya!" He hadn't gotten the chance to warn them yet.

"I already told them, Basen," Effie said.

"Easy." Alabell supported his back. "You've overexerted yourself."

"So that's why everything's spinning."

"Yes, lie down."

"What's steaming?" The light fog clouded his vision.

"You, now lie down."

He obeyed and closed his eyes as they continued to fan him. He cooled as quickly as a hot coal tossed into a barrel of water.

"I'm fine now."

He sat up only to be struck by dizziness again.

"It's going to take much longer than that," Alabell said. "Here, have more water."

Basen put up his hand to refuse. He knew how scarce water was for everyone. "I won't have any more until we're back in the city."

"Basen."

"I insist." He forced himself to stand, ignoring the dizziness as best he could. "Where's Jack?"

"He's already speaking with Steffen and Gabby about turning the akorell metal into stones," Alabell said. "Are you sure you don't want to rest a little more? I think you might need it."

"I'm sure." He took his shirt back, put it on as he thanked Alabell, and found the group of chemists.

"What do you need to get the akorell metal to the capital?" Basen interrupted.

"Just a ladder and a mining pick," answered Jack. "But if you can get us two of each, it will go twice as fast."

"I will." He cupped his hands around his mouth to ask the army, "Where are Reela and Annah?" The cavern was only dimly lit, and hundreds of shadows looked alike. "Reela and Annah, come here!"

"Coming," answered Annah first, then Reela.

When they arrived, Basen told them, "We need someone to get us ladders and mining picks from the city. It can't be me, because I need to make a portal for everyone afterward. Two psychics as strong as you should be able to avoid suspicion. We have a friend in the capital by the name of Millry, and she just happens to be Jackrie's sister. You can trust her if you have questions about where to buy these items. She owns the tavern next door to where I'm taking you."

He went on to describe the district, his experiences with guards and the citizenry, and everything else he could think of that might keep them out of trouble.

When they had no more questions, Basen walked to put himself in front of the enormous group. "Quiet, please!" he announced, and the murmurs died down. "In a moment, I'm going to make a portal to our sanctuary in the capital. Only two psychics, Reela and Annah, will be going through at the moment. They will purchase supplies for mining the akorell metal and meet back in the sanctuary to await my next portal, which I will make in an hour. At that point, they will bring the supplies back to this colony. Using the same portal, everyone except for those responsible for akorell will go through to the capital, where you will be fed."

Many looked apprehensive, so Basen decided to emphasize something. "We're not running. This is the next step of many to winning this war. Reela and Annah, meet me beneath the akorell."

Many more than just the two psychics came to the alcove for a glimpse at another portal. They made room for Basen and the two women.

"Are you ready?" Basen asked them.

"Yes," Reela answered.

Annah seemed hesitant.

"What is it?" Basen asked.

"What if we cannot buy what we need?"

"I'll make a portal every hour, or when I perceive an hour to have passed. It's difficult to tell the time in here. If you can't get the supplies by the first hour, meet back at the sanctuary before the next." He pointed up at the glow of light. "The akorell has plenty of energy stored for multiple portals."

Annah still looked as if she didn't want to go. "I think you should send someone for us if we don't return by the second hour."

"I promise I will."

Basen pulled energy from the akorell metal above and made the first of what he figured would be many portals in this colony. Reela and Annah entered, and he closed it.

He used the following hour to discuss strategy with his father and Sneary. Shortly into their conversation, however, Wilfre came to join them. The liaison only listened, though he wore a practiced expression of confidence to make himself look comfortable joining the discussion without an invitation.

Jack and Trela were the next to join them, and Penny followed. Soon, there were dozens of officers and Basen found himself to be the only one speaking until he asked his instructors a question.

"How much money do we have?"

He was surprised when it was Wilfre who answered so competently, "With everyone's coins together, we have three hundred and thirty kymarks, one acrown, and some pennies. We also have a few items of jewelry that can be sold or traded for two hundred more kymarks to my estimation. In total, that should buy enough food to feed everyone for a week, but if we take additional costs into consideration, which there will be, then we're looking at five days."

"Thank you," Basen said, still unable to hide his surprise at Wilfre's usefulness. From his few experiences with the former liaison, and how people at the Academy had talked about Wilfre, Basen had assumed the man would be nothing but an annoyance in this dire situation.

Basen didn't know who was rich enough to possess an acrown at the Academy, but he was glad. That one person had given about two hundred people one more day of food. "But we'll need more than five days. Some of the troops will need to find work."

"A thousand young men and women looking for work will be too suspicious," Sneary said.

"Some," Basen repeated. "No more than a hundred. The rest will be busy anyway."

His father asked him, "Where have you decided people should sleep?"

"Fifty can fit in the dilapidated building in the capital that I will soon be bringing everyone to. Millry should have room for ten, perhaps twenty if we stuff the rooms. The rest can pay for lodging. We'll have to distribute the coins to them, a daily allowance for food and sleep until we get everything settled."

"One hundred working jobs won't pay for nine hundred," Sneary said. He glanced over at Henry. "We're still in Raywhite Forest. It's not too late to send everyone back."

His father actually seemed to be deliberating it in the pause that followed.

"You worry about the lack of money," Basen said, "but the lack of food and water will kill them first. I'll figure out a source of money. In the meantime, everyone will be safe in the capital so long as Ulric doesn't find out where we are. There's always time to return to the forest later, when the plan calls for it."

"This is too complicated," Sneary complained. "There will be problems."

"That's why I need the help of officers to oversee each group once we separate."

By the time he was finally done, Basen felt as if he'd spent half the time arguing rather than strategizing. He was glad he'd already spent hours plotting out everything beforehand or Sneary's badgering might've created doubts.

It would be a relief when Reela and Annah returned and Basen could take everyone to the capital. Then all would be playing his game, including their enemies, a game he knew he could win.

It was difficult to draw out only some of the energy from the akorell metal above, akin to swallowing only a quarter of food already at the back of his throat. He accidentally took more than he needed and lost some into the air as he ripped open the portal.

Vithos was one of the few crowding the small alcove around Basen. The Elf hadn't voiced his worry about his half-sister, but Basen could see from Vithos' face that he would be relieved at her safe return.

Basen peered into the portal but saw only the charred walls of the basement. "Move around for a look," he told the small audience. "See if you can find them."

They circled around.

"Nothing," Vithos said. "Not here."

The others agreed.

Basen held the portal open for a few minutes anyway, but there were no signs of the young women. He let it close.

"They'll be back by the next hour," he assured everyone.

"What happened?" It was Sneary's voice from the cavern behind them.

"They haven't gotten the supplies yet," Basen told him and the many listening. "We need to give them another hour."

Many people took it upon themselves to investigate the colony during this time, but Basen remained near the akorell to speak with his father. They needed to prepare for every contingency. The hardest to discuss was if Reela and Annah had been killed and the plan to bring everyone to the capital had been discovered. There was no way to overcome that, so it would mean returning to the forest to fight. Basen could only hope it wasn't the case.

He noticed Sanya sitting alone against a dirt wall. She'd hardly moved the entire time Basen strategized, almost as if all these people didn't exist. Many watched her the way they might watch a prisoner, and in the rare moments she got up, people moved away.

Basen didn't know where Effie had built the sartious pen for the febeetles, but he trusted it had been done. She stayed in company with Cleve, Steffen, and her sister. Neeko and Shara spent a little time with them until Neeko decided to take this opportunity to gather the few remaining pyforial students and work with them to improve their skills. Basen was glad to see the initiative, especially as it seemed to be contagious. Swordsmen engaged in instructive combat, and mages gathered around instructors to fiddle with energy. Even psychics looked to be practicing against each other.

It was easy to forget that these people weren't just Basen's allies who he now felt responsible for. They were the elite of each class. Family name and wealth made no difference between them, only their training and experience.

He was pleased when Wilfre came to join discussions with him and his father, filling in details that Basen and Henry had only been able to guess until then. Wilfre knew how many soldiers were of each class and how many years they'd been at the Academy. He knew how many uniforms looked to Henry as their leader, and how many of these men were graduates of the Academy. The liaison spoke about the school with the utmost respect, as if he believed those who'd attended or graduated had skills that could be trusted completely.

"How many here are family of students, unable to fight?" Basen asked.

"An even one hundred and ten, but Warrior Sneary had expected them to fight nonetheless. He convinced all of them they should, so I assume they would for you if necessary."

Basen had already confirmed from Henry that Juliana was not among them. Neither had seen her during the battle at any point, but Basen could feel that she was still alive. He tried to imagine what it would be like if she was here and Sneary demanded that she fight.

"No," Basen said. "Only those who volunteer."

Eventually it felt as if the hour was up. People agreed it was time, so Basen walked beneath the akorell metal once again. An even larger crowd gathered in the cavern just outside the alcove, more than half. He could feel their eagerness to get out of this dark cavern. Worse, they were probably as hungry as he was.

Whether or not Reela and Annah were waiting on the other side of the portal, it was time to go to the capital. It took a little while to gather everyone and organize them into a line like before. Basen put the people he trusted most at the front, Alabell, Neeko, Cleve, and other close friends, who could quickly look into the portal from all sides and confirm if the psychics were there. If not, they would jump in quickly, but one at a time. Cleve had carried Basen through the portal, but for all Basen knew they'd been lucky something horrible hadn't happened. Now was not the time to test the consequences of two people entering the portal at the same time again.

Only half of the energy remained in the akorell metal. Basen accidentally used all of it as he opened the gateway.

There still were no signs of Reela and Annah. The small group within the alcove confirmed this quickly, then entered. Basen knew he should be worried about the two young women, but he didn't have the focus as everything went into maintaining the portal.

His allies ran in. Only a few lost their balance once inside and required the help of others to get out of the way. Basen had made enough portals by now to realize the distance traveled determined the level of dizziness. It wasn't far from here to the capital, but the difference between these two worlds was as if they'd gone to another continent.

Everyone will be safe now, he reminded himself to allay his growing concerns.

Now if only he thought the same about Reela and Annah.

CHAPTER TWENTY-THREE

One thousand people took up a lot of room. They knew not to crowd around the outside of the dilapidated building, so they had to spread out and fill the taverns and bars of the poor district as they waited for further orders.

By the time Basen had gotten through his own portal, his father already had a report ready.

"Millry hasn't seen Reela or Annah since they came by hours ago to ask about purchasing ladders and mining picks. We discussed this possibility."

"I remember. Sneary should be ready."

"He's waiting for us at Millry's."

With Basen's mind full of details for every contingency, he couldn't feel the panic he knew to be buried somewhere inside himself. Sneary had agreed he would lead the team to purchase the mining supplies, but that didn't mean he would be happy about it.

"If we don't return in an hour..." Sneary began.

"Another team will be sent for you," Basen concluded. They'd already covered this, as well as every possible situation, and Basen didn't like Sneary testing his memory.

"I still think it's not a good idea for you to leave this district, Basen," Sneary said. "I can send out another group to look for them instead of you."

"That will arouse suspicion, and we both know where they're most likely to be."

The other officers had already left to investigate the

locations Basen had memorized from his earlier trips around the city. It would be up to them to lead the information-gathering teams and develop a system to report back to Basen without getting caught. Soon enough, every ally would be busy. But for now, he'd let them enjoy a real meal.

"Besides," Basen said. "I'm the only one with a fitting uniform and hat. And I'm the only one who's tested it before."

"If you're caught—"

"I won't tell them anything. You'll find a way to win without me."

Sneary seemed satisfied as he walked away without a word.

"Basen," Henry said, "If you're caught, don't give up hope. I will find a way to get you out."

"If anyone's going to get me out, it'll be myself. Don't waste anyone's life trying to get to me."

Henry gave no reply.

"Promise me," Basen pleaded. "This cause has become bigger than me, and I'm ready to accept any sacrifice."

"That's something I'd like to hear from any good leader, but not from my son."

He hugged his father, then returned to the basement of the burned building to change into the enemy's uniform.

When he was done, Alabell was waiting for him on the other side of the charred wall.

"You look annoyingly handsome in that," she said.

Basen gave her his akorell stone. "Will you be

alright?"

"I should be asking you that, not the other way around."

"I'll be fine."

He kissed her. After he pulled back, he made the mistake of looking into her eyes. He almost forgot everything he was doing in that instant, as the urge to stay came over him.

"I'll be looking forward to seeing your face when I return," he said.

*****

There was one big difference Basen felt within himself from the last time he was in the capital: the anger. Now that he'd seen just how few of his allies were left, and how they could've been killed in the forest just a few hours ago, it was clear their enemies were not only willing but eager to exterminate Basen and his comrades like pests.

Kyrro's Allies had done nothing to deserve this. It was Ulric and his followers who should be exterminated. They were cockroaches. If only there weren't so damn many of them.

You're one of them, for now. Focus.

He had to keep his head on straight. Entering the castle would put him in danger leagues beyond causing trouble around the training center.

The overconfident enemies had the door to the castle

open, but there were two guards standing in front of it. Basen tried to make it look like he was on patrol when really he was watching for other guards coming or leaving. It took a while, but eventually he confirmed that the guards weren't questioning each other. As one of them, he should be able to enter freely like he saw many others doing.

He walked up the long road in as natural a gait as he could. Wrong-doers kept their heads down, so he showed confidence as he looked each man in the eye. They paid him little mind as he walked past them and into the great hall.

Kyrro's castle wasn't quite as big as Tenred's, but it was at least as tall. If his psychics were in here, there was only one floor where they could be.

Cleve had wanted to volunteer to be in Basen's shoes right now, but none of the unsoiled uniforms could fit him. Besides, Basen felt responsible for these women. He needed to be the one to get them back. He followed Cleve's instructions to go through a door from the great hall to get to the portcullis separating the castle from the dungeon. In the few halls it took to get there, he encountered no one else. But here, a man sat upon a large vase turned upside down.

He didn't care to hide his boredom as he coldly greeted Basen with a slight lift of his chin. Basen looked down at the man but said nothing as he went straight for the door handle. To his delight, it was unlocked.

"What are you doing?" asked the guard.

"Business. I'll be back soon."

The guard grumbled something but didn't object.

Basen descended the stairs into shadow. He was thankful to be a mage, as there seemed to be no torches lit down here. Every cell was empty.

They aren't taking any of us prisoner! Everyone captured was killed. The gravity of it reached down into him, grabbed his anger, and brought it to the surface. *Calm down and think.* What about the prisoners before the war? Perhaps they were elsewhere, along with Reela and Annah.

"Basen?" It was Annah's voice.

He froze to listen for guards. Would Annah be foolish enough to reveal his identity if there were others around? No, she must've sensed they were alone.

He came up to her cell and was relieved to find Reela in there with her. But how was he going to get them out?

"What in god's world happened for you to end up here!"

They coiled back, clearly surprised by his anger.

"I'm sorry," he said. "Misplaced frustration. What happened?"

"There's a ladder-maker in the capital," Annah said. "The only one Millry knew of. So we were on our way there—"

"Guards were harassing people and we stupidly intervened," Reela interrupted.

Basen let out his light to focus on figuring out a plan, putting them in complete darkness.

"Please keep it going," Annah whimpered. "I can't believe they haven't even lit a torch for us."

"You were supposed to remain unnoticed," Basen scolded as he created the light again. "If we don't overthrow Ulric, it won't matter how many people we save. All of us will die."

"We thought it would be easy to stop them and get away unnoticed," Annah said. "But so many guards came so quickly."

"They don't know we're rebels," Reela whispered. "They just believe us to be psychics who went against them. They don't know the extent of our power because we didn't fight once it was clear we'd be arrested."

"Did they tell you anything about what they might do with you?" Basen asked. "You're the only ones in this entire prison. It doesn't look good."

"Aren't you going to get us out?" Annah's voice held an unspoken plea.

"I will," Basen promised. "But first I need a plan."

"They didn't tell us anything," Reela said. "The best plan might be for you to do nothing."

"That's a terrible plan," Basen countered.

"I think I can lie to their psychics," Reela continued. "Sanya taught me how, and I've been practicing every day with Vithos since the battle. I'll convince them we can be loyal, and then we'll spy."

"That's too risky. They just need to ask Annah one question of loyalty, and both of you could be killed."

"I agree with Basen. It's terrible, Reela."

"Any plan to free us," she said, "would involve more risk. Take a moment to actually consider your options for us."

So he did and realized Reela was right. But how could he do nothing?

"Annah, what are your thoughts?"

"I don't know."

"I might be able to change your energy in the same way I need to change mine," Reela said.

"Their psychics will know."

"They won't."

"No, just let them do whatever they want with me. I'll probably live."

She had to know the truth, as hard as it sounded. "They're going to kill you, Annah," Basen informed her.

"No, I've heard of some of us being captured. It was only Terren who they needed to kill."

"But the prison is empty!" Basen whispered through his teeth. "They're killing us, and you are one of our most powerful psychics. They won't risk keeping you alive. You have to let Reela try."

"Let out the light!" Reela whispered. "People are coming."

Pale lamplight entered their hall, at least a dozen shadows behind. The man at the lead had his eyes set on Basen.

"What were you whispering?"

Basen forced a chuckle. "I wanted to hear what nasty things they'd offer me to release them, not that I could or would."

The guard sneered at Reela and Annah. "Pretty, aren't they?" He raised his eyebrows at Basen. "And what did they tell you?"

"The tall one said I'd regret propositioning them." He laughed and moved out of the way as the man in front of him drew a set of keys.

"All psychics are overconfident." He inserted his key.

"Young women, if you try to hurt any of us, you will wish you had been killed."

"We don't plan to fight," Reela said.

Was this true? With Basen's help, the three of them should be able to kill these armed men. They even had a decent chance of escaping the castle, but not without pursuit. Ulric would learn rebels had entered the capital. That might make it impossible to carry out his plan.

But if Reela and Annah chose to fight, Basen would join them.

The group of guards surrounded the women as they came out, forcing Basen to the back.

"Where are you taking us?" Reela asked.

"To be questioned. Psychics like you aren't often found in cities. You will explain where you've been and what you've been doing."

"To prove what? You can't possibly think we're rebels."

"That's not for me to decide."

Basen followed, but the men in front of him shot suspicious looks over their shoulders as if his presence bothered them. He hung back a bit, but it did no good. They started to ask each other about him, and eventually the lead man turned around.

"Who is your reporting officer?"

Basen could only think of one name. "Cassius Lane. He sent me here."

"To spy?"

"He didn't tell me the purpose. He just wants me to observe the happenings of the castle and the prison."

The lead man asked the others, "How long has he

been here?"

A few muttered that they didn't know while the rest remained silent.

He asked Basen, "What does Cassius hope to accomplish by sending you?"

"He didn't tell me, but it seems to me that he's worried."

"Worried?" The man spoke through a chuckle that got the other men laughing. "The war is already won, and Ulric was already questioned by Crea's psychic. Tenred and Kyrro will go back to their alliance when this is over. Tell Cassius that Ulric isn't interested in your territory, so stop sending his men to the castle unless he wants Ulric to start doubting their alliance. Understand?"

"Yes."

"Don't let me see you here again."

They all waited for Basen to leave. He maneuvered through them, passing between Reela and Annah to get to the front. He almost reached out to squeeze their hands, to silently tell them his thoughts would be with them, but he resisted the urge as it was too great a risk. He set a quick pace to get out of the castle.

It wasn't until he was a few streets away that he felt as if he could breathe again. The whole way back, he tried to think of some way to get them out, but he came up with nothing. Only a direct attack on the castle might save them, but it was even more likely to get everyone killed. The castle was a fortress designed to stand against any army. Basen doubted his comrades would even be able to get through the door before they were slain.

Ulric's time would come, but there was much that had

to be done in preparation.

When Basen realized he'd have to tell Cleve where Reela was and what she planned to do, he stopped where he stood and nearly vomited.

It became difficult to keep up his quick pace when he knew Cleve awaited news, but Basen managed. He returned to the basement and had only removed his cap when he heard Cleve's heavy boots behind him.

"What happened?"

"She and Annah are alive and not hurt."

"In prison," Cleve realized. There was no sadness in his voice, only determination. He looked ready to run to the castle if Basen didn't stop him.

Vithos and a few others Basen didn't recognize came closer. The Elf had to remain in the basement at all times, unfortunately. Like the Krepps, he was too conspicuous to be seen anywhere in the capital. He looked just as eager as Cleve to get out of there and do something about Reela.

"I know you want to get them back," Basen said, "but it's impossible right now. Reela doesn't want us to do anything. She has learned from Sanya how to lie to psychics. Isn't that true, Vithos?"

"Oh, yes. Cleve, we trust her to lie. She find her way out."

"Well, not exactly," Basen said. "She doesn't believe she can convince them to let her go, only to let her and Annah join them."

He expected Cleve to take up arms and storm the castle. Basen especially hated to be wearing the uniform of their enemies as he thought he might have to put his hands on Cleve to stop him. But the warrior surprised him by taking his time to consider the situation.

Eventually he asked Basen, "How confident was she?"

"As confident as she always is."

Cleve looked around for someone, then seemed to locate her nearby. "What do you think?" he asked the older woman in the group.

"I think Reela will keep herself alive no matter what."

"I agree," Vithos said. "I trust her."

They didn't mention Annah, but it wasn't Basen's place to remind them. He felt at fault for this. If anything happened to anyone, it was because they were following his plan.

The older woman added, "And it doesn't seem like we have any other options."

Cleve looked toward the stairs as if he still might march out of there. He sighed and asked Basen, "How much more time do we need before we can kill them all?"

"At least a few weeks, Cleve. I'm sorry."

"Is there any way to hear from Reela again? We must at least find out if she's alive every day."

Both Vithos and the older woman seemed just as interested. Basen didn't see how it was possible to communicate with Reela and Annah, but he couldn't tell these caring people no either.

"I'll see if I can figure out something."

"Thank you," said the older woman. She offered her hand. "We haven't met yet. I'm Airy, Reela's mother."

God's mercy. Basen felt sick again as he shook the woman's hand.

CHAPTER TWENTY-FOUR

There was so much to do, it almost felt impossible. To keep track of it all required more than memory. Basen purchased parchment and ink and made a little spot for himself in the corner of the basement near his stash of enemy uniforms. There was nothing smooth to write on, and nowhere to sit, so he hunched over the floor and scribbled away until his back ached.

Psychics were needed to help his spies establish their route of information gathering, but his most powerful psychics were unavailable. Reela and Annah probably wouldn't be seen for a while, and Vithos and Sanya were both too conspicuous. Unfortunately, the few psychics from the Academy who were still alive had admitted to Basen that they didn't have the necessary skill to read and manipulate emotions. All they could do was cause pain, and even some of them couldn't do that. But his side needed spies, so Basen sent people off to the locations he'd chosen and hoped he wasn't making a mistake.

He stayed in the basement the rest of the day, his throat dry from talking, his wrist and back sore from writing. Hundreds of people came to him with either questions or a status report. There were times that he realized exactly what he had done, taken responsibility for all their lives, and the nausea attacked.

However, no new problems had been reported by the end of the day, and Basen's confidence returned. Sneary had purchased the ladders and mining picks and handed them off to Jack, who would lead the team to excavate the akorell metal tomorrow. They would rest in the capital where they had beds, and Basen would make them a portal in the morning.

"I'm wasting away in here," Sanya complained as Basen settled down on a pile of clothing to snatch some sleep.

"I said you can sleep in Millry's tavern where there's no risk of someone recognizing you."

"No, I'll sleep here during the night to save beds for others. It's during the day when I should be doing more."

He sat up when she started to make a bed out of clothing beside him. "You're going to sleep there?"

She looked dejected. "No." She bundled the garments in her arms and started to leave.

It was easy to forget that he was the closest thing she had to a friend because she treated him as if he did nothing but bother her.

"Stay," he invited.

She did. "I'm not the only one tired of feeling wasted here. You should hear what the Krepps are saying."

"You'll be helping me with portals soon enough. What are they saying?"

"Rickik and the others want to venture out and kill guards. Nebre's words barely do enough to keep them here."

He sighed.

"What are you going to do?" Sanya asked.

"I don't know yet."

She fell silent, and slumber took him.

*****

After much thought, Basen realized that it was important to give their enemies someone to chase in forest. He hadn't considered the option of sending anyone back because it felt inhumane, but after speaking with Rickik and finding out that the Krepps wanted to go back and fight, it was an easy choice.

He needed to make a portal for Jack, Steffen, and Gabby back to the Slugari colony anyway, so it was decided the Krepps would go through with them.

"I go with Rickik," Vithos told Basen. "Better for everyone with me in forest."

"You don't have to," Basen said quietly to keep it from the Krepps. "There still must be thousands of enemies there."

"I want to."

Sanya walked over and opened her mouth, but no words came out when she looked at Vithos and Rickik and saw no signs of welcome.

"I'm going to make a portal into the Slugari colony at the end of each day," Basen told Vithos and the Krepps. "If you have anything to report or if you wish to return, be inside the colony by nightfall. Remember not to stand directly beneath the akorell metal."

"We remember," Rickik said.

Of their group, Nebre was the only one who looked as if he wanted to stay as he glanced down at the floor.

"Nebre, you aren't required to leave."

He looked up and puffed out his chest. "I want to."

Jack arrived with the two chemists. They'd spent the morning filling their bellies with Millry's cooking and showed Basen they were ready to work with heads held high.

Gabby stood in front of Basen. With her long dark hair and pixie face, she looked remarkably like Effie. "Have you sent anyone to Oakshen?"

"I haven't had the energy for a portal yet. I can't send anyone until tomorrow because at night I'm bringing you back to the capital."

"Good. I want to go to Oakshen. I'm familiar with the city and already know who rebels against the Takarys. Effie wants to go with me."

"But won't someone recognize one or both of you and know you've been at the Academy?"

"No one loyal to the Takarys."

It seemed accurate enough. Remembering Steffen had come from Oakshen as well, Basen glanced over and expected the chemist to tell him the same thing. But Steffen shook his head.

"I can't go even though I want to see my mother. I don't trust her to handle the situation appropriately. Effie and Gabby will check on her without her noticing. Instead, I should be with them in the forest." He pointed at Vithos and the Krepps. "They have no chemist, and I don't have the skills needed to spy."

Gabby nodded. "He doesn't, unfortunately."

"You can fight, chemist?" Rickik asked.

Vithos answered for him. "Very well. He use bow and sword."

"Good," Rickik said.

"You're making this easy for me," Basen told them. "Thank you."

He checked to make sure they had food, water, and the highest quality weapons their army possessed. Then he opened a portal.

"I almost forgot," he said through the strain. "If you see Abith, try to tell him we know he's not the traitor. He should be fighting with us."

"We tell him," Vithos said. He was the first into the portal. The Krepps ran in after, leaving the more hesitant chemist for last.

Besides Sanya, there was still one last person who had to remain in the basement. The old king's liaison was too easily recognizable. But Wilfre seemed perfectly happy to stay here as long as he could.

Basen went to visit him on the first floor and found him sitting in a chair and using a half-burned desk to write. "You shouldn't stay up here," Basen said. "The floor might give out and collapse onto the others below."

"It's stable here."

Basen looked over Wilfre's shoulder to see him not writing but drawing. Wilfre leaned back and gestured at it like a proud father showing off his heir.

The parchment nearly took up the entire desk. The drawing was of this three-story building, Basen realized, but with so much more than its outline. Each room was drawn separately, one on top of another. Wilfre had added numbers next to each image that seemed to represent more than just height and width.

"What is all of this?" Basen asked.

"People are getting suspicious of the activity around this building," Wilfre said.

"I realize that, but there's little we can do about it. Besides, everyone here hates the Takarys. They wouldn't go to guards with suspicions."

"Why take the risk when we can give ourselves the excuse we need?" He tapped his parchment at the small part at the bottom where there was no ink. "Our team has been contracted to rebuild this place."

"How sure are you that if we follow your guidelines it won't topple down and kill us all?"

"Certain. I was a carpenter before a liaison."

"*You?*" Shock made the word come out before Basen had the chance to stop it.

"Can't imagine me getting my hands dirty?"

"No, I can't."

"Well, you're right." Wilfre chuckled. "I would design, then leave the building to others. With a team of the right people we could get the floors and walls up in a week."

"That seems impossible."

"Neeko was a carpenter as well, did you know?"

"No."

"He's modest, unlike me, but I was able to get the truth out of him eventually that he's something of a prodigy. With his pyforial energy and experience, it can be done. There's just one problem."

"The money," Basen realized.

"Exactly. It's going to run out in a week even without purchasing the supplies we need. Have you found a way to expedite the attack you've spent so long planning?"

"No. It takes time to learn the whereabouts of our

enemies and get everyone in position."

"Then we need more money, lots of it. I wish I had taken more than my one acrown from the Academy."

"That was yours?"

Wilfre stood to stretch his back, letting out a groan as he answered, "Yes. I had two more I should've taken, but that one was already in my pocket. Have you figured out how we will get more money?"

"That, I will figure out soon." Something had come to mind right after Basen had woken up, when he turned to see Sanya bored and sulking as she leaned against the wall. He could use her; he just had to determine how.

He returned to his corner of the basement. He'd paced back and forth here so many times he half expected to have worn down a trail, but there was only scattered soot upon blackened wood.

The best place to get money was directly from his enemies, but the person he most wanted to take it from was his cousin Crea. She didn't deserve whatever amount of wealth she'd clung to after the execution of her father.

Basen could make portals to many places by now. If he knew where she was, he was certain he could devise a plan to take her money.

Actually, I only have to know where she keeps her money, not where she is. And this he did know: the treasury in Tenred castle. Nearly all troops loyal to her were already in Kyrro, betraying Basen and his allies. Only those necessary to govern the territory remained.

Once he had two akorell stones, Basen could teleport into the castle and then out again, but how could he get into the treasury? Getting past the guards might be possible, but not the steel door.

Crea's younger sister, Gayla, should be somewhere in the castle if Crea wasn't. She'd know the way in, probably even had the keys.

Basen had to stop himself at this point, for it was becoming too tempting to follow through with this plan. His gut told him it was a bad idea, and in the few instances he'd gone against his instincts, he'd regretted it. The warden had already told Basen never to return when he came with Krepps to intimidate the man into letting Juliana out of prison. His presence would alert every guard.

But Nebre should be welcomed back to the castle. As the only one able to provide insight on Krepps, he was valuable. He hadn't wanted to leave when he'd been taken by his father, so it would make sense. *He'll tell them he had a wretched time with his kind and wants to return.*

No, he will be questioned by psychics. Besides, Basen had already told himself to stop speculating about stealing his family's money.

An unbidden voice returned as much as he tried to keep it silent: *Don't forget about Sanya.* She'd spoken about stealing and leaving Kyrro as if it were easy. She could find a way to get herself an audience with Gayla.

Sanya will say her father's still alive and has been following the progress of the war. He wants to offer his services to Tenred by returning to be the inventor of military potions. He'll threaten to offer his services to Ulric if the Hillers aren't interested, through Sanya of course.

She'd be questioned by a psychic the whole time, which wouldn't be a problem.

This would work, so why did he feel something regrettable would happen?

"Sanya," he called out.

Her shoulders slumped as she walked. "What?"

"How would you like to get out of here and steal from Crea and Gayla Hiller?"

She perked up. "I'm listening."

CHAPTER TWENTY-FIVE

Sanya voiced no concerns about Basen's plan. The only thing she told him she was worried about was making sure the febeetles would be fed each day.

"They're completely irrelevant to this," Basen said. It was a concern that she might be losing her mind if she thought so.

"I know that—I'm not stupid! I've put in a lot of effort and lost sleep because of those creatures, so you'd better keep them alive."

"Effie knows to feed them and rebuild the sartious pen. They are important to me as well." She seemed like a volcano about to erupt. "You're going to have to control your emotions for us to get away with the money. Are you sure this is something you can do?"

She actually seemed to ponder the question as she glanced at the floor. "We can't go until we have two akorell stones tomorrow, so I'll tell you then."

"It was more of a rhetorical question, Sanya."

"Oh."

"What aren't you telling me?"

"Nothing."

She was acting too strangely for that to be true. "Can I trust you to do exactly what I need while we're there?"

"I said I'd tell you tomorrow," she said to the floor, then went back to her corner of the basement to sulk in the shadows again.

People generally stayed away from her, and she

looked at them as if she resented them for this, which only made people keep more distance. Basen didn't know how to end this cycle, but doing nothing didn't mean he was ignoring it.

Neeko and Shara came by to speak with Wilfre and inspect the building closely. Neeko agreed with Wilfre that it would only take a week to replace the walls and floors, so Basen gladly let them take full control of the project.

Most of the instructors—or officers—as Basen thought of them now, worked well together and had already relayed information to Basen about their district and associated team. So it came as a surprise that Basen's father was one of the few who hadn't gotten back to him yet, especially considering that the district of his team's responsibility was the closest one. It was this poor area, with many houses burned like the one Basen and others spent so much time within.

He had begun to fear something had happened before Henry finally showed up looking even worse than when Basen had reunited with him in the forest. There were no signs of youth left on Henry's weathered face, his hair graying more every day.

"What happened?" Basen asked.

"Nothing. It took this long to be thorough, and we've already begun recruiting."

Recruiting? His instincts told him not to scold his father. "Are you sure these people can be trusted?"

"They have nothing to gain by reporting us. The guards will do nothing to better the lives of these wretched souls."

"That might be true," Basen said, "but it only matters if these people *think* they have something to gain by betraying us."

"They're too angry. No guards patrol this district anymore, as if Ulric has deemed it invisible. We've already added fifty people to our army, and I expect more to follow."

There was at least one guard still patrolling last Basen had checked. Was Henry lying or had the guard given up on this district?

"I appreciate your effort, Father, so don't take what I'm about to say as a slight against your work. None of these people are trained to fight, and we have no weapons for them." Early recruitment wasn't part of the plan. Basen wasn't sure why his father had taken it upon himself to pad their numbers without asking Basen first, but it was too awkward to claim rank over his father.

"When we get more money, we can buy steel. There's a blacksmith in this district who could help us with the making of akorell bracelets and swords."

"Trela has already claimed there is a blacksmith in her district who wants to support us."

"So we'll have two."

"That just increases the risk. Even if both blacksmiths are loyal, someone entering their forge at the wrong time could see the extent of their project and inform a guard."

"Then tell Trela not to bother with her blacksmith. The people in this district are loyal to us. I'll speak with the blacksmith later today."

It bothered Basen how hasty his father could be about something in which subtlety was of the utmost importance. "You can't possibly be certain everyone's loyal to us."

"My son, I know these things." Henry clearly didn't use their bond as an endearment but to invoke his perceived rank over Basen. "You focus on where we're going to get the money we need and let me handle this district."

"When did you speak to Wilfre?"

"Last night. You were sleeping."

Basen didn't like his father going around him, but there was nothing he could say. "All right. I'm trusting you."

Henry left just as quickly as he'd come.

Sanya walked around the wall from where she'd obviously been eavesdropping. "He's lying," she said.

Basen shushed her. "Keep your voice down. What did he lie about?"

She came closer and whispered, "When he answered your question of what happened."

So something *had* caused his father's delay. Basen wasn't sure he wanted to know.

"I'm going for a walk," Sanya said, though she looked to be waiting for his permission.

"Doesn't Ulric know you abandoned him?"

"Yes."

"Then it's not a good idea. All it takes is one person to recognize you, and the whole district will be investigated."

"What's not a good idea would be sending me into Tenred castle to steal the Hillers' fortune having done little more than stretch my legs in the past week."

"Fine, but try not to be noticed."

As she left, he got the sense that she was no different from his father in that there was something she didn't want him to know.

Henry had always been secretive. Basen and Juliana never pried because they knew it had to do with Henry's brother, Tegry, and not them. But Sanya's secrets were different. They were potentially deadly to Basen.

As he looked through their sanctuary and then Millry's tavern for someone he trusted to follow her, Cleve confronted him. As soon as Basen caught sight of the subdued fury in his friend's narrowed eyes, he realized what this would be about.

"Why didn't you tell me you were sending a group back to the forest?" Cleve demanded.

"I should've, I'm sorry. But I didn't think of it until I saw you just now. I can take you there tonight when I make a portal to the Slugari colony."

His expression softened. "All right." But it looked as if there was more he needed to say.

"What is it?"

"I suppose Wilfre told you about my money?"

"He didn't mention anything about you."

Cleve looked surprisingly abashed as his eyes rolled down. "I had many acrowns that I left behind. Wilfre really didn't say anything?"

"Nothing."

"That's a surprise considering the hard time he gave me for leaving it in the hands of our enemies."

"How much money, Cleve?"

"You don't want to know. It was a gift from a friend, a

rich friend. You don't know him."

Crea probably has it now. "Is there a chance your rich friend could still help us?"

"I hoped long ago that he might, but no. I just needed to tell you about the money. I'm sorry."

"It's fine. We'll get what we need and more. I have to be going, though. I'm sorry."

"Of course."

Why couldn't more people be as easy to manage as Cleve? Basen almost asked the warrior to follow Sanya for him, but Cleve was not known for subtlety. Basen didn't have time to look for anyone else, so he took it upon himself to track her down before she got too far.

She could probably tell with psyche if someone was spying on her, so Basen made sure to keep as much distance as he could. There were many narrow streets in this poorer district of the city, but Sanya chose to stroll down the main roads instead. She walked without purpose, chewing on a finger most of the time. She appeared oblivious to the people passing by, wistful even as she often stopped and looked up at the sky.

A few times, Basen caught her balling her fists as if to punch an invisible foe, only to drop them and visibly force herself to relax with a deep breath. It was only once that she glanced around to check for anyone spying, nearly catching Basen before he ducked behind the side of yet another burned building barely standing.

He wondered how his father had come to trust these people so quickly and what method he used to recruit them. They must be happy about the febeetles being taken away by a rebel psychic, but such information was dangerous to spread.

Could that be what bothered Henry—something Henry had done to gain trust that could come back to bite them? Yes, that was most likely it. Knowing Henry, he probably had promised coin to some of the people he'd recruited. *The blacksmith.* Henry was too desperate for political power. Trela could've taken care of the making of the akorell stones, but Henry needed it to be him.

After following Sanya for a while, Basen had seen enough of her pointless wandering to realize she must be in the midst of an inner dialogue. He turned back before she found him, wishing there was someone else he could bring to Tenred castle who he trusted more.

*****

Sanya spent the day walking around the district. The rebels referred to it as H district, or home, but the people who lived here seemed to think of it more as punishment, for they named it "the claw." Once you were in its grip, you couldn't get out.

She found a few more febeetles that she'd missed the first time around. She drew them out into the street and stomped them dead.

If Basen saw, he'd probably bar her from ever leaving their "sanctuary" again, and it would become the second prison she'd be forced to escape from.

None of this mattered in the end. Her "allies" were going to be killed no matter how hard she fought to keep them alive, and she would be far from here when it happened.

Basen had distributed the collective money to Wilfre, his father, Sneary, Trela, Jack, and Alabell to hold. Sanya would never be part of that inner circle, even after she put her life at risk to steal from Tenred castle. The only person who would look after her was herself.

A young man started walking beside her by evening. He purposely seemed to keep a gap between them, but he slowed and sped up whenever she changed her pace. He didn't look as if he was dimwitted, but Sanya could think of no other excuse for his behavior. It seemed as if he'd washed recently, his combed-back hair damp and his face cleanly shaven. He was probably a year or two older than Sanya, strong and distractingly tall, matching Cleve's height.

He hardly glanced over at her, but she could feel from psyche that he wasn't just walking the same way by chance. He was following and as curious as a cat.

She had learned to ignore people over the years of harassment in Tenred castle, so it was easy to pretend he didn't exist. Soon she felt the presence of more creatures, this time in an inn where some of her "allies" were staying, no doubt. Dutifully, she called the creatures out into the street. She frowned when two rats were among the ten febeetles. She didn't so much mind killing the rats, but it was a hassle.

Some people came out of the inn, probably to thank her, but stopped and held their stomachs when they saw the febeetles devouring the disabled rats alive. When it was done, she squished each black beetle with the heel of her boot.

It was a shock to see the young man still there, not even slightly perturbed by the sight. He even smiled. Meanwhile, the entire street had cleared.

"Something's wrong with you," she told him.

He laughed. "I'm not the one scaring people."

"I'm helping them. They're grateful."

"And scared."

It was true, she did frighten everyone. "What do you want with me?"

"To get to know you."

She wrinkled her nose. "Why?"

"I think you're beautiful."

It was such a shock that Sanya couldn't even get a word out. "Yu...wh...mm?"

"Yes, beautiful in a dark kind of way, like the moon glimmering through the fog."

"You're bleeding."

She felt his embarrassment as he touched around his upper lip. He found the wet spot and frowned at his red finger.

"I would apologize," he said, "but you don't strike me as the kind of woman who hates the sight of blood." He gestured at the mess she'd left on the street.

"Did you just come from shaving?"

He nodded. "But there are more interesting topics for us to talk about. What's your name?"

"Why were you shaving in such a hurry?"

"I wasn't in a hurry. Sometimes men cut themselves shaving. It..." His gaping mouth slowly closed into a smile. "I just remembered I've heard psychics can tell when we lie."

"Yes. What's the truth?"

"It seems like you already know, so why don't we skip forward and you tell me your name."

She did already know. She'd recognized him by then. He was the blacksmith's apprentice, but without the shaggy beard and greased dirt on his face. Their eyes had made contact when she'd passed the forge, but Sanya had thought nothing of it. Nothing good could come of this... but he wasn't hard to look at.

"My name is Sanya."

"I'm Greg. You must've moved here recently."

"You don't get a lot of psychics, I assume."

"Nor do we get a lot of beautiful women close to my age."

"What aren't you telling me about that?"

Lines formed across his forehead as if he might back up his lie with more lies. He opened his mouth but then caught himself.

"You're not making it easy to flatter you," he said.

"You're wasting my time."

She started back.

"Fine, I'll only speak the complete truth." As she turned around, he was pulling away the collar of his shirt as if it bothered his neck.

"That doesn't quite fit you anymore," she observed. The buttons barely held the fabric together.

He curled his lips inward. "I've had it for years."

And it's probably his only unstained shirt. "What about these other beautiful women? What was your lie?"

He sighed. "There *are* others."

"And?"

"I already know them."

"You've already lain with them."

"Yes, but that makes me sound much worse than I am." Greg suddenly looked confused as he tilted his head. "Do you put all your suitors through this type of interrogation?"

"Yes."

He grinned. "It's not fair to require the truth out of me when you're going to lie."

How did he know? But she felt little confidence from him, the opposite of what she saw in his expression. He was just guessing.

"It's getting late," he said. "May I walk you to your home?"

Had Henry already spoken with this man when he'd visited the blacksmith? She wasn't sure, and she couldn't risk him seeing the others, not until they had the cover of construction. It would be too obvious that they were rebels.

"No."

"All right."

"I'm sorry."

"I understand." He offered his hand for a shake. "It was nice meeting you, Sanya."

As his long fingers enveloped hers, a sudden urge to make him keep holding on came over her. It was as if she hadn't known she was thirsty until a tall glass of water was put down in front of her.

He was too tall, so she cupped the back of his head and pulled him toward her lips. He didn't hesitate to return her kiss as their lips came together. Waves of pleasure and sparks of excitement traveled over her skin.

She leaned away, but their hands were still connected. He let go and smiled.

"Oh." He suddenly looked embarrassed as he pointed at the top corner of her mouth. "You have some…"

She noticed the wetness, then. She took it off her mouth with the tip of her finger, then held it in front of her eyes for a look. How strange this was to have the blood of someone on her hands who she hadn't harmed. She wiped it off on her pants.

"I have to go," she said.

"Come by the forge tomorrow."

"I can't."

As she turned to leave, he frowned.

"Goodbye, Sanya."

"Goodbye."

Tomorrow will be a dark day.

On her way back, she noticed the shimmering moon through the clouds like the description he'd given of her beauty. It filled her with a strange feeling, as if she were a girl again dreaming of a better life. Her father had taken away her teen years, when the only thing she could rely on was her imagination. Sometime between then and now, she'd stopped imagining and started planning. But right now she could imagine going to the forge, wrapping herself around Greg, and kissing him until morning.

She glanced down at the faint stain on her pants from his blood and smiled for the first time in a week.

CHAPTER TWENTY-SIX

Sanya had to part with her stolen dagger before entering Tenred castle. The Takary inscription on the handle could bring up questions that she couldn't answer.

"Keep it safe until I return," she said as she handed it to Alabell.

"I will." Alabell traded Sanya's dagger for an unmarked one, giving it over hesitantly. It was obvious she didn't want Sanya to kill anyone with it, so Sanya told the healer what she needed to hear.

"No blood will be shed so long as they cooperate."

"They won't want to, so keep in mind that threats proven truthful through a psychic will go a long way."

"I see Basen has told you of the plan."

Alabell nodded. She then handed Sanya the other weapon she'd need, a small knife.

Sanya started to leave.

"Wait," Alabell called.

"What?"

"I've wanted to ask you something for a while."

And she thinks I might die, so she's choosing now. "Get on with it."

Basen still had to come to Millry's tavern and say goodbye to Alabell before they could leave, and Sanya needed to get this over with before she had any doubts.

"I think back to when we were friends at the Academy and I wonder: Are you at all the person you were back then?"

"I don't know anymore," Sanya admitted.

Alabell rubbed the back of her neck, clearly uncomfortable. "Are you interested in finding out? We could try to be friends again."

"How would we do that?"

"Uh." Alabell let out a nervous chuckle. "I guess the first step would be to try to care about each other. I'm already worried about you, but it doesn't seem like you have any thoughts about the rest of us."

There was some truth to that, but only because Sanya thought no one cared what happened to her. She investigated Alabell's energy to find genuine worry, like the healer said.

"Now I will care."

"Just like that?"

"I will care about *you*," Sanya specified.

Alabell formed an awkward smile. "At least it's a start. Be safe."

"Thank you."

Strangely, she felt a little better about living in this world she'd created for herself now that she knew Alabell cared.

As Sanya waited for Basen in the basement, the very doubts she'd worried would come finally did, with full force. She might not have the will to go through with this after all, if there were people like Alabell willing to give her a second chance.

She'd stored her doubts in the dark cabinets of her mind by the time Basen arrived.

"Are you ready?" he asked.

"Yes."

Their side finally had two akorell stones by then, and they would have three more before the end of the day thanks to Jack and his team. So long as Sanya made it through this, she could start helping Basen with portals. She just needed a little bit of practice.

Basen gave one akorell stone to Sanya to hold away from him as he drew the energy out of the other and formed a portal. As Sanya walked into it, she reminded herself of Basen's suggestion to be nice and smile to the kitchen staff if they encountered any in the castle.

She landed on her side and muffled a sound of pain with gritted teeth. She tried to roll out of the way, knowing Basen was coming in behind her, but dizziness made it difficult to tell exactly how far she was from the swaying kitchen counters around her and she slammed into one.

Basen toppled through the portal and stumbled over to fall on her legs. This time, she couldn't muffle her yelp.

"*Shh*," Basen whispered.

She was up before he was. He clung to her pants to try to get himself up quickly, as if expecting to run, but all he managed to do was pull down her pants just past her hips.

"Get off!" she snapped, grabbing her pants with one hand and prying loose his fingers with the other.

He fell as she glanced around. The kitchen was empty. Their decision to come in the time between breakfast and lunch was a good one.

"No one's here," Sanya whispered. "I'm going."

"Hurry," Basen said as he clung to a counter for balance.

She'd already visualized the route to the king's

chambers, where she expected to find Gayla, but actually walking through the castle was a far different experience than she'd anticipated. Memories of her father returned like attacks of a sword. She made fists and even lifted her arms to defend herself as she winced, recalling the feeling of interminable anger and then sadness as he forced her to ingest bitter potions.

The trials he'd designed, however, were the worst part of his supposed "training to unlock her full potential." She'd roamed these halls blindfolded, barefoot, and backward too many times to count. The castle was already a dangerous place, spiral stairs without railings and lavish rooms with exquisite flower vases that could fall and shatter after a slight bump to the table they stood upon.

The servants and the inhabitants hated her equally but for different reasons, and the other children teased her to no end, Basen included. She only learned what a friend was through her sister and mother, both taken by Spiro. To pretend he was alive and that she was helping him would be a trial in itself.

She lost her way, but it didn't matter. Eventually she encountered an armored man.

"I'm Sanya Grayhart, and I need to speak to Gayla Hiller."

He looked confused as he glanced around Sanya. "Where are your escorts?"

"They let me in because they know who I am." This man obviously didn't. "Gayla wants to speak with me."

He scratched his chin as he pondered. "Let me check you for weapons."

She lifted her arms. "There's a dagger around my ankle that I'd like back when this is over."

He went for it first, then patted down the rest of her. "Follow me."

They walked for a while. Eventually he remarked, "It's strange they'd let you in by yourself."

"They knew someone like you would find me and escort me the rest of the way."

"Who are you?"

"Have you heard of Spiro Grayhart?"

"Ah. His daughter."

Sanya recognized some of the people who passed them, but they didn't recognize her. It was her polite smile, an expression she'd never showed anyone in the castle. They smiled back and carried on without the slightest idea of what she was capable of.

She'd only been in the throne room a few times, but it looked just as she remembered. Statues of kings surrounded the throne. It was built upon a pedestal, with steps painted red and black to match the colors representative of the territory. Banners of family names hung on the walls, the Hillers and the Grayharts side by side. The room bled pride, soaking Sanya in a feeling of filth. At least Gayla wasn't on the throne but standing beside it at a table covered in a map with figurines, probably representing soldiers.

"Who is this?" Gayla had the same air of superiority in her tone as her sister.

"Sanya Grayhart," answered the escort.

Sanya pointed at the banner with her family name. Gayla glanced over at it, then looked at Sanya as if she were risen from the dead.

"You must be Spiro's daughter. What are you doing here?" She climbed up the steps to sit upon the throne, beckoning for someone. A short man rushed up the steps to stand by her side, and Sanya felt psyche invade her.

There were only three other armed men besides the one who'd escorted her here. This shouldn't be too difficult. It was the psychic who made things complicated. Fortunately, Tenred wasn't known for its psychics like Kyrro was, and anyone powerful enough to fight with psyche probably would've joined Crea already.

"My father needs to speak with you," Sanya said.

"I thought he was dead."

"It was a ruse." Though he really was dead now. It felt like a lifetime ago that she'd killed him in the spiritual world. "He's still alive and wants to offer his services to Tenred by working on military potions again."

Gayla didn't seem to believe it, waiting for her psychic to tell her it was a lie.

"The truth," he squeaked.

"How is he still alive?" Gayla asked, skepticism dripping in her voice.

Sanya tried to maintain her smile. "I don't see how that's relevant." No one had questioned his suicide in the past. No one had even asked to see his body. The only reason he wasn't as hated as Sanya was because people had feared him. They all told Sanya how horrible it was that he'd killed himself, but the only people who meant it were those who'd never met him.

"I just want to ensure he's not going to try to trick us."

"He won't, but he will offer his services to Ulric if

you're not interested."

Gayla had the black hair of almost all the Hillers. She slowly ran her fingers down through it along the front of her shoulder, eyeing Sanya as if she knew this was a trap.

"What does he want in exchange for his service?"

"A life at the castle, a salary." Sanya thought for a moment about what else he might want if he were still alive. "Respect." It would be what he'd craved most.

"He'll have to earn it back."

"He wishes to do that. And I would like a room in the castle, not with him."

"That can be arranged."

"I will return to him and tell him to come to the castle."

"Yes, do that."

Sanya walked toward the throne. It stirred the guards.

She smiled in a disarming manner. "I'd just like to bow in front of my new queen."

Sanya's escort said, "She's already been stripped of weapons."

Gayla gestured for her to come forward, and the guards let her.

They would regret this for the rest of their lives.

Sanya put one foot on the first step and knelt. "Gayla Hiller, everything I told you is true," she lied. "But there is one more thing that I need to tell you, the final reason I came here. I ask that you cooperate with my request to make this easier for everyone."

"What request would that be?" Gayla already sounded irritated.

Sanya's escort hadn't searched her boot properly, for

he'd figured the only weapon was the dagger she'd willingly shown him. But there was another, small yet sharp enough to kill, that she drew quickly as she sprang up onto the pedestal of the throne.

She grabbed Gayla as the woman screamed and pressed the knife against her throat.

"Gayla!" shouted the small psychic as he danced around unsure what to do.

"Get off." Sanya kicked him in the hip. He rolled off with a grunt. The guards were already rushing Sanya. "Stop, or I'll kill her!" Gayla tried to squirm free, so Sanya increased her grip and pierced the other woman's neck slightly with the blade. "Don't move or I'll run it across."

The guards froze. Gayla didn't speak.

"Psychic," Sanya called out. "Say whether I'm telling the truth or not. I will kill Gayla if I don't get what I want!"

"It's the truth."

"As soon as you kill me, you're dead," Gayla said.

"I'm prepared to take us both to the next world if I must."

"Truth, Gayla! This bitch is mad!"

"I am. *Get back!*" she yelled as loud as she could. "I will kill Gayla if anyone tries to stop me!"

It worked to get the attention of the guards in the hall outside. They came in, took one look, then separated to go alert more of their ranks.

"What do you want?" Gayla asked.

"First I want my dagger back." She gestured with her foot at the one who'd escorted her. "Leave it at the bottom of the stairs, then get against the wall. Everyone against the walls!"

None of them moved.

"Gayla?" one of the guards asked.

"She's going to live," Sanya told them. "Everyone will live if you cooperate."

"It's the truth," said the psychic.

Sanya could feel Gayla relax slightly. "Do as she says."

All but one guard moved to the side walls to make a wide path. The one Sanya specified left her dagger and then joined the rest.

"Now we're going to walk down slowly and collect my dagger."

She and Gayla descended the three steps and bent down, Sanya pressing her small blade firmly against Gayla's throat.

"Stop," Gayla groaned. "You're hurting me."

"As soon as you put my dagger into my other hand, the pain will stop." She slung her arm around Gayla's shoulders and opened her palm. She felt absolute terror from Gayla's energy. This woman wouldn't think to go against Sanya until this was over, and then she would demand Sanya's head.

Once Sanya had her dagger, she put it against Gayla's neck and dropped the knife.

"Out of the throne room," Sanya demanded.

"To where?"

"The vault."

Gayla tensed again.

CHAPTER TWENTY-SEVEN

"Leave your weapons here," Sanya demanded.

No one obeyed her.

"You think I won't do it? Psychic, tell them!"

"She'll kill Gayla."

"Get rid of your weapons," Gayla said.

A clash of swords hit the floor.

"Do you have any psychics in this castle who can cause pain?" Sanya asked. "Before you lie to me, you should know that I'm waiting for an excuse to kill you. And I care more about taking your life than I do about saving mine."

Even now, Gayla turned her head toward her psychic in disbelief.

"It's all true," the psychic said.

"Yes, there is one who can cause pain here."

"You will order them not to as soon as you see them. I'm trained to resist the spell. If I feel it even for a moment, I will kill you. You will continue to tell any guards we see to put down their weapons and keep their distance."

Sanya dragged Gayla along toward the vault. It was one of many places in the castle Sanya remembered clearly. Everyone knew where it was. The glass door separating the room containing the vault from its adjacent hall was designed to let everyone see the guards standing in front of the steel door. It would keep the people of the castle honest and the guards as well, but children like Sanya would come to the vault to stare through the glass and wonder just how much treasure was inside.

It was common knowledge that the vault guards held neither of the two keys to get in. One key was always with the king, and the other was hidden. But if Sanya knew anything about the Hillers, Gayla had them both now.

"I know you have one key with you and one somewhere else," Sanya said. "Tell me where the other one is."

"In my apartment."

"Do you stay in the king's chambers?"

"Yes, but now it is called the queen's."

This would be easy; they were already close to both the vault and the queen's chambers. The guards shuffled around nervously as Sanya kept her eyes on them while walking backward with Gayla.

Sanya used psyche to sense if others were trying to sneak up behind her, or if there was anyone around corners. At first there was no one to sense, but soon she felt herself walking into a trap as she neared the end of the hall.

She pretended to guess what she already knew. "If there is anyone waiting around the corner, it would be wise for you to drop your weapons and show yourselves now. If anyone tries to surprise me, I'm running my dagger across her neck."

She waited, but none of the many people she sensed came out. There was movement behind her, the guards edging closer. She spun around and pricked Gayla's skin deep enough to draw blood. Gayla whimpered as Sanya threatened them.

"Try it again and see what happens."

She felt Gayla panicking as the queen reached up reflexively to grip Sanya's arm.

"Drop your hand," Sanya ordered. "If you squirm again, I will kill you."

She pulled Gayla against one wall for a glimpse around the corner, spotting a few swordsmen before they were quick enough to get out of sight.

"Come out and join the others. Put down your weapons. I will not tell you again."

"Do it," Gayla commanded, her voice rising in near hysteria.

Several of the men discarded bows, but Sanya noticed a few with no weapon to throw down.

"Mages. I see who you are." It was impossible to tell if any of them were skilled enough to cast without a wand. Sanya quickly counted them. "The three of you will walk to the other end of this hall and wait there. If I spot any of you even for a moment, she dies."

"Wait," Gayla said.

The two men and one woman stopped. Hostility filled the air, but Sanya sensed no aggression from Gayla.

"She's a psychic." Gayla pointed to the woman and told her, "Don't try anything. Sanya will resist."

Sanya's smile came off as more of a sneer. "I'm glad to see you're learning. We might both get out of this alive."

"You know no one can escape if they steal from the kingdom of Tenred," Gayla warned with surprising confidence. "But if you leave now, no harm will come to you or your father."

"No, you and I are going this way."

There were no more traps en route to the queen's chambers. Most of the guards in the castle had already come running in defense of their queen, Sanya figured, so there were very few others who could be a threat to her. There were too many in her vicinity for one psychic spell of pain to disable them all, but she trusted in Basen's plan that she wouldn't need it.

It was a painfully long process to get Gayla into her lavish quarters to fetch the key from a locked box. It took a different key to unlock, this key hidden beneath a corner of the mattress. Eventually, they returned to the hall and walked over to the vault.

"Order your guards out," Sanya demanded as they stood in front of the glass door.

"Come out here," Gayla called to them. "Don't try to stop her." She fidgeted in Sanya's grasp as a thin line of blood ran down the queen's neck.

The guards exited the antechamber to join the others in the hall.

Sanya pointed at one man with a friendlier face than most others. "Come here." He hadn't shown any signs of aggression toward her, unlike the others. "Inside," Sanya ordered.

The guard walked in, then Sanya and her prisoner followed. She called back into the hall, "If I see anyone else come in, I'll kill her."

"It's the truth!" shouted the psychic.

"Shut up!" Gayla yelled back. "That's not needed anymore. She's clearly insane."

"You, guard," Sanya directed. "Slowly reach into

Gayla's pocket and fetch the two keys."

She sensed nothing but mild alarm from his energy as he obliged.

"Now go open the vault." Sanya felt a wave of disappointment from a few people's psyche, Gayla's included. The secret trap within the vault was known only by a few. Sanya hadn't heard anything about it, but Basen was a Hiller, so he knew it, as well as other secrets of the castle.

"We can go in together," Gayla goaded. "I'll give you all the acrowns you can carry."

Basen had warned Sanya that if she walked into the vault with Gayla, someone outside the chamber would take a painting off the wall to reveal a lever. Once Sanya arrived at a certain spot, Gayla would shout for the lever to be pulled as she ducked, and spears would jut out from the wall to kill Sanya.

"No, we're staying out here." She gestured for the guard to go. "Open it and fetch me three acrowns."

The guard seemed confused, but he headed toward the steel door anyway. Gayla shared his surprise for the small amount Sanya had requested.

He could barely open the door by himself, revealing a chamber much smaller than Sanya had imagined. There was probably just enough room for four people to stand inside and make a square. Shelves containing bags lined each wall.

"Which one?" the guard asked Gayla.

"Doesn't matter."

He took one off the shelf and reached his other hand within. He plucked out three coins as many more tinkled against each other.

"Three, you said?"

"Yes she said three!" Gayla bellowed. "Get on with it."

"I realize it's less than you expected," Sanya said. "But I don't need much. I figure my chances of escape are much better now. What do you say, Gayla?"

"Yes, we will let you out of here." It was a lie. She wanted Sanya to die just as if she'd taken hundreds of acrowns. That was the Hiller greed that somehow had never sunk its claws into Basen.

"Close the door," Sanya told the guard. "Then put the acrowns and keys in the small pouch in my pocket and return to the others."

He did, leaving her with Gayla in the antechamber of the vault.

Sanya made her way out with her captive. The guards inched forward like wolves approaching prey.

"Back!" Sanya demanded. "Get back."

They shoved against each other to make room. Sanya took Gayla the other way down the hall. Suddenly she sensed someone coming behind her. She shot a look over her shoulder to see two swordsmen running.

"Stop, or she dies."

They'd already dropped their weapons and put up their hands as soon as Sanya spotted them. Sanya ordered them to go around her and Gayla to join the others.

"Now get into the antechamber," Sanya demanded. "Everyone."

"Why?" Gayla asked.

"Once everyone's there, I will release you and run out

of the castle. You will see my father tomorrow, but you won't see me again." Sanya spoke loud enough for everyone to hear. "It's only three acrowns. Let's just get this over with."

It was a tight fit for all the guards, but they managed to get into the antechamber. She made Gayla close the glass door to separate the two of them from the rest of her guards.

"Now push the table in front of the door," she told them. "And then put the chairs on top of the table. The sooner you get this done, the sooner I leave."

The psychic's squeaky voice rang out from among them, "And will you leave without harming Gayla?"

"Yes."

"Do as she says," the queen echoed.

The guards shuffled as the table came into sight from the side.

"Leave the keys," Gayla ordered. "Or we will have to come after you."

"Fine. I'm going to let go of you for a moment so you can see me discard them, but if you try to run I will chase you down and kill you. Will you cooperate?"

"Yes."

Sanya released her grip around the top of Gayla's torso, giving her arm a much needed rest. With a quick spin, Sanya tossed the two keys as hard as she could to get them as close as possible to the end of the hall.

Gayla grumbled. "You could've just dropped them here."

Sanya gestured Gayla toward her. With a sigh, Gayla returned to the original position, then groaned as Sanya put the blade against her neck once more.

"Why only three acrowns?" Gayla asked as chairs were passed along the rows of men and pushed onto the table. The doors only opened inward. This wouldn't delay the guards for more than a minute, but it should give Sanya the time she needed to escape.

"I'm only taking what I can easily conceal."

"Why would you need to hide the money? Everyone in Tenred will know what you've done. They won't accept stolen coin. It's better that you leave it and just go."

Her greed was palpable. "I won't need to hide the coins from anyone in this territory."

The fleet of unarmed guards finished stacking the chairs atop the table. "They're done," Gayla said. "Let go of me."

"You will answer my questions first, and then I will leave."

"If you hurry up." It was astonishing that even now Gayla spoke as if she was in control.

"Did you and your sister know what Spiro was doing with my older sister?"

"Of course not, and I never planned to work with your father now because of the kind of man he was when he worked for my father. I just needed time to figure out what to do before he went to Ulric."

Some of the men began to shout from within the antechamber for Sanya to leave Gayla and go.

"Shut up!" she yelled, losing control of her anger for a moment. Some of them reached for the chairs after hearing her tone. "Stay there! Or I bury this dagger in her throat. I still have more questions for her. Psychic, are you listening to her answers?"

"Yes, they are all true!"

"Good, then she stays alive for now."

She felt Gayla tremble with fear.

Sanya asked, "If you had known what my father was doing to my sister would you have done anything to help? Be honest."

"I would've put a stop to it."

"Did you know it was my father's experiments that killed her?"

"Bastial stars, no! I'm sorry, Sanya. He deserved imprisonment. No, worse!"

"Are you now going to tell me that you had no idea that he continued his experiments after her death...on me?"

"I had no idea! I'm sorry. I wish I'd known!"

"You are a liar! Liar!"

"It's the truth!"

The psychic crawled onto the table and put his hands against the glass. "It is true! She would've helped."

"No. She knew and she did *nothing*. You are both lying!"

*****

Basen waited just around the corner of the hall as he listened to Sanya order the guards into the vault's antechamber. He couldn't make out much of what was said but it didn't matter; he was waiting for one thing only.

Then it happened, the keys clanging against the wall. He waited, as it sounded as if Gayla might be facing him. Sanya would turn her away as soon as she had the chance.

He risked a peek. One key was much closer than the other, but it would still require him to run out into sight. But both Sanya's and Gayla's backs were to him for the moment. He hurried out as silently as he could, grabbed one key, then hurried back. He pocketed it and waited for a shout to indicate that Gayla had seen him, but there was only the muffled sound of her and Sanya speaking.

Basen ran. One of the best kept secrets of the castle was the second treasury. It contained only a fraction of the valuables in the main vault, but there still should be more than enough acrowns for Basen and his allies. The money had been hidden in case someone did manage to steal from the main vault. It would provide a reserve to run the kingdom while they attempted to recover what was taken.

Others knew the location of the small treasury only for its other purpose, a waiting room. It was connected to the throne room. Guards were always stationed there, though only a few people knew their true purpose had nothing to do with keeping guests from entering the throne room before the king was ready to see them.

This "treasury" was actually just a simple safe behind a painting on the wall, requiring a single key. More often than not, only one trusted guard in the waiting room even knew of its existence.

Basen's speed took him there in a flash. He flung open the door and gasped in shock to see not only one swordsmen but three. Why hadn't they gone with the others to protect Gayla? The answer was important, because it would tell Basen whether they'd obeyed an order to remain here or if they cared little about Gayla and Crea and stayed because they were lazy. One would mean a fight while the other would mean Basen could bribe them.

"Gayla's under attack!" he spewed out before they could recognize him, hopefully. "What are the three of you doing here?"

"What are *you* doing here, Basen Hiller?"

So they already knew of Gayla and didn't care. Bribe.

He produced a key. "All of us can split the coin, but we must hurry."

The younger of the three men was the only one to glance toward the painting of Crea and Gayla standing beside each other with equally stern expressions. The other two guards probably had worked in the castle for ten or twenty years, because they appeared worn out, as if time had taken away all their spirit. They'd risen slowly from their chairs when Basen entered, and even the one who'd recognized him showed no inclination to draw his weapon.

The younger, however, had already been standing. His feet shuffled as he put his hand on his hilt.

"There's a hole in the wall behind that painting," Basen explained to the older men. "I have the key to open the small locked door to reach what's inside." He started toward the painting, but all three of them took out their swords and pointed the tips at Basen. He played the confident fool as he casually removed the painting and inserted the key, glancing back to them as if they were mad to stop him. "Are the three of you interested or not?" He retrieved the large pouch of coins.

Both older men let down their swords as they glanced at each other.

"How much is in there?" asked the younger.

Basen lowered the pouch and tilted it toward them so they could see the gold coins. "Probably forty acrowns. We could each take ten." It would still be enough for Basen's army, though he might have to rely on more from another source. He would find a way to make it work.

The older men ignored the younger guard as they considered Basen's proposal. "We'd have to disappear," said one.

The other nodded, but he didn't see the younger guard pulling back his arm to plunge his sword through his companion's back.

"What the bastial hell are you doing!" screamed the other one. He got up his sword just in time to block the thrust as his ally went down.

Basen couldn't decide whether to try running around them to escape with the coins or waiting. His hesitation decided for him, as the younger worked his way through the older's defenses and stuck him in the thigh. As both older men struggled to get up from the ground, the younger stabbed them each in the heart.

"Throw me the pouch, and I'll give you half," said the younger, now the only remaining person in Basen's way.

But someone greedy enough to kill his comrades for money would certainly try to kill Basen for more.

"No, *I'll* give you half," Basen said.

"I won't know it's half unless I count it myself."

"There's no time." Basen grabbed a handful of acrowns and stuffed them in his pocket after showing the coins to the guard. "I've taken less than half. You can have the rest, but you have to make way."

He rushed Basen, but he didn't know Basen had already been gathering energy. It wasn't enough for a fireball, but it served its purpose as Basen forced it into his attacker's face.

His eyes shut as he flinched, but he still swung with surprising strength. Basen ducked and heard a clash as the sword must've struck the wall. Like a shield, it deflected the sword hard enough to knock it out of the man's grip. Basen grabbed it and stabbed him in the leg. As the man howled in what sounded to be more anger than pain, Basen fled the room.

It was important to keep the last one of the three alive. He'd be questioned by psychics, and Crea and Gayla would find out that it was Basen who took from them. He wanted them to suffer from the Hiller fury he'd seen in their father. They would send someone after the end of the war to try to take it back. It would lead to his cousins' capture, for the hired sword would be questioned until he revealed where to find them if they'd gone into hiding.

Basen returned to the kitchen and took out the second akorell stone he'd brought. He broke the sartious encasing and hoped to see Sanya soon. He readied his sword as he heard someone sprinting, then lowered it when he saw her.

"Let's go," she said in a rush.

Basen made the portal back to Kyrro's capital. Sanya went in first, then he followed.

The basement was full of people pushing each other away to make room as Basen tumbled in after Sanya. He didn't know why she was in such a hurry to get away from him, colliding into people as she told them to move.

"We got it," Basen said as he started after her. People began to clap. He found Alabell among them and handed her the pouch. "I'll be right back."

He nearly lost his balance from vertigo several times as he followed the trail Sanya had made between people. He chased her to the other side of the basement, where he'd done most of his plotting. She came to the wall and looked back, clearly not pleased to see Basen there.

"What happened?" Basen asked.

She wouldn't fully turn around.

"Sanya, I already saw the blood on your hand. Don't try to hide it."

She turned and knelt down to take the bloody dagger out of the holster on her ankle. She tossed it onto the floor as if it disgusted her, then covered her eyes with her sleeve.

"What happened?" Basen asked again.

"I had to kill a psychic," she said.

Was that it? He knelt down beside her, surprised to see her barely holding back tears.

"We knew we might have to kill when we went to the castle," he said. "It's all right."

His words didn't seem to help.

"I'm proud of you," he told her.

"I'm not proud of myself."

"You should be. The old Sanya wouldn't have felt pain like this from killing. You're changing."

She shook her head, then showed him a hard look as if she needed to tell him grave news.

"What is it?" Basen asked.

She sucked in a few breaths until her eyes glazed over and her mouth relaxed. "Nothing. I'm fine."

CHAPTER TWENTY-EIGHT

The plethora of acrowns gave the army a boost in morale, but most people didn't realize that spending these acrowns on food, lodging, and weaponry without alerting Ulric would require more careful planning than what had gone into obtaining them. Wilfre told Basen with confidence that he could handle it, and Basen gladly surrendered the responsibility so he could focus on other matters.

They needed spies at Oakshen a day ago, but with both akorell stones depleted, Basen wouldn't be able to make a portal until tonight. Sanya had withdrawn from the world again, sulking in the shadows of the basement.

Most of the spies in the capital posed as workers reporting to Trela, Sneary, and other instructors. Penny admitted that she had little use besides battle...or training for battle, so Basen had no idea what she was doing with her time. Soon she would be needed. When spies were in place in Oakshen, it would be time for their first attack.

Alabell paid Basen a visit. He halted the discussion with Wilfre to greet her with his warmest smile.

"How are you?"

"Good, but I can see you're busy," she said. "I'll come back."

"We're almost done. I'll meet you at Millry's." He knew she spent most of her time helping out the overworked tavern keeper. It was a good thing not to need a healer, though he did worry about her getting bored.

Wilfre got right back into their conversation about money as soon as she left. "It's important to trade our acrowns for kymarks as soon as possible. They will be less suspicious to spend. Our spies should be able to tell us of the sellers of higher quality items who wouldn't blink at the sight of an acrown. I know of a few myself, but we'll need to do business with many."

"I'll let our officers know when they give me their evening report."

"That's all for now." Wilfre gestured toward the front of the building for Basen to leave, obviously knowing he was eager to meet Alabell.

Basen would've run out of their headquarters and into the tavern next door if the scene wouldn't have caused a commotion. The rest of his allies would storm out of the basement like an army of ants to look for an enemy. So he maintained his calm all the way to Alabell and even kept from grinning excitedly like a fool when she led him into an empty room.

"I need to speak with you about your father...why are you looking at me like I'm dinner?"

"I'm just happy to see you."

"You're always happy to see me." She slid her arms around his lower back and gave him a kiss. "But it isn't good news of your father." She let go. "He's taken charge of the akorell stone making."

Basen sighed. "I told him it's under control. I'm beginning to see how my father has worked his way into high positions. He pretends to be in the position he wants until he gets it, but he doesn't seem to realize there is no power left for him to take."

Alabell pursed her lips.

"You disagree?" Basen asked.

"There is power for him to take...from you. Everyone sees that you're the first link in the chain."

Part of Basen had already figured he was their leader if one had to be chosen, but it felt too surreal to be true. "It doesn't need to be that way."

"No, and I might have more time with you if it weren't, but we can all see that it's working. Even Sneary has backed down. It's only your father who vies for your authority."

"I'd let him have it if it was something I could give, but he doesn't know everything I do. I'm the one making the portals and keeping track of where everyone is. I'm giving the orders. I'd have to tell Henry what to tell others if he were to take charge, and that's a waste of time."

"I know." She took his hands. "You don't have to convince me. I wanted you to know he's convinced Jack to work with the blacksmith in this district. Henry has deemed both he and his apprentice trustworthy. From what Millry has told me about them, I would agree. It was just the way Henry went around you that troubled me. He's making sure all of us know of his success with the akorell bracelets, as if he was the one to mine the metal and stone and build the bracelets himself."

"I'm not going to compete with him."

"Jack doesn't seem to want to either. It's probably for the best."

"How many akorell bracelets are being made?"

"Four more to make six in total. All are about done,

now cooling."

"Then I'll tell Trela not to bother with her blacksmith anymore. I have to get back. You're welcome to come with me."

"I'd rather keep myself busy here than stand idle over there."

Soon after Basen returned, he received the visit from his father he'd expected. Basen spoke before Henry could.

"You've taken over control of the akorell bracelets." Basen made sure to smile to dissolve any contention. "Now I'll have six. I'll need to use two soon, so when can I expect them?"

"Two should be ready by the hour."

"Thank you," Basen said. "Was it Jack who thought of making six?"

Basen caught a hint of confusion in his father's eyes before Henry fixed his expression to show the usual look of complete control. "Yes."

"It's the perfect amount. I'll thank him next time I see him."

Henry nodded. Clearly, he didn't know why six was perfect. Basen could use two a day every day without needing to worry about running out because it took two days for them to charge. If a portal was needed sooner, he could have mages gathering energy nearby to charge one of the bracelets.

"I have an idea to get Mother back to us," Basen said in hopes of breaking the invisible barrier he felt growing between him and his father.

"So long as you don't risk your own life. She wouldn't want that, and neither do I."

Finally Basen could smile genuinely as he felt Henry become his father again.

"There is risk involved," Basen admitted. "But there's more risk if we wait. I don't want her in Crea's clutches when she finds out we've stolen from her. We need to free Mother before then, and only I can do it with a portal." His father started to speak, but Basen continued. "The first step will be to get information about the present condition of the Academy and what they have Mother doing there—if she is there at all. Then we will come back here and return to the Academy later after we have a plan."

Basen actually figured he should be able to formulate the plan for her escape the moment he saw her, but Henry was more likely to let Basen go without interference this way.

"You and I are both recognizable by the betrayers loyal to Crea," Henry pointed out. "Going to gather information is too risky."

"Which is why I'll be sending someone else."

"Who?"

"Sanya."

"Basen..." Henry's tone made it clear he didn't approve. "It was the right choice to send her to Tenred castle to lie to psychics, but getting your mother out of the Academy requires a set of skills that Sanya does not have."

"I do." Sanya emerged from the other section of the basement. "I can bring her back safely."

Basen hadn't discussed this with her yet, but he wasn't about to let his father know that. He gestured at

Sanya as if presenting her. "There you go, Father. She can do it."

"Not by herself. All of Crea's troops are men. She'll be recognized as an outsider."

"Not if she plays the role of a kitchen worker or a farmer. There were many women working at the Academy, so many of them should still be there."

"Nearly all of them are older than Sanya."

"She's going to keep her distance and spy. Her age won't make a difference."

Henry tilted his head. "You're creating this plan as we speak, aren't you?"

"No. I just haven't figured out every detail yet." Basen put up his hands. "We're getting ahead of ourselves. First we need to convince our enemies we're still in the forest and trying to win this war, otherwise they will search for us in every city. I need to speak with Trela and Penny, and that's after I teleport a team to Oakshen. So I need the akorell stones from you as soon as they're ready."

"I'll have the two bracelets brought to you whenever they're cool enough to handle." Henry glared at Sanya for reasons Basen couldn't understand. It was the first time he did more than just glance her way. She stared back at him in confusion.

Eventually Henry asked her, "What did you do to the blacksmith's apprentice?"

Sanya suddenly had an unreadable expression that would've gotten her far at any card table, even without her psychic ability. "What did he say?"

"First tell me what you did."

"I kissed him."

"You what?" Basen blurted. "No, this has to be a joke," he told Henry.

Sanya ignored him. "What did Greg say about me?"

"She knows his name!" Basen whispered to no one in particular. "God's mercy, you really did it, didn't you?"

Now both were ignoring him as Henry spoke. "When the blacksmith trusted him enough to tell him we were rebels, he guessed you were one of us. He wants to know where to find you. Seeing as how you shouldn't leave the headquarters because of how easily you could be recognized, it's not smart to get involved with men who will come looking for you. He might be stupid enough to start asking around about a woman named Sanya, which could reach the ears of guards in other districts and bring them over to us. I shouldn't have to explain this to you. There's only one more time you should see him, and that's to convince him—and I *mean convince* him—not to pursue you."

They'd gathered a little audience that seemed to be enjoying the news about Sanya's kiss. She silenced their babbling with a mere glance.

"I'll take care of it," she told Henry before shifting her eyes to Basen. "You know where I'll be when it's time to discuss getting your mother out."

Not wanting their audience to see the hostility between him and his father, Basen smiled at Henry. "Thank you for getting the akorell stones to me as soon as possible. We'll speak later."

"Yes, I have a lot to do," he said, though Basen figured it was mostly for others' ears.

After Henry left, Basen sent for Effie and her sister.

When he found out they were in Millry's tavern, he decided to join them there for supper.

As he spoke with them, his eyes were treated to glimpses of Alabell as she rushed in and out of the kitchen to help Millry.

"How many more do you need to help you?" Basen asked. "I can get a team together as soon as we finish eating."

He'd directed the question at Effie, but it was Gabby who answered.

"It should only be Effie and me because more will cause suspicion. People in Oakshen know each other better than the people here. Well, not *here* in this district. The people all seem to know each other here. I mean in the rest of the capital."

"It's true," Effie confirmed.

Gabby wasn't finished. "They'll recognize anyone as an outsider, and there are no outsiders during this time because of the walls and the guards. Anyway, I should be able to organize a small team of spies."

"You alone?" Basen asked.

"Both of us," Gabby corrected. "Well, mostly me. Effie doesn't know how the city or the people have changed since the beginning of this war. I do."

Basen didn't know much about Gabby other than she was Effie's fifteen-year-old sister. She didn't look three years younger than Effie, but she did speak and sound younger. Could Basen rely on her to take command of gathering information on the entire city?

His face must've betrayed his thoughts because Effie leaned forward and told him, "You can trust her."

"I do," Basen lied. "I'm just trying to understand the details."

"I'm not going to take control like you have here," Gabby said. "There are many people who others already come to with information. I just need to get involved with them and find some way to get information back to you."

"*We* just need to get involved with them," Effie corrected.

"We, sorry."

"All right. You can get information back to me in the same way I plan to keep in contact with those in the forest," Basen replied. "At sundown each day, I'll make a portal to Worender training center in Oakshen. Please be there but not in the exact spot of the portal. One or both of you can come through and give me your report." He took a scroll out of his pocket. "This is everything I need to know about the city before tomorrow so that we can attack. It also has instructions on where to be during the attack. Read it until you've memorized what you need to do, then burn it."

"Bastial hell, Basen." Effie grabbed the scroll and gestured with it. "You just made this all too real for me."

"Good. It'll prepare you for what I'm about to say next." He gestured for her to hide the document, so she put it under her shirt against her belly. "If that gets into enemy hands, we're all dead."

Both sisters stopped eating. They had the same wide dark eyes.

"We'll, uh, memorize it and...destroy it before we leave," Gabby stammered.

CHAPTER TWENTY-NINE

By the time Basen spoke with Trela and Penny about tomorrow's attack, the Elegin sisters had memorized what they needed to do and burned the scroll. An audience had gathered around Basen to watch him make his first of two portals, this one to Oakshen.

"I'll see one or both of you tomorrow," he told Effie and Gabby.

"At sundown," Effie said.

"Wait." Gabby lifted her hands. "What if there are people at the training center?"

"I doubt there will be." Basen hadn't been there since his test to get into the Academy. Remembering brought on a pang of grief about Jackrie that he quickly suppressed. He gestured at the audience circled around him. "But if there are, someone here will see them through the portal before you enter. I'll then close the portal, and we'll try again later."

He set his mind back in Oakshen. The workhouse haunted him like a bad dream—walking toward the training center with his filthy comrades; seeing the line of warriors he'd be competing against, losing hope. His memories sped through the rest of the tense experience at double speed and stopped right as he was about to show Jackrie his attempt of a fireball with an empty wand.

Suddenly he was there again, but everyone had disappeared. It was night instead of day, the moon shining through the treetops as some pressed against the fence of the training center. Never had he been here during the night, so why did he have this strangely realistic memory? He felt the cold air as if he were there right now. He tried to make a sound, unable to tell if he'd failed or if he just couldn't hear it.

He returned to the basement with such force that he started to fall, only to discover that he was already on his back and rolling around as many pairs of hands struggled to keep him steady.

"Can you hear us?" Steffen asked.

"Yes."

They helped him to sit up. Steffen lifted a finger in front of Basen's eyes. "Follow it."

Basen tried but his eyes forced themselves shut as a spell of dizziness crashed into him.

"I think you should lie down until we figure out what's wrong," Steffen advised. He heard others muttering to get Alabell.

"I'm fine." With the dizziness gone as quickly as it had come, Basen stood. "I want to make the portal while the memory is fresh. I haven't been to Oakshen in a while."

Many began to object until he broke the sartious casing around the first akorell bracelet and put it on his wrist. "I already know the training center is empty," Basen told them. "No need to wait." He sucked out all the energy in the akorell stone and ripped open a portal. People looked into it deeply anyway, Effie and Gabby included.

"Empty," Basen said. "Go."

Effie and Gabby jumped inside, then Basen let it close.

He took a few breaths to gather himself as he tried to

recall the Slugari colony without putting himself there this time. Shutting his eyes, he started with something that reminded him of that interminable darkness. He was in the entrance tunnel again...he opened his eyes as he felt himself falling into the memory, flinching as if he'd slipped on a stair.

He got the idea to pinch his leg to keep his mind grounded. Squeezing hard, he felt pain he couldn't ignore. He closed his eyes again and raced down the entrance tunnel. Half his mind remained on the pain, telling him he was still in the basement, while the other half waded through the darkness.

There was a gap of time he couldn't account for, and suddenly he was beneath the akorell metal. It was a fraction of what it used to be, just a subtle glow. He focused on the pain until he snapped back into the basement. He stumbled forward and started to fall but Steffen caught him.

"I'm fine," Basen said before anyone could ask. He broke the sartious casing on the next akorell bracelet and replaced the used one with it. "No one is there," he told Steffen. "Wait for Cleve and the others in the cavern. They know to come for you."

"How can you be sure they aren't there already?"

"I don't know how to explain it right now. Let me focus on making a portal."

Basen withdrew the energy and created the gateway to the cavern. Steffen had already memorized everything he needed the forest team to accomplish. Basen's only fear was that Cleve, Vithos, and the Krepps had been caught.

Steffen ran into the portal, and Basen let it close with relief.

He felt as if he'd spent the day running in circles. He stumbled over toward his side of the basement.

"Are you all right?" Sanya asked. He hadn't seen her join the group.

"I'll be fine. I'm going to sleep."

"You need a healer."

"I just need quiet."

He hoped Sanya would take the hint to leave him alone, but she followed him over to his bed of clothing.

"It's time I started practicing portal making. You need help."

"I can't disagree, but we don't have any akorell stones to spare yet. All of them will be used tomorrow. If you waste one, it will cost us many lives. I need to sleep, Sanya. Please."

She huffed as she left.

Basen closed his eyes and lost himself. Three different images stuck to the back of his eyelids: the training grounds at the Academy, the abandoned cavern, and Worender training center. They overlapped, as messy as three paintings spliced into one. He fell into them to stand in all three at once. Panic set in as they started to separate.

Pressure built in his head as each location dug a corner into his brain and tugged. Finding no escape, he could only fight against them. He wrapped his mind around each location and tried to force them together again. They fought back with such force it was as if the turn of time was against him.

The harder he wrestled, the more his body materialized. He grabbed hold with arms and legs. The locations threatened to rip him apart, but he couldn't let go now. There was nowhere else he could exist. It had to be here in all of them.

He collapsed his body in on itself, bringing all together. There was a small pop within a loud crash.

Everything red. Hills, ground, but no sky.

Nothing but bursts of light.

Thoughts couldn't fully....bad. Stuck. Bad!

SPIRITS! DEATH?

Death?

death...

peace.

Basen took a breath. He looked down at his hands. There was no flesh, no bone, only energy. It sizzled without sound as it took the shape of his body. Was he really dead?

He bent down and touched the ground. Ripples of blue and white undulated out from him. He felt a sudden surge of control over this place as he stood, the spirits skittering away as if afraid of him. He waved and a living image of Basen, dirty and hungry, was created in a trail behind his hand. All his power went into each slam of his hammer as he worked beside his father.

Basen brought his hand back, and the image disappeared. He waved his hand toward him, and Alabell appeared walking in his direction. He reached out to touch her, but his hand passed through her, freezing Alabell midstride. He backed up, and soon she began walking toward him again. He moved out of the way so as not to disturb her. A medical cart appeared in front of her as she began to wheel it toward the fence of Worender training center.

Basen saw himself within the training center and could feel Alabell drawn to the image of him in the same way he could feel the cavern was empty before sending Steffen there. Basen watched himself try to cast a fireball only to create a red tear within the training center. This whole world of energy jerked toward it for a blink, then eased back as the rip dissolved.

Something began to pull him, the real him. He slid into the training center and stood in front of Jackrie.

"Go ahead," she urged.

He looked down to find himself holding her wand.

Everyone in the training center had their gaze on him.

"I'm not supposed to be here."

They all went completely still as if Basen had given the wrong line in a play. The fence began to fall. The ground curled. The blackest of holes opened in the middle of it all. It started to gain color as it sucked in Jackrie and the others.

Basen ran. He jumped over the undulating ground as it turned red, but a gust of wind with the strength of a hurricane whipped him into the hole.

He fell into the Dajrik Mountains, the sea of lava hot behind him. Annah lay unconscious with her head on Alabell's lap. Cleve towered over Basen. "Where's Peter?"

"I have to get out of here."

They froze. Another hole opened. Lava began to flow toward it. Basen tried to run, but his legs were numb. The lava came up in a wave so high it nearly touched the roof of rock.

"Basen!" It was Alabell's voice. Somehow he knew she was trying to help him.

"Where are you?"

"I'm here with you in the basement. You need to wake up."

"I can't. I'm in some other world." The same gust of wind carried him toward the hole. He screamed as he came down into it just as the lava crashed down on top of him. He pulled his arms and legs in as he expected agony. To his surprise, he only felt something cold and hard against his palms.

"Everyone who threatens the Elves will die."

Basen rolled over to find Fatholl standing over him. He could feel himself back in the Elven village, but this wasn't a memory like the others. The sounds were cleaner, the colors more vivid. He ran out the door as Fatholl chased after him.

Alabell's voice came from the clouds. "Basen!"

"I can hear you."

"Then wake up!"

"I don't know how."

He came to the hill with stepping stones beside the waterfall. Something touched his cheek but not here in this world.

He started to float off the ground, picking up speed.

"Can you feel that?"

"I think so. Whatever you're doing, do more."

The warm feeling of comfort filled his face as the same sensation came to his other cheek. He floated higher and soon started to fear he might fall.

When he felt her lips press against his, he rolled out of the dream and back into the real world, taking Alabell with him and coming to a stop on top of her.

"Thank you." Overjoyed to return, he showed his appreciation with another kiss. Then his strength gave out and he rolled off her and onto his back. "God's mercy, I thought I would be stuck there forever."

Sanya spoke, "You were in the spiritual world."

He sat up. "How did you know?"

"I could feel it. I tried to get you out with psyche but it was like you were behind a solid wall."

"How well have you been sleeping?" Alabell asked him.

"About as well on a pile of clothes as you could imagine."

"Come with me."

She helped him up and took him to the tavern. He followed her into the same empty room where they'd last spoken. She pointed at the bed. "Sleep."

"I don't want to take a bed from someone else."

"You won't be because I'm going to be right beside you."

Basen lay on his back and closed his eyes.

Something started to pull him back into the nightmare. He sat up and shook his head. "It's going to happen again."

"Don't think about it." Alabell lay beside him and took his hand. "You're not going anywhere. Relax."

Focusing on her touch, he closed his eyes and slowly slipped into slumber.

He awoke later and realized he hadn't dreamed; his mind had stayed put. It was dark out, still night.

His confidence returned when he realized he could now fall asleep soundly again. But first he spent a few moments enjoying the moonlight coming in through the window to illuminate Alabell's sleeping face.

CHAPTER THIRTY

Basen had to make his first portal of the day before lunch. He feared the same splitting of his mind would occur, so he asked Alabell to be there with him. She grounded him the most of anyone. It was her effect on both his mind and body that did it, for every time he saw her, he felt as if this was exactly where he needed to be.

Relief came over him when he opened the portal to the cavern without a problem and the entire team he'd sent to the forest came through. No one appeared to be injured as they rose up and shook off the dizziness.

"What's happening in the forest?" Basen asked.

Cleve took it upon himself to answer. "They continue to hunt and beat their drum. There are allies still out there, but we haven't been able to find them."

"How many beats have you heard?"

Vithos answered, "Three."

"We kill ten for every one," Rickik said, looking proud.

"You killed thirty of them?" Basen asked Nebre for confirmation.

"Thirty-one."

Hopefully Ulric still believes we're all in the forest, but it's best to make sure.

"It's time for our first battle."

The Krepps hissed and smiled at one another, even Nebre, though he didn't share the same level of enthusiasm. Steffen came over to Basen's side and whispered, "They won't agree with your plan. They expect to fight."

"Rickik," Basen said. "You will have your chance to kill our enemies, but only if you help us during this battle by staying back."

"No, Krepps fight. Humans spy."

"We need your Kreppen eyes, and you know the forest now better than any of us here." He wasn't sure of this, so he looked to Steffen, who nodded.

"We know where they go when they're not hunting us," Steffen said. "Most of them still return to the camp they've set up along the northern end of the forest. Others sleep in groups throughout the forest, but fewer of them do that now that we've killed thirty-one enemies during the night. I believe all of us should monitor their northern camp during the attack."

Rickik stomped his foot. "And we kill when we can."

"It's important that you do not let them know you are there," Basen said. "No light, no sound, and certainly no killing. We don't want them to think we're coordinating between the cities and the forest."

Rickik looked confused, so Basen tried again.

"We don't want them to know the truth about where we are and what we're doing."

Rickik didn't agree, only glowered.

Cleve told him, "We will continue to surprise them. We kill more this way. We kill *all*."

"Yes," Rickik said. "But I fight next battle after!"

"You will."

*****

When night came, Basen brought every akorell stone with a decent charge into the Slugari colony. Cleve's forest group had been given half the day in the city, the Krepps confined to the headquarters. Construction had begun, but Basen pulled Neeko away to join them for this attack.

Henry's struggle for political power was put on hold as he led his few hundred allegiant men into the cavern with Basen. They didn't have more than a dozen shields between them, but those would have to do. Not only did this attack need to happen, but Basen had to survive. The rest of his plan couldn't come to fruition without him. Others must've realized the same thing, for they looked at him as if he was ill and trying to sneak out of bed when he readied to join them.

"You don't need to be with them," Henry reasoned. "At least wait in the cavern for us to return."

It's what everyone else had expected. "If there's trouble, I know I can help," Basen insisted.

In the end, Basen didn't convince his father to change his mind. He just made Henry realize that arguing was pointless.

The sense of danger trilled in Basen's chest as he walked with his team of mages through the dark forest. Penny led, with Henry beside her. Henry had claimed to be able to get them to the western wall of Oakshen, but he and Penny had to stop several times to look at a compass and consult a couple of their soldiers.

Their army consisted mostly of Henry's troops and mages from the Academy. A surprising number of mages were of Group One. Basen was glad to see so many had survived the battle when the betrayal had come to light. There was no denying that Penny had done a marvelous job training them, and their coordination with each other would be needed now more than ever.

It took longer than Basen would've liked, but eventually they reached the wall of Oakshen. The wood was built up taller than the Academy's wall, but this one lacked strength. The guards stood on an unseen walkway. They appeared as mere shadows, most resting their forearms on the thin top of the wall as they slumped over.

Basen moved back into the shadows. The rebels wouldn't have to see the wall from where they shot. There was no way to miss it.

Henry's soldiers with shields positioned themselves between the trees. Basen stood behind them with the line of mages.

"Fire," Penny ordered.

They shot their fireballs over the heads of their comrades. As fire bombarded it, the wall complained with squeals and cracks.

The guards began to scream announcements of an attack as they moved away and disappeared.

Although there was urgency among Basen and the other mages, he could feel that they were just as calm as he was as they continued to cast. Penny joined in as they all fired away, shooting without challenge from their enemies.

Fire soon blanketed the wall and climbed up to dance above it.

Basen shot his enormous fireballs one after another.

They beat against the wall as he began to tire. Some of the mages beside him stopped as they huffed for breath, but Basen didn't relent. His fireballs grew in size as his training took over. When was the last time he'd casted without pause like this? It had to be in Penny's class, a lifetime ago.

As soon as chunks of the wall started to come down, the mages gained momentum. They cast bigger and faster fireballs. There were still no enemies in sight. Basen listened for the sound of an order, but all he could hear was the whoosh and crash of each fireball.

More of the wall came down, then huge chunks began to topple.

"Hold!" Penny ordered.

There was no more wall left in front of them, only the shanties on the outskirts of Oakshen. The rest of the wall still surrounded the city, but this gaping hole would hurt Ulric's army more than they could possibly realize.

Time to run.

Penny and Henry took the lead while Basen waited to put himself in the back. Neeko took to his side. The screams of his enemies finally reached his ears. Basen looked over his shoulder to see them charging out of the city.

They were too far behind. Basen's allies could easily win this race, but getting to the Slugari colony first would win them nothing. They needed to make sure not a single enemy saw them go into the colony. Otherwise, their disappearance would raise questions.

"Pick up the pace!" Basen yelled to the front.

But to his horror, they began to stop in front of him.

Before Basen could ask why, his father was shouting to turn north. It must be to avoid more enemies.

Basen took the lead as he came to realize what was happening. Ulric's soldiers had come around to drive them north, straight into the enemy camp at the edge of the forest. Thousands of enemies were probably leaving the camp to surround them.

Basen ran until all enemies charging from the city and those who'd come around to intercept were on the same side. Here he stopped.

"Get beside me," he told the others. "We fight here."

They created the same formation as before, shields in front and mages behind. Neeko stayed to Basen's right and pulled his swords from their sheaths. Penny and Henry took their spots on opposite sides of the lines.

"Fire to keep them back," Penny ordered.

The onslaught of fireballs turned this into the only type of battle that Basen and his allies could win, one of combat at range. All enemies tried to take cover but many were too slow to get behind the trees. Basen hadn't yet seen the men on horseback until he heard the sharp cry from one of the animals. Of those Basen spotted, they dismounted to take quicker cover as their horses darted off.

Basen and the others shot wave after wave of fireballs. These were the best mages in Ovira. They would not be out-cast. No enemies got a chance to shoot back.

There was still one problem.

"They'll be coming from behind soon," Basen announced. "We have to advance."

"March on my order!" Henry yelled. "One, two, one,

two!" His men moved in stride. Basen and the mages walked behind their armored allies as they continued to burn all the forest in front of them.

"Face them!" yelled a familiar baritone. When he came out from behind a tree, fear broke through Basen's concentration and forced him to a complete halt. Rockbreak had a shield taller than any man or Krepp and wide enough to protect him from every angle Basen's allies could reach.

"What the bastial hell is that?" shrieked one of the mages beside Basen.

"A man. One who can be killed." Basen found his courage and fired, but the ball of swirling flame—deadly in most circumstances—slammed into Rockbreak's shield and only knocked him back a single step.

As nearly every mage focused their fire on the giant taking to the front, the enemies used this as their chance to pop out and shoot arrows. Most were caught by the shields of Henry's men, but one made it through to fell a mage. The effect was a hundred times more devastating than just losing one person, as their lines began to break.

More enemy archers stepped out and shot freely. Two more mages fell. Rockbreak inched forward as he continued to take the brunt of fireballs.

"Let our swordsmen deal with the giant!" Basen yelled. His fireball exploded against the chest of an archer and shattered his bow. "Shoot the archers."

But the enemies from the city had joined Rockbreak's battalion by then. Basen's allies lost their momentum. Some began to hide behind trees to avoid being shot.

"Stay and fight," Basen growled. "Henry's men need

our support."

He noticed Neeko making two claws in Rockbreak's direction. The giant's shield wobbled as Rockbreak grunted.

"I don't think I can get it," Neeko grunted.

"Keep trying." It was the only thing preventing Rockbreak from charging into them.

The mountain of a man had almost reached the allies' front line when he suddenly spun and turned his shield. An enormous fireball blasted it out of his hands and knocked him over, the shield soaring through the trees as Neeko's pyforial energy went unchallenged. Basen fired upon the fallen giant as another fireball came from the side. The forest ground exploded all around Rockbreak as he bounded back behind the line of his men.

"It's the damn sword-mage again!" yelled Rockbreak. "Move to surround him."

Basen could barely make out the shadow of a man standing between both armies. It could only be one person.

Basen opened his mouth to yell to Abith, but what could he say? He couldn't call out for Abith to meet him in the abandoned colony.

"We know you're an ally!" was all Basen could think to scream. But Abith had already disappeared into the darkness. There was no way to know if he'd heard.

Half the enemies chased after Abith, but there were still more than enough to stand in Basen's way. Even without Rockbreak, his allies wouldn't be getting through anytime soon. Earlier Basen had thought of making a portal to the spiritual world in case they were about to be trapped, just like now. Sanya said it could be made from anywhere, and after Basen's journey into the red world while he slept, he felt he could easily go back whenever he wanted. But it was too experimental. There was no telling if he could ever get them back into the world of the living.

He still had four fully charged akorell stones, though, and that gave him an idea.

"Father, give the mages a minute of protection but be ready for my order to move."

"Better hurry!"

His father's voice faded to the back of Basen's thoughts as Henry ordered his men to change formation.

"Neeko, help Henry's troops. Penny, I need every mage with me behind cover."

"Back into cover!" she yelled as Neeko joined the fray. "Stay with Basen. Use the trees."

Basen led them back behind a couple rows of trees. "We're taking out all the energy from three of these akorell stones." He slid them onto his arms. "It's too much energy for me to handle on my own, so I need help from all of you to keep it steady as we add to it."

"Basen, mages do not train holding energy with each other. If one person pulls more than another, we could all lose control."

"It must be done," Basen told Penny. "They'll come behind us at any moment."

Penny looked behind them, then back at Henry's men.

"I *need* your cooperation," Basen said.

"All right. But no mage should take a firm hold," she told the team. "If your grasp slips while holding on with the full force of your mind, it might be too much of a jolt for the rest of us. Only take on what you can maintain easily."

Basen pulled out the energy from the first akorell stone. Although it was heavy, he had a good hold. The mages around him lifted their arms. They took the weight off his mind, but the white ball of energy began to shake. It started to the left, so everyone forced it to the right. Then it shot to the right, so everyone compensated again.

"Let me get it under control," Basen said. "Everyone else just hold on. Don't move it." He closed his mind around it like cupping his hands around a bee.

It fought to free itself but there were just too many mages holding it, as if they all had strings to the same kite. Basen easily overpowered it as his allies took most of its weight. The wobbles ceased. He released his hold.

"I'm going to draw out another," Basen said. "I'll move it into the first cluster, and that's exactly when all of us will grab hold of both together. For now, just hold onto the first."

He drew out the energy from the second akorell stone to form two equally bright clusters so silvery-white they acted as mirrors to the forest. Each were about the size of his fist. Bastial energy had a tendency to stay together, so he expected them to merge on their own as he moved his energy cluster close to the other.

But he had not expected the blast of light.

He flinched and almost lost his concentration. All he could see was white. He tried to rub it away so he could see the energy, as it felt out of control. When the forest came back into view, the size of the white cluster had nearly doubled. It shook as if it were trying to break out of a cage.

"I'll steady it!" Basen announced. Once again, he closed his mind around it until it stopped moving. Carefully, he released his hold.

The mages all began to groan as the strain wore on them.

"Basen," Penny said, "that's enough."

"It's not enough. There are hundreds of enemies who won't be affected by the explosion. I'm taking out the third now."

He drew out the energy and directed it toward the cluster. This time, he shut his eyes and turned his head. But the flash still felt like squinting into the sun. Tears formed that he quickly wiped away.

The energy was out of control.

It looked as if they'd taken a piece of a star out of the black sky and stuck it in the forest. It didn't belong here, shaking as if it might erupt. Basen's eyes burned as he forced himself to look at it to better gain control. The white darkened to orange, shifting quickly to red.

"Hold it!" Basen yelled. "I will steady it!"

It began to catch the leaves and branches on fire. Waves of heat blew out and singed Basen's face. He stepped back like everyone else, but the strain became almost unbearable.

There was no controlling this beast. *What was I thinking?* But they still had to feed sartious energy to it, then aim and release. It was impossible for two mages to shoot a single fireball at a target, and Basen expected twenty to work together? It might shoot straight down and kill them all or fly into the sky to eventually land in one of the cities.

No, it had to be only one person who took complete control. It could only be him.

He strained his mind to lift the energy, testing its strength against his own. It might just be for a moment, but he would manage to control it even if it broke him.

"I need everyone to let go one at a time, starting from the right side," Basen announced. "I'll take over."

"Basen, no one can hold that amount of energy!"

"I can. Penny, I'll need you to feed sartious energy to it when I'm the last one holding."

"Start releasing now!" Penny ordered.

"Releasing!" called the first mage down the line.

Basen felt no difference.

"Releasing," said the second.

Whoever this mage was had a good hold until then. The energy jolted before Basen got control.

They continued releasing one by one, soon passing by Basen in the center of the line. His body shook as every muscle clenched.

"Faster," he urged, as it felt as if his chest might collapse.

Three more released in three seconds, but it became too much. The energy was as red as the spiritual world, catching a nearby tree trunk aflame.

"Stop," Basen said. He could barely speak through the strain, his mind screaming to let go. "I need everyone left to release their hold on the count of three. Penny feeds it. I aim. Now, Henry, get them out of the way! One, two, three!"

Bastial energy could not sit still unless forced, so all Basen had to do was direct it at his enemies. It was like rolling a boulder down a hill, only he'd been holding the boulder with his mind.

He released and directed it as it caught flame. It traveled slower than Basen's other fireballs, but speed wasn't important here. The massive thing barely made it down the forest lane, bouncing between the edges of trunks and releasing small explosions every place it touched.

It finally came down among the lot of Ulric's troops too slow to get out of the way and exploded with a sound like the belch of a god. Fire burst out in every direction as if it had been awaiting its chance to escape. Trees cracked and began to fall as flames climbed up their burning limbs. Bodies spun up into the air.

A wave of hot air collected all the loose leaves and dust along the ground as it stormed past Henry's men and into the line of mages. Everyone turned and covered their faces.

Basen lost himself momentarily in the stunning display of destruction as a chunk of the forest was completely demolished. Fire raged everywhere around the crater.

"Now we run!" Penny yelled, bringing Basen back.

They took a wide path around the enemy army. Below the loud roar of flame and the sharp cracks of wood, Basen barely made out the sounds of screams as he watched for signs of retaliation.

There was no pursuit.

Basen and his allies made it back to the colony with time to spare, giving them the opportunity to cover their tracks near their hideout.

No one said a word as they made their way down the tunnel with mages illuminating it.

"How many did we lose?" Basen asked his father.

"Not many. Ulric's cowards were hesitant to approach."

They reached the bottom of the tunnel and waited, impatient and scared. Basen could feel it in the air, and he knew the others could, too. What if their enemies found them before Cleve and the Krepps came to meet them?

But no one spoke. No one complained about waiting.

Finally, the group with the Krepps arrived.

"Were you followed?" Basen asked Cleve.

"No. And now we know what they do during an attack. Let's go."

They rushed into the depths of the cavern until they reached the alcove with the akorell metal. Basen opened a portal for them to return to the city. He would be the last one to go through, but not before first enjoying a breath of relief. He marched into his portal with a proud grin.

CHAPTER THIRTY-ONE

The Krepps had spread out to spy on the northern camp during the attack on the wall. Cleve, Vithos, and Steffen had stayed nearby to help fight in case something went wrong. At least that's what Basen had told Rickik. The truth was that Basen's three designees—especially Vithos—were there to convince Rickik not to attack.

The army that had gone with Basen had lost two of Henry's soldiers and three mages. Basen promised himself their deaths would not be in vain. He was glad to be out of the forest and back in the headquarters where he couldn't hear the drumming soon to come. Wilfre's builders had done good work in the little time they'd been given. With interior walls and doors, the place was finally beginning to feel like a real building.

Basen's "quarters" were the first with a door inside the building, so he could have privacy while he paced and plotted, though he spoke with Rickik in the open.

"What did you see?"

Basen had become accustomed to a small audience listening in every time strategy was discussed. Instead of sleeping, many had come to the headquarters now to hear news of the attack.

"Tell him." Rickik slapped his hand down on his son's back.

"Two humans...I don't know the word. They went into the enemy camp in the forest on horse."

"They rode on horseback," Cleve corrected.

"Messengers. Rickik was closest."

"Is there any chance you were seen?" Basen asked the Krepp.

"No."

"Good. What else did you see?"

"Two humans rode south out of the camp on horseback," Nebre answered. "They were too fast to follow."

"I want kill them," Rickik said. "Easy."

"It's important that you didn't. They must've gone to find Rockbreak's hunting group, because the giant surprised us from the south."

The audience perked up, and Basen realized that most were here just for these details. He breezed through them as quickly as he could until he suddenly remembered an important detail. "Abith was there. He helped us get into better position."

Henry asked, "Are you sure it was him? Did you actually see him?"

Penny confirmed, "I was close enough. It was definitely him."

A few of her mages agreed for good measure.

"Rockbreak sent men after him. He had to run, so he couldn't join us." Basen looked at Rickik. "Do you wish to return to the forest?"

"Yes. I kill who kill Krepps."

"I'll be with them," Cleve volunteered.

Vithos and Steffen did as well.

"If you see Abith, bring him back to the Slugari colony at night and wait for the portal," Basen directed. "That goes for any other allies you find out there. I don't know how they've survived this long in the forest on their own, but they deserve to be here with us."

Wilfre made a face. "But if Rockbreak has only the Krepps to hunt in the forest, they'll realize we're elsewhere."

Basen didn't have to say anything. The collective complaints of the audience made Wilfre put up his hands. "All right, they should join us if they can."

Basen fetched one of the two akorell stones he hadn't brought. "I'm going to need to make a portal to Oakshen to get the report from Effie and Gabby soon. I know we're exhausted, but can any mages help me by charging this?"

Three volunteered. Basen thanked them.

He asked Nebre, "What else can you tell me about the horsemen you saw?"

"I saw none of them. Rickik saw all." He asked his father a question in Kreppen. Rickik appeared confused and responded with a question of his own. Nebre shook his head as if he, too, was perplexed.

"Neither of us know what you want to find out," he told Basen.

"I'm asking what other details you noticed."

"They humans on horses," Rickik said, leaning over as if about to spit. But he straightened and swallowed with a sour face. "No other..."

"Details," Nebre finished the sentence for him. "We still don't know what you mean. They were just two men on horses."

"I'll be more specific. Were the first group of messengers different than the second?"

"No know," Rickik answered.

"Are the rest of you certain you didn't see them?" Basen asked dubiously.

Rickik thumped his chest and glared. "Best eyes in Krepps."

"They rode right below him while he was hidden in a tree," Nebre added.

"I might've seen one horseman," Steffen said. "Or it could've been my imagination."

Basen sighed as he realized he'd only be dealing with Rickik. "What were they wearing?"

Rickik understood this question and seemed excited to answer as he smiled and pinched Basen's shirt.

"Human clothing."

Basen refrained from sighing again.

"Was it a tunic like this or the enemy uniform that we've seen before?"

Nebre translated, but Rickik just looked more confused.

"He doesn't know," Nebre reported.

"Was there a symbol of any kind? What about color?"

In response, Rickik gritted his crocodile-like teeth.

Basen went to his quarters and fetched the enemy uniform he'd worn into the castle. "Did it look exactly like this or different?"

"Different." Rickik transitioned into Kreppen and spoke to Nebre for a long while. Nebre's yellow eyes widened as he seemed to come to an understanding.

"It was the same as that uniform," Nebre said. "Except there was a bird on their back."

"The Takary sigil of spread wings?" Basen asked.

"No, a full bird. I don't know the name."

"*Jiya*," said Rickik.

"The Kreppen word doesn't help me. Wilfre, can you get them some ink and parchment so they can draw it?"

He nodded and walked off.

"I don't draw well," Nebre said.

"We just need a sketch. Collaborate with your father to make sure the position and size of the bird are as accurate as possible. Someone with more skill to draw can create a better version by working with the two of you."

"I'll do it," Steffen said. "I see where you're going with this, Basen. If we can't get it almost exactly as it was on the scout's back, we won't use it."

"I don't get it," Cleve said. "Why do you need to know?"

"It's not just their exact clothing we need." Basen lifted his hand to regain Rickik and Nebre's attention as the Krepps spoke to each other. "We also need the height and age of the scouts, and if they had any weapons with them. What about their horses? What color and how big?"

Nebre translated. Rickik clawed his chin softly as they spoke. Finally, Nebre gave an answer.

"Two small men on large horses. Not old but not young."

"Smaller than me?" Basen asked, as he was about average height.

"I think same," Rickik answered. "Young to father, but...old to Basen." He looked to Nebre and spoke in Kreppen.

"Only a few years older than you, he thinks."

"Weapons?" Basen asked.

"None."

"Steffen, can you and Nebre write down all of these details?"

"I still don't understand," Cleve said.

Basen brought him and Vithos toward the audience as father and son stayed with Steffen.

"The Krepps might not find what we're doing honorable," Basen noted, "so it's better we don't discuss it with them until they've given us all the details they can."

Cleve's head tilted back. "Oh. I understand now."

Vithos grinned as he shook his finger. "Sneaky, Basen. I like."

*****

Effie and Gabby reported gaining the trust of hundreds of spies in Oakshen. It wasn't so much that they'd gathered rebels. They'd just given them a cause. Part of the sisters' mission was to watch the wall around the time of the attack. They reported the same thing as Rickik: two men leaving the city on horseback. They had something embroidered on the back shoulder of their uniform, but neither Effie nor Gabby was close enough to see any details. Eventually Steffen came to Basen with a drawing of a hawk. He told Basen that Rickik was certain it looked just like this. Basen hoped Millry could replicate it with her needle and thread.

The following days passed quickly. Dressed in an

enemy uniform, Basen walked to the back wall of the castle during the night. He gathered energy until he noticed a guard catching sight of him, then drunkenly pretended to be looking for a place to relieve himself. He went back to his home district, then sent another mage who could fit in a uniform to continue drawing energy behind the castle.

Jack had gathered the supplies he needed to make a potion that would slowly disintegrate stone. Each time a mage in an enemy uniform returned to the castle at night, he or she would pour a little more of the potion onto the same spot.

The officers in charge of each group of spies continued to get logistical information about their enemies. Basen learned where Ulric's soldiers tended to go on business, where they went for pleasure, and most importantly, the areas of each city they neglected. They'd soon collected so much information that Basen needed more than just Wilfre's help to use it to their best advantage for a final plan.

"I need your guidance," Basen told his father one day. Henry had organized all the rebels in Trentyre, when Tauwin had just come to power, to successfully defend the city even though they were outnumbered. Such experience would be invaluable now, Basen was certain.

Henry appeared delighted by Basen's request, though his prideful expression slowly changed to a look of concentration as Basen reminded Henry of everything he hoped to accomplish. By the end, Henry had the same embarrassing grin as when he'd put the medal around Basen's neck in Redfield.

"It sounds like you don't need my help at all. You have this under control."

"But I don't know what to do about the northern district in Oakshen that the guards completely ignore. The people there are just as frustrated as they are in our district. I'm sure we can use them somehow."

"As you said earlier, there is risk in recruiting, even if the people want to join."

"But if we supplied them with swords, it could add three hundred more to fight with us."

"Let me tell you a secret. The day Tauwin took over the castle, I didn't have a plan like yours. All I cared about was recruiting and getting them somewhere to mount a defense. When Trentyre came under attack the first time, we didn't need to find a way to recruit. Everyone who wanted to fight came to us. When you take the fight to Ulric, they will join you just the same."

"So you don't recommend we attempt to get the message to them before we strike."

"No, it's too risky. Trust that they want the same thing as you—they will jump at the opportunity you create for them."

Basen thought for a while. "What if we give them a hundred swords right before the attack and tell them to get ready?"

"Now there's an idea."

Basen never would've figured it could be that simple. He began to think differently about some of his other problems and came up with similar solutions, all involving trust of the citizenry without needing to prepare them.

However, there was one problem that couldn't be

made simpler. If he didn't get his mother out of the Academy soon, she would be in danger. Crea Hiller was not in her castle; only her sister had been there. Basen could feel that Crea was at the Academy. He wanted to go there and kill her for setting up this betrayal that led to so many deaths, but he would have to wait until just before the final battle.

Basen spent most of his days bouncing ideas off Wilfre and speaking with the officers. He received reports from Effie and Gabby about Oakshen, reports from everyone else about the capital, and reports from Cleve about the forest. Trentyre went ignored, as there was no hope of getting anyone in and out of the city without being seen. It shouldn't matter in the end.

All walls and floors of the headquarters had been rebuilt. The workers focused on beds next, offering to build Basen's first. He told Neeko that he had a place to sleep already. Alabell always waited up for him.

Cleve became more inquisitive about the plan each night he reported in, and eventually he asked to speak privately in Basen's quarters.

"I want to check on Reela and Annah. No one has heard anything about them."

Basen frowned, wishing he didn't have to explain what he'd told Cleve days ago.

"I know I can't go because my size makes me too conspicuous," Cleve agreed. "But you're already sending mages in enemy uniforms to the castle at night. One might be able to find out something."

Basen opened his mouth to object, but Cleve put up his hand.

"Or if there was some other idea you could come up with. A better one."

"I'm worried about them as well, but it's too dangerous for anyone to go inside the castle or ask about them from outside. If Ulric finds out someone from the Academy is wearing an enemy's uniform within the city, the entire capital will be searched. Sending the mage at night is a risk as well but not as big as trying to find out about Reela and Annah."

"I know what you're planning with the castle. I see that it's necessary, but what is to happen with Reela and Annah if they are within the castle during that time?" Basen was thankful only to hear worry in Cleve's voice instead of judgment.

"I haven't decided for certain. I need more time. But I promise that Reela and Annah will be made aware if we can't get them out first."

"All right, I trust you." Cleve seemed as satisfied as one could be with such a worrisome topic. "I have one other request."

"Anything."

"There aren't enough of us in the forest to continue to give the impression that our army is still there, and it's becoming more difficult to catch our enemies unaware. We need more in these final days, enough to attack the damaged wall sporadically and make it appear that we're trying to break into the city."

"How many more do you need?"

"As many mages and psychics as possible and whatever swordsmen are available."

Cleve probably didn't realize the difficult spot he'd

just put Basen in.

"Cleve, a certain number of mages, psychics, and swordsmen will be required soon. If too many of them fall before we're ready, we won't be able to win this war. I don't want to ask you for the minimum number of men required to keep yourselves alive as you fight, but neither can I give you everyone available. If something goes wrong out there and many of us die, that would be it for everyone. Allow me to speak to Wilfre to look at our numbers again, and I'll give you as many as can be spared."

"That's fair."

"You're still able to feed the febeetles?"

"Every day they feast on the flesh of our enemies. I like to believe they've acquired a strong taste for bastard men and should ravage our enemies when the time comes."

Basen grinned. "Did Cleve the Beastslayer just make a joke?"

Cleve confirmed it with a rise of his eyebrows and a twinkle in his eyes.

"Be careful out there," Basen said. "Ulric and his officers are smart. They might leave one part of the wall unguarded to lure you there as a trap."

"We will stay safe."

"Good."

"I must admit," Cleve said, "you've given me hope."

He gave Basen a heartfelt look, but Basen could see the anger burning just beneath it. Revenge had motivated Cleve until now, Basen realized. The warrior probably would've died to achieve it, even figured he would. Now all that had changed, and he was thanking Basen for it.

Basen didn't know what he was supposed to say to fill this silence. Perhaps Cleve didn't expect him to say anything.

Eventually Cleve extended his hand. They reached past each other's palms to grab arms. Cleve's was like smooth rock, a warrior down to his soul. Basen would've feared for the lives of his enemies if he'd had even a bit of empathy for them.

CHAPTER THIRTY-TWO

Alabell was often writing by lamplight by the time Basen came to her room to sleep. Although always curious, Basen figured she'd tell him what it was if she wanted him to know. Besides, he was usually more exhausted than curious, so he never asked. But this night, she was looking out her window and didn't seem to hear him come in.

She turned when he shut the door. They usually greeted each other with the kind of kiss that led to them intertwined on top of the sheets, but Alabell had a serious look in her eyes.

"Are you going to the Academy for your mother tomorrow?"

"Yes." He'd told Alabell of his plan days ago. She hadn't disagreed, but she'd paused before telling him it seemed sound.

They hadn't discussed it since, and he hoped she wouldn't have a problem now that he was so close to leaving. He wasn't sure anything could convince him to change his mind at this point, no matter how much he might agree there were potential problems.

"Neither you nor Sanya can explore the campus to look for your mother," she said. "Both of you could be recognized."

"Not so much Sanya. I didn't recognize her the first time I'd seen her since Tenred."

"But if Ulric has sent any of his men to the Academy, they just need to glance at her and there would be no way to get Juliana out of there."

"I realize that is one of many risks. It's why we'll go at night. With Sanya's psyche, she should be able to avoid people as she looks for my mother."

"But it's even more likely that someone would recognize Sanya as an outsider if she's creeping around the campus in the dark."

"What are you getting at?" Basen asked.

"Someone else should go with you two."

"Who?"

She looked down for just a blink, losing confidence for the quickest of moments. It was enough to tell Basen the answer.

"Alabell, no."

"There's no one better for the task. You need someone who knows the Academy well enough to figure out where Juliana might be kept. It needs to be someone who will recognize your mother upon sight, and who wouldn't be recognized by the people of Tenred. I'm the only one who fits all three categories. And don't tell me how dangerous it is. I've already spent days building up the courage. I want to go."

"I won't tell you how dangerous it is," Basen agreed. "But there's something you're not thinking about. Even though no one from Tenred knows you, the chances they'll realize you're an outsider are higher than them recognizing Sanya."

"But why?"

"Because of how beautiful you are." She scoffed. He put up his palms. "I'm not just saying that to flatter you. I mean it in an unbiased way; you are strikingly beautiful.

Most men—and some women, no doubt—would notice you immediately as someone their eyes hadn't had the pleasure of seeing before."

"You're exaggerating."

"I'm really not."

She walked over to put herself in front of the mirror on her desk. She turned her face to every angle as if seeing it for the first time.

"You only think that," she said, "because I put in the effort to look good for you. I can make myself uglier for tomorrow."

"I sincerely doubt it, but you can try and we'll decide then."

He removed his shirt and got into bed. She stood at her side of the bed with arms akimbo as if she wanted to continue the conversation but eventually sighed and slid in next to him. She nuzzled against his side. He moved his arm around her to pull her even closer.

"Is there ever an opportunity to compliment me that you let pass?"

"Every time I look at you, I have to resist the urge to spew out expletives about your appearance."

She chuckled and gave him a playful swat. "Like what?"

"The usual stuff you might hear walking past a bar while showing skin late at night."

"No!" she objected with a high to low pitch. "Words that crude go through your mind?"

"On occasion."

"Have you ever told a girl any of these thoughts?"

"You're the only one who makes me think them."

She was silent for a moment, and Basen wondered if he'd said too much.

"I can't tell if I find that funny and adorable or slightly disturbing. I think I'm going to need an example."

"I don't think so."

"I insist."

Basen took in a breath as he sat up, then looked her up and down with a lustful gleam. "God's mercy!" She had already begun to laugh as she tried to shush him. But that only made him get louder. "If I'm dreaming this body, let me never wake up! Oh sweet god, stop all future work because *she* is perfection!"

Alabell shushed louder as she tried to muffle him with her pillow.

"I would be her...twwaaallii...if she...mmrra fuur." He lay down and turned away in hopes of escaping her pillow, but she kept it against his face.

"The whole tavern can hear you at this hour!"

He didn't move or speak. She took off the pillow.

"I should not have asked you for an example. Basen? Basen." She shook him. "Stop pretending to be dead."

"But you have killed me. The only thing that can bring me back to life is THAT SWEET NAKED...brrroii." She muffled his mouth again as she laughed.

*****

Sanya had not felt nerves like this since her declaration of joining Kyrro's Allies at Redfield. All she had to do was find Juliana and get her back to Basen, who would be waiting at the Group One training grounds. Juliana might be guarded or just watched. In both cases, Sanya would have to kill again. That wasn't the issue. In fact, she had come to enjoy killing her enemies. It was the thought of encountering Crea that filled her with worry.

She ate her breakfast as slowly as she could. They wouldn't leave until night, and Sanya had nothing to do until then. Her only form of entertainment, Greg, had been taken from her by Henry. It had been a week since she'd seen him, but the taste of his lips returned every time she noticed the light stain of blood on her pants. She knew she should've gone to see him by now to tell him to stop looking for her, but she couldn't bring herself to do it.

Sanya scoffed at her own thoughts. He was probably chasing some other woman by now anyway.

Basen and Alabell came down the stairs together. They drew a few smirks from other rebels packed in the tavern, not that Sanya knew why. The only available places to sit were near Sanya, and Basen and Alabell took the spots in front of her without hesitance, to Sanya's surprise.

Alabell looked as if she hadn't slept well. Her cheeks sagged as if it was too much effort for her skin to stick tightly against bone. Her eyes appeared smaller, less vibrant. She wore a shirt too big for her body. She looked as uninteresting as this undecorated eating room.

Basen took his first spoonful of porridge, then said, "Alabell's coming with us. It'll be the two of you who retrieve my mother. Let her lead and talk to anyone who questions you. You're there for her protection."

Sanya shrugged. "All right."

Basen and Alabell looked at each other in surprise. He glanced back at Sanya.

"And we're leaving right after breakfast. It's better than going during the night."

"Good." Not wanting them to see how nervous she was, she quickly finished her food and left.

It wasn't long before Basen and Alabell arrived in the basement. As word spread that they were leaving for the Academy now, a group of students with nothing better to do gathered around to wish Basen and Alabell luck. Sanya leaned against the far wall with her arms folded. Not a single person so much as glanced her way. Out of curiosity, she read their psyche to find they were all aware of her behind them, but they didn't know what to say.

Basen and Alabell were the only two people who felt anything for Sanya. They worried, mostly, and wanted her to be happy. She was thankful to be going to the Academy with the two of them and no one else who saw Sanya only as a weapon. But she feared that an encounter with Crea would turn the last two people who cared about her against her.

"Sanya," Basen called. The crowd parted to let her through. "We finally have enough spare akorell stones for you to practice." He handed her one of the bracelets.

An immense fear flooded out from everyone's psyche as Sanya put on the akorell bracelet. They didn't want her making portals like Basen, even if she would use them to help. They didn't trust her with that kind of power.

She handed back the bracelet. "You have portal

making under control."

He looked confused as he accepted the bracelet back.

"They don't want this," she whispered.

His face took on a disappointed expression as he understood. "We'll talk later," he whispered.

"No, it's fine." It wouldn't matter. She could steal an akorell stone when the time came to leave, then practice on her own.

Basen opened the portal. The students called out "clear" from each angle. Sanya went in first. She'd grown to like the sense of freedom of leaving the basement, even when Basen's portal spat her out across the sand and gave her a sick feeling in her stomach. Alabell and Basen followed as Sanya got up and brushed herself off.

Alabell seemed too distracted by the blackened walls of the training grounds to realize she had sand stuck to her knees. Sanya wiped it off her.

"We can't have people thinking we've been rolling around in the dirt. Let's go. The longer it takes to find Juliana, the greater the chances we'll be caught."

"It's hard to believe we're back here that quickly." Alabell took in a long breath as if the air was sweeter here. "I forgot how much I missed this place."

"I'll wait here," Basen said. He had on the uniform of one of Ulric's troops. It would buy him time if someone found him here, though he would probably have to kill whoever discovered him to keep from being caught.

"You lead," Sanya told Alabell. "Go."

"Right." Alabell walked out of the training grounds with the small bag on her back swaying with each step.

It didn't take long for them to realize that there was

no one around any of the mage or psychic classrooms. In fact, from here the entire Academy seemed empty. They made their way north. Sanya had only a dagger in a holster on her leg, hidden by her pants, but she was still confident she could kill anyone who discovered them so long as it wasn't a mage or an archer who got the jump.

There was no hidden way to the northern side of the campus, so they took the main road and soon came to Warrior's Field. She and Alabell still saw no one.

"We have to figure out if the school has been deserted before we find ourselves stumbling into somewhere we can't escape from," Alabell said. "Let's check on the gardens and the farms. If the animals are still alive, there must be people here tending to them. If not, the Academy is likely abandoned."

Sanya followed her east. Alabell kept them as hidden as she could now, taking a route through the mage and psychic classrooms. Sanya smelled the animals before she saw them.

Alabell took them south before they came out onto any roads. She climbed on top of a psychic classroom and Sanya followed. They got down on their bellies and crawled to the edge to overlook the gardens and farms. Sanya could make out people working among the plants and animals sectioned off by fences as Alabell got the spyglass out of her bag and took a look.

"I recognize many of them," she said. "They're the same Academy staff from before. Hopefully that means Juliana is still alive and working in the kitchen."

"Do you see anyone guarding them?" Sanya asked.

Alabell looked for a while. "Two men in Tenred

uniforms."

"Can we get around them?" The dining hall was all the way on the northern side of the campus, but it was large enough for Sanya to make out from here.

"Not without being seen but perhaps without being scrutinized."

"You should leave the bag and spyglass here on the roof. They might search us."

"I can explain the spyglass and bag better than you can explain your dagger."

But Sanya couldn't stand the thought of parting with her weapon. "Let's wait here first and see what we can observe."

"That's a good idea. We should watch what they do during lunch. We might get lucky and spot Juliana."

Sanya turned on her back and put her arm over her eyes to shield herself from the sun. "Tell me when you want me to take over."

"Basen's going to be worried when he doesn't hear from us," Alabell muttered.

"Is he stupid enough to come looking for us?"

"I don't think so."

Sanya fell asleep eventually. She awoke to Alabell rousing her. "I need a break."

"What did you see?"

"People working, nothing else."

Sanya took watch as Alabell took her turn napping. There was nothing of interest. Sanya soon grew bored, but she remained vigilant.

An hour passed. Sanya had tried every position imaginable to continue looking out over the ledge of the roof without sitting up, but she could no longer find any comfort. She was just about to wake Alabell, when she noticed movement to the east.

The two uniforms hurried toward the gate. The workers stopped to gawk as the soldiers got it open and a single man walked through. Alabell awoke and shifted to lie on her stomach beside Sanya.

"What's happening?"

"I'm not sure."

Basen's voice asked from somewhere below, "Alabell is that you?"

"Yes."

Sanya heard him climbing up the back of the building. As Alabell went to offer him help, Sanya kept watching ahead. The uniform of the third man was dirty as if he'd had a long trek to get here. Perhaps he'd been taken in for questioning by Ulric's men controlling the Fjallejon Pathway. The other two men took him north across the farm as he removed a scroll from his bag.

"It seems like a messenger has come," Sanya told Alabell and Basen as they went down on their stomachs beside her. "What are you doing here, Basen?"

"I feared something had happened, so I went looking for you. I couldn't find you, so I started watching the workers. Then I heard your voices."

"Is that Crea?" Alabell asked.

"Yes," Sanya said. She'd come out of the dining hall to greet the messenger. "He's handing her the scroll."

"Have you seen my mother?" Basen asked.

"Not yet," Alabell said. "We were going to wait until lunch to see what happens. She might leave the dining hall afterward, and that would be our best chance."

Crea suddenly began to shout at the messenger. He backed up a step and lowered his head. Crea went on screaming at no one in particular. She threw down the scroll and kicked the fence of the farm, scaring the pigs and chickens in nearby pens.

"She must've just heard about the money you and Basen stole," Alabell said.

Blood rushed to Sanya's face. Unable to watch what she knew was coming, she handed Alabell the spyglass as Crea stormed toward the dining hall.

Basen shouldn't be here for this.

Crea screamed something over her shoulder. The three uniforms ran to catch up.

"We'd better get closer," Sanya said.

"God's mercy," Basen said, "she's going for my mother, isn't she?"

Alabell gasped.

"Yes." Sanya climbed down the front of the building.

"They'll see us," Alabell warned, though she and Basen climbed down anyway.

"No one will notice until it's too late." They hurried down the road beside the garden.

Everyone had stopped work to stare as Crea pulled Juliana out of the back of the dining hall by her hair. Chains around her ankles forced her to take small steps to keep up. She fell several times, reaching up to grab Crea's arms but stopping herself as if worried about further punishment.

One of the uniforms tried to console Crea as he put his hand on her back, but she elbowed him in the side and shrieked in fury. The Academy workers murmured to each other as they moved in haste toward Crea, but none did or said anything to the enraged Hiller.

Sanya stopped just behind the workers. She knelt to retrieve her dagger and hid it up her sleeve as best she could. More uniforms arrived, circling around Crea with worried expressions matching those of the Academy staff.

Crea walked over to the nearest uniform and grabbed the sword out of his sheath. Juliana started to back away as Crea stomped toward her with a rabid look.

"Hold her," Crea demanded.

"She did nothing wrong," a farmer objected.

"Anyone who says anything will be next after her. Hold her!" Crea pointed at two guards, who took Juliana by her thin arms. She struggled as they easily pushed her down to her knees.

"This is an overreaction, even for Crea," Basen muttered as he looked panicked about what to do. "It doesn't make sense. She wouldn't kill my mother for our theft, would she?"

"Crea, don't do this," Juliana pleaded. "It won't help anything."

Crea didn't slow as she plodded closer. "Juliana Hiller, you are to pay for the crimes of your son."

Just as Sanya was about to ask Basen for the plan, he ran out from the crowd. "Ulric has urgent news, Crea!"

Glancing over, she appeared too preoccupied to recognize Basen in uniform, but she certainly would at any moment.

"What?"

"The capital is under attack! Ulric needs your troops

now!"

Crea straightened as confusion twisted her face. "Why isn't a wall guard with you?"

"They are slow and I'm fast. Hurry!"

"After I kill this woman for her son's crimes." She turned back to Juliana and brought back her arms.

Basen drew his wand. "Get out of the way!"

Crea looked over, unsure what to make of his order. Juliana seized her opportunity to twist out of the grasp of the confused men of Tenred. She stumbled away from them as Basen cast a fireball. It exploded into the dirt just in front of the group, sending Crea into a backward tumble.

Basen sprinted to his mother and lifted her over his shoulder before anyone could tell what was happening.

"It's Basen!" Crea screamed. "And that's *Sanya* with him! Don't let her out."

Sanya pained the three nearest uniforms and started after Crea with her dagger. But the Hiller ran the opposite way with eyes full of fear. That didn't stop her from yelling, "You will die for what you've done!"

Sanya turned and fled, soon catching up to her party.

"What did you do?" Juliana asked.

"Just stole some money from the castle," Basen answered. He began to slow as he huffed for breath. "We won't make it."

"Let me help." Sanya grabbed Juliana by her legs as she, Basen, and Alabell ran sideways.

"Leave me," Juliana said. "It's the only way you'll make it out."

"We'll kill them," Sanya said as she stopped to face

their pursuers. "There are only six."

But as soon as she'd finished speaking, swordsmen and archers flooded out from the dining hall. Crea yelled for them to stop Sanya from leaving.

"We run!" Alabell shouted.

Sanya got her arms underneath Juliana's rear this time. But even with the three of them carrying the woman, they couldn't run as fast as they needed.

"Around the southern side of the psychic classrooms," Alabell directed. "We might be able to lose them for long enough to get to a mage training ground."

Alabell was right—Basen should be able to make a portal from any training ground. They ran between the buildings. Sanya kept out a constant net of psyche and soon felt the enemy closing in behind them.

The first to arrive was an archer, but they took a left at the next opening to block his view. A swordsman was next, jumping out in front to intercept them. Sanya sent him to the ground with psyche as they veered right to avoid his fallen body.

They didn't get far before two more swordsmen and an archer confronted them. Alabell stopped while Basen tried to keep going, causing Juliana to fall. Sanya tried to floor the three enemies blocking their path, but she could only cause them to scream as exhaustion sapped most of her strength.

The archer lifted his bow through the pain, nocked an arrow, and shot. Alabell ducked as Basen seemed to be unaware, scooping up his mother. The arrow missed high as the swordsmen rushed toward them.

"They're coming from behind and from the sides,"

Sanya announced as she felt their presence with psyche.

Basen gave up trying to lift his mother, and she hobbled backward to escape the swordsmen about to run their blades through her and Alabell. She was about to back up into another enemy when Sanya flung open the window of the psychic classroom beside them.

"In here." She pained the three swordsmen, this time severely enough to knock them down.

"Come on, Mother." Basen took her hand. "Go, Alabell."

Sanya felt an arrow zip over her shoulder as she was the last one in. She shut the window onto an enemy's reaching hand. He screamed and fell back. Another reached in and grabbed Sanya by the wrist before she could get the window shut. She went for her dagger to stab him, only to realize she must've dropped it before helping to carry Juliana.

He screamed and convulsed as she pained him, and finally let go. The archer appeared next with no intention of coming in the window as he aimed his arrow.

"Get down," Sanya yelled.

The arrow shattered the glass but missed its mark, leaving a crack in the wall near Alabell.

"Move, Sanya!" Basen called as he aimed his wand.

She dove out of the way as he shot. There was a thud as the archer yelped, heat coming back in through the window to brush over Sanya's head.

"The far window!" Sanya announced as she felt someone moving toward it.

Basen shot just as the man got it open. The glass shattered as he screamed.

"Toward the middle!" Sanya called. But no one appeared.

"He's moving to the far end," she said. "Crawling below the windows."

Basen held his wand ready. An archer popped up as if to shoot through the window. Basen shot first and broke it, but the archer had spun out of the way. He returned right away and was about to shoot when Sanya hit him with a spell of pain. He crumpled out of sight.

Although three windows were broken, the shards of glass remaining around the edges would keep anyone from getting through quickly. Every other wall was solid. The door to the classroom stood between the windows.

"They're gathering around the edges," Sanya whispered. "About ten of them."

"How far to the nearest training grounds?" Basen asked.

"Not far," Alabell said. "We could get there quickly if we could run."

"How long would it take while going the speed my mother can walk?" Basen asked. "We could fight our way there."

"Minutes."

"I have no weapon," Sanya reminded them. "And they have archers."

"If you can pain them all—"

"We still might not make it," Sanya interrupted Basen. "They could be gathering right now to stop our escape. There's no way to know how many they have."

"Break the chain," Alabell said. She picked up a chair and gave it to Sanya. "You're stronger than I am. Basen can watch the windows."

Juliana's face blanched as she stood against the far wall. She spread her feet as far as she could, a little longer than Sanya's hand, and Sanya slammed one leg of the chair down onto the chain.

She heard Basen cast at someone and turned to see an archer spinning away from the window. The bowman tried to line up a shot after the fireball, but Sanya crippled him with pain. He fell forward into the shards of glass and got caught. Basen shot again and ended his screaming as he blew the archer away.

Sanya slammed the chair leg against the chain over and over, but it did nothing.

"I have an idea," Alabell whispered. "Basen, stand at the front of the classroom and see if you can feel for a portal. Psychics duel each other up there."

Basen watched the windows as he sidestepped over to put himself beside the lecturing podium. "Nothing."

"We just need to find the right classroom. One where powerful psychics have battled frequently enough."

"Which one would that be?" Basen asked.

"I don't know."

Sanya could feel the minds of at least twenty people now, though she couldn't locate their exact locations through the walls. "We can't make it to another classroom."

Crea announced, "The building is surrounded, and every building around here is surrounded as well! You cannot escape!"

"Is it true?" Basen whispered.

"I don't know," Sanya said as her throat went dry.

"She's too far and there's too much in the way."

"We will let the rest of you walk out of here if Sanya comes out without resistance," Crea continued.

The three of them glanced at Sanya with confusion. She couldn't hide the dread any longer as she swallowed a lump.

"Sanya, what did you do?" Basen whispered.

"I'm sorry."

Someone tossed in a pair of chains with open shackles.

"Sanya will put the shackles around her wrists and ankles and come out first," Crea said. "The rest of you will be free to leave afterward. That's the only way you will live."

"Come closer and say that again," Sanya called back. "Tell me exactly who's going to live."

There was a pause, then Crea's voice rang out from just beside the last window. "If you come out shackled, then Basen, Juliana, and whoever that younger woman is will live. If you try to resist, all of you will die eventually."

"You didn't follow the plan," Basen muttered to Sanya in anger.

"I did."

"But you must've done something we hadn't discussed!"

Crea yelled, "There is no other way out of this building alive!"

"The truth doesn't matter," Basen whispered in a lie as he watched the windows. "We're going to have to fight our way out."

"Basen…" Alabell paused as she stared into Sanya's eyes. "We…we won't make it."

"She's right. And this is my fault," Sanya admitted.

There was a long moment of silence.

Sanya announced, "I'm going to put on the chains now!"

"Don't," Basen said. "Give me time to think."

"There's nothing to think about. I couldn't stop myself, Basen. I knew right before I did it that this might happen, and I let myself do it anyway." She put the shackles around her ankles. "Crea's telling the truth. She'll let the rest of you live."

"Why, Sanya?" Basen asked, no doubt realizing by then what she had done.

The answer to this, Sanya announced to everyone. "Gayla knew exactly what my father was doing to my sister with his experiments. She knew that he killed her! She didn't say one thing to her father to stop mine, even when he began experimenting on me. Gayla needed to be punished. I stabbed her in the stomach and let fate decide whether she would live or die. She must've had a slow and painful death for the message to get to you only now, Crea! She must've been in terrible pain, and you deserve the same!"

What was she doing? Anger had taken control.

"Sanya..." Basen wiped away a tear. "I can't help you now. You should've told me this earlier." Anger crossed his face with his next breath. "My mother would've been killed because of your actions."

Realizing that this would be the end, Sanya felt a sudden peace as she took the tiny money pouch from her pocket. She tossed it to Basen but could say nothing to explain, or Crea would hear and seize it back.

It didn't matter. Basen understood as he opened it to find the three acrowns. "You were going to leave."

"Only once this was over."

"Come out, Sanya," Crea demanded.

"You will let the rest of my party go first and will not follow them. Then I will come out."

"Fine. None of you will be harmed except Sanya. It's her I want."

Alabell stood in front of Sanya, seemingly unsure what to do. Eventually she grabbed Sanya in what felt to be an angry embrace. Juliana cried, staring deeply into Sanya's eyes as she walked past her. Sanya felt a burst of empathy, of complete understanding of her pain. Pushing all of these feelings to the surface were needles of guilt, breaking through the blanket of emotion and causing physical pain.

"It's all right, Juliana," Sanya said. "I figured this day would come."

Basen stood in front of Sanya with a mixture of anger and sadness as his lips pressed together tightly. "I wish I'd known the truth earlier. About everything."

"Don't blame yourself. My choices have led me here."

"Come on," Alabell said as she pulled Basen toward the door. She opened it for them and walked out. Juliana followed. Sanya put the last shackles around her wrists and came out to face Crea. The woman looked as if she'd been waiting for her dinner for too long and now that it had finally come, her anger had ruined her appetite.

Sanya spat in her face.

CHAPTER THIRTY-THREE

Basen said only one thing when they returned to headquarters. "Give me some time." He locked himself in his room. It was clear they could retake the Academy today and save Sanya, but was there any way to do it without eventually losing the war? He raced through each possible outcome. In the basement outside his quarters he could hear Alabell telling everyone what had happened. He blocked it out as he paced around in thought.

He always came back to the same conclusion. Yes, they could attack the Academy to free Sanya and take back the school if they wanted, but it would cost them their advantage of position and surprise. Ulric would become aware that they could get their armies out of the forest through a portal, as there was no other way around the enemy camp on the northern side of the forest. Every city would be searched for other rebels. Citizens would be questioned and possibly hurt or killed for information. The only way to get Sanya and keep everyone alive would be to first gather everyone loyal to the rebels and take them *all* to the Academy. Then this would turn into a war of numbers, a war they could not win.

Someone knocked. "Basen?"

He let Alabell inside.

"Have you come up with something?" she asked.

"No, and we're running out of time. It won't be long before Crea kills her. She's probably being tortured right now."

"Basen, this might feel impossible to accept, but Sanya chose to sacrifice herself."

"Yet I keep thinking about what I would do if it were you instead, and there would be no hesitation to go back with an army."

"I wouldn't want you to if it meant losing the war. Would you want me to come for you?"

He let out his breath. "No, but that doesn't mean I'm ready to give up on her yet."

"All right. Take as much time as you need."

She left him with his thoughts. If he could just get Sanya out of the Academy then they wouldn't need to retake it. He could go back with a small team and break her out. But it would be clear Basen could make a portal when betrayers chased his group back to the mage training grounds and watched him disappear into one. Still, he had to try.

He flung his door open and stalked out into the basement. Basen needed to get in contact with the team in the forest. He would teleport to the Slugari colony and look for them...but he had no idea where they were.

Would Cleve and Vithos even be willing to risk everything to retrieve Sanya?

No, they most definitely wouldn't. Would anyone else be willing to help? Only if Basen forced them to, which he couldn't bring himself to do.

He felt tears wet his eyes. He forced a smile as he watched his father reunite with his mother. No one would know that his tears were not for his family but for Sanya. She had suffered every day since this began, and if she was still alive, she would be in terrible pain until her last breath. He'd been feeling more pity for her than anger, as she seemed to be completely hopeless. This had finally pushed him over the limit of emotion he could handle.

"Basen, let's not let Juliana suffer in chains one moment longer." Henry didn't even notice they'd come back with one fewer.

"We'll get them off right away."

*****

Juliana eagerly offered to help Millry feed so many mouths just after Henry finished explaining everything he and Basen had set up. His mother gave Basen a kiss, told him she was proud, then put herself to work. She looked as if she was trying to smile, but there was no doubt in Basen's mind that her guilt about not saving Sanya from her father was the cause of her tears.

Basen spent the rest of the day getting information to his officers in preparation for tomorrow. By now, Basen knew his enemies almost as well as they knew themselves. He knew which soldiers were expected to patrol which districts of each city, who would be guarding the walls at different times, and who was sent out to the forest to provide supplies or fresh troops. He was aware of who had horses and even what kind of soldiers were in each spot: mages, archers, or swordsmen.

There was one key piece of information still lacking. Where were the enemy psychics? There were only two ways to find them. One was listening to the soldiers discussing their psychic comrades rather impolitely in bars, taverns, brothels, and even while strolling around the city. Basen doubted these men had been told to keep their mouths shut about each other because they chatted and gossiped like Academy students. The other was for Basen's ally psychics to put themselves close to their enemies and feel for the manipulation of energy. However, no psychic could be manipulating energy at all times, so there was a lesser chance of locating them this way. Thus, they relied on the first method. They'd confirmed only a few psychics, but from what Sanya had told Basen, this number was likely to be correct because psychics were extremely rare in Greenedge, the previous home to most of these intruders.

Basen assumed there had to be at least one psychic in the castle with Ulric at all times to act as a lie detector. Two psychics have been confirmed to be with Rockbreak in the forest trying to flush out hiding rebels. These psychics would be of some concern but not compared to the psychic general in charge of the capital's walls. Basen had asked Sneary for more information about this general, and Sneary eventually came to give Basen a report that included absolutely nothing about him.

"No rebels have been able to get near him without risking detection, and he has no visible weaknesses," Sneary said. "He has all his meals brought to him on duty, and he sleeps in his private house close to the southeastern edge of the wall."

"How did he get a private house?" Most of the soldiers slept at inns for free.

"Ulric has purchased houses in strategic locations for some of his higher ranking officials."

"At a fair rate I assume?" Basen asked sarcastically.

Sneary frowned. "Many of the citizens have been displaced."

"They'll be able to go home soon enough."

"I have a team ready to kill the general tonight."

Basen thought for a while. "No, there's a chance they might fail. We don't know yet how strong he is. Don't disturb his sleep. Kill the degenerate soldiers as we've discussed."

"It's not wise to leave him alive."

Basen almost told Sneary that his mind was made up, but it would just spark an argument. Sneary had never taken the subservient role as Basen had wanted.

Henry came through the cellar doors, probably to give his report on this district. "Sneary, Basen tells me how successful your team has been spying on our enemy general and officers."

"Without him," Basen said, "we would be fighting blind through most of the capital tomorrow."

Henry shook Sneary's hand. "Thank you for working with my son. I know he can be stubborn at times."

"We were just discussing the psychic general," Sneary grumbled.

"He will die with the rest of them," Henry said.

"He's said to be smart," Sneary said. "He has the potential to ruin our plan if we don't kill him during the night."

Basen gave his father a look to show he disagreed. Fortunately, Henry had learned to trust Basen's judgment during this time.

"The only way this is going to work," Henry said, "is if we follow Basen's plan. It's too late now to alter a single detail."

This wasn't exactly true, however Henry spoke with such authority that Sneary didn't argue.

"Fine." The warrior instructor gave Basen a defeated look. "He will live through the night."

"And it will be his last," Basen vowed.

When Sneary left, Basen thanked his father. "I wonder if he doesn't trust me or if he just doesn't like to be told what to do."

"No one likes to be told what to do."

"That's not true. We gladly accepted orders from Terren, and your men have turned to you for guidance since joining you in Trentyre. But when I give an order, I often need to explain myself."

"Because you're young and you speak as if it's a suggestion."

"To my ears, I'm demanding."

"You're too nice. When you want your men to follow your command with loyalty instead of reluctance, sometimes you need to talk to them like the dog you want them to be in that moment."

The cellar doors came open with a crash. Mage Trela flew down the stairs. "I only have a moment before I have to return. Annah is sitting in a tavern near the castle, but not for much longer. I spoke with her."

"In front of guards?"

"No one saw."

"What's she doing?"

"Ulric believed her and Reela when they told him they would join him. Annah has been walking around the city and speaking to citizens to find out their mood."

"What? Their mood?"

"Yes, Ulric feels as if this war has already been won. Now he's interested in pleasing the people. He believes all the rebels still alive are in the forest or have left Kyrro. Annah is waiting for me to return to tell her what to do. I said we'd find a safe route for her to get here without any uniforms seeing. She believes some of them are waiting to see if she runs. It's her first time out of the castle, and it might be her last when she tells Ulric that everyone despises him. Basen, this could be our only chance to help her."

Basen knew Annah; she frightened easily. She must've infected Trela with this fear or filled the mage with guilt because Trela wasn't seeing the risk anymore.

"What did she say about Reela?" Basen asked before delivering the bad news.

"Ulric is having her teach psyche to him a few hours a day. She spends the rest training in the castle. He wants her to go out and hunt rebels, but she's convinced him to let her stay for now as it's the only way to keep teaching him. I have to get back to Annah."

"She has to go back to the castle," Basen insisted. "She won't want to, but it's the only way to keep her safe and to keep all of us from getting caught. We need her there with Reela. This is the perfect opportunity to explain what she'll have to do. Go back and tell her about the febeetles tomorrow."

Trela's brows hung low above her squinted eyes.

"Basen—"

"I know she wants to come back here with you, but she must return to Ulric and tell him whatever she needs to say to remain in the castle tomorrow. Tell her I was going to send someone in with this message before this chance presented itself. We haven't forgotten. We will keep her safe."

"She's terrified." Trela seemed surprised that Basen showed no empathy.

"That's nothing new for her. We need bravery from everyone. Go," Basen ordered. "And Mage Trela, you can't tell her any more details than she needs to know. Just mention the febeetles. That's all. If Ulric loses trust in her and she's questioned by a psychic without Reela to help, she could tell him everything. All of us would be killed tomorrow. I know she can be brave for one more day."

"All right." Trela moved quickly up the stairs for a woman in her middle years.

"That was better," Henry said.

But Basen felt as if he'd eaten a worm.

*****

Alabell helped Basen transport sacks of food and flasks of water into the Slugari colony. Basen held open the portal as she tossed in everything they needed to give to Cleve's group in the forest. Basen walked toward the portal when they were done. "I'll be back soon."

"Take care."

There had been more episodes of his mind splitting, but none like the first. Whenever he felt himself drifting into what he thought of as the dream world, he pinched his leg to keep hold of reality. When that didn't work, he reached out for Alabell's hand. She always stabilized the tilting.

Cleve and his group were already within the cavern when Basen arrived. There was a woman with them who Basen had never met. She looked to be at least a few years older than Terren had been, probably close to forty. Basen hardly noticed how short she was until Cleve came to stand beside her.

"This is Quessa Polken," Cleve said. "My cousin."

"This young man is your leader?" Quessa asked Cleve in disbelief. She looked Basen up and down and seemed unimpressed. Didn't she see the portal he'd stepped through to get here? Who in god's world *was* this woman?

"He's done very well," Cleve said. "Quessa was hired by Annah's parents to find and protect her until they can determine what to do."

"Now I'm trying to figure out how much I can tell them," Quessa grumbled. "You've gotten her into a mess that, if I got her out, will create more of a mess."

Basen had forgotten Annah came from wealth. He wondered if any other parents had sent people like Quessa for their children.

"You can't tell her parents anything yet," Basen said. "She'll be returned to them safely by the end of tomorrow."

"Forgive me if I don't believe you, but they're paying me a lot of money to make sure she's safe, and that's what I'm going to do."

Cleve jumped in, "She could at least check on Annah and Reela in the castle."

There were a few hundred people behind the Polkens, some of them Krepps. They rifled through the supplies and ate, but slowly, no doubt to listen. Basen noticed them quieting before he spoke. None of them would say it, but they all had to know that letting Quessa into the castle was too big a risk.

"If a psychic questions her," Basen explained, "everything would be ruined. The best way to protect Annah would be to fight with us and ensure we win."

"Cleve told me what you hope to accomplish tomorrow. Your chances are slim," Quessa argued. "Take me back to the capital with you and I'll go into the castle before it's time to attack to keep Annah safe."

"And Reela," Cleve added.

"If Reela is the same woman I remember, she won't need much protection."

"Annah doesn't either," Basen argued. "Her parents don't know the psychic soldier she's become. I won't bring you back to the capital if you're going to demand to enter the castle before the attack. There's too great of a chance that Ulric will see your presence as a threat. He must die for this war to end."

"You underestimate me," Quessa challenged. She had the expression of an old, impatient woman getting in back of a long line. "I'll fight you for it."

"For what?"

"Quessa," Cleve chided.

"I'll fight you for the portal. For whether I go or stay."

"You're half mad," Basen remarked.

She drew her sword. "If you're not going to fight for it, then you're taking me back with you or you're staying here with us."

"Quessa!" Cleve bellowed. "Put away your weapon."

She didn't. He placed his hand on Basen's back and guided him away from the group to speak in private.

"You're right, she is half mad," Cleve agreed. "But believe it or not, she also knows how to be subtle when she needs to be. She won't take any risks that could hurt us. She cares too much about Terren to lose her opportunity to avenge his death. I'm sure you can find a way to coordinate with her."

Oh, her behavior was partly about Terren. It made more sense now.

"She doesn't seem very cooperative," Basen observed.

"She's only like that when she disagrees."

"And how often is that?"

Cleve glanced back at her over his shoulder. "I'll be honest. I've only seen her a few times in my life, so I don't know. But Reela knows her better than I do. She'll know how to handle Quessa once they meet in the castle, so long as Reela has already been warned about the attack."

"We got a message to her," Basen assured. He went on to explain Trela's encounter with Annah.

"Good. Let Quessa into the castle to protect them. Please, Basen."

He sighed as he looked at the small woman. "How much can she really do to help?"

"More than you'd imagine."

He supposed her arms were thick, and her legs looked strong and agile. "All right. Come on, Quessa. I'd better get you back and explain everything to you before the fun begins."

"We attack tonight?"

"Only some of us. Everyone joins in tomorrow, including me."

Basen relished how thousands of his enemies would die while he was sleeping. He had spent weeks stacking the tiles and now it was finally time to knock one over.

CHAPTER THIRTY-FOUR

There was nowhere Steffen wanted to be more than Oakshen tonight. Basen did him the favor of giving him a portal to Worender training center after he convinced Basen it was worth the risk. Steffen knew Oakshen well and would kill the men who'd taken the city from those he cared about.

Steffen went to check on his mother, peering in through her window to find her staring at the drawing he'd made of her before he'd left for the Academy. She seemed to be admiring it as she held her hand over her mouth. He wished he could tell her he was alive, but she would latch on to him in hopes of preventing him from fighting. The neighbors would hear her yelling, and guards might come.

Steffen had always gone back to the capital with Cleve to give their reports to Basen, but Steffen would read through Gabby and Effie's report about Oakshen before letting Basen teleport him and Cleve back. Although Steffen hadn't spoken with either sister in many days, he still felt connected to them through Gabby's writing. He'd watched Basen's plan come to life and wanted to be a part of it in Oakshen so much that he'd convinced Basen to let him take on the most difficult role.

There were a total of two thousand troops of Kyrro's Allies throughout Oakshen, the capital, and the forest. One thousand were citizen rebels who had no training at fighting. Steffen and his allies wouldn't have to kill all of their ten thousand enemies to win this war, but most needed to die before the rest would give up.

Steffen knocked on the door to the local brothel and waited. A woman a few years his senior with a plunging bodice opened the door. She smiled as if happy to see him. It was so convincing he started to believe Gabby had given her his description.

So I don't need the password, I suppose. "May I come in?"

Her mouth twisted at the corner. "Um, yes."

He stepped in. She shut the door after him. "Have a seat, and I'll bring someone out for you."

"Uh, wait. Do you have any rats?"

She glanced at the empty staircase behind her, then turned back to Steffen and grabbed his hand to seat him at a table in the far corner. Without her smile now, she looked older and angrier.

"So it *is* you. People don't knock, and *no one* asks politely to come in." She *was* angry. He didn't understand.

"I'm sorry."

"Wait here." She scampered across the room and then up the stairs. She disappeared for a moment before coming back to wave for him to follow. "Make no sound," she whispered. "Walk quietly and go through door six."

A red carpet covered the entire length of the hallway. Paintings of women with exaggerated busts decorated the red walls. The moans of women and grunts of men accompanied a chorus of smacking flesh and rocking beds.

Steffen went through the door with a "6" made out of leather on it.

"Bastial hell," he muttered as pity froze him. A girl

who appeared younger than Gabby sat on her knees against the bed post with her arm covering a nearly flat chest. Steffen looked away, but not before he noticed the bruises all over her naked body...not before he noticed her tears.

He kept his head down as he walked around the far side of the bed, got on his stomach, and slid underneath. She stood. Her legs disappeared above the bedframe as she got on the mattress, but a chain remained attached to her ankle and the post.

Steffen waited. Basen had needed assurance that Steffen could do this, but if Basen had seen this girl he would've realized that assurance wasn't necessary.

The officer's name was irrelevant, but that didn't stop Steffen from wanting to know. The other uniforms called him by his last name, Coal, spelled just like the material that so resembled his nature. He wasn't the one who organized Ulric's troops in Oakshen, but he managed them. Most of the soldiers were less severe to the citizenry here than in the capital, no psychics found to be among them. The troops received their wages at the end of the week, so this was high time for them to visit brothels and weapon shops, and to gamble, drink, and indulge themselves with exorbitant meals. Coal was known to be the worst among them.

There were three possible shifts any soldier could take, and it was up to Coal to decide who worked the morning, the evening, and overnight. It was no secret that he took bribes to change a soldier's shift, but what he did with most of the money was only known to this brothel.

Although his favorite girl was ordered to remain

chained with no idea when he would come, rebel spies finally noticed his pattern. He visited the brothel whenever his glance caught a boy of the age between child and young man. Right now, Micklin should be walking near Oakshen's southeastern wall so Coal could get a good look.

Steffen didn't want to think about what Coal did to this girl on the bed, but Steffen couldn't keep such thoughts away while he waited. Coal had taken all the hair off her head, probably elsewhere as well, in an obvious attempt to make her appear even younger and boyish.

"You will kill him, won't you?" she whispered from above him.

"Yes, but I have to wait until I can catch him from behind to slit his throat. We need to keep him from screaming. The longer it takes for any of his men to know he's dead, the better."

"Please don't let him touch me."

"I'll try."

"Promise you won't. Promise."

"I promise I won't let him hurt you. Now stop talking."

She cried softly as they waited. Steffen held the dagger ready.

The girl startled as the door opened. Steffen could only see a pair of boots as he remained far beneath the bed. They walked into the room and turned. The door shut. They turned back to face the bed.

Steffen waited, but there was no movement or sound for some time. Something seemed wrong. Finally, Coal spoke.

"Why aren't you crying?"

"What is that around your neck?"

"Protection. The city's different tonight. Something's happening." His belt fell to the floor. "I'll have to be quicker than I'd like, rougher. I asked you a question."

She began to cry again. "I don't know why I ever stop."

She'd done well to give Steffen the hint of Coal wearing some sort of neck shield. Steffen tried to think of a new plan as Coal's clothes puddled around his shifting feet. The girl let out the start of a scream as Coal walked toward her. Her chain whipped against the bedframe as she shifted above Steffen.

Coal stopped at the base close enough for Steffen to stab his dagger through Coal's foot. "Come here," he said.

Her bare feet came down on the floor.

"Turn around," Coal demanded.

She cried louder as she turned. Coal was too close for Steffen to move without being heard.

"Bend over," Coal ordered.

She cried even louder.

"Don't make me repeat myself," he warned.

There was a thud as Steffen imagined him striking her. She yelped and fell forward, coming down onto her hands. There was another sound like the first, then Coal's boot forced her flat against the ground. She showed Steffen a look of malice. He'd already broken his promise.

"Are you looking at something down there?" Coal asked with a chuckle. "Perhaps you hid a weapon in hopes of fighting me?"

Steffen's pulse raced.

"No."

A hand reached down and grabbed her by the ear. Her eyes changed to plead with Steffen for help just before her face coiled in pain. But if Steffen came out at the wrong moment and was caught, not only would he be killed with the girl, the entire takeover of Oakshen might be ruined. Everyone would die.

He held his dagger ready, hoping Coal would lean down for a look. But the officer seemed satisfied by her answer, or he was more interested by what wasn't under the bed. Their feet shuffled around together. She seemed to be squirming.

Turn him around.

There was a slap that knocked her to her knees, then Coal yanked her into the air. She came back down on her feet and began to struggle again.

Finally she maneuvered around to face Coal away from Steffen. He inched toward the opening, but there was another slap—this time accompanied by a laugh— and the two of them scuffled again.

"You want to fight back *tonight*?" he asked. "The very night I need to do this quick?"

He hit her with a solid punch. She fell gripping her stomach and groaning, crying uncontrollably. As Coal bent to pick her up by her hair, Steffen could wait no longer.

He lunged with the knife and drove it through Coal's foot. The man screamed as he swung, catching Steffen in the face with the back of his hand just as Steffen was getting up. He lost his balance and slammed his back into a dresser. Coal ripped the dagger out and had begun to turn to Steffen when the girl bit him on the leg.

He screamed and bent his elbow to stab her but Steffen was there, catching his arm. With the girl continuing to gnaw on Coal's leg, Steffen easily toppled him with a shove. The metal guard around his neck clanked as he hit the ground. Steffen stepped on his arm and twisted the dagger out of his hand, ignoring Coal's pounding against Steffen's leg.

He came down with all his weight, plunging the dagger into Coal's chest. He threw his hands over Coal's mouth before the officer could scream. He wasn't dying fast enough as he thrashed. Steffen must've missed the heart.

"Take out the dagger and stab him again," he told the girl. She was standing by with her hands up as if ready to help but unsure how.

She screamed as she bent down behind Steffen. He could hear the dagger ripping out of Coal's chest just to be thrust back in. She didn't relent. Coal managed to pry Steffen's hands off his mouth long enough to let out a yelp before Steffen could adjust his knees over Coal's arms and muffle his screams again.

Finally, he went limp.

Someone knocked on the door. "Sir, are you all right?"

Damn. Steffen cleared his throat to find the right sound. "Leave me alone!" he yelled in his best imitation of Coal's voice. Many familiar voices weren't recognizable at a shout, so he could only hope Coal had never screamed at this soldier before.

At any moment, there could be a dozen of them in the brothel. Steffen could not afford to start a fight in the hall. He pulled the dagger out of Coal's chest and crept toward the door.

He waited, waited, then waited some more, but the soldier must've returned to his room. Steffen looked down to find blood on his pants and hands. He cursed. He didn't have time for this.

"How much of it is on my back?" he asked the girl without looking at her.

She didn't respond. He took a quick glance to see her standing over the corpse with a faraway stare, no longer hiding her nudity.

"How much blood is on my back?" Steffen asked again as he backed toward her. She still wouldn't answer. "If it's noticeable, I need to change all my clothing before I leave."

He heard her gasp. "Very noticeable."

"I have to be elsewhere. Does he have any clothing in here I can use?" She said nothing. "What about in that dresser?"

"Yes."

Steffen wiped his hands on his soiled clothing as best he could, then disrobed. He looked through every drawer, finding only "bedroom outfits" for women until he came to the last drawer. There were a few shirts of varying degrees of stench and a single pair of pants slightly too large, but they would have to do.

"No one can know that he's dead," Steffen murmured to the stunned girl. "Help me get him beneath the bed."

She finally recovered from her shock, covering herself as best she could with her arms as she turned away from Steffen.

"I have to leave now. I'm not looking at you, so just

help me."

It wasn't easy, but they got the job done eventually. Fortunately, the rug was red and mostly hid the trail of blood. Steffen started toward the door.

"Wait," she whispered.

He stopped. "I really need to leave."

"Will anyone else come?"

"To help? Yes. To hurt, no."

"Thank you."

"You're welcome."

CHAPTER THIRTY-FIVE

With no officer to direct them, Steffen had been told that command would fall to the four sergeants on each side of the wall around Oakshen. He didn't see how it was possible Gabby could know exactly what they would do during an attack on the wall, but he had to trust her report was accurate. Everything that would follow Steffen's ambush would only work if she was right.

He couldn't afford to be seen sprinting through the city, as eager as he was to get to his next destination. Eventually, he walked through an alley and opened the first barrel along his path to find a bow with a quiver of arrows waiting for him. He looked around for an open window. It was nowhere in sight, so he continued down the alley and soon found it on his left. He put the bow and quiver through first, then climbed in after.

A man and woman old enough to be his grandparents sat at their kitchen table cradling cups of tea. The woman took one look at Steffen, then glanced back and whistled. A man in his twenties walked into the room. He had both hands on the handle of his sword as he carried it awkwardly. No sheath. No armor.

"It's an honor," he said.

Steffen got his quiver over his shoulder. "We're grateful for the help."

The older man asked, "How much longer?"

"Any moment now." Steffen crouched beside the window facing the wall and moved the curtain for a peek.

"Do you have the torch?"

The woman reached beneath the table and retrieved the club wrapped in cloth. The man Steffen assumed to be her grandson walked toward it with his outstretched arm, but his grandfather stood and grabbed it first.

"I'm doing this."

The younger man reached for it. "You can barely lift a sword. Give it to me."

"I'm not bringing a sword."

"You're not fast enough. They'll shoot you before you get to the wall."

"Then the others will have a better chance to make it. I'm doing this."

The grandmother stood and hugged her husband. She couldn't seem to get out anything clear, but the sounds she made while crying expressed her gratitude clearly enough.

"Stop or you'll make me cry." The grandfather wiped his eyes.

Steffen would rather the younger fellow took the torch, but there was no time to argue about it. "Go now," he told the old man.

The grandson took the candle from the center of the table. He and the old man left the kitchen together. Steffen heard the door to the house open as he watched the wall from the window. The old man ran with the flaming torch, though his speed was no faster than a jog.

The wall was a good distance away, and a soldier spotted him early. Steffen could only see three of them from his limited purview, each standing on the walkway toward the top of the wall. One had a bow; the other two had swords.

"What are you doing, old man?" yelled the archer with a light tone of entertainment.

"There are others," said one of the swordsmen with a grave voice.

Steffen could feel a change in the air as light illuminated the wall. He heard shouting farther down. The three soldiers began to panic, all talking at once and moving in different directions. The archer tried to line up a shot but Steffen's arrow impaled his stomach. He stumbled back against the wall and toppled over. The two swordsmen ran toward the ramp to get down.

Steffen missed his next shot. One uniform made it down the ramp. The old man wouldn't reach the wall before he was killed. Steffen shot again and hit his mark in the shoulder. The soldier came to a stop as he threw his hand over his wound, then ran the other way, giving up on the old man. "Light the beacon!"

Steffen shot an arrow in front of the scared uniform to miss on purpose this time. He needed to give his enemies the idea the rebels didn't want the beacon lit when really it was the opposite.

The old man held the torch to the wall with fifty others doing the same while spread out beside him. Up against the wood, they were directly below the walkway. Enemy archers who weren't fleeing began to lean over to get a shot at them. Steffen had already taken care of his archer and now ran out of the house for a better line of sight. He shot down another archer, then another. But the torchbearers began to fall as enemy swordsmen got to them.

It was too late, the wall already lit. The old man ran back, his grandson taking his place as a flood of rebel swordsmen rushed the wall. Their lack of skill did not matter as they overwhelmed their enemies, forcing many to run.

Steffen shot down a few of them until there were none left standing. The enemies had lit the beacon atop part of the wall, as Steffen had expected. But it hardly had a chance to burn before the wall started to come down. The more wood that crashed to the ground, the quicker the rest fell.

Steffen grabbed a plank of wood and stuck it in the flame until it was lit. He ran farther down and used it to set more of the wall aflame.

Others began to mimic him. Soon, the wall burned for as far as Steffen could see.

*****

Effie watched the fire from atop her house. Her entire family stood beside her. When she and Gabby had first come to Oakshen, it had taken hours of pleading before they had finally convinced their mother and father not to flee the city. They had begged for Effie and Gabby to go with them, but Effie would rather die fighting than run.

Each day, her parents' cowardice had disappointed Effie more. But eventually they'd seen results from her and Gabby's efforts and realized just how possible an uprising would be with the right organization and leadership.

But it was Gabby who impressed Effie the most of her family. Gabby wrote every report for Basen, being the faster writer with better handwriting. She knew who to speak to about rebellion in the city and who to avoid. She brought food back from the headquarters in the capital to those most in need and was repaid in loyalty. No doubt she'd been preparing to rebel soon after the war had begun, though she wouldn't admit this when Effie asked.

Gabby had done more than Effie could've hoped to accomplish if she'd been here in her sister's stead. But now was Effie's time. She grinned as she saw the first soldiers running down the empty street. The night was too dark for them to see the oil ahead.

She let these few uniforms pass. As they ran through the oil, one slipped while another questioned why the ground was wet if it hadn't rained. The first got up and put his sword in his sheath before running again. The others did the same, no doubt fearful of falling and stabbing themselves. They would all have their weapons drawn by the time they reached the burning wall on the other end of the city, but they would find no one to fight until it was too late.

Effie had been instructed to let the first twenty men through her street. A few looked up to see the people atop houses. Only a couple yelled at them to get back inside or they would be marked as rebels.

When Effie spotted the large battalion on its way to the wall, she let loose her first fireball. Flame rose up from the glistening street to block the path of the sergeant leading his small army. The man, marked by the silver stars on his shoulders, came to an abrupt stop and yelled for his men to hold. But there were hundreds behind him, and the ground was slick with oil.

"Now," Effie told her sister as the soldiers collided into each other's backs and began to slip. Gabby threw a small bucket at them. Oil poured out as it spun, then splashed up as it hit the ground. By the time Gabby was throwing the second bucket, rebels from every rooftop had joined her in dousing the men from Greenedge.

Effie greedily cast the first fireball upon her panicking enemies before telling her parents to fire. Many of Effie's classmates had been killed in the battle that drove her from the Academy, and those still alive were split between here and the capital, but there were still enough to burn nearly every soldier in the city with the help of torch- and oil-flinging citizens.

The uniforms tried to flee, some kicking at doors of nearby homes to escape the street. But every rebel had barricaded the entrance with their heaviest furniture in preparation of this. Other soldiers went for the windows as their struggling comrades blocked the doorways. Citizens waited within. They stabbed the soldiers with meat knives before the uniforms could get up their swords.

The smart soldiers removed their burning clothes and stayed in the street, some singeing their hands in the process. Others tried to flee back the way they'd come, while more began to search for another way through. But this location of the city had been chosen for a reason. Just like the ten other spots in Oakshen where similar traps had been set, there were no alleys or side streets for the men to take.

Walls of flame trapped these intruders. Some uniforms began to realize that their best chance of escape was to run through the fire. Most would make it who tried, but not without injury.

Many of these wounded enemies would eventually arrive at the burning wall, no doubt furious and ready to kill. But they would find no one to face. They might gather to look for rebels or they might search the empty houses. No matter what they decided, they would soon be overwhelmed.

Effie continued to rain down fireballs without mercy. The blaze ate through the survivors until nearly all the men had fled or died. Effie jumped down from the roof, then helped her mother and father down with Gabby's assistance from the top.

Effie looked through the broken window into the home where she'd grown up. Micklin was covered in blood as he panted, but his smile showed Effie that none of it was his own. Bodies were scattered around him.

"Effie!" someone yelled. "Effie, come here."

She rushed down the street littered with corpses. Some of the soldiers still squirmed and groaned, while others were half naked and alive enough to make a run for it. But every rebel had come to the streets with a dagger or a knife, stealing the last vestiges of life like voracious lions swarming a sick beast.

"Here, Effie." She recognized Penny's voice as she came to the fire. Her instructor was gathering sartious energy and holding it against hungry flames searching for fresh wood.

Effie helped Penny smother the flames with sartious energy, all the while wishing Jackrie was here. They ran from house to house as their allies cleared the streets, stomping out life and taking their enemies' weapons. Everything had gone better than Effie had hoped, but celebrating too early was the easiest way to ruin a victory.

"With me!" Sneary announced. Effie and Penny were the last ones there after they extinguished each threatening flame.

Sneary set their army's pace at a quick jog. If citizens weren't cowering in their homes, they were running into the street to join the ever-growing rebellion.

Soon, Sneary joined their group with Steffen's. The wall still burned, the flames dancing above the rooftops in Effie's way.

She grabbed Steffen's hand and squeezed. "Any problems?" she asked.

"None. You?"

Gabby kissed him. "None for us, either."

"It isn't over," Effie felt the need to mention.

"You'll stay back, right?" Steffen asked Gabby.

"Yes."

She would wait with their parents. Effie stood on her toes but was still too short to see over her surrounding comrades. "Are the others here?"

Steffen stretched his neck to look around. "Just arriving now."

The other officers and their corresponding groups came together with Penny and Sneary. Penny announced, "Front mages, follow my voice."

"Front swordsmen, here!" Sneary called out.

"Everyone else, line up behind."

There were only twenty mages with Effie. Penny took them to the last street before the wall. It hadn't yet caught fire. Every enemy had run past long ago.

"They're trying to put out the fire," Penny said after a peek down the last street before the wall. "We quietly ascend the ramp. Now."

Effie stayed close as Penny led them up the steep incline. They filed into place on the walkway. The fire approaching along the wall was nearly blinding, smoke burning Effie's throat.

"Move back," Penny ordered, no doubt having underestimated the heat and smoke.

The twenty mages hurried away from the flames, but their enemies appeared to have underestimated the fire as well, moving away from the wall.

"Fire, now!" Penny called out.

Effie cast with the others, a hail of fireballs exploding among the hundreds of dispersing soldiers. They yelled as they fled down the streets to use shanties as cover, most probably terrified of fire by now. Screams of agony and aggression beat against the roar of the fire, steel clanging. They'd run straight into Sneary's swordsmen waiting to surprise them. Uniforms ran back toward the wall to escape the army of rebels, but there was only death for them out here as Effie continued to cast fireballs one after another.

Soon there was no more movement she could see. Effie ran down the ramp with her mages to come behind their remaining enemies around the turn, exchanging her wand for a dagger. But by the time she made it to the battle, though, every enemy had been cut down.

She could feel the urge to cheer bubbling up in her chest. The city was theirs. It was a temptation to stay and knock down the rest of the wall, but she and everyone here had orders to follow.

A few had begun to cheer, but Sneary stopped them with a shout. "We still have a long way to go. Don't be overconfident. Take what weapons you want from the bodies and follow me."

He led them through the broken chunks of charred wall and into Raywhite Forest.

CHAPTER THIRTY-SIX

Basen slept a few hours before Alabell woke him. Having only drifted into a light sleep, he sat up and felt as if he'd merely shut his eyes for a few moments.

"The sun's almost up." Alabell stood at the window. Knowing her, she'd probably been too worried to sleep. She opened the curtains so Basen could see the faintest of light coming over the top of the wall.

He devoured the fruit and bread Alabell had somehow quietly gotten into their room, dressing as he chewed.

"I'll be as careful as I can," he promised.

She took his face and kissed him with such emotion he wished he could linger with her longer.

He went downstairs to greet his mother in the kitchen as she helped Millry prepare a feast that might mostly go uneaten on account of nerves dampening many appetites.

"Has anyone returned yet?" Basen asked. The tavern appeared to be empty.

He heard voices outside as his mother pointed at the exit. As he got the last buttons of his shirt in place, he went out to find hundreds of his allies gathered outside the tavern. They stopped at the sight of him.

"Anything wrong?" he asked no one in particular.

His father pushed through to face Basen. "Nothing yet."

"So all of our assassins in the capital—?"

"Killed their marks and escaped. Although most of the enemies who died during the night were whoremongers and gamblers, the loss of five hundred men should hurt them nonetheless."

"Let's hope everyone in Oakshen was just as successful." There was no way to know how Sneary and Penny's brigades had done. Basen couldn't get even a glimpse of the city to look for smoke without climbing the wall, where he could be spotted by guards. "Vithos, where are you?"

"Here." People made way for the Elf. He had a grin as if this was all entertainment to him. "Febeetles now?"

"That's right. Neeko and Shara, are you here?"

They came through the crowd together. "We're ready," Neeko confirmed.

Basen told his father, "Gather all the citizens who are joining us. We'll be back soon."

"They're already on the way."

"Good."

Basen led Neeko and Shara down into the basement of the headquarters. Its emptiness reminded him of the void created by Sanya. If she was still alive, Crea would be making her wish she was dead. *Hold on a little while longer, Sanya. One more day.*

All six akorell stones were charged. He put one on each wrist, then opened the portal to the abandoned Slugari colony. Vithos practically skipped into the portal, then Neeko and Shara followed. Basen entered last.

He came down with his hands onto the hard dirt, staring at the ground until it stopped tilting. Then he got up and followed his group to the cage of sartious energy.

"Oh, they very hungry," Vithos said.

"They'll eat soon."

Shara waved her hand and the sartious cage shattered into dust. The energy became a dense cloud covering the febeetles until it fell to the ground and sprinkled on their backs. Vithos moved his arm and they followed his direction, forming a line of black and green as they swerved around to get in front of Basen. They made a light patter, like a tiny army charging into battle.

Basen returned to the alcove and used the energy in the akorell metal to create a portal back to the basement. He'd brought the extra akorell bracelet in case there wasn't enough energy in this cavern and was glad he didn't have to use it. He would need every weapon in his arsenal to get through the day.

"Go, small monsters!" Vithos laughed like a villain in a play.

"You will feast soon!" Shara added in the same evil tone.

As soon as the last of the febeetles crawled into the black hole of shimmering energy, Vithos followed, then the rest of them entered.

The Elf had regained control by the time Basen's dizziness had worn off. He waited with Neeko and Shara as Vithos walked up the stairs, then called up the febeetles after him. They climbed the wooden staircase with ease. Hopefully they could crawl up stone just as easily.

Basen's allies had moved to surround the headquarters. They appeared panicked by the sight of the febeetles, or so Basen thought. He realized his mistake when they began calling out, "Basen's here. Tell him."

A novice psychic of the Academy shuffled through,

many people taking to her sides. Her hands and face were covered in soot. She seemed to be having trouble keeping her breath steady as she sniffled and teared.

"He must've found out," she murmured.

"Who?"

Henry took it upon himself to speak for her. "The psychic officer must've become aware of his missing soldiers and went searching for them. He questioned people and burned their houses when they couldn't provide answers."

"I should've done more," the psychic said as she found her voice. "I ran straight here, but I should've fought."

"No, it's good you came here," Basen assured her. "Where did this start?"

"Near the eastern wall, close to his residence. People tried to fight him as he stuck a torch against their homes, but his psyche is strong enough to hurt them all. His men came to support him as they woke up. He'll burn half the city looking for us."

Basen thought quickly. None of the citizenry knew the details of the plan. In fact, the only people who knew about the rebels in the capital were already here. The army had nearly doubled in size as they filled the streets outside the headquarters. But it wasn't time yet.

"Has the wall come under attack?" he asked the woman.

"Not while I was there."

Basen should've eliminated the officer during the night like Sneary said. No, it was too risky to take on such a dangerous psychic. And his plan could still work.

"Let's go now," Henry urged Basen.

"But if we get to the castle before Sneary and Penny get to the wall, this day will result in failure." Basen put his hand over his eyes to look for the sun to the west. "Lift me up," he told his army.

A few people took his legs and hoisted him up. He could see the treetops over the unguarded wall just ahead of him, but there was no sphere of the sun, only a wave of light blending into the dark sky. They let him down.

"It isn't time yet," he said.

"People aren't letting their homes be destroyed without a fight," the psychic argued. "More are dying every minute that passes."

An extraordinarily tall man a few years older than Basen made his way through the army as he looked around and called Sanya's name. He pushed through to the front and took the brief silence as his chance to ask Henry, "Where is Sanya?"

"We don't have time for you right now. She's not here."

"Where is she?"

"You must be Greg," Basen said. "She was captured." *Probably dead.* "We'll try to get her back soon. Fight with us until we get to her."

"Why are we just standing here?"

Henry whistled and a few of his men in gray uniforms rushed over. He warned Greg, "Give us a moment to finish strategizing."

Greg looked at the men giving him hard glares and slunk back into the crowd. Nearly a head taller than everyone, he stared at Henry, waiting for him to speak.

Henry ignored him to look at Basen.

"How much longer, if not now?"

"Sneary knows to attack as soon as the sun can be seen on the horizon. We are to wait until after we see it to march to the castle. I don't know how much longer until then, perhaps ten minutes."

The psychic turned to face east and let out a mournful gasp. Others turned to catch the same sight of smoke towering into the sky less than a mile away.

Basen fought back his guilt as he refused to give the order. They waited a while longer. Every second that passed became less bearable as his army stirred, many staring at him like Greg.

"Fine," Basen said, unable to control his guilt any longer. "We leave now. Let's just hope Sneary's group was successful in Oakshen and is as eager to fight as we are."

Otherwise we're all dead.

*****

Marching to the castle from the edge of the city was the easiest way to be noticed by Ulric's scouts. No matter how many enemy soldiers were sent to the wall, every troop would be called to defend the castle. The fight would become impossible. So instead, Basen's army in the capital lined up outside their headquarters.

"Soon all of you will be walking into a portal," Henry announced to the one thousand allied troops. "If you are a citizen here, this will be the first time you see a portal. It might look like it will rip your body apart, but everyone else here has gone through one safely. Some of us have gone through many. You will not be harmed. We do not have time for hesitance, so build up your courage now to rush into the portal as soon as it's your turn."

Basen opened the cellar doors. Alabell walked down the stairs behind him. She would accompany him as he strained his mind to hold open the portal. She said it was in case his mind slipped into another realm and she needed to pull him back, but Basen figured she really wanted to stand close to him until it was time to go. He wouldn't have had it any other way.

With five akorell stones left, he hoped to use only one for this portal and save four for the rest of the day. His army lined up out of the basement. The stairs would slow them getting to the portal, but Basen resolved to keep it open as long as it took. He felt pride as he watched the strongest men in his army get in position to slide the enormous battering ram into the portal first.

He ripped open the gateway. After men slid in the battering ram endways to fit it in the opening, Henry and his troops were the first ones in. Basen's swelling pride gave him strength as he watched person after person rush into his portal with the same determined look.

Then the citizens of the capital started showing up in line, scattered among the soldiers. Even after Henry's warning, some hesitated with obvious trepidation. Others were struck with awe and momentarily forgot they were supposed to run into the portal instead of admire it.

Greg stood out among everyone. Without Cleve here,

he might've been the tallest one. *But nowhere near Rockbreak's height.* The giant was the only one with the potential to wreck Basen's plan worse than the psychic officer.

It was Alabell who'd told Basen how the castle called for help when it came under attack. There were launchers on top of the castle designed to fling burning clusters of some kind of plant high into the air, leaving trails of smoke thick enough to be seen from the other cities. He asked Alabell if Cleve's cousin might be able to enter the castle disguised in enemy uniform and stop these flares from launching, but Alabell had told him it would be impossible to convince anyone to let her near the flares. So the flares would be launched no matter what; Basen would have to take the castle before help arrived.

As he strained to keep the portal open, he wished he'd had more time to keep up his battle casting training. Perhaps if Abith had made it to the city...Basen hoped to see the sword master today, but more than that, he hoped to see the rest of his army alive when everything was done.

"How many more?" Alabell asked from the bottom of the stairs.

"About a third," Wilfre called from outside headquarters. "The flares have been launched."

Already? They must've spotted the armored troops pouring out of Basen's portal into the training center. *We should've waited longer to make sure Sneary had reached the wall by now.*

Basen focused his mind on the task at hand as the portal became heavier and harder to manage.

Eventually, Wilfre called from outside, "That's almost everyone."

Soon Vithos came down the stairs with his febeetles in tow. Cleve's cousin, Quessa, took her place at the top of the stairs when the febeetles had cleared. The enemy uniform was slightly too large for her, but she'd convinced Basen earlier it wouldn't keep her from getting into the castle.

Now that the flare had gone off early, however, he wasn't so sure.

"We are last," she said. The three of them were the only ones in enemy uniforms.

Basen would gladly let the portal close but not before taking his first and only glance within. Alabell had watched for him to ensure everyone tumbling through the portal was able to move out of the way quickly enough, and now they all appeared to be drawing their weapons in preparation for battle.

Basen discarded the used akorell bracelet. He still had two on each arm but he used another to open a portal to the back of the castle. Vithos sent in the febeetles first, then followed them in. Quessa went in afterward.

"I'll be safe," Basen told Alabell as Wilfre came into the basement to watch from the stairs.

"I'm in love with you," she blurted.

"Alabell!" Wilfre scolded as Basen went into shock. "Now is not the time!"

Alabell ignored him. "I needed to tell you before you left. There was no time earlier. Go, don't let the portal close."

"Go, Basen!" Wilfre demanded. "Vithos is vulnerable

behind the castle right now."

Wilfre was right. But the delay had given Basen enough time to realize that he couldn't imagine his life without Alabell. If that wasn't love, he wasn't sure what was.

"I'm in love with you, too."

Alabell squeezed his arm before running up the stairs.

Basen walked into the portal and then tumbled out. Overwhelmed by the dizziness of his emotions, he barely felt the vertigo.

"Why you smile?" Vithos asked. "We still need hurry?"

"Yes." Basen focused on his task, searching the stone wall for any kind of discoloration.

"It's here." With what appeared to be a bored look, Quessa pointed at a circle that was lighter in color than the rest.

Basen stabbed his sword into it as he heard shouting from within the castle. The febeetles squirmed around their feet while Basen took out a chunk of partially melted stone.

"That's it?" Quessa complained. The hole only appeared deep enough for a finger. "The wall is at least three times as thick as that hole!"

"No that's not it." Basen stuck his sword deeper into the wall and scraped it around to loosen the rock shoved in by his allies to hide the hole. Every night, he'd made a portal for a mage in enemy uniform to spread Jack's stone-softening substance deeper into the hole. Then the mages would push energy as far into the hole as possible. It was up to them when to walk back to H district.

Basen scraped out all the loose rock he could, then

pointed his wand over the hole and made light for a look. It was deep but stopped short of opening up into the great hall of the castle.

Basen stepped back and put his hand over the small opening. Quessa stood right beside it with a scowl.

"Move," Basen said.

She took a single step away, not even glancing down to ensure she didn't crush the febeetles.

Without using any of the four akorell bracelets remaining, Basen gathered bastial energy into the hole. He packed it together as deep as he could, then opened a portal inside the wall. He forced it to expand. It ate away at the edges of the wall weakened by potion.

The stone creaked in complaint.

"The whole wall is going to come down," Quessa warned him.

"It won't. The portal isn't strong enough to eat solid blocks of stone, only the loosened parts."

He could feel the portal pushing against the edges like water pressing against his head in a deep lake. He pushed harder and harder until he felt something give in front of the portal. He let go and the portal devoured the energy and sucked up some of the pebbles remaining in the tunnel. Basen put his eye against it and could see light coming through from the other end.

He heard movement behind him and turned to see Vithos aiming his hand straight up. "Quiet," the Elf whispered. "Scout on edge of top."

"Quessa," Basen whispered, "go around and get in the castle now. Find Reela and Annah."

She rushed around the castle. Eventually Basen heard

her shouting at the uniforms guarding the entrance.

"Let me in! I know what the rebels are planning." She sounded so angry yet sure of herself that Basen had trouble believing it was the same emotionless woman.

He looked up with Vithos, ready for someone to peer over the edge. "Can you pain him from here?" Basen asked.

"Yes but only—"

A head appeared. "What are you doing down there?"

"Wait," Basen whispered to Vithos. He called up to the watcher, "Finally, you heard us calling to you. We will ambush them when they attack. I have many more waiting for instruction. Are the others coming from the wall or are they still engaged in combat?"

"What is that on the ground?" asked the watcher.

"Beetles!" Basen yelled with annoyed urgency. "We must've disturbed a colony down here, so hurry up and answer me."

"They're coming from the wall. Join them when they get here."

Basen muttered a curse. "We have to do everything at twice the speed we planned. Now, Vithos."

Vithos grunted and gave his arm a shake. The watcher screamed and fell, but the parapets caught him. Basen fired straight up. The enemy caught the fireball with his face and stopped screaming.

He disappeared, only smoke remaining. *Probably dead.* Basen wouldn't let himself feel guilty about any of this until the end.

Vithos put his hand against the wall. The febeetles moved at blinding speed in a line of pure black up from the ground into the hole. Basen cursed again. In all their haste, he'd forgotten a plug for the hole. Vithos would lose control of the febeetles shortly after sending them through. They could go anywhere within in the castle, even back from where they came. Hopefully Reela and Annah would take control sooner rather than later.

Basen figured Quessa would still be shouting for their enemies to open the door if she hadn't gotten inside yet. She would now fight her way to Reela and Annah to protect them, while the febeetles should give her the distraction she needed.

"Done," Vithos said.

Basen found a rock that should do. He jammed it into the hole. There were two gaps on either corner, none big enough for the large beetles.

"Let's go."

The two of them ran around the side of the castle.

"What are you doing?" shouted someone from above as they came around front. Basen looked up to see a team of archers on top of the castle ready to shoot at his approaching allies.

"Too far for pain," Vithos told Basen quietly. "And too many."

Their uniforms should protect them for now. "We'll kill them all!" Basen shouted to the archers.

The enemies' confusion lasted long enough for Basen and Vithos to get all the way down the hill the castle was built upon before arrows began breaking against the ground around them. They took the first turn available to put shops between them and the castle. Here they shed the blue uniforms and rejoined their army.

"Their archers are ready for us, unfortunately," Basen informed his father. "Can febeetles get to the top of the castle?" Having spent some time inside, Henry knew the layout better than Basen did.

"Unlikely. They'd have to climb a ladder. I don't imagine our psychics having the time to stand nearby and direct the beetles up one."

"Then we'll need to counterattack the archers as we approach."

The entirety of their plan revolved around getting into the castle before enemy reinforcements arrived. The door had to be opened.

Basen's officers helped him organize their ranks quickly. Then they marched down the main road as the frightened and unaware citizenry ran past them the opposite way. Basen let loose soaring fireballs with his fellow mages as their ally archers shot into the sky. With numbers on their side, the archers atop the castle disappeared far behind the parapets, hopefully taking cover in the castle rather than attempting to fire back.

"We rush!" Henry commanded.

They sprinted up the hill, the drum of their boots making Basen feel as if they could storm right through the ironbark door. He dispelled that foolish thought as soon as it came.

Once they made it to the top, they circled around the door. Basen moved close to one of the arrow slits beside it. Everyone waited for his order.

He witnessed an empty great hall. Distant shrieks echoed. Something moved in front of him. Basen spun away as a sword stuck through. He kicked the flat end before his attacker could pull it back. It dropped and fell out of the thin opening. The fool ran up the stairs.

Quessa and our psychics must be busy elsewhere. He had hoped to get into the castle while keeping the massive ironbark door intact, but there was no time to waste on hope.

"Break it down," Basen said.

The strongest of their men were still making their way up the hill with the battering ram. Basen turned his attention back to the arrow slit. Perhaps the febeetles weren't as vicious and terrifying as he'd thought. They were supposed to drive the castle folk and troops out, opening the door for Basen's army to come in swiftly and kill Ulric. Or perhaps the task was just too much for Quessa, Reela, and Annah to handle on their own.

Basen started to step back as his men got the battering ram in place but something within the castle caught his eye. "Wait. They're coming."

Quessa and the two psychics bounded down the stairs. "Behind us," Quessa announced.

Reela turned and thrust out her hand. Two soldiers upon the balcony collapsed. Quessa started up toward them, but they crawled away as they screamed, and she soon gave up.

As the three women got the door open from the other side, and Basen's army started to pour in, he took time to scan the city. Black smoke rose up from the east. He could not see the wall past it. Citizens fled, no doubt as word got around of the psychic officer's interrogations in which homes would be burned when no answers were provided. But the streets were clear of soldiers as far as Basen could see. *They must've been summoned to defend the wall against Sneary's attack. Good.*

Basen was the last one in the castle. "Help me get the door shut." Members of his army helped him close the heavy ironbark door and shift the nearby lever to raise unseen locks from the ground. Then they moved the battering ram to sit just in front of the door.

His army knew to search the castle in teams and began this task without delay. Basen found Reela and Annah in the great hall catching their breaths. Before he could ask about Ulric, Reela was already telling him what he needed to know.

"He's gone to the top of the eastern tower with a few hundred below ready to fight for him. We sent those beetles after every soldier we could find and managed to kill quite a few, but every enemy still alive should be gathered below the tower now. The beetles will probably be dead by the time we get there."

"How many mages, archers, and psychics do they have?"

"A few mages, a dozen archers, and one psychic," Reela said.

"Any chance of a trap?"

"No. You took them by surprise."

"What now?" Annah asked.

"We kill Ulric."

Basen chose a small team to remain around the door while everyone else rushed up the stairways. Jack volunteered to head the team.

"I'll shout when we see them coming," Jack said with a proud grin. "I have an excellent shouting voice that's rarely used."

It was a long way up, and not a single person made it to the top without gasping for breath. Basen bolted around the slow-moving line of his troops and eventually came to his father and a group of soldiers standing at the edge just before another hall. The rest gathered behind Basen. He figured the enemies must be waiting right around the turn.

"No more beetles to distract them," Henry informed him. "The hall is wide enough for five men. We're waiting on shields."

Greg appeared to be the most competitive of their army to get at the front, shoving his way there and then peering around the corner. "They come!"

Basen heard a stampede of boots. *They know most of us are tired from the stairs.*

"Back away from the corner," he ordered. "Give me space." They moved behind him.

"What are you doing?" his father asked in horror.

Basen was too busy concentrating to answer. He drew out the energy from one of his four remaining akorell bracelets as he stepped into the hall. Basen fed sartious energy to the heavy cluster of swirling white energy while his charging enemies let out a roar of aggression. He willed it forward as it caught fire.

Heat rapped against Basen's back as he turned. The fireball growled as it exploded. Then it crackled and sizzled.

Basen turned back. It had cleared half of the hall, the troops in the other half stunned. As their wits returned, archers and mages lining up their shots, Basen fled around the corner. A barrage of arrows and fireballs pelted the balcony, others exploding against the far castle wall.

"Shields ready," Henry announced. A swarm of his troops came together in front of Basen. Archers took to his sides. Vithos, Reela, and Annah squeezed in behind him.

"Now," Henry said.

They made their way around the corner and immediately blocked an array of arrows. Basen and the archers beside him shot over the heads of his ally shield bearers, but their enemies had lined up shields as well.

There was a flash of light as an enemy mage let loose a fireball. The shield bearer in front of Basen intercepted it but fell backward into him. Basen caught and steadied him, but the shield slipped free from his hands. Two arrows pelted the man's torso, felling him. Before Basen could reach down to grab the shield, Greg had already taken it and stepped into line. He blocked the few arrows that would've pierced Basen, then broke into a sudden charge.

Everyone followed suit, enemies included. Basen put away his wand and drew his sword. Shields clashed as swords found flesh. Basen stabbed around Greg and felt his blade slide into something that screamed.

They tore through the first line of enemies, and their psychics took down the next. Now with no shields in their way, their attacking army plowed through the third and fourth lines.

They ravaged their enemies and soon came to the end of the hall. Littered among the corpses were hundreds of dead febeetles. A short ladder rose up to a closed hatch made of black ironbark.

"Ulric is up there," Reela said.

Greg was the first one on the ladder, practically snarling at Basen when he put his hands on the rung.

"Let me," Greg said. "My parents were killed because of him and Tauwin."

Basen backed off. Greg climbed up and pushed against the square hatch. Metal clinked louder the harder he pushed, no doubt locked from above. He groaned as he shoved even harder, veins bulging in his neck. Basen feared Greg might fall as he thrust his sword against the wood with Cleve-like strength.

Basen turned and asked his father, "Is there another way up?"

"Not to that platform, but to another that might give us a line of sight. Follow me."

Jack Rose was screaming from the great hall as Basen followed his father along the balcony.

"They've arrived!"

"How many?" Basen shouted back.

"Too many."

"We need more time. How long until they get here?"

"Minutes."

Basen gave his father a dire look.

"There might be enough time," Henry said.

They broke into a sprint.

CHAPTER THIRTY-SEVEN

Cleve felt as if he could barely breathe. The buttons of his pilfered uniform dug into his chest each time he took a deep breath. It was the largest they could find on any of their slain enemies, and it had been cleaned and altered with a hawk on its back.

He'd waited for this night for weeks: vengeance. He'd taken a little of it every night before this as he'd roamed the forest to hunt their hunters with some of the most capable troops in the ally army. But Basen's orders prevented him from taking on Rockbreak's hunting party, and for good reason. There were too many.

Tonight and tomorrow, however, everything would change.

He waited with his army outside Oakshen as his allies within the city set the wall aflame. Penny led the mages and Sneary led the others. Cleve trusted them to keep Steffen and Effie safe.

"Here!" yelled a soldier in Cleve's army. The first enemy messenger was on his way.

The ally soldier had called from too far away for Cleve to offer his support, so he continued to watch the wall, bow in hand.

The second horseman rode out from the burning wall, the flames licking his back. "Here!" Cleve shouted as he took aim.

His allies moved to get in front of the messenger, stopping the horse and causing the animal to buck. The messenger tried to turn his mount around, but Cleve put an arrow into his chest before he could regain control.

Cleve ran there as he latched his bow behind his back. His allies swarmed the fallen messenger as others attempted to get the frightened horse under control. Cleve jumped on its back, his allies handing him the reins.

"Make room," he announced as he pulled to get the horse going in a tight circle. "Back away."

He gained control quickly, then figured out which way was north and gave the animal a gentle kick.

As the only one here who'd been to Greenedge, he was the only one who could ride a horse. The few psychics powerful enough to control the animal were busy with more important tasks. Cleve took a lamp from one of his allies to fight back the darkness. He set a decent pace.

His thoughts didn't deviate from his task the entire way to the northern end of the forest. If all went according to plan, Oakshen would soon be cleared of Ulric's trespassers and Sneary would be heading toward the capital to divert enemies away from the castle. Support for Ulric would come from Trentyre to the south but too late to matter.

There were terribly many things that could go wrong. Without any method of sending a message of distress to their allies, each group would have to rely on the other to succeed or all would fall by the end of the day. This risk didn't bother Cleve. He'd planned to die weeks ago, gladly giving up his life, if it came to that, for a chance at retaliation. He'd felt as if he'd been coming down with an illness in which battle was the ailment and peace was the cure.

The first rays of morning light cast upon the forest as Cleve arrived at the enemy camp. He was most certainly seen by scouts on the way, but the uniform of his enemies kept him protected better than any armor. *So long as I don't get too close to be recognized.* Cleve wasn't camouflaged very well, his broad shoulders practically bursting through the seams.

Not one of Kyrro's Allies had made it this far north and lived. Cleve's horse entered the clearing of the enormous camp. There had to be at least two thousand scattered across the entire edge of the forest, most still sleeping in tents.

"Oakshen is under attack by the entire rebel army!" Cleve rode parallel to the camp as he continued to shout. "Everyone must get to Oakshen now!"

His enemies didn't seem to be in much of a hurry as they shook off their grogginess and went for their horses.

"Everyone to Oakshen. The entire rebel—"

A flood of anger stopped Cleve midsentence as he saw Rockbreak. The giant emerged from his tent at the center of camp, the only one grinning. Cleve could shoot him right now before he donned his armor. *It would ruin everything,* Cleve reminded himself to calm his twitching fingers.

He rode along the rest of the camp and spread the message of battle. He only noticed a few glancing at his uniform, but none of their expressions held suspicion. Instead, they looked at him with shock as if he'd brought news of the sudden end of the war. Smiles finally began to spread as the men told each other it was about time.

They mounted up and left the camp, riding southeast toward Oakshen.

By the time the last of them had disappeared behind the dense trees of Raywhite Forest, Cleve noticed something horrible in the sky above the capital. Flares.

Basen has attacked too early! Cleve cursed as he dismounted and ran to hide behind the enemy tents. His horse ran off into the trees, leaving only Cleve in the camp.

What could he do to stop Rockbreak's army if one of them caught a glimpse of the flares through the canopy of treetops? *Nothing*, Cleve soon realized. They would turn back and kill him as soon as they realized he was lying about Oakshen. Or worse, they might ignore Cleve and go straight for the capital. He cursed again as he made his way west.

Cleve climbed a hillock where he could get a better view, and where he could shoot from if he did see the horrible sight of Rockbreak leading his army toward the capital. Cleve waited and watched, his hands never unclenching except to remove his restricting uniform. He would gladly die just to delay them, if it meant Basen had taken the castle.

The plain tunics of boiled leather of his allies came into sight first. He nearly fell and broke his leg in his rush to climb down.

"Did you see a flare?" he asked them.

They shook their heads. Cleve asked others, but none of them had. *Then Rockbreak's army couldn't have seen, either.* He took a breath of relief.

"The camp is clear," he told them.

It felt like a waste to walk through without setting fire to a single tent. Rickik and his Krepps began to let their saliva loose in all directions. Cleve more than understood—he felt the urge to join them.

Their enemies had enjoyed comfort and safety every night since Tenred's betrayal, while Cleve and his allies had been disturbed nearly every night by hunters. Rickik tore his claws through the side of one tent. His fellow Krepps followed suit. Soon all of them were on a rampage.

Seeing as how there was no stopping the spitting and thrashing creatures now—Nebre included—Cleve decided to join them. They demolished the enemy camp as they made their way through.

When the last of the forest was behind them, Cleve wanted to bask in the morning sun and take time to admire the view. The Academy, his home, was in sight, but this also meant that Tenred scouts on the walls had seen him. He took a breath to harden himself, then started to run.

There had been no one man elected to lead them. They didn't need one. Together, they charged and screamed like jackals. The Krepps took the lead with their superior speed, screeching out a terrifying sound that made Cleve smiled wickedly. It was finally time to teach Crea and her followers that going against the Academy was a death wish. He tried to make out the faces of the two wall guards before the men ran down the ramp and disappeared, but they were too far.

Cleve's joy was gone as he realized his enemies wouldn't stand and face him but instead would run back to Tenred. Crea would escape. There would be no glorious battle within the walls as Cleve had imagined. Of course not; these men were cowards.

Basen had been right to send only three hundred troops with Cleve into the forest. He'd been right not to give them any of the valuable psychics nor any of the powerful mages. Cleve would've joined Basen to take and defend the castle if it weren't for his ability to ride a horse.

Disappointment started to eat away at him by the time he arrived at the school. The Krepps had hopped up to pull themselves over the wall and opened the gate for the rest of the small army. The Academy looked just as they'd left it except no one was in sight. If only Cleve's army could've come from the north instead, then none could've escaped. But there had been no chance of going around without being seen.

He sullenly took his position upon the wall and waited for his allies to fail or succeed. He peered north through the spyglass for a look across the barren Academy. The last of Crea's troops were leaving through the opposite gate, too far for Cleve to discern if Crea was among them.

A team of his allies were volunteering to search the Academy for any remaining enemies when Rickik pointed south and hollered, "They come!"

Cleve glanced toward the forest. Thousands of enemies seeped out from the trees and searched through their destroyed camp.

"Get down," Cleve announced. Everyone on the wall ducked below the parapets. Those on the ground cleared away from the gate.

"Why have they returned?" Nebre asked Cleve.

"They might've thought something about me to be

suspicious, or a scout we failed to intercept told them the truth about the attack. They could've even seen one of the flares. There's no way to know." He handed Nebre the spyglass. "Take this and tell me what you see, but keep your head as low as possible."

Nebre watched for a while in silence. Eventually he handed the spyglass back to Cleve and straightened his back all the way. "They're coming with weapons drawn. They know we're here."

Cleve stood beside Nebre to look for himself. The entire forest army with Rockbreak was marching toward them. There had to be at least two thousand with the giant in full steel armor.

"Battle!" Rockbreak yelled.

His army boomed in echo.

Cleve drew his sword. Everyone around him took out their weapons. Rickik hissed and grinned. He grabbed Cleve's shoulder.

"For honor."

For Terren.

*****

Basen's father showed him to the ladder before sprinting back from where they'd come, needing to organize everyone into the proper positions to defend the castle. Basen climbed up the ladder and pushed up the hatch at the top. Then he ascended to stand upon the castle's tower.

He glanced in all directions before finding a man his father's age, in a separate tower, the backdrop of the blue morning sky behind him. Basen lifted his wand, but Ulric spotted him before Basen could cast. He fired anyway, Ulric ducking from sight. Basen's fireball cleared the tower and crashed into the next, blasting off a Takary flag.

Basen stood on his toes and fired again at his unseen foe. His fireball exploded against the front side of Ulric's tower, but flames squeezed through the parapets. Basen couldn't tell if he'd hit his target, so he fired again and again. Basen was certain he would hit Ulric soon enough. Their towers weren't that far from each other.

Ulric began to scream like a madman, "Jaol! Jaol! A mage is on the near tower. Shoot him! Shoot him!"

Ulric must've seen the other man approaching. Jaol was the psychic officer who'd been burning down homes for information on rebels. Basen took a moment to scan the city below and found Jaol with an army quickly approaching the bottom of the castle's hill. Basen changed his strategy to shoot the fireball high into the air in hopes of it coming down on top of Ulric. But he had no training for shots like this, and his fireballs missed the tower every time, sizzling against the roof of the castle.

He felt something pass by overhead and turned in the direction it had come. He cursed and ducked below the parapets as ten more arrows arced toward him. He'd only gotten a glimpse of the men with Jaol before hiding, but it was clear the psychic officer had taken his time to gather all the available troops in the city. If any had been distracted by Sneary's attack on the capital's wall, none were likely there now. They'd filled the street and the alleys up to the castle, halting just before the hill.

Basen stayed below the edge of the stone as arrows continued to fly overhead. He shot more fireballs into the sky at Ulric's tower but couldn't tell how close he was getting.

Ulric continued to scream for help. "Shoot him down, then get inside the castle! They've almost broken through to get to me."

So Greg was making progress with the ironbark hatch. But the arc of the arrows changed to match Basen's fireballs, soaring high into the air and coming down around him. He cursed again as he went back through the hatch and started to close it after him. He would be of better use alive and in the great hall in preparation of Jaol's assault than firing random fireballs into the air. But what he heard from Jaol stopped Basen from shutting the hatch completely so he could listen.

"King Ulric, I need to first determine their plan before I attack." His voice came from somewhere outside the castle, Basen unsure how close.

"Their plan is to kill me and then take the rest of Kyrro! They've almost broken through the hatch, get here *now*, Jaol!"

"There is but one entrance to the castle," Jaol shouted back without fear or panic. "There's no doubt that the rebels are waiting for my men to squeeze through it so they can ambush us. We have kept you safe from fireballs for now, but we'll all die if we rush this. We need to determine how they expect to take back all of Kyrro. What have you seen from up there?"

"What have I seen?" Ulric sounded manic. "It doesn't

matter what I've seen! I order you to enter the castle and kill them all!"

"I believe one of them can make portals, as you suspected," Jaol shouted. "Part of the wall of Oakshen has fallen—the city might have been taken. Yet we've received no news. The capital's wall has fallen as well. You must tell us where you see the rebels heading."

"Trentyre is untouched," Ulric yelled. "A small army is headed to the Academy, but don't ask me how they've gotten past Rockbreak because I don't know. They took the castle with less than a thousand." It was actually an even thousand. "You can easily take it back. Most of their army is coming to the castle through the broken wall, and the hatch is breaking!"

The longer Jaol waited to attack, the greater the chances that Basen's allies could get to Ulric. However, they still had to worry about the most capable enemy group: Rockbreak's. Basen was thankful Sneary was on his way to aid their allies within the castle, but Rockbreak's group would soon realize there was no battle at Oakshen if they hadn't already seen the flares. They could come to the capital and flank Sneary or they could go to the Academy and overwhelm Cleve.

There was only one solution. The rebels had to kill Ulric soon and force Jaol to attack Basen's comrades within the castle, because a battle on the streets would lead to complete annihilation of Basen's and Sneary's brigades.

Basen ran back through the castle, unable to hear the rest of the conversation between Ulric and Jaol. When he arrived below Ulric's tower, the only people remaining were Greg and a few of Henry's soldiers. Greg was just descending the ladder, his hands shaking and bloody. The hatch looked chipped and cracked around the edge.

Basen took out his sword to finish what Greg started, but the men put up their hands to stop him, no doubt to listen to Jaol.

"We will wait for their army to arrive and face them on the street," the psychic officer shouted. "After we kill them, we will devise a plan to retake the castle."

Basen climbed up the ladder and started bashing the tip of his sword against the hatch.

"You have your order!" Ulric screamed. Basen stopped again to listen.

"If you want any chance of your army surviving the day, you will be patient," Jaol retorted.

"It's not an issue of patience, you imbecile. My life is at stake here. I'm your king, giving you an order! I don't care what they have planned. We have ten times their numbers."

As much as Basen enjoyed picturing Ulric sweating up there, he didn't have time for this. He started slamming the blade against the hatch again. Sneary's forces could not face Jaol's outside the castle with any hope of winning.

Ulric's hoarse voice screeched out the most manic of sounds yet. "Whoever kills Jaol and assumes command of retaking the castle will receive twenty acrowns and a promotion to the rank of officer!"

"*You* are the imbecile!" Jaol yelled. He screamed something at his men that Basen couldn't understand.

Basen bashed away at the hatch until he nearly fell off the ladder from giddiness.

"I am taking command!" shouted a different man. "We're coming, your highness. Anyone who refuses to attack these rebels will have every finger and toe broken before being executed. We will not stand here and do nothing!"

Having made no progress on the hatch, Basen got down from the ladder, wincing from the pain in his hands. "Someone needs to stay to make sure he doesn't come down while we're away."

None of the four looked as if they would volunteer. Basen couldn't blame them for wanting to engage their enemies, but he couldn't stay as he had something more important to do. It had to be one of these other men.

"I will," Greg said, a resigned look on his face. "I am the newest to this rebellion, the least deserving of glory. Don't let a single one of them survive."

The men followed Henry down the stairs while Basen returned to the top of the second tower to face the one where Ulric hid. By the time Basen made it back up there, all his allies would be in place in the great hall. They would fill the stairs and the balcony while their best archers positioned themselves inside each of the many shooting windows. The arrow slits were too thin for Basen to safely cast his fireballs, hence his ascension into the tower.

The view of the city was majestic enough to make any man feel like a king up here. He could see all of Kyrro, including the Academy. He lost his breath as he witnessed an army far too large to be part of his own rushing the southern wall of the school. Rockbreak...*Cleve needs help!* This had to end soon, but Basen's immediate enemies still appeared to be preparing to charge. Basen turned to Ulric's tower to find the false king staring back with uneasy eyes.

"Are you the portal mage?"

There was no point for either of them to lie now. "I am."

"So are you the one responsible for all this?" Ulric gestured with both hands at the territory surrounding them.

"That's one way of looking at it."

"You should've come to me when this began."

"Why would I do that?"

"I see you haven't considered what will happen to you if you do manage to take this territory back."

"Enlighten me."

"Whoever takes my place will use your portal ability not to improve the lives of these citizens but for his own desires. You will become the soldier you once were but lowly and dutiful. You will never have the opportunity to organize, to take your own power. It's not too late to change your mind. I can make you a god, a commander with unlimited authority. You will be revered by everyone."

Basen ignored Ulric as he glanced back at his enemies, eager for this to begin. They made their way up the hill to the castle at a slow pace, marching behind the cover of their shields. Soon they would be in range for Basen to shoot them.

"All I've been trying to do is clean up Tauwin's mess," Ulric continued. "I don't want to control these working citizens. The war has forced me into a position I despise."

"You could've stayed in Greenedge where you belong."

"There is only wealth without power in Greenedge. Money corrupts us all, as it did Tauwin. It would've corrupted me eventually. What else am I to do when I hear of the Takarys in Kyrro planning to retake control of the continent and expecting to do so in a single day? Tauwin and his father came from a line of tyrannical madmen. They would've ruled this territory the way a coldhearted master treats his slaves."

"Stop lying," Basen interrupted. "I know you were planning with Yeso to steal power from someone somewhere before Tauwin's father wrote to ask you for money. I just don't know where. If it wasn't here, it would've been somewhere else."

"I *was* going to steal power," Ulric admitted to Basen's surprise. "But not by taking control of Kyrro. I wished to help Greenedge. If you know about my past, you must know the dire circumstance the continent was in. Yeso and I were going to take over every territory held by men and Elves to end the conflict. Only then could we band together to stand against the desmarls taking over our land. Fatholl is a narcissist trumpeter who blares the tune of his own philanthropy while refusing the help of other rulers. It was mostly by luck that he succeeded."

Ulric paused and looked out toward his approaching army. "I ask you again, what was I supposed to do when I heard of the plan to take Kyrro? I couldn't let Kyrro's Takarys sully our family name more. Our reputation in Kyrro was already bad enough. I needed to get involved to remove them from power."

"You could've stopped this war when Tauwin died."

"No. A promise was made to thousands of men. If I'd reneged, they would've hung me and chosen someone else to lead them. My staying in power was the only way to make Kyrro better. To do that, I had to win the war first. I don't enjoy killing your comrades, but it must be done. Crea Hiller is a brat waiting to steal from the cookie jar as soon as no one's looking. There are others like her, Cassius Lane, my now dead officer Jaol, and Crea's own uncle, Henry Hiller. You probably know him as a leader among the rebels, but he's just another Hiller who takes power where he can get it. If I'd moved toward ending the war, all it would've done was get me killed. At least I can make Kyrro thrive again. Others won't."

As much as Basen wanted to shoot fireballs at him again, Ulric would just duck and Basen would be wasting his energy. Instead, he lined up his first shot at the approaching enemies, but part of his focus was torn away. Could Ulric be telling the truth? Could he be right about Henry?

Yes, he could be, but that didn't matter. The blood of thousands was on Ulric's hands, and he and his greedy soldiers stood in the way of restoring Kyrro.

The arrows of Basen's allied archers shot out from the castle, pelting the shields of their enemies. Some staggered while their officer yelled for them to remain in formation. They inched closer to the castle as Basen drew out the energy from one of his three remaining akorell bracelets. He shot his enormous fireball into the sky. His practice shooting at Ulric had paid off, the fireball arcing down to explode into the middle of the oncoming troops.

Basen took out the energy from another akorell bracelet and fired his second fireball, too focused on aiming to watch the effects of his first. He did relish the screams, though. He saved his last akorell bracelet as he shot a regular fireball, then another.

Finally, he took the time to look. The formation had broken apart. Those in front still had their shields out ahead of them, but many men had separated to take aim at Basen and his allies inside the castle.

A storm of arrows was traded between the castle and the road, some soaring up into the sky in desperate hope of stopping Basen.

He fired upward as well, gravity pulling his fireballs fast onto their heads. Meanwhile, the arrows of his allies mowed over them like a scythe across grass.

There were still so damn many.

The enemies in front reached the door. Basen couldn't see them from his vantage point, nor could he shoot them. But he knew the arrow slits of the castle provided a clear view for his allies to defend their positions.

He heard Ulric's forces screaming as they tried to break down the door. Basen couldn't help himself, indulging in a glance over at Ulric to enjoy his panic. His face was as white as a cloud as he leaned over the edge to watch.

Basen continued to shoot upon his enemies as he heard the door to the castle breaking. He opened the hatch, rushed down the ladder, and sprinted through the castle to get to the stairs. It was a long way down, forcing him to watch the battle migrate into the great hall.

There were no other orders for his army to follow, no

tricks to be played. Basen's allies faced their enemies with sword on sword, fighting against the disadvantage of numbers even after all they'd killed and wounded.

The castle was supposed to protect the true king of Kyrro; these pretenders didn't deserve to be standing within its great hall. These men—who'd killed Alabell's family—would die.

Basen finally joined the fray as he descended the last set of stairs, his allies now falling back. He had just enough time to gather energy and shoot a pillar of fire into the faces of his swarming enemies. They tumbled backward into each other, many of them continuing all the way down the stairs.

Momentum shifted as Basen pulled out his sword. The rebels drove their enemies back. He fought with calculated fury, soon finding himself beside Neeko. The pyforial mage grabbed enemy weapons with the clear energy and ripped them out of their owners' hands. Other times, Basen caught sight of Neeko flinging enemies off the stairs with tremendous power.

Basen fought them back to the base of the stairs, then circled around to come behind the enemies pressing his allies farther into the rooms of the castle. Soon he came up on Quessa's side, not recognizing her until she jabbed her sword through the enemy Basen was about to stab. She fought with fluidity and surprising strength, blocking and swiping similar to how Terren had fought against Abith. But Quessa's enemies were nowhere near Abith's master level, and she made quick work of all who came near.

Basen found Annah and Reela together and told them

to separate to either end of the great hall. They obeyed, while he yelled for Vithos to take the center.

"Put everything you have into it now!" he announced to the rest of his army. "Get to the edges and close in on them!"

Basen and his allies overwhelmed their enemies, forcing them back through the broken door. Many tripped on the battering ram still in the way and were killed before they could rise up again.

There was no hesitance or mercy as Basen plunged his blade through the flesh of his enemies. It did not matter if they were on the ground or had their backs to him.

He fought his way over the battering ram and onto the road. Some of the enemies began to back away as if to flee, but they all came back to the fray, to Basen's surprise. Soon he saw why.

Abith Max led the charge up the hill, his bastial steel sword whirling. Krepps fought on either side of him, Sneary just behind with the rest of Basen's army, save Cleve and those at the Academy.

The battle was won, every enemy realizing so as they dropped their weapons in surrender. Basen's allies quickly surrounded them. Cheering erupted. Basen didn't partake as he pushed his way through to Abith.

"I thought I might never see you again," Basen said as he threw one arm over Abith's shoulder for a quick half-embrace.

Abith returned the gesture with a grin splitting his face. "And I thought all of you would be killed before I found a way to join."

"Abith and his Krepps found us on our way to the

capital," Sneary said, slapping Basen on the back, then extending his hand for Basen to shake.

"I couldn't let them have all the glory." Abith slapped Sneary's back. Basen had never seen the warrior leader smile before, but he did now.

CHAPTER THIRTY-EIGHT

Cleve tried to keep them off the walls. He fought with near perfection, every arrow finding a home in an enemy soldier's chest, every swipe of his sword cutting down one who'd gotten over the wall.

After leading the charge, Cassius had ordered his men to spread out along the base of the wall and help each other up. The barrier was too long, and there were too many for Cleve's small army of three hundred to stop them all. Cleve alternated between slicing them up and shooting them down, sometimes forced to shoot around his allies to get enemies behind them on the walkway along the wall.

Rickik and Nebre covered Cleve's back, but soon their enemies stopped trying to climb up near enough for the Krepps to reach them. Instead, the attackers ran along the wall until no one waited above them. Only half of the enemies could make it up, as they needed to help each other to reach the parapets. But half of them still outnumbered Cleve's army by more than two to one.

Rockbreak was one of the last men to reach the wall. Cleve had managed to get a few arrows off at the armored giant, but none had pierced his steel. Rockbreak didn't need his men's support, as he could reach the parapets with a small hop. With inhuman strength, he pulled himself up, armor and all. Cleve wasn't close enough to stop Rockbreak from swiping two rebels off the wall before reaching back over to grab his bastial steel sword handed to him by his comrades.

Cleve's army had mostly managed to hold everyone back until then. The change of momentum came so suddenly that no order of retreat needed to be given, all allies fleeing from the wall. Some even jumped down and risked a sprained ankle to escape certain death as swordsmen closed in around them.

"No run!" complained Rickik, the last one on the wall.

Cleve came back to the walkway from the ramp to slash someone about to stab Rickik in the back. "We still fight, but we need to move to survive! Come on."

Rickik ran with Cleve, their enemies close behind.

"No!" Rockbreak whined as he threw off pieces of his armor to catch up. "You won't escape Rockbreak this time!"

There wasn't much dirt left before the mage classrooms. "Stop and fight here!" Cleve yelled. "Keep the buildings at your backs." It was the only way to prevent them from being surrounded.

Rickik and Nebre lined up together beside Cleve. There was a strange pause in the battle as their enemies stopped ten yards short. All looked back. Cleve assumed they were waiting for Rockbreak to lead the charge, but it was Cassius who came to the front. The Tenred officer, the betrayer. Cleve would see him and Rockbreak dead if it was the last thing he did.

Cassius drew Cleve's bastial steel sword from his sheath. "Why get yourself killed just to hold the Academy for a breath? Of course we would return to check on the camp when we realized we were tricked. Did you think we wouldn't look for you at the Academy?" He chuckled.

"After all this time in the forest, this must be your way of giving up."

Rickik shocked Cleve by charging straight at Cassius while spitting and screeching. "Betrayer!"

Stunned, Cleve couldn't move. Fortunately, his enemies didn't seem ready for this either. None attacked as Rickik lifted his sword. Cassius shuffled backward and Cleve lost sight of him as the others finally rushed in after Rickik. They stabbed at the Krepp from every angle, but he moved too quickly for them to land more than a glancing blow. Cleve caught them by surprise as he shouldered one soldier into a group of others.

The other Krepps came to flank Cleve, knocking down their enemies and slashing wildly. With his retreat slowed by the wall of his troops, Cassius was forced to turn and face a crazed Rickik. The enormous Krepp twisted his torso to swipe his blade everywhere, nearly cutting Cleve as he tried to get close to offer support. Rickik spat and flung dirt with his feet. Blades ran across the hard flesh of his arms and sides but did nothing to slow him. He bled but did not tire as he took everyone's focus. Cleve killed a dozen in Rickik's path as he heard his allies coming into the fray behind him with battle cries.

Cassius no longer appeared shocked or even afraid as he stepped toward Rickik. Their swords clashed, giving the enemies around the Krepp a chance to jump on him. They grabbed his arms and neck and tried to take him down. He shook like a dog drying his fur, flinging them off. One tumbled into Cassius. The betrayer fell forward past the Krepps.

Rickik brought his sword down with a hiss. There was

a crack as it pierced through Cassius' back. His arms splayed and he dropped Cleve's bastial steel sword.

Rickik left his weapon in the corpse and picked up Cleve's sword. Whether he recognized it as Cleve's or not, it wouldn't matter. Rickik believed it belonged to him now. Cleve was too busy fending off three assailants to care. He blocked one attack while bringing up his forearm to intercept the arm of another, but he could do little about the third who tried to stab Cleve in the heart. He turned and cried out as the blade sliced through his leather armor to cut across his chest. They would have to do a lot worse than that to kill him.

He retaliated with his own strike, lodging his sword into the neck of the swordsman. Before he could pry it out to defend himself from the two others, Rickik swiped his blade from behind Cleve's assailants and cut them clean in half.

"Make room!" growled a man with a voice of a bear. The enemies in front of Cleve bolted out of the way of Rockbreak, creating a clear path. Rickik stepped in front of Cleve.

"Move!" Cleve shouted. "He's mine."

"No, he's mine." Rickik spat into the face of an enemy trying to catch him off guard from the side, then pushed his blade through the man's chest in an almost lazy manner. The rest stayed back as Rickik charged Rockbreak.

The two largest creatures on the battlefield collided, both holding their bastial steel swords across their bodies to block the other's sword. They jumped into each other upon impact.

Rickik screeched as he flew backward. Cleve tried to

stick his sword through Rockbreak's leg as he closed in on the fallen Krepp, but Rockbreak swiped Cleve's blade away from his body without his gaze leaving Rickik. He jumped as if to crush the Krepp. A flash of gray stole Rockbreak out of the air as Nebre tackled him from the side.

They crashed through enemies and allies, bouncing off one another to roll away. Nebre had lost his sword and now looked around for it as enemies swarmed him. Cleve focused energy and jumped, striking one in the head with his boot. Then he ran his blade through the back of another.

Nebre wrestled two men, using one arm for each, while Cleve circle around to fend off the others coming up behind the Krepp. There were too many. One blade got through to stab Nebre in the leg before Cleve could stop it. The Krepp fell beneath the grappling enemies as both pulled out daggers.

More enemies swarmed around Cleve. "Rickik!" he shouted as he kicked them back. "Nebre's on the ground!"

Rickik leapt into the fray. Cleve lost him for a moment. An enemy flew up and landed on another, no doubt tossed by Rickik. Soon Rickik and Nebre were up and fighting back to back. Enemies closed in around them and Cleve, forcing the three of them back toward the classrooms. Rockbreak fought at the front of the enemy line, killing Cleve's allies while Cleve found no opening to attack the giant as he was too busy defending himself.

It was as if the enemy army had doubled. *Or half of our troops have been killed.* Cleve had trained against two and three swordsmen at once, but even he had no way of keeping up with five.

Soon he was fighting with his back against a building. Enemy swordsmen continued to make it through his defenses little by little, striking his leg, his arm, and eventually his stomach. None of the wounds were deep enough to threaten his life, but he could feel himself slowing as he bled.

*****

"We have to get to the Academy!" Basen announced to stop the cheering. "The enemy army in the forest went for the school instead of the castle."

"Let them have it," Abith said as he wiped the blood off his bastial steel blade on a fresh corpse. "We'll take it back."

A couple of Krepps crouched in front of Basen to meet his gaze. "Rickik is where?" one asked.

"Fighting for his life in the Academy." Basen turned to Abith. "Including Cleve and others. We have to go now. Henry, where are you?"

"To the Academy!" Sneary announced. "Everyone behind the castle for a portal!"

Basen located his father in the scramble, Henry grinning with the rest of them. "Can you organize a team to imprison the surviving enemies and capture Ulric? I need to—"

"I will take care of everything here. Go help the

others."

*****

It dawned on Cleve that this was how his life would end, fighting to his last breath in battle. He'd figured that this was how he'd die one day, but he'd hoped it wouldn't be so soon. The only solace was that Basen should've taken the castle by now. They would have a chance against Rockbreak eventually. Cleve just wished he'd had his own opportunity.

Suddenly, allied fighters poured out through the openings between classrooms. Arrows and fireballs rained down from the roofs up and behind Cleve. Psyche took down dozens at a time. It was as if a tidal wave had crashed upon the enemy troops.

Cleve went with the momentum, riding the turning tide. He recognized Steffen, then Reela. He turned back to see Effie standing on the roof behind him, unleashing fireballs nearly half her size. Abith Max jumped in front of Cleve, slashing his bastial steel sword down across two men.

Feeling so proud he could almost fly, Cleve stormed through his enemies. They couldn't get away fast enough, some tripping over each other as they backed away from Cleve's rampage.

"Get around them!" Sneary was yelling. "Don't let them escape."

Realizing he was near the front, Cleve took the

responsibility of rushing through his enemies rather than killing them. Half had already begun to flee, but Abith was right there with Cleve, going through to block their path.

As soon as one enemy threw down his weapon and put up his hands, all others did the same. They surrendered, a third of them bloody and barely standing. There was only one who continued to fight.

"Cowards! You're all cowards!" Rockbreak swung his massive bastial steel sword at anyone who came close, no matter the color of their uniform. "I'll fight everyone here!"

A wide berth formed around him as Cleve made his way over.

"Don't shoot him," Cleve said to the archers taking aim.

Rockbreak grinned and pointed his weapon at Cleve. "You wish to die like Terren?"

Basen came to his friend's side. "Don't do this, Cleve. Just let us kill him."

"I have to be the one to do it."

"Don't embarrass yourself," Rockbreak teased. "All of you fight me, and all of you lose." He swung his blade around him as he spun. "All at once!"

"I will kill you by myself," Cleve said with certainty.

Basen looked as if he wanted to stop Cleve but said nothing more.

Cleve found Reela staring at him with a terrified look. He told her with his eyes that he needed to do this. She frowned for a moment, but then finally nodded. A strong hand came down on Cleve's shoulder. He turned to see Rickik offering the bastial steel sword.

"You use it. For honor."

"For Terren," Cleve corrected him as he took back his sword.

"For Terren," Rickik agreed.

During every moment at night when Cleve had tried to sleep but couldn't, his mind had replayed the scene over and over again of his uncle fighting Rockbreak. Terren had fought well only to lose when he'd tried to match Rockbreak's strength by charging at the oncoming giant. Cleve also was used to being the stronger swordsman in any fight, but he'd trained Sanya how to win with skill over strength.

Cleve had imagined his clash against Rockbreak countless times. Slaying him was the only way to avenge Terren and Jackrie, and everyone else who this beast had killed. Cleve would not let himself fail.

With his beloved bastial steel sword back in his hands, he felt as if he were holding a thin stick. He spun it through the air as he advanced, his wrist never resting. Rockbreak didn't back away from Cleve but tried to advance. Cleve stopped and blocked Rockbreak's two heavy attacks, then retaliated with flicks of his wrist to move his sword in small circles. Rockbreak stepped back and laughed as if to taunt Cleve, but Cleve didn't want to get close enough for his opponent to add more wounds to his already bleeding torso.

Rockbreak grunted as he swung at Cleve, but Cleve kept his distance.

"You fight like the coward you are!" Rockbreak complained as Cleve continued to circle. Cleve had seen the giant's frustration against Terren and knew he could draw out Rockbreak's anger, but it erupted faster than he'd anticipated. Rockbreak charged like a crazed bull.

Cleve danced back as he whipped his sword around. His motions might've seemed random to a novice, but really Cleve attacked and defended with meticulous care. Terren had taught him this method long ago, when Cleve was too little to face his uncle in a battle of strength. One of his little flails caught Rockbreak on the back of his wrist. Or at least it seemed so. But Rockbreak didn't cringe or even slow. Cleve danced farther away to give himself time for a good look and spotted blood on Rockbreak's wrist after all. *It's as if he doesn't feel pain.*

Rockbreak inhaled and exhaled with fury. He roared as he spun toward Cleve with a slash strong enough to cut him in half. Cleve ducked under and poked Rockbreak in the arm.

"You're terrible at this," Cleve taunted him.

"Fight me!" he screamed.

Cleve shrugged. He rested the flat end of his blade on his shoulder as he sauntered toward Rockbreak. The giant lunged, but Cleve whipped his blade around to strike Rockbreak's sword away. With a little twirl of his wrist, Cleve brought his blade back and left another cut on Rockbreak's wrist.

Blood ran down Rockbreak's hand. He backed off Cleve to wipe it on his shirt. Then he took his hilt with both hands and came at Cleve with an overhead slash. Cleve spun and was about to counterattack when he was surprised by Rockbreak's second attack, spinning to deliver a back fist at Cleve's face. He ducked. Rockbreak kept up his turning momentum to swing his sword. Cleve barely got his own blade up in time to catch Rockbreak on the back of his arm.

This was the deepest cut yet, though it still seemed to cause the giant no pain. Rockbreak flinched but chased after Cleve with growing desperation.

Rockbreak fought with his full momentum behind him, each blow potentially more devastating than the last, but none landed. Cleve dodged and parried, chipping away at Rockbreak's hand and arm as it was the only part of the giant's body Cleve could reach.

Soon Rockbreak was bleeding so much he had to use both hands at all times. That didn't stop his rage as he chased Cleve around the circle while allies and enemies watched. If anyone in the audience said a word, Cleve didn't hear it. He focused everything into finding flesh while avoiding bastial steel.

Rockbreak finally began to slow as he huffed for breath. He backed away from Cleve. Once again, Cleve put the blade over his shoulder nonchalantly. He belied his inner fury with a leisurely gait toward the giant. Rockbreak grunted in anger and darted toward him, so Cleve swatted his sword around as if shooing a fly, batting Rockbreak's sword away. Enraged, Rockbreak screamed as he lunged at Cleve, but Cleve was ready. He made a good long gash down Rockbreak's uninjured arm with his first powerful swipe of the duel.

This only seemed to anger the giant more as he rushed to get past Cleve's defenses. Cleve hopped away and continued to keep himself alive with whips of his light sword. Eventually Rockbreak came after Cleve with a full on sprint. Cleve backed away, only to stop suddenly and duck under Rockbreak's slash. He cut Rockbreak's side as he moved beneath the blade. Coming up behind his opponent, Cleve swiped his blade down Rockbreak's leg.

The giant's sword was red with blood as it ran down his arms. It stained the side of his shirt and one of his enormous pant legs. He charged Cleve, swinging with sword and fist. Rockbreak's blood sprayed across Cleve's face and chest as he ducked and weaved. The giant continued to chase him around, finally beginning to slow. His face grew white, his breathing ragged.

Suddenly he dropped his sword and keeled over. He did not move as Cleve came over and grabbed his weapon out of his limp hand. Cleve glanced around the audience to find faces he recognized, hundreds of them. His friends beamed with pride. The Krepps thumped their chests and hollered.

Cleve gave Rockbreak's enormous sword to Rickik.

"For you." Cleve lifted his own blade, wet with blood. "I'll keep this one."

CHAPTER THIRTY-NINE

The victory of the battle cleared Basen's mind of all the strategy that had seeped into his nightmares, all the planning and detailing, all the stress. It was as if a fog had covered his entire world since the war began and now it had finally lifted and dissipated. He cheered with the others as relief washed over him.

"Are there any other enemies here?" he asked Cleve.

"Crea and the betrayers fled as we arrived. There's no one else here."

They had several hundred prisoners to take care of, and there was no place in the Academy that could fit them all. Basen would have to teleport them to the castle and lock them in the dungeons with the prisoners from the capital until it was decided what to do with them.

The day was quickly coming to a close, and Basen was starving. He longed to go back to Alabell and tell her the war was won so he could see it through her eyes. But a nagging thought brought his mind back to business.

"If Sanya is still alive, she would be here somewhere," he realized aloud.

He gathered hundreds to go looking for her. Basen wasn't surprised when Cleve and Reela came with them, but he was when he saw Effie tagging along.

They made it all the way to the northern side of the campus without seeing anyone but their comrades. Basen went behind the dining hall and into the kitchen to find what appeared to be the Academy staff huddled together, gardeners, farmers, and all.

"It's over," he announced.

None seemed to understand as they stared back in confusion.

"The war," he specified. "Kyrro's Allies have won."

They grabbed each other and jumped up and down as they cheered. Some even kissed.

"Have any of you seen Sanya Grayhart?"

The few who heard Basen immediately stopped their cheering.

They led Basen out of the dining hall and toward the storage building. *The very place she was imprisoned last time she was here.* Basen could think of no worse place for her to die. The Academy staff was running to get to Sanya as if she was still in danger, setting Basen's nerves on edge. Cleve and the others who saw them joined in.

Rather than taking Basen within the storage building, the staff went around back. Many began to give the excuse that there was nothing they could do, and then Basen saw her. Sanya hung supple, her body roped to one plank of wood and her outstretched arms tied to another going across. Bloody bruises covered her face down to her feet. Rocks lay scattered around. Basen had no doubt that Crea and her cronies had spent the last day and a half pelting Sanya with stones, probably at a distance too far away for Sanya to hurt them with psyche.

"Sanya!" Basen ran to her.

She didn't respond.

He put his fingers against her neck.

"She's still alive!"

"Water," Cleve called. He was right—she was severely

dehydrated, her lips cracked. One of the staff gave Basen a pouch. He held it to her mouth.

"Drink," Basen said.

Her eyes rolled open. "Where am I?"

"You have to drink." He turned to shout over his shoulder. "Does anyone have caregelow?"

No one answered. She had a small sip of water before passing out again.

Cleve cut the ropes with his blade to free her, and Basen carried her away from the post. Greg bolted through the crowd.

"Sanya!" He took her limp body from Basen's arms.

"We need to get her to the capital for caregelow," Basen said.

They ran south. Greg seemed as if he had her on his own, so Basen didn't offer to help.

"Did you break through the hatch before my father came back up?" Basen asked him.

"No. Ulric might still be up there."

Sanya moaned and lifted her head. "Water."

They set her down and let her drink again. She looked slightly better as some color returned to her face, but she passed out again as soon as Greg helped her up.

"I don't know what injuries she sustained from her torture," Basen said. "We need to get her to a healer."

"I won't let her die." Greg ran with her again.

Basen realized something with dismay. There had been no talk of caregelow since they'd left the Academy. Why would Alabell have any with her in the capital?

Fortunately, some of the staff were still following. Basen asked them again if there was any caregelow left in the school. None gave an answer as they all turned to each other with questioning looks.

*****

Sanya didn't know where she was or how many days she'd been asleep. She tried to think back to where she was last but all she could remember was pain. Rocks still pelted her in her mind. She flinched to escape them but ropes held her tight.

"It's all right." Alabell leaned over Sanya. "You're safe."

She sat up for a look at herself. Bruises covered her. Her body ached with dull pain. She glanced around to find herself in an unmistakable bedroom of the Academy. It might've even been her own from her brief time here as a student. Yes, there was the familiar crack on the wall beside the bed.

"How long have I been asleep?" Sanya ran her hand down the crack.

"Almost two days."

Fragments of memories came back to her: Alabell's voice, drinking something, shifting around in bed. "I'm starving."

Alabell grinned. "Good. Can you make it to the dining hall if I help you?"

"Let's find out."

Alabell offered her arm, but Sanya didn't take it. "I'm fine." Her legs shook as she made her way out of the campus home. Alabell offered her arm again, and this time Sanya clasped it to steady herself.

She heard others talking within their houses, younger voices just like when she was first here. It suddenly occurred to her that the war must've been won for this to be possible.

"He did it, didn't he?"

Alabell nodded. "It's over."

I never thought I would see this day. Sanya swallowed. "What will happen with me now?"

Alabell looked confused. "Oh, I haven't even thought of that."

She let go of Alabell's arm. "There's been no talk of prison?"

"Nothing that I've heard."

Sanya looked behind her at the southern gate. *I'm too damn hungry and tired to run.* Besides, she'd already given her traveling money to Basen. She sighed as she resigned herself to whatever fate they would decide.

She'd prayed for a quick death while confined by rope and pelted with rocks. But Crea's aim was horrendous. She threw stone after stone, none with enough force to kill Sanya even when striking her in the head. The idiot had refused to get closer, nor did she let anyone else throw. Sanya had laughed in the beginning, taunting Crea. But by the end, she was heaving out dry sobs. She hoped Crea had been killed.

"What happened after I surrendered myself to Crea?"

"All plans were followed, though there were some surprises. The takeover of Oakshen went perfectly. Ulric's troops were...removed with no casualties on our side.

Some rebels stayed behind to take control of the city while Sneary and Penny led our troops to the capital. They had just reached the wall by the time Ulric sent out the flare from the castle. The psychic officer gathered all his men and took them to the castle."

"That's too early. Was Basen able to kill Ulric before then?"

"No, Ulric locked himself atop a castle tower. They couldn't get to him until after the battle. Almost everyone came straight here and scared off Crea. She must be back in Tenred by now."

Sanya didn't care about the woman at the moment if the Takary was still alive. "What about Ulric?"

"He's dead. Jumped off the castle tower after they broke through the hatch. We believe he was trying to jump to a different platform and didn't make it."

Sanya stopped. "Are you sure it was him who died and not someone else?"

"Well, none of us knows what he looks like except for you. I was going to ask you after you ate…"

"Take me to his body now."

Alabell chuckled as she put up her hands. "You need sustenance or you'll collapse."

Sanya supposed that was true. "Then as soon as we're done. Where is it?"

"Somewhere in the Academy. They brought it here for you. I'm to take you to Wilfre when you're able."

"He's the new headmaster?"

"No one knows for certain, but he's acting the part."

Sanya didn't know enough about the politics of the school to think of anyone more suitable, though Basen did come to mind. After all, he was the one who had taken charge and led them to victory.

"Reela and Annah never saw Ulric?"

"Only with a mask. They'd heard rumors he had something else planned involving hiding his identity from the people of Kyrro."

Sanya could think of a great number of things Ulric could've done with his identity hidden once more. He could spread the rumor that he liked to take walks around his city without his mask, unrecognizable by his citizenry so he could hear the real thoughts of his people. They would be too scared to speak poorly of him.

The mask could also protect him from assassination if he hired another man with a similar build and hair to wear an identical one. She was glad she didn't have to worry about his deceptions anymore.

When they arrived at the dining hall, Sanya felt as if she'd gone back in time to when she'd come to the Academy as the first female warrior full of pretend hope. In the glances and stares she attracted, she saw no hatred as she'd expected. The people she recognized welcomed her into the dining hall with proud looks, some even nodding. The others she didn't know couldn't see past Alabell's beauty to even notice her.

There was one face that she'd completely forgotten about. The sparkle in his eyes set a small fire in her chest.

"You have an admirer," Alabell remarked with a sly smile.

Greg made his way over from his table to stop Sanya in the aisle. "It's good to see you up and walking. I visited often."

Sanya couldn't help but appreciate how he poured his focus on her and how little he noticed of Alabell. *But why is he so drawn to me?* Sanya wondered. She was fire and he was a moth seeking warmth. *He doesn't know that.*

"I'll get you some food," Alabell said as she left.

"No one must've told you what I've done," Sanya realized aloud. *It was the only reason he was still interested.* "You shouldn't be seen speaking with me."

"I know what you've done. You helped the portal mage establish headquarters in my district."

"That's not what I mean—"

"You took out all the febeetles, to my neighbors' immense relief."

"I've done a lot of bad as well."

He ignored her. "You took money your army required from the people who deserved it the least."

"And I killed. Shut up and listen to me."

Greg grabbed her hand. "Do you know what else you did, Sanya Grayhart? I shouldn't have to tell you for you to see it."

"Let go."

"You risked your life to fight for people who wanted you dead. You sacrificed yourself for them."

She broke out of his hold, then stormed past him while grumbling about how little he actually knew of her.

"No one else can say the same thing about themselves, Sanya," he called after her. "If I'm the only one who can see it, then it's my task to tell you."

Had he spent all his time here pestering others about Sanya's accomplishments just to flatter her? So much work just to take her to bed. Pathetic. She turned back to him. If she hadn't been so weak from hunger she would've screamed her question.

"Tell me what?"

"It's over. Whatever battle you've fought with yourself, it's done. It ended with the war. Now it's time to live."

By jumping into bed with you? He probably gathered information about every woman who caught his eye, then attempted to inspire them with a speech just like this one. She wished she wasn't so weak so she could catch his insincerity with psyche and expose his deception in front of their gawking audience. But as her anger rose, her head began to spin.

She came to on the cold floor. Alabell and Greg hovered over her.

"She's fine," Alabell announced. "No more talking, Sanya. You need to eat."

"I'm sorry," Greg said. "Crea almost let you starve and yet I stood in your way of food."

Feeling strangely calm, Sanya let him help her up. Psyche was the only explanation for this serene veneer, so she wasn't surprised when she looked over at Reela crouching beside Effie and Cleve. But it was Effie's look of pity that soon stole Sanya's focus. She ached to delve into the small mage's mind, but all of her strength went into remaining standing.

"Go back to your table, Greg," Sanya told him.

"But I—"

"Please. You're overwhelming me. I need time to settle."

"All right," he agreed reluctantly. "Take care. If you

need anything—"

"Alabell will see to it."

He gave a slight nod and walked away.

"Do you feel as if you'll faint again?" Alabell asked.

"No. Reela, cut the psyche."

Effie and Cleve left, but the half Elf remained. "You should believe Greg," she told Sanya. "He might be a fool for all I know, but he genuinely believes everything he told you."

"And what does Effie think about me?"

"She has words for you when you're ready." Reela turned and left.

"I have a table for us where no one will disturb you," Alabell said.

They walked to the corner of the dining hall, Alabell holding out her hands to catch Sanya if she fell. With her gait unsteady, she didn't object.

They sat at the otherwise empty table, Sanya's stomach feeling as if it had begun to devour itself out of hunger. Basen's mother came by and set two plates in front of them.

"Sanya, there's much I want to say to you. I'll make it quick, but I do hope we can speak more when you're better. Thank you for your sacrifice with Crea. We wouldn't have survived if not for you. About your father..." Tears wet Juliana's eyes. "I failed to stop him. I regret not treating the situation as if you were my own child, for I'm sure I would've found some way to remove you from him. I blame him for all your misguided...behavior. And you should as well."

Sanya stuffed her mouth with food. Neither Juliana

nor Greg understood her half as much as they thought they did. Her father wasn't responsible for her murdering, only for her pain and loneliness. But she didn't care right now that they were wrong about her. All she cared about was finding a way to atone.

"I'll let you eat." Juliana smiled halfheartedly before she left.

Sanya was thankful when Alabell said only two words during their entire meal. "Go slow."

She ignored the advice and spent the entire walk back groaning with pains in her stomach, earning exactly zero sympathy from the healer. Eventually they made it back, and Alabell got Sanya into bed.

"I'll be in the other room. Call if you need anything."

"What about Ulric's body?" Sanya asked.

"They'll deliver it to our door when they can. You can rest until then." Someone knocked. "Oh." Alabell perked. "That was fast."

She offered her hand to help Sanya out of bed, but it was unnecessary. Sanya showed a glimmer of her old strength by answering the door. She was disappointed to find Greg standing there with an awkward grin. Alabell seemed to feel the same disappointment, grumbling at him like an old shrew.

"Come back tomorrow," Alabell told him.

"I just wanted to make sure you're all right." Greg ignored Alabell as he leaned down to Sanya's eye level.

"Come in." She turned and started toward her room. At feeling Alabell's shock, she said, "I'm fine, Alabell. You've done a marvelous job."

Greg followed her into her room. She didn't bother

closing the door, needing Alabell to hear what she had to say to him. But first, there was something she'd wanted to do from the moment she'd seen him again. She grabbed his cheeks and pulled him down to plant a kiss square on his lips.

It turned out that one wasn't enough. She kissed him two more times, finishing only when she could still taste him.

"I can't be with you," she told him as she let go of his face.

"I didn't ask."

"You didn't have to."

He shrugged and turned up his hands. "Of course, we don't know each other yet."

"It wouldn't matter if we did. I still couldn't. I don't know who I am. I keep jumping from one path to the next without taking time to see where the first leads. For reasons I don't yet understand, I've been given another chance; I've been put on another path. I'm not ready to jump off this one to join a path with anyone else. I have to give myself the chance to like myself. Because if I never do, then why should I expect anyone else to?"

His brow furrowed. "Then why kiss me?"

"I wanted to, and I knew you wouldn't mind."

He leaned forward and raised his eyebrows. "If that's the kind of relationship you want, you should've said so. Kissing is only where the fun begins."

"Get out."

Anger briefly crossed his face before he forced a gentlemanly smile and left. He wasn't gone for more than a moment before Alabell entered Sanya's room. She smiled like a proud mother.

"I don't want to hear anything," Sanya told her.

Alabell stepped in close and wrapped her arms around Sanya. It surprised Sanya how supported she felt. Alabell shined with love, pouring it over Sanya like a bath she'd forgone for years. She had to push Alabell away before a tear escaped her eye.

"That's enough of that."

There was another knock. Alabell grumbled. "If that's Greg again—"

"It's not."

Sanya answered the door. Wilfre stood beside a mobile bed with a sheet draped over it, the contours of a body beneath. Ten people stood behind him, all of them Henry's uniformed men except for one. Reela.

Why was there such regret among everyone's psyche? Even their faces expressed terrible sorrow. Wilfre peeled back the sheet. Sanya barely had to glance at his cracked skull before she recognized him.

"It's definitely Ulric."

Wilfre nodded as if he'd already known. "I'm sorry about this, Sanya."

"What?"

One of the men brought a pair of cuffs out from behind his back. He handed them to Wilfre.

"This is *not* necessary!" Alabell complained.

"It's fine." Sanya extended her wrists. As Wilfre locked each shackle, Sanya put all of her strength into holding back her tears. It would be the toughest battle of her life to make it all the way to the jail in the storage building without shedding a single tear, but she would do it.

CHAPTER FORTY

Sanya didn't resist. They walked beside her rather than held on to her, swords sheathed. It was only when she got to the entrance to the prison cell that she could go no farther. She'd spent days in there wondering whether she would live or die, and she would rather accept death than endure the agony any longer.

"How long must I stay here before a decision is made?"

"A decision will be made soon," Wilfre said.

"How soon?"

"Soon," he repeated.

"How will it be decided?"

"You will receive a visitor who will provide you with the details of your trial."

"When?"

"Soon," he repeated again.

"What's soon to you is an eternity to me! I refuse to get back in that cage until I know the details of how and when my fate will be decided."

"Sanya." Reela approached.

"If you use psyche on me, I will retaliate."

"There is to be a Redfield announcement now," Reela explained. "Afterward, Effie is going to visit you and discuss the details of your trial. It *will* be soon."

Sanya took a deep breath and stepped into her cell.

If Effie was going to decide her fate, perhaps she should escape. But would doing so really be better than fighting them as they attempted to execute her, killing as many as she could?

It didn't take long after they left her alone for her to realize how tired she was of running and how sick she was of killing. She'd done everything in her power to help them. If they still decided she deserved to die for her crimes, so be it.

It was a depressing thought that she wouldn't have the chance to spend her life atoning for her murders, but she was exhausted of the battle. Death would be a welcome release.

No one had bothered to take Sanya's dagger. She'd looted it not long after the betrayal from some dead soldier she couldn't picture anymore. Dried blood stained the Takary sigil on the handle. She'd lost it during the botched escape with Basen's mother. Someone must've found it and put it on her desk. *Probably Basen.*

She wanted to cut something.

She grabbed a handful of her long hair and hacked it off.

*****

When the Redfield announcement came to an intermission, Effie made her way north toward the storage building. Gabby tried to tag along.

"I need to speak to her alone," Effie said.

"At least tell me what you've decided for her."

"I haven't decided anything yet."

Gabby squinted as if Effie might be lying, then seemed to believe her, leaning back with a nod. "All right. Then I'm going back to watch the discussion."

"Make sure to remember all and tell me after."

"I will."

They shared a hug.

Effie's younger sister had been admitted to the Academy, along with many other rebels who would've otherwise been too young or old to join. Wilfre and Jack were still sorting everyone into appropriate positions, but one thing had become abundantly clear. There weren't many loyalists to the Academy left in the cities because almost all were here. Basen's father depended on support to assist his claim to king, but hardly any of his men were willing to go to the cities. Doing so would mean campaigning against the citizenry of Kyrro, who wished no Hiller to be king, their wounds too fresh from the war before this one. It didn't seem to matter that Henry had fought against the Takarys from the start. They had no interest in him leading them.

Basen and his mother had spent many nights arguing with Henry to give up this play for the crown. "He doesn't care that every king of Kyrro was killed long before dying of old age," Basen had told Effie the last time she'd seen him in the dining hall. "He thinks he'll be the first to escape that fate."

All pieces of the political game were already moving toward crowning a different king. Another wealthy man. Surely by the end of his reign, his son would have twice the wealth that the king had, and *his* son would have twice the wealth of the other.

All that money and power would've disgusted Effie, but there was something different this time around. Annah remained in the capital to monitor all the candidates for kingship as they answered questions from the people. And all candidates had lied and lied, eventually removing themselves from consideration. Except for one: Fernan Estlander, who swore to use his wealth for Kyrro to prosper.

Fernan seemed to be the subject of every other conversation in the Academy, and Effie couldn't help being just as curious about him as everyone else. Fernan was young at thirty years old, described as being so handsome that Effie was certain details had been exaggerated. His wealth didn't compare to the Takarys, but Ulric still had enlisted his help during the war. Fernan told the people during a hearing that he regretted helping Ulric, but he would've been killed and all of his money would've been used to fuel Ulric's army if he'd disobeyed.

Effie wouldn't have believed this soon-to-be-king if it weren't for Annah's psyche, especially when he said he would've helped the rebels if he'd known how. If the rumors were correct, it was this answer that finally led the other candidates to remove themselves before the people made them regret their decision to stay.

Everyone talked about a vote in the near future— something Fernan suggested when the other candidates, Henry included, attempted to dishonor him by saying he would use his wealth to take the crown no matter what the people wanted. Effie didn't know when this vote would be, but if it were today, she would choose Fernan instead of Henry, for she'd promised Basen she would.

And she just might have anyway.

The other talk around campus had to do with the prisoners of war. Most of Ulric's few hundred men in Trentyre had come to the Academy to surrender while the rest fled. Nearly half a thousand men now filled the dungeons of the castle, and no one wanted the responsibility of feeding or cleaning up after them, but someone had to do it until their fate was decided.

Among the many issues to be settled, one of the more important was who would be headmaster of the Academy. Wilfre and Jack currently shared the responsibility, Wilfre because he wanted it all to himself, and Jack because he'd worked the closest with Terren over the years and was forced into helping Wilfre by the other instructors. During the recent announcement at Redfield, Wilfre had revealed their plan to select a permanent leader for the school.

"In the spirit of a new order of leadership chosen by the people, all the instructors will remain in the stadium to give their opinions on who should be the new leader of the Academy. After an hour of discussion, the instructors will vote. Everyone is free to stay and watch, but we ask that you do not comment or applaud. We will begin shortly."

It was then that Effie had left, but not before noticing Basen's father entering the sandy arena to put himself in the discussion. Only a few others didn't stay to watch, though Effie didn't know who they were or what they'd be doing instead.

Everyone was too busy to deal with Sanya. In fact, Effie seemed to be the only one who wanted her back in prison. Even when she encouraged the friends of Nick and Alex to join her demand that Sanya be imprisoned, they were too tired from all the killing to take on such a responsibility. Effie was surprised when most of them told her they trusted her to do the right thing about Sanya. As the family and close friends of Sanya's victims, it would've been their responsibility to argue for a severe sentence if this had happened before the war. The king or his appointed judge would then make a decision, and it would be done.

Effie gladly accepted the sole responsibility of this task. Unfortunately, it meant missing the discussion about the new headmaster.

Effie was shocked when she arrived at the makeshift prison and it took her a moment to recognize Sanya. "What have you done to yourself?"

"I felt the need to change my appearance, and I couldn't exactly pick out a new outfit."

Sanya stood in the center of a circle of hair, continuing to saw off any strands she could find long enough to reach her neck. Effie didn't know what to say as she stared, fearful Sanya had gone mad.

"I'm perfectly sane, Effie. Can you get on with this trial?" She put down her dagger and focused on pulling the loose strands out of her hair.

"It's not a trial," Effie corrected. "I already know what you've done."

"Then what is it?"

"It's just a discussion before I make a decision."

Sanya let out a loud sigh.

"Do you even want to be free?" Effie asked.

Sanya approached the bars. "What do *you* want, Effie? Do you want to hear me beg? Perhaps it's tears you want. No, maybe anger." She shook the bars and screamed. "Let me out! Let me out! Let me OUT! Is this what you want to hear?"

Sanya let go and walked back to sit on her straw bed, fiddling with her hair once again.

"If this is a joke to you—"

"This is my life, but it's starting to feel like a joke." Sanya ran to the bars and grabbed them again. "You have no psychic here! Where is Reela? Don't torment me just to question me again later!" She turned away and looked down. "I can't take any more of this. Just make your decision quickly and end my suffering. I have made many mistakes, but never have I deliberately put others in agony like you're doing to me."

Effie kicked the bar in front of her. "You don't know agony until you lose someone you love!"

"I lost my sister and then my mother, Effie! You're not the only one here who knows agony! But have you ever felt prolonged loneliness? Have you felt *years* of isolation to the point of believing there must be a reason you have no one? Any rational person starts to wonder if they are scum and no one will ever be their friend. And if no one will be their friend, there's *definitely no chance* to be loved! Don't play this game of who suffers worse with me, mage. You will lose!"

Effie stormed out of the storage building. She slammed the door, letting out all the rage she could. But it wasn't enough. She opened it again to slam it once more, then kicked it with her heel until she feared the door might break. She went around to the outside of Sanya's cell, unsure what she would yell, but it would be vicious.

She stopped when she heard Sanya sobbing. Guilt mixed in with her fury and brought tears to Effie's eyes.

She missed Alex less each day, the memories of him fading. Sometimes she'd cry at night when she realized this. But in this moment of confusion as she tried to figure out what to do about Sanya, she missed him as strongly as if he'd left this world yesterday. Effie needed his guidance. He was so wise, too good of a man for her. She didn't even care if they would be together anymore so long as he was back. He deserved to live.

He's at peace, she reminded herself. *It's me who isn't.*

*****

Sanya could feel Effie just outside, but the walls were too thick to read the mage's emotions. Sanya couldn't stop crying. It felt as if a dam had burst within her. But then she noticed Effie walking back around. She held her breath to listen and heard the door opening to the storage building. Wiping her tears, Sanya turned away as Effie approached. Loose hair stuck to Sanya's cheeks. She picked it off her face as best she could.

"There have been arguments about what to do with our captured enemies," Effie told Sanya. "Many people want them dead. They've killed our allies, people I...we love. Tauwin took all the prisoners while he was king and sent them away. Ulric continued the exile treatment. Anyone breaking the law was removed from Kyrro."

Sanya hated that her best chance of freedom was playing the part of the interested listener Effie wanted her to be, when really Sanya wanted to scream at her to hurry and make a decision.

"Where did the Takarys send them?"

"To Kanoan."

Then we'll never see them again. The small continent wasn't as far as Greenedge, but only the edges had been mapped. All the explorers who ventured deeper never made it back to Kyrro.

Effie said, "We might send our prisoners there."

"And what does that have to do with me?"

"You have a lot in common with them: You've killed our allies—people we love. Perhaps you should be sent away as well."

Sanya had been prepared to leave for Greenedge when the war was over. She didn't know what creatures or men resided in Kanoan, but she was confident she could survive.

"Is that what you want?"

"I don't know."

Sanya rolled her eyes.

"I understand you killed Gayla Hiller because she did nothing to stop your father," Effie said. "He killed your sister, right?"

"Yes." *And I killed him for it.*

"I'm finding it difficult to decide you should be free when *you* decided to kill Gayla. She didn't murder your sister. She just stood by idly. You did murder Nick and

Alex."

Grinding her teeth, Sanya told Effie, "I'm sick of trying to defend myself only for it to result in a wasted effort. It's embarrassing, pitiful, and it makes me hate myself even more to keep at it. There is a difference between Gayla and me. I have done everything I can, including preparing to sacrifice my life for Kyrro's Allies. Gayla sacrificed nothing for others and never would've if she'd survived her stab wound. She wouldn't wish to make up for her crimes like I do. I will spend the rest of my life doing so. If you decide that your anger is too much to allow me to help Kyrro, then fine. Send me away. I'll still spend my life trying to make up for my crimes."

Effie stared at Sanya. Then she glanced down as her brow furrowed.

Sanya's heart jumped. *Don't send me away.*

"You're right," Effie said. "You're different from Gayla. In fact, you're different than you used to be."

Sanya was glad she'd cut her hair. She was probably hideous, but the change felt like finally sleeping through the night after so many fitful slumbers. She was ready to start her new day.

Effie looked up as she produced a key and unlocked the cell. "I'm not sure if I'll ever be able to forgive you, but I don't want to be the only one in Kyrro arguing for your execution or exile." She moved to let Sanya out.

But Sanya couldn't leave the prison just yet. She hated herself for asking, but she needed to know. "What about the family of Nick and Alex?" She couldn't bear leaving the cell only to return at a later time. She had to know this was it.

"All of Nick's family had joined us when we retook Kyrro. When Basen found out who they were, he spoke to them about his friendship with Nick and his dealings with you. They didn't want to punish you more so long as you continued to fight for Kyrro and regretted your actions for the rest of your life. Alex only has one family member left, his mother. I visited her yesterday to speak with her about you. She's tired of death, like many of us. She asked me if you will spend your life atoning for your crime, and I said I would find out. But with everything you've done, it's hard for any of us to believe you'll suddenly stop causing harm. You'll have to prove that you can." She stepped into the cell and unlocked the shackles around Sanya's wrists. "Don't expect any of us to forgive you."

"I won't."

Effie turned to leave.

"I'm sorry," Sanya said. "I've never been sorrier."

Effie looked back at Sanya, her eyes glistening with tears. "If you hurry you might be able to make the end of the headmaster discussion at Redfield."

Sanya hoped Effie didn't notice her legs shaking.

As soon as Effie left, Sanya collapsed onto her scattered hair and wept with relief.

*****

Basen sat beside Alabell at Redfield as the discussion between instructors became heated. Basen was embarrassed to realize that it was mostly due to his father putting himself into the discussion without an invitation and turning it into a debate of why *he* should be headmaster. Had Ulric been right about Henry's wish for power? Was there something in Hiller blood that would eventually cause Basen to thirst for control? Basen had wanted it recently, as he'd taken command over this army, but that was only because he knew his stratagem would succeed so long as every detail was followed, and he'd trusted himself more than anyone to carry it out.

Basen hadn't remembered his father acting this way in Tenred castle, and Henry certainly wasn't this entitled during their time in the workhouse. Basen hoped everything would go back to normal once Henry failed to become king and headmaster.

Alabell had calmed down since watching Sanya be arrested, though Basen knew she wouldn't let Sanya be executed or exiled without doing everything she could to stop it.

"Don't worry," Basen had told her. "I'm sure Effie will let her go free."

It still seemed strange to him that one eighteen-year-old woman could decide Sanya's fate, but he supposed it wasn't any worse than a king who'd never met Sanya making the decision.

Henry had taken control of the discussion once again. "The headmaster should be someone who's not only proven he or she can lead in times of war, but skilled enough with magic, psyche, or sword to defend him or herself. The two headmasters before now have been attacked. Terren would've been assassinated on the first day this began if he hadn't had the skill to defend himself, in which case we might've lost the war."

Basen supposed his father had a point. From the nods of the instructors, it seemed they agreed as well.

Henry had been the only one clearly speaking about himself during this discussion. Even Wilfre had refrained from lobbying for himself with such ferocity during his statements about the headmaster needing to be smart and experienced. Jack seemed to have even less interest in being selected, declining to participate except to add that the headmaster should be someone who wasn't already burdened by other important tasks.

The audience had given little reaction to any of it until Abith stood and asked, "May I speak?"

Suddenly everyone seemed to be whispering at once and stirring in their seats. The entire discussion had gone by without Basen once thinking of his recent instructor, and he supposed he wasn't the only one. Abith hadn't gotten the chance to make himself more known as an ally.

Had Abith been more involved in Basen's stratagem, he might've been an equal contender for the headmaster position. He'd proven his loyalty by going against the traitors, killing Ulric's men in the forest each and every day with his small team of Krepps. But it didn't feel right to give him leadership over the Academy. Even Henry had proven himself to be a better leader than Abith.

If the decision of choosing the headmaster went to Basen, he didn't know who he would select. None seemed as if they could replace Terren.

"What do you have to say?" Wilfre asked in response to Abith.

"I was stuck in the forest until the very end, so I only

heard about everything the rest of you accomplished. From what I've gathered, it seems to me that none of us would be here if it weren't for many people. But there's one in particular who continues to come up in my thoughts as the right person to take the job. I'm still waiting for his name to be mentioned."

Alabell glanced at Basen as she squeezed his hand.

He laughed through his nose and shook his head. Abith couldn't possibly be talking about him.

"The headmaster of the Academy should be someone who has the ability to turn this great place into something even greater," Abith continued. "It should be someone who not only can organize a large army but can do so in a way to overcome a nearly impossible challenge."

Some people began to clap. Basen started to sweat as he realized what Abith was really saying.

"Like many of you have mentioned," Abith went on, "the headmaster should be someone with experience leading. He should be wise and trusted, but he should also be someone who will never be corrupted by power. He needs to be able to outthink the enemies of the Academy. He needs to be a true soldier who can defend himself against any foe. He needs to understand the limitations and the power of the people here but with more hope than anyone as to what we can accomplish. There's only one person still living who not only understood how to fight this war against the Takarys but implemented it to perfection, despite initial resistance from his allies."

At least half the audience started to applaud, forcing Abith to raise his voice. "I say we've been at this long enough and it's time to make a decision. I might not have a vote, but if I did, it would be for Basen Hiller."

The applause grew to a roar. They began to chant Basen's name. Alabell grabbed his hand and pulled him up.

He felt as if he were standing on a cloud, unable to feel his feet against the ground. Shock and pride swelled in his chest with such force he felt as if his heart might burst. He became dizzy from it all, his face burning with heat.

His father gave him a stern look but slowly began to smile. He waved for Basen to join him in the arena. Basen shook his head. This was too much for him to handle. He could wage war against the Takarys and win, but he couldn't fathom the idea of going down there into the arena, even with the zealous support of those in the stadium. He would melt from embarrassment as soon as his feet touched the sand.

"It's no longer your decision." Alabell beamed with a bright smile. "You have to go!"

When he realized she was right, he made his way down. He didn't think the applause could get even louder, but it did as soon as he started down the stairs. He couldn't remove the shock from his face as hard as he tried. He slipped on one of the stairs but caught himself. Laughter erupted with the cheering.

He made it onto the hard sand and walked over to join his father. Although they were the same height, Basen felt like a child wanting to cower behind Henry's leg as his father put his hand on his shoulder.

Wilfre put up his arms for silence but was ignored. He began to wave them.

The applause finally quieted after some time, though

the air still buzzed with excitement. Basen had a feeling Wilfre was about to bring everyone back to reality with a more than reasonable response to all this.

"He is much too young to be headmaster."

As much as Basen was disappointed, Wilfre was right. But he wasn't done.

"Even Terren was considered young at twenty-five when he took on the task. None of you applauding knew him when he first began, with the exception of Cleve. He wasn't the same confident leader as the headmaster you knew. He learned through his mistakes and became wiser as he aged. It took many years.

"Kyrro has been reborn—there is no time for mistakes now. The headmaster must take the Academy in the proper direction. If Basen became headmaster, his portal and combat training would cease. As excellent as he did leading us recently, I'm sure you would all agree that he would be of better use continuing his training and advising the headmaster when necessary."

"He *is* too young," Penny said. "Wilfre is right about everything. And that's why I propose that Basen spend the rest of his two and a half years at the Academy continuing his training as a combat portal mage under Abith's guidance. Wilfre and Jack should split the responsibility of headmaster. Jack, we all know how much you helped Terren. And Wilfre's probably the only person here who knows everyone's name as well as their function in the school. I'm sure all of you have had at least one conversation with him that he initiated."

The audience seemed dejected, some nodding along.

"And Basen." Penny looked right at him. There was

something new in her eyes that hadn't been there when she used to instruct him, a look like a mother realizing her child was now a man. "Basen should begin his training as the headmaster's apprentice in between his lessons with Abith." There was a hum of energy as the crowd began to murmur. "And when his time at the Academy is up, he will be appointed headmaster."

The roar of the audience was near deafening, though none was as loud as Henry.

EPILOGUE

It had been a month since the instructors had voted for Basen to begin his headmaster apprenticeship. Since then, Wilfre had spent the beginning of every lesson pouring out his concerns about Basen being too young and how fast he had to learn, but eventually Wilfre resigned himself to instructing.

Basen had gone with Wilfre several times to meet the new king, Fernan Estlander. The most recent had been to accept the acrowns Fernan had promised the Academy before his coronation.

It had taken a few days afterward to discover Ulric's hidden treasury. Sanya had been the one to suggest searching for passages in the dungeons of the castle by testing for parts of the wall that had give. After the treasure was found, Fernan swore to use part of it to employ all the people out of work from the recent war, not as soldiers but as farmers, masons, tailors, blacksmiths, miners, woodworkers, and even scullions if they couldn't find another line of work. Another portion of the money would be used to pay employers a stipend if they took on an apprentice. And some of it would remain in the treasury of the kingdom, while the rest would go toward the Academy. Workers and instructors needed to be paid, and construction would allow the school to grow.

Basen had taken a cautious liking to the new king, especially when Fernan showed enthusiasm for working with Basen once he was headmaster. "I expect us to turn

Kyrro into the greatest nation in the world," Fernan had said. It helped that Annah was there to confirm everything he said was genuine.

Basen had gotten only a quick moment alone with her before needing to return to the Academy with Wilfre. Annah would go back to the school once the transition of kingship was settled, but for now she said she enjoyed staying at the castle. Basen suspected she had a small infatuation with Fernan, but Basen could probably assume the same about most people and be correct.

The Krepps had lost many of their kin, and now totaled only thirteen. There were too few of them to build their own village as they'd first wanted upon joining the humans. It didn't matter to Rickik, who was as happy as a dog with a bone now that he possessed Rockbreak's imposing bastial steel sword. Rather than start a new village for his followers, he wanted to return to his tribe of Krepps. Basen believed him when he said he had new pride for his kin, for his son, and even for humans. They wouldn't let the other Krepps attack human territory.

"Allies," Rickik had said just before Basen opened the portal to Regash Forest.

"Allies," Basen agreed.

Cleve had come to see them off. Rickik put his hand on Cleve's head and said something in Kreppen before entering the portal. The rest of his Krepps followed.

"What did he say?" Basen asked after it closed.

"That I am like a Krepp. It's supposed to be a compliment."

When a woman showed up to join Basen in training with Abith, Basen thought she looked familiar but couldn't figure out who she was. She wore a nervous smile and had hair shorter than Basen's. It was only after she scowled at him for staring that he recognized her.

"God's mercy, Sanya?"

"What?"

"You look...different."

"That's the point." It wasn't her hair so much as her polite smile that had really thrown him off.

Abith had grown even stronger in his time apart from the army, thinking of new methods to use energy in combat. It was as if he'd planned to return to this very position at the Academy from the start. Basen was eager to learn everything he could, and he could see the same eagerness in Sanya's twinkling eyes at the beginning of each of their lessons.

Eventually others began to train with them. All still had to climb up and down the wall each day as they waited for a training area to be built, but Basen didn't mind. He would often be called away during training to join Wilfre in some task, and he enjoyed showing off his skill by leaping up to grab the wall rather than using the rope.

Neeko continued to teach the manipulation of pyforial energy in Redfield stadium, though he too would need a more suitable training area as people showed real promise with the skill. Micklin turned out to be Neeko's hardest working student. Basen walked by Micklin in the dining hall once and found the boy using the energy to move food from his plate into his mouth. It was almost painful to watch the agonizingly slow process, but Micklin was so intent on succeeding he didn't notice Basen.

Wilfre had sent demands to Tenred to bring Crea Hiller to the Academy, alive or dead. Everyone was prepared to get Fernan involved when Tenred refused, so it came as a surprise when an envoy came in a carriage to present her dead body. She'd been stabbed in the heart but also in the back. Basen found it fitting considering everything she'd done to the Academy. He just wished the envoy would tell them who had done it so Basen knew who to thank if they ever met.

Kyrro scouts investigating the neighboring territory reported battles beginning in Tenred as men tried to claim the crown. After all the deaths in both territories, but more so in Kyrro, the armies were of nearly equal strength now. Basen was glad when Wilfre agreed that they shouldn't get involved, and he was even more glad when Fernan came to the same conclusion.

Fernan gave Alabell the choice to return to the castle to be the head healer as she'd been training to do before this all began, but she'd already decided to stay at the Academy. She spent her days in the medical building treating the injured from the war. Basen didn't know whether she would stay there as a healer or become an instructor, but she seemed happy to do either, and so was he.

Eventually she told him what she'd been writing: a true story of the war. Many people undoubtedly would write and sell the tale in hopes of exploiting the people's natural interest, but no account would be as accurate as hers. She felt obligated, for her mother had spent years teaching her to write well, and she was one of the few people at the Academy who would have time to finish it.

Basen was flattered to the point of embarrassment when she told him he would be the hero of the story, but he could tell from the way she spoke about this project that it was bigger than the two of them. He would never ask her to change anything or stop, as uncomfortable as it made him.

It was a solemn day when all the new names were added to the red wall of Redfield. The number of fallen exceeded those still alive who had been with the Academy from the beginning. Many came by to pay respects, Basen included. He took his time to think about Nick and Alex when he found their names, specifically how much he missed both of them even though he'd barely gotten to know them. Many people would rekindle their anger for Sanya that day, but she would not be put back in prison. Everyone could see how hard she was trying to fit in. She showed up at one point and spent most of the brief time staring at the ground with a guilty look.

Basen thought of Peter next. He'd been angry enough at Basen for abandoning him in the Fjallejon Mountains that he'd gone against the Academy, protecting Abith when he had tried to kill Terren. The act must've taken more bravery than most men could muster, especially when Peter realized the kind of company he'd associated himself with and returned to the Academy's side. Basen would try to honor the warrior's brave spirit as he continued to use his sword.

Eventually his thoughts shifted to Jackrie, reminding him of his test to get into the Academy. Had Basen performed for someone less understanding, like Penny for example, he might've failed right after his botched fireball and never would've made it into the Academy. Jackrie reminded him of Alabell in how much she cared about everyone. He would never forget how she'd given her life so Cleve and Annah could escape.

Terren...the school seemed less alive without him. Whenever Basen found himself wondering if his ideas about the Academy were good, he'd ask himself what Terren would say, and he'd always gain confidence. Everyone here might've been killed if it wasn't for Terren's quick thinking to get them into the forest. Basen was certain that if the late headmaster had survived, he would've come up with a plan similar to the one Basen used to win the war.

He somehow felt close to all of these people while standing here near the wall. He was thankful that no one disturbed him and he was able to stay here and remember his fallen comrades for hours. By the time he finally left, he felt changed, as if part of them had come with him.

Basen participated in many of the discussions between Wilfre, Jack, and Fernan about their prisoners of war. Eventually they came to the conclusion to send them back to Greenedge. Everyone agreed there was little risk of them returning to Kyrro.

Cleve had resumed his warrior training for the first week since the Redfield announcement, dominating the surviving Group One warriors. Eventually Sneary suggested Cleve try a few training sessions with Abith to see if it would be a good fit. Cleve might not have the same skill over bastial energy as Basen and Sanya, but he'd demonstrated the ability to focus the energy into his muscles already, and he didn't have much room to grow among the other swordsmen.

Cleve seemed to relish the challenge of facing Abith, Basen, and Sanya, but all for different reasons. Abith seemed to be the only swordsmen left who could beat Cleve in an honest duel, though he would lose just as many as he won. Basen could catch Cleve off guard with surprise blasts of energy and bursts of speed, though it was his only chance to score against the superior swordsman. Cleve still beat him most of the time.

Sanya had the strongest weapon of all, her psyche. She was still learning how to use bastial energy to fight with more speed and strength, but even without honing that talent, she could beat any of the rest of them when she pained her opponent with psyche.

Basen knew her advantage wouldn't last long. The three of them were already talented at resisting psyche and would only get stronger as the year went on.

Tauwin's mother was still alive, as Sanya noted to Basen one day.

"Is she a threat?" he'd asked.

"No. She's always avoided conflict, and she has no incentive to cause problems. There are other Takarys in Greenedge, though. I know nothing about them."

"If they didn't get involved with Tauwin and Ulric, they probably won't now." It was the best Basen could hope for. They weren't about to go to war with the most powerful family in Greenedge.

Sanya still ate alone most of the time. Greg made several more attempts to court her but eventually gave up. Basen and Alabell would've accompanied Sanya during meals in the dining hall, but Basen already spent most of each day with Sanya, and that was enough. Her abrasive personality hadn't exactly gone away, though he could tell she was working on it. Her biggest problem was severity, as nothing was casual to her. Every meal was to fuel her for training, and all her time spent training was to improve. During their time in the Tenred castle, she'd never learned to enjoy herself, and he worried she was gravitating toward the same disposition. Fortunately for Sanya, Reela had taken an interest in helping her. In rare occasions, even Effie would sit with the two of them during meals.

Basen had seen Sanya and Effie speaking but they'd always fall silent whenever he or anyone else came near, so eventually he stopped coming over to bother them.

"What do you talk about with her?" Basen had asked Sanya one day while watching Cleve work up a sweat trying to get through Abith's defenses.

"Severe topics," Sanya had answered. "The exact opposite of what you think I should do."

Basen had constantly given her the advice to take life more casually, but he stopped after that. Whatever Sanya was doing with Effie and Reela seemed to be helping her.

*****

Because of Sanya's crimes, she wasn't allowed to be seen anywhere at the Academy alone at night, and she wasn't allowed to leave the campus without permission from Wilfre or Jack. It didn't bother her. Considering what she'd done, she felt she deserved much worse.

It was the first time in years that she had no plan for her future. She often went to bed worried that if she didn't come up with a goal to work toward, she would wake up one day done with the Academy, having wasted her time. She had to continually remind herself that she had years to think of something, and it was important to relax. At least that's what Basen had kept telling her until recently.

But relaxing was impossible when she saw Effie so frequently. The mage had demanded that Sanya visit her campus home every other night. The first time Sanya went, she didn't know what to expect. The decision of whether or not to bring a weapon made her chew her nails off in deliberation. She was glad after she arrived that she'd decided not to.

With Gabby, Steffen, Reela, and Cleve all living in the small home, Effie met Sanya outside and said they would go for a walk. The mage had remained silent until they were out of the large area of campus homes. Sanya was surprised when Effie had told her that she would be taking Reela's advice to speak about her feelings.

The first walk had been painfully awkward and full of anger and tears, but after weeks of the same routine, Sanya's nerves were no longer on edge around Effie. The mage began to speak about Alex not as Sanya's murder victim but as a memory. She would talk about the things he used to do, but never for very long. Instead, she had many questions about Sanya's feelings toward her dead family.

Sanya hadn't realized until then that there was much more than just anger buried in her heart. The agony of loneliness had been the worst of her childhood, but if she searched long enough she did find moments of joy she'd forgotten. She never questioned why Effie decided to keep up their clandestine walks, and she never skipped a meeting, as painful as some of them were.

Tonight was the first change of their routine. Effie requested that Sanya meet her in the training grounds of the Group One mages. Effie was late, making Sanya nervous as she paced around in the very place she'd killed Alex. She half expected the mage to come through the single opening in the wall with her wand out.

Effie was shaking when she arrived.

"What's wrong?" Sanya asked.

"This is hard for me."

It can't be the place. She trains here every day, so she must be used to coming here by now. "What is?"

Effie took an akorell bracelet from her pocket, then broke the sartious casing around it. "I want you to take me to the spiritual world. I want to say goodbye to Alex."

"I told you it's dangerous to go there."

"I remember everything you said about it. I still want to go."

"I'm not sure he'll even be able to hear you."

"Then you can use psyche to speak to him for me."

Sanya had gotten to know Effie well enough by now to realize that there was no changing her mind when it was set.

"All right," Sanya said. "Do you have any questions

before I open the portal?"

Effie handed her the akorell bracelet, and Sanya put it on.

"How long will we have?" Effie asked.

"A few minutes. Are you ready?"

"Yes."

Sanya had been practicing everything she was capable of, including opening portals to the spiritual world. It was easy compared to forming gateways to other places in their world, which Basen now did with ease. Though he still hadn't figured out how to open a portal to a place he'd never been before. Nor could he create a portal unless energy had been gathered in the same spot over time.

Sanya believed she would one day be able to maintain a gateway from one location in the physical world to another that was large enough to walk through, but for now she could barely make one bigger than her fist.

She opened the red sphere. Effie took a breath and stepped in. Sanya followed.

Effie muttered something in shock as she looked around. Sanya could see it through the mage's eyes: the sharp, pure color, reds and oranges too vibrant to compare to the otherwise dull colors of the natural world. It was as if the energy here was alive, breathing. And everything was made of it.

Effie's black hair was as white as snow, dancing around her back as she spun to look in every direction. The tint of her human shape was between orange and red, a shade darker than Sanya's. Spirits wafted around them, floating clusters of energy. They were more complex than the energy of the landscape around them. Trying to read them was like looking at a page of jumbled letters. Only when their message was clear could Sanya understand them. She sensed them stronger than she could see them, like smelling freshly baked bread before spotting it.

She'd felt her mother's spirit draining during the war. Sometimes Sanya would fall into the spiritual world during sleep and immediately start to nurture her mother, only to remember that she had to let go.

It seemed so long ago that she'd lost the feeling of contact. No one had noticed or cared when she'd spent that day in the corner of the basement of their temporary headquarters in the capital crying softly.

"What am I feeling?" Effie asked. "What is this? It's like a bundle of emotions, with edges and colors. I can't see it, and yet I can."

"I thought only psychics could feel that. It's psyche."

"Alex!" she yelled.

"He's already here." Sanya pointed.

The clusters parted to leave one glowing sphere of yellow, like the sun breaking through clouds.

"It *is* him," Effie whispered to herself. "It's you. I can feel you close to me again!"

He hovered nearby. *worry.*

"I'm fine," Effie assured him. "I just wanted to see you one last time."

safe. tranquil. together with brother.

"Your mother misses you both, and so do I."

love. He drifted toward Sanya. *her?*

"I've spent my life atoning for my crimes," Sanya said. "And I don't plan to stop until I die. I'm sorry, Alex."

peace here. i forgave already.

Sanya's eyes prickled with tears.

"I don't know what I'm supposed to do," Effie said. "I'm losing memories of how you used to look, how you felt...I don't want to say goodbye, but everyone tells me I need to let go."

let go. live and love.

"I don't know how." She began to cry, clear blue lines down her cheeks.

forgive is the answer.

"I don't think I can."

A spirit of vibrant red drifted over to them. Effie let out a gasp. "Terren?"

yes.

A third spirit joined them, this one with a hint of blue among the red. Sanya felt a wave of comfort flowing through her as she recognized Jackrie.

The three spirits huddled together and spoke at once, each with the same message.

in death there is peace...do not regret.

you can cry but you must laugh too.

you can hurt but you must rejoice too.

live and love...we will always be with you.

Sanya suddenly felt her sister's and her mother's presences and collapsed to her knees. She couldn't reach out to either like she had with her mother before, but she knew both of them still existed. It might've only been in Sanya's heart where they lived, but it was strong enough for Sanya to know she would never lose them completely.

The spirits spoke in one final word, though it came out with such force that it lifted Effie and Sanya up from the ground.

proud.

The two young women drifted back through the portal and landed on the sand as the gateway shut. Effie cried into her hands. Sanya shed her own tears in quiet, cherishing the feeling of her mother in her heart.

"He's always been with me," Effie said. "And he always will be. Thank you for letting me see that. I forgive you, Sanya. I do."

END

New Releases

Please consider leaving a review on Amazon. They are extremely important. Thank you.

The next series will take place in the same world.

Author Information

Thank you so much for reading. I hope you enjoyed the series.

If you want to discuss the series with me or just want to say hello, look me up on Facebook or email me at brian@btnarro.com. Or feel free to start a forum discussion on my author profile page.

Come visit my website at www.btnarro.com and chat with me. I post updates about my progress with the new series and provide insight about the creative process.